A QUARTET OF
RUSSIAN MASTERPIECES

FIRST LOVE *by Turgenev*

  The awakening of love in a 16-year-old
  youth brings him joy, torment, and a shat-
  tering revelation about his rival.

THE GAMBLER *by Dostoyevsky*

  A young Russian gentleman at a German
  resort succumbs to a morbid craving for
  the roulette wheel.

MASTER AND MAN *by Tolstoy*

  A rich merchant faces death with his servant in a snowstorm and learns an ultimate
  truth about life.

THE DUEL *by Chekhov*

  A man and his mistress degenerate in a
  small town on the Black Sea coast while
  pursuing a Tolstoyan life of simplification
  and Christian love.

FOUR
GREAT RUSSIAN
SHORT
NOVELS

*Translated by Constance Garnett
and Nathan Haskell Dole*

ACKNOWLEDGMENTS

THE DUEL, by Anton P. Chekhov, translated by Constance Garnett,
copyrighted 1916 by The Macmillan Company, copyright re-
newed 1944 by Constance Garnett, reprinted by permission of
The Macmillan Company, New York.

THE GAMBLER, by Fyodor Dostoyevsky, translated by Constance
Garnett, reprinted by permission of The Macmillan Company,
New York, and William Heinemann, Ltd., London.

FIRST LOVE, by Ivan Turgenev, translated by Constance Garnett,
reprinted by permission of The Macmillan Company, New
York, and William Heinemann, Ltd., London.

The translation of MASTER AND MAN, by Leo Tolstoy, reprinted
here is by Nathan Haskell Dole.

First printing—June, 1959
Second printing—May, 1961
Third printing—May, 1964
Fourth printing—January, 1966
Fifth printing—March, 1969

Printed in U.S.A.

CONTENTS

FIRST LOVE

FIRST LOVE

by *Ivan Turgenev*

The party had long ago broken up. The clock struck half-past twelve. There was left in the room only the master of the house and Sergei Nikolaevitch and Vladimir Petrovitch.

The master of the house rang and ordered the remains of the supper to be cleared away. "And so it's settled," he observed, sitting back farther in his easy-chair and lighting a cigar; "each of us is to tell the story of his first love. It's your turn, Sergei Nikolaevitch."

Sergei Nikolaevitch, a round little man with a plump, light-complexioned face, gazed first at the master of the house, then raised his eyes to the ceiling. "I had no first love," he said at last; "I began with the second."

"How was that?"

"It's very simple. I was eighteen when I had my first flirtation with a charming young lady, but I courted her just as though it were nothing new to me; just as I courted others later on. To speak accurately, the first and last time I was in love was with my nurse when I was six years old; but that's in the remote past. The details of our relations have slipped out of my memory, and even if I remembered them, whom could they interest?"

"Then how's it to be?" began the master of the house. "There was nothing much of interest about my first love either; I never fell in love with any one till I met Anna Nikolaevna, now my wife,—and everything went as smoothly as possible with us; our parents arranged the match, we were very soon in love with each other, and got married without loss of time. My story can be told in a couple of words. I must confess, gentlemen, in bringing up the subject of first love, I reckoned upon you, I won't say old, but no longer young, bachelors. Can't you enliven us with something, Vladimir Petrovitch?"

"My first love, certainly, was not quite an ordinary one," responded, with some reluctance, Vladimir Petrovitch, a man of forty, with black hair turning grey.

"Ah!" said the master of the house and Sergei Nikolaevitch with one voice: "So much the better. . . . Tell us about it."

"If you wish it . . . or no; I won't tell the story; I'm no hand at telling a story; I make it dry and brief, or spun out and affected. If you'll allow me, I'll write out all I remember and read it you."

His friends at first would not agree, but Vladimir Petrovitch insisted on his own way. A fortnight later they were together again, and Vladimir Petrovitch kept his word.

His manuscript contained the following story: —

1

I was sixteen then. It happened in the summer of 1833.

I lived in Moscow with my parents. They had taken a country house for the summer near the Kalouga gate, facing the Neskutchny gardens. I was preparing for the university, but did not work much and was in no hurry.

No one interfered with my freedom. I did what I liked, especially after parting with my last tutor, a Frenchman who had never been able to get used to the idea that he had fallen "like a bomb" (*comme une bombe*) into Russia, and would lie sluggishly in bed with an expression of exasperation on his face for days together. My father treated me with careless kindness; my mother scarcely noticed me, though she had no children except me; other cares completely absorbed her. My father, a man still young and very handsome, had married her from mercenary considerations; she was ten years older than he. My mother led a melancholy life; she was for ever agitated, jealous and angry, but not in my father's presence; she was very much afraid of him, and he was severe, cold, and distant in his behaviour. . . . I have never seen a man more elaborately serene, self-confident, and commanding.

I shall never forget the first weeks I spent at the country

house. The weather was magnificent; we left town on the 9th of May, on St. Nicholas's day. I used to walk about in our garden, in the Neskutchny gardens, and beyond the town gates; I would take some book with me—Keidanov's Course, for instance—but I rarely looked into it, and more often than anything declaimed verses aloud; I knew a great deal of poetry by heart; my blood was in a ferment and my heart ached—so sweetly and absurdly; I was all hope and anticipation, was a little frightened of something, and full of wonder at everything, and was on the tiptoe of expectation; my imagination played continually, fluttering rapidly about the same fancies, like martins about a bell-tower at dawn; I dreamed, was sad, even wept; but through the tears and through the sadness, inspired by a musical verse, or the beauty of evening, shot up like grass in spring the delicious sense of youth and effervescent life.

I had a horse to ride; I used to saddle it myself and set off alone for long rides, break into a rapid gallop and fancy myself a knight at a tournament. How gaily the wind whistled in my ears; or turning my face towards the sky, I would absorb its shining radiance and blue into my soul, that opened wide to welcome it.

I remember that at that time the image of woman, the vision of love, scarcely ever arose in definite shape in my brain; but in all I thought, in all I felt, lay hidden a half-conscious, shamefaced presentiment of something new, unutterably sweet, feminine. . . .

This presentiment, this expectation, permeated my whole being; I breathed in it, it coursed through my veins with every drop of blood . . . it was destined to be soon fulfilled.

The place, where we settled for the summer, consisted of a wooden manor-house with columns and two small lodges; in the lodge on the left there was a tiny factory for the manufacture of cheap wall-papers. . . . I had more than once strolled that way to look at about a dozen thin and dishevelled boys with greasy smocks and worn faces, who were perpetually jumping on to wooden levers, that pressed down the square blocks of the press, and so by the weight of their feeble bodies struck off the variegated patterns of the wall-papers. The lodge on the right stood empty, and was to let. One day—three weeks after the 9th of May—the blinds in the windows of this lodge were drawn up, women's faces appeared at them—some family had installed themselves in it. I remember the same day at dinner, my mother inquired of the butler who were our new neighbours, and hearing the name of the Princess Zasyekin, first observed with some respect, "Ah! a princess!" . . . and then added, "A poor one, I suppose?"

"They arrived in three hired flies," the butler remarked deferentially, as he handed a dish: "they don't keep their own carriage, and the furniture's of the poorest."

"Ah," replied my mother, "so much the better."

My father gave her a chilly glance; she was silent.

Certainly the Princess Zasyekin could not be a rich woman; the lodge she had taken was so dilapidated and small and low-pitched that people, even moderately well-off in the world, would hardly have consented to occupy it. At the time, however, all this went in at one ear and out at the other. The princely title had very little effect on me; I had just been reading Schiller's *Robbers*.

2

I was in the habit of wandering about our garden every evening on the look-out for rooks. I had long cherished a hatred for those wary, sly, and rapacious birds. On the day of which I have been speaking, I went as usual into the garden, and after patrolling all the walks without success (the rooks knew me, and merely cawed spasmodically at a distance), I chanced to go close to the low fence which separated our domain from the narrow strip of garden stretching beyond the lodge to the right, and belonging to it. I was walking along, my eyes on the ground. Suddenly I heard a voice; I looked across the fence, and was thunderstruck. . . . I was confronted with a curious spectacle.

A few paces from me on the grass between the green raspberry bushes stood a tall slender girl in a striped pink dress, with a white kerchief on her head; four young men were close round her, and she was slapping them by turns on the forehead with those small grey flowers, the name of which I don't know, though they are well known to children; the flowers form little bags, and burst open with a pop when you strike them against anything hard. The young men presented their foreheads so eagerly, and in the gestures of the girl (I saw her in profile), there was something so fascinating, imperious, caressing, mocking, and charming, that I almost cried out with admiration and delight, and would, I thought, have given everything in the world on the spot only to have had those exquisite fingers strike me on the forehead. My gun slipped on to the grass, I forgot everything, I devoured with my eyes the graceful shape and neck and lovely arms and the slightly disordered fair hair under the white kerchief, and the half-closed clever eye, and the eyelashes and the soft cheek beneath them. . . .

"Young man, hey, young man," said a voice suddenly near me: "is it quite permissible to stare so at unknown young ladies?"

I started, I was struck dumb. . . . Near me, the other side of the fence, stood a man with close-cropped black hair, looking ironically at me. At the same instant the girl too turned towards me. . . . I caught sight of big grey eyes in a bright mobile face, and the whole face suddenly quivered and laughed, there was a flash of white teeth, a droll lifting of the eyebrows. . . . I crimsoned, picked up my gun from the ground, and pursued by a musical but not ill-natured laugh, fled to my own room, flung myself on the bed, and hid my face in my hands. My heart was fairly leaping; I was greatly ashamed and overjoyed; I felt an excitement I had never known before.

After a rest, I brushed my hair, washed, and went downstairs to tea. The image of the young girl floated before me, my heart was no longer leaping, but was full of a sort of sweet oppression.

"What's the matter?" my father asked me all at once: "have you killed a rook?"

I was on the point of telling him all about it, but I checked myself, and merely smiled to myself. As I was going to bed, I rotated—I don't know why—three times on one leg, pomaded my hair, got into bed, and slept like a top all night. Before morning I woke up for an instant, raised my head, looked round me in ecstasy, and fell asleep again.

3

"How can I make their acquaintance?" was my first thought when I waked in the morning. I went out in the garden before morning tea, but I did not go too near the fence, and saw no one. After drinking tea, I walked several times up and down the street before the house, and looked into the windows from a distance. . . . I fancied her face at a curtain, and I hurried away in alarm.

"I must make her acquaintance, though," I thought, pacing distractedly about the sandy plain that stretches before Neskutchny park . . . "but how, that is the question." I recalled the minutest details of our meeting yesterday; I had for some reason or other a particularly vivid recollection of how she had laughed at me. . . . But while I racked my brains, and made various plans, fate had already provided for me.

In my absence my mother had received from her new neighbour a letter on grey paper, sealed with brown wax, such as is only used in notices from the post-office or on the corks of bottles of cheap wine. In this letter, which was written in illiterate language and in a slovenly hand, the princess begged my mother to use her powerful influence in her behalf; my mother, in the words of the princess, was very intimate with persons of high position, upon whom her fortunes and her children's fortunes depended, as she had some very important business in hand. "I address myself to you," she wrote, "as one gentlewoman to another gentlewoman, and for that reason am glad to avail myself of the opportunity. Concluding, she begged my mother's permission to call upon her. I found my mother in an unpleasant state of indecision; my father was not at home, and she had no one of whom to ask advice. Not to answer a gentlewoman, and a princess into the bargain, was impossible. But my mother was in a difficulty as to how to answer her. To write a note in French struck her as unsuitable, and Russian spelling was not a strong point with my mother herself, and she was aware of it, and did not care to expose herself. She was overjoyed when I made my appearance, and at once told me to go round to the princess's, and to explain to her by word of mouth that my mother would always be glad to do her excellency any service within her powers, and begged her to come to see her at one o'clock. This unexpectedly rapid fulfilment of my secret desires both delighted and appalled me. I made no sign, however, of the perturbation which came over me, and as a preliminary step went to my own room to put on a new necktie and tail coat; at home I still wore short jackets and laydown collars, much as I abominated them.

4

In the narrow and untidy passage of the lodge, which I entered with an involuntary tremor in all my limbs, I was met by an old grey-headed servant with a dark coppercoloured face, surly little pig's eyes, and such deep furrows on his forehead and temples as I had never beheld in my life. He was carrying a plate containing the spine of a herring that had been gnawed at; and shutting the door that led into the room with his foot, he jerked out, "What do you want?"

"Is the Princess Zasyekin at home?" I inquired.

"Vonifaty!" a jarring female voice screamed from within.

The man without a word turned his back on me, exhibiting as he did so the extremely threadbare hindpart of his livery with a solitary reddish heraldic button on it; he put the plate down on the floor, and went away.

"Did you go to the police station?" the same female voice called again. The man muttered something in reply. "Eh. . . . Has some one come?" I heard again. . . . "The young gentleman from next door. Ask him in, then."

"Will you step into the drawing-room?" said the servant, making his appearance once more, and picking up the plate from the floor. I mastered my emotions, and went into the drawing-room.

I found myself in a small and not over clean apartment, containing some poor furniture that looked as if it had been hurriedly set down where it stood. At the window in an easy-chair with a broken arm was sitting a woman of fifty, bareheaded and ugly, in an old green dress, and a striped worsted wrap about her neck. Her small black eyes fixed me like pins.

I went up to her and bowed.

"I have the honour of addressing the Princess Zasyekin?"

"I am the Princess Zasyekin; and you are the son of Mr. V.?"

"Yes. I have come to you with a message from my mother."

"Sit down, please. Vonifaty, where are my keys, have you seen them?"

I communicated to Madame Zasyekin my mother's reply to her note. She heard me out, drumming with her fat red fingers on the window-pane, and when I had finished, she stared at me once more.

"Very good; I'll be sure to come," she observed at last. "But how young you are! How old are you, may I ask?"

"Sixteen," I replied, with an involuntary stammer.

The princess drew out of her pocket some greasy papers covered with writing, raised them right up to her nose, and began looking through them.

"A good age," she ejaculated suddenly, turning round restlessly on her chair. "And do you, pray, make yourself at home. I don't stand on ceremony."

"No, indeed," I thought, scanning her unprepossessing person with a disgust I could not restrain.

At that instant another door flew open quickly, and in the doorway stood the girl I had seen the previous evening in the garden. She lifted her hand, and a mocking smile gleamed in her face.

"Here is my daughter," observed the princess, indicating her with her elbow. "Zinotchka, the son of our neighbour, Mr. V. What is your name, allow me to ask?"

"Vladimir," I answered, getting up, and stuttering in my excitement.

"And your father's name?"

"Petrovitch."

"Ah! I used to know a commissioner of police whose

name was Vladimir Petrovitch too. Vonifaty! don't look
for my keys; the keys are in my pocket."

The young girl was still looking at me with the same
smile, faintly fluttering her eyelids, and putting her head
a little on one side.

"I have seen Monsieur Voldemar before," she began.
(The silvery note of her voice ran through me with a sort
of sweet shiver.) "You will let me call you so?"

"Oh, please," I faltered.

"Where was that?" asked the princess.

The young princess did not answer her mother.

"Have you anything to do just now?" she said, not taking her eyes off me.

"Oh, no."

"Would you like to help me wind some wool? Come in
here, to me."

She nodded to me and went out of the drawing-room. I
followed her.

In the room we went into, the furniture was a little better, and was arranged with more taste. Though, indeed,
at the moment, I was scarcely capable of noticing anything; I moved as in a dream and felt all through my being
a sort of intense blissfulness that verged on imbecility.

The young princess sat down, took out a skein of red
wool and, motioning me to a seat opposite her, carefully
untied the skein and laid it across my hands. All this she
did in silence with a sort of droll deliberation and with
the same bright sly smile on her slightly parted lips. She
began to wind the wool on a bent card, and all at once she
dazzled me with a glance so brilliant and rapid, that I
could not help dropping my eyes. When her eyes, which
were generally half closed, opened to their full extent, her
face was completely transfigured; it was as though it were
flooded with light.

"What did you think of me yesterday, M'sieu Voldemar?" she asked after a brief pause. "You thought ill of
me, I expect?"

"I . . . princess . . . I thought nothing . . . how can
I? . . ." I answered in confusion.

"Listen," she rejoined. "You don't know me yet. I'm a
very strange person; I like always to be told the truth. You,
I have just heard, are sixteen, and I am twenty-one: you
see I'm a great deal older than you, and so you ought al-

ways to tell me the truth ... and to do what I tell you,"
she added. "Look at me: why don't you look at me?"

I was still more abashed; however, I raised my eyes to
her. She smiled, not her former smile, but a smile of appro-
bation. "Look at me," she said, dropping her voice caress-
ingly: "I don't dislike that ... I like your face; I have a
presentiment we shall be friends. But do you like me?"
she added slyly.

"Princess ..." I was beginning.

"In the first place, you must call me Zinaïda Alexandrovna, and in the second place it's a bad habit for children"—(she corrected herself) "for young people—not to
say straight out what they feel. That's all very well for
grown-up people. You like me, don't you?"

Though I was greatly delighted that she talked so freely
to me, still I was a little hurt. I wanted to show her that
she had not a mere boy to deal with, and assuming as easy
and serious an air as I could, I observed, "Certainly. I like
you very much, Zinaïda Alexandrovna; I have no wish to
conceal it."

She shook her head very deliberately. "Have you a tutor?" she asked suddenly.

"No; I've not had a tutor for a long, long while."

I told a lie; it was not a month since I had parted with
my Frenchman.

"Oh! I see then—you are quite grown-up."

She tapped me lightly on the fingers. "Hold your hands
straight!" And she applied herself busily to winding the
ball.

I seized the opportunity when she was looking down
and fell to watching her, at first stealthily, then more and
more boldly. Her face struck me as even more charming
than on the previous evening; everything in it was so delicate, clever, and sweet. She was sitting with her back to a
window covered with a white blind, the sunshine, streaming in through the blind, shed a soft light over her fluffy
golden curls, her innocent neck, her sloping shoulders, and
tender untroubled bosom. I gazed at her, and how dear
and near she was already to me! It seemed to me I had
known her a long while and had never known anything
nor lived at all till I met her. ... She was wearing a dark
and rather shabby dress and an apron; I would gladly, I
felt, have kissed every fold of that dress and apron. The

tips of her little shoes peeped out from under her skirt; I could have bowed down in adoration to those shoes. . . . "And here I am sitting before her," I thought; "I have made acquaintance with her . . . what happiness, my God!" I could hardly keep from jumping up from my chair in ecstasy, but I only swung my legs a little, like a small child who has been given sweetmeats.

I was as happy as a fish in water, and I could have stayed in that room for ever, have never left that place.

Her eyelids were slowly lifted, and once more her clear eyes shone kindly upon me, and again she smiled.

"How you look at me!" she said slowly, and she held up a threatening finger.

I blushed . . . "She understands it all, she sees all," flashed through my mind. "And how could she fail to understand and see it all?"

All at once there was a sound in the next room—the clink of a sabre.

"Zina!" screamed the princess in the drawing-room, "Byelovzorov has brought you a kitten."

"A kitten!" cried Zinaïda, and getting up from her chair impetuously, she flung the ball of worsted on my knees and ran away.

I too got up and, laying the skein and the ball of wool on the window-sill, I went into the drawing-room and stood still, hesitating. In the middle of the room, a tabby kitten was lying with outstretched paws; Zinaïda was on her knees before it, cautiously lifting up its little face. Near the old princess, and filling up almost the whole space between the two windows, was a flaxen curly-headed young man, a hussar, with a rosy face and prominent eyes.

"What a funny little thing!" Zinaïda was saying; "and its eyes are not grey, but green, and what long ears! Thank you, Viktor Yegoritch! you are very kind."

The hussar, in whom I recognised one of the young men I had seen the evening before, smiled and bowed with a clink of his spurs and a jingle of the chain of his sabre.

"You were pleased to say yesterday that you wished to possess a tabby kitten with long ears . . . so I obtained it. Your word is law." And he bowed again.

The kitten gave a feeble mew and began sniffing the ground.

"It's hungry!" cried Zinaïda. "Vonifaty, Sonia! bring some milk."

A maid, in an old yellow gown with a faded kerchief at her neck, came in with a saucer of milk and set it before the kitten. The kitten started, blinked, and began lapping.

"What a pink little tongue it has!" remarked Zinaïda, putting her head almost on the ground and peeping at it sideways under its very nose.

The kitten having had enough began to purr and move its paws affectedly. Zinaïda got up, and turning to the maid said carelessly, "Take it away."

"For the kitten—your little hand," said the hussar, with a simper and a shrug of his strongly-built frame, which was tightly buttoned up in a new uniform.

"Both," replied Zinaïda, and she held out her hands to him. While he was kissing them, she looked at me over his shoulder.

I stood stockstill in the same place and did not know whether to laugh, to say something, or to be silent. Suddenly through the open door into the passage I caught sight of our footman, Fyodor. He was making signs to me. Mechanically I went out to him.

"What do you want?" I asked.

"Your mamma has sent for you," he said in a whisper. "She is angry that you have not come back with the answer."

"Why, have I been here long?"

"Over an hour."

"Over an hour!" I repeated unconsciously, and going back to the drawing-room I began to make bows and scrape with my heels.

"Where are you off to?" the young princess asked, glancing at me from behind the hussar.

"I must go home. So I am to say," I added, addressing the old lady, "that you will come to us about two."

"Do you say so, my good sir."

The princess hurriedly pulled out her snuff-box and took snuff so loudly that I positively jumped. "Do you say so," she repeated, blinking tearfully and sneezing.

I bowed once more, turned, and went out of the room with that sensation of awkwardness in my spine which a very young man feels when he knows he is being looked at from behind.

"Mind you come and see us again, M'sieu Voldemar," Zinaïda called, and she laughed again.

"Why is it she's always laughing?" I thought, as I went back home escorted by Fyodor, who said nothing to me, but walked behind me with an air of disapprobation. My mother scolded me and wondered what ever I could have been doing so long at the princess's. I made her no reply and went off to my own room. I felt suddenly very sad. . . . I tried hard not to cry. . . . I was jealous of the hussar.

5

The princess called on my mother as she had promised and made a disagreeable impression on her. I was not present at their interview, but at table my mother told my father that this Princess Zasyekin struck her as a *femme très vulgaire,* that she had quite worn her out begging her to interest Prince Sergei in their behalf, that she seemed to have no end of lawsuits and affairs on hand—*de vilaines affaires d'argent*—and must be a very troublesome and litigious person. My mother added, however, that she had asked her and her daughter to dinner the next day (hearing the word "daughter" I buried my nose in my plate), for after all she was a neighbour and a person of title. Upon this my father informed my mother that he remembered now who this lady was; that he had in his youth known the deceased Prince Zasyekin, a very well-bred, but frivolous and absurd person; that he had been nicknamed in society *"le Parisien,"* from having lived a long while in Paris; that he had been very rich, but had gambled away all his property; and for some unknown reason, probably for money, though indeed he might have chosen better, if so, my father added with a cold smile, he had married the daughter of an agent, and after his marriage had entered upon speculations and ruined himself utterly. "If only she doesn't try to borrow money," observed my mother.

"That's exceedingly possible," my father responded tranquilly. "Does she speak French?"

"Very badly."

"H'm. It's of no consequence anyway. I think you said you had asked the daughter too; some one was telling me she was a very charming and cultivated girl."

"Ah! Then she can't take after her mother."

"Nor her father either," rejoined my father. "He was cultivated indeed, but a fool."

My mother sighed and sank into thought. My father said no more. I felt very uncomfortable during this conversation.

After dinner I went into the garden, but without my gun. I swore to myself that I would not go near the Zasyekins' garden, but an irresistible force drew me thither, and not in vain. I had hardly reached the fence when I caught sight of Zinaïda. This time she was alone. She held a book in her hands, and was coming slowly along the path. She did not notice me.

I almost let her pass by; but all at once I changed my mind and coughed.

She turned round, but did not stop, pushed back with one hand the broad blue ribbon of her round straw hat, looked at me, smiled slowly, and again bent her eyes on the book.

I took off my cap, and after hesitating a moment, walked away with a heavy heart. "*Que suis-je pour elle?*" I thought (God knows why) in French.

Familiar footsteps sounded behind me; I looked round, my father came up to me with his light, rapid walk.

"Is that the young princess?" he asked me.

"Yes."

"Why, do you know her?"

"I saw her this morning at the princess's."

My father stopped, and, turning sharply on his heel, went back. When he was on a level with Zinaïda, he made her a courteous bow. She, too, bowed to him, with some astonishment on her face, and dropped her book. I saw how she looked after him. My father was always irreproachably dressed, simple and in a style of his own; but his figure had never struck me as more graceful, never had his grey hat sat more becomingly on his curls, which were scarcely perceptibly thinner than they had once been.

I bent my steps toward Zinaïda, but she did not even glance at me; she picked up her book again and went away.

6

The whole evening and the following day I spent in a sort of dejected apathy. I remember I tried to work and took up Keidanov, but the boldly printed lines and pages of the famous text-book passed before my eyes in vain. I read ten times over the words: "Julius Caesar was distinguished by warlike courage." I did not understand anything and threw the book aside. Before dinner-time I pomaded myself once more, and once more put on my tail-coat and necktie.

"What's that for?" my mother demanded. "You're not a student yet, and God knows whether you'll get through the examination. And you've not long had a new jacket! You can't throw it away!"

"There will be visitors," I murmured almost in despair.

"What nonsense! fine visitors indeed!"

I had to submit. I changed my tail-coat for my jacket, but I did not take off the necktie. The princess and her daughter made their appearance half an hour before dinner-time; the old lady had put on, in addition to the green dress with which I was already acquainted, a yellow shawl, and an old-fashioned cap adorned with flame-coloured ribbons. She began talking at once about her money difficulties, sighing, complaining of her poverty, and imploring assistance, but she made herself at home; she took snuff as noisily, and fidgeted and lolled about in her chair as freely as ever. It never seemed to have struck her that she was a princess. Zinaïda on the other hand was rigid, almost haughty in her demeanour, every inch a princess. There was a cold immobility and dignity in her face. I should not have recognised it; I should not have known her smiles, her glances, though I thought her exquisite in this new aspect too. She wore a light barége dress with pale blue flowers on it; her hair fell in long curls down her cheek in the English fashion; this style went well with the cold expression of her face. My father sat beside her during dinner, and entertained his neighbour with the finished and serene courtesy peculiar to him. He glanced at her from time to time, and she glanced at him, but so strangely, almost with hostility. Their conversation was carried on in French; I was surprised, I remember, at the purity of Zinaïda's accent. The princess, while we were at table, as before made no ceremony; she ate a great deal, and praised the dishes. My mother was obviously bored by her, and answered her with a sort of weary indifference; my father faintly frowned now and then. My mother did not like Zinaïda either. "A conceited minx," she said next day. "And fancy, what she has to be conceited about, *avec sa mine de grisette!*"

"It's clear you have never seen any grisettes," my father observed to her.

"Thank God, I haven't!"

"Thank God, to be sure . . . only how can you form an opinion of them, then?"

To me Zinaïda had paid no attention whatever. Soon after dinner the princess got up to go.

"I shall rely on your kind offices, Maria Nikolaevna and Piotr Vassilitch," she said in a doleful sing-song to my mother and father. "I've no help for it! There were days, but they are over. Here I am, an excellency, and a poor honour it is with nothing to eat!"

My father made her a respectful bow and escorted her to the door of the hall. I was standing there in my short jacket, staring at the floor, like a man under sentence of death. Zinaïda's treatment of me had crushed me utterly. What was my astonishment, when, as she passed me, she whispered quickly with her former kind expression in her eyes: "Come to see us at eight, do you hear, be sure. . . ." I simply threw up my hands, but already she was gone, flinging a white scarf over her head.

7

At eight o'clock precisely, in my tail-coat and with my hair brushed up into a tuft on my head, I entered the passage of the lodge, where the princess lived. The old servant looked crossly at me and got up unwillingly from his bench. There was a sound of merry voices in the drawing-room. I opened the door and fell back in amazement. In the middle of the room was the young princess, standing on a chair, holding a man's hat in front of her; round the chair crowded some half a dozen men. They were trying to put their hands into the hat, while she held it above their heads, shaking it violently. On seeing me, she cried, "Stay, stay, another guest, he must have a ticket too," and leaping lightly down from the chair she took me by the cuff of my coat. "Come along," she said, "why are you standing still? *Messieurs,* let me make you acquainted: this is M'sieu Voldemar, the son of our neighbour. And this," she went on, addressing me, and indicating her guests in turn, "Count Malevsky, Doctor Lushin, Meidanov the poet, the retired captain Nirmatsky, and Byelovzorov the hussar, whom you've seen already. I hope you will be good friends."

I was so confused that I did not even bow to any one; in Doctor Lushin I recognised the dark man who had so mercilessly put me to shame in the garden; the others were unknown to me.

"Count!" continued Zinaïda, "write M'sieu Voldemar a ticket."

"That's not fair," was objected in a slight Polish accent by the count, a very handsome and fashionably dressed brunette, with expressive brown eyes, a thin little white nose, and delicate little moustaches over a tiny mouth. "This gentleman has not been playing forfeits with us."

"It's unfair," repeated in chorus Byelovzorov and the gentleman described as a retired captain, a man of forty, pock-marked to a hideous degree, curly-headed as a Negro, round-shouldered, bandy-legged, and dressed in a military coat without epaulets, worn unbuttoned.

"Write him a ticket, I tell you," repeated the young princess. "What's this mutiny? M'sieu Voldemar is with us for the first time, and there are no rules for him yet. It's no use grumbling—write it, I wish it."

The count shrugged his shoulders but bowed submissively, took the pen in his white, ring-bedecked fingers, tore off a scrap of paper and wrote on it.

"At least let us explain to Mr. Voldemar what we are about," Lushin began in a sarcastic voice, "or else he will

be quite lost. Do you see, young man, we are playing forfeits? the princess has to pay a forfeit, and the one who
draws the lucky lot is to have the privilege of kissing her
hand. Do you understand what I've told you?"

I simply stared at him, and continued to stand still in
bewilderment, while the young princess jumped up on the
chair again, and again began waving the hat. They all
stretched up to her, and I went after the rest.

"Meidanov," said the princess to a tall young man with
a thin face, little dim-sighted eyes, and exceedingly long
black hair, "you as a poet ought to be magnanimous, and
give up your number to M'sieu Voldemar so that he may
have two chances instead of one."

But Meidanov shook his head in refusal, and tossed his
hair. After all the others I put my hand into the hat, and
unfolded my lot. . . . Heavens! what was my condition
when I saw on it the word, Kiss!

"Kiss!" I could not help crying aloud.

"Bravo! he has won it," the princess said quickly. "How
glad I am!" She came down from the chair and gave me
such a bright sweet look, that my heart bounded. "Are
you glad?" she asked me.

"Me?" . . . I faltered.

"Sell me your lot," Byelovzorov growled suddenly just in
my ear. "I'll give you a hundred roubles."

I answered the hussar with such an indignant look, that
Zinaïda clapped her hands, while Lushin cried, "He's a
fine fellow!"

"But, as master of the ceremonies," he went on, "it's my
duty to see that all the rules are kept. M'sieu Voldemar, go
down on one knee. That is our regulation."

Zinaïda stood in front of me, her head a little on one
side as though to get a better look at me; she held out her
hand to me with dignity. A mist passed before my eyes; I
meant to drop on one knee, sank on both, and pressed my
lips to Zinaïda's fingers so awkwardly that I scratched myself a little with the tip of her nail.

"Well done!" cried Lushin, and helped me to get up.

The game of forfeits went on. Zinaïda sat me down beside her. She invented all sorts of extraordinary forfeits!
She had among other things to represent a "statue," and
she chose as a pedestal the hideous Nirmatsky, told him
to bow down in an arch, and bend his head down on his

breast. The laughter never paused for an instant. For me, a boy constantly brought up in the seclusion of a dignified manor-house, all this noise and uproar, this unceremonious, almost riotous gaiety, these relations with unknown persons, were simply intoxicating. My head went round, as though from wine. I began laughing and talking louder than the others, so much so that the old princess, who was sitting in the next room with some sort of clerk from the Tversky gate, invited by her for consultation on business, positively came in to look at me. But I felt so happy that I did not mind anything, I didn't care a straw for any one's jeers, or dubious looks. Zinaïda continued to show me a preference, and kept me at her side. In one forfeit, I had to sit by her, both hidden under one silk handkerchief: I was to tell her *my secret*. I remember our two heads being all at once in a warm, half-transparent, fragrant darkness, the soft, close brightness of her eyes in the dark, and the burning breath from her parted lips, and the gleam of her teeth and the ends of her hair tickling me and setting me on fire. I was silent. She smiled slyly and mysteriously, and at last whispered to me, "Well, what is it?" but I merely blushed and laughed, and turned away, catching my breath. We got tired of forfeits—we began to play a game with a string. My God! what were my transports when, for not paying attention, I got a sharp and vigorous slap on my fingers from her, and how I tried afterwards to pretend that I was absent-minded, and she teased me, and would not touch the hands I held out to her! What didn't we do that evening! We played the piano, and sang and danced and acted a gypsy encampment. Nirmatsky was dressed up as a bear, and made to drink salt water. Count Malevsky showed us several sorts of card tricks, and finished, after shuffling the cards, by dealing himself all the trumps at whist, on which Lushin "had the honour of congratulating him." Meidanov recited portions from his poem "The Manslayer" (romanticism was at its height at this period), which he intended to bring out in a black cover with the title in blood-red letters; they stole the clerk's cap off his knee, and made him dance a Cossack dance by way of ransom for it; they dressed up old Vonifaty in a woman's cap, and the young princess put on a man's hat. . . . I could not enumerate all we did. Only Byelovzorov kept more and more in the background, scowl-

ing and angry. . . . Sometimes his eyes looked bloodshot,
he flushed all over, and it seemed every minute as though
he would rush out upon us all and scatter us like shavings
in all directions; but the young princess would glance at
him, and shake her finger at him, and he would retire into
his corner again.

We were quite worn out at last. Even the old princess,
though she was ready for anything, as she expressed it,
and no noise wearied her, felt tired at last, and longed for
peace and quiet. At twelve o'clock at night, supper was
served, consisting of a piece of stale dry cheese, and some
cold turnovers of minced ham, which seemed to me more
delicious than any pastry I had ever tasted; there was only
one bottle of wine, and that was a strange one; a dark-
coloured bottle with a wide neck, and the wine in it was of
a pink hue; no one drank it, however. Tired out and faint
with happiness, I left the lodge; at parting Zinaïda pressed
my hand warmly, and again smiled mysteriously.

The night air was heavy and damp in my heated face; a
storm seemed to be gathering; black stormclouds grew
and crept across the sky, their smoky outlines visibly
changing. A gust of wind shivered restlessly in the dark
trees, and somewhere, far away on the horizon, muffled
thunder angrily muttered as it were to itself.

I made my way up to my room by the back stairs. My
old man-nurse was asleep on the floor, and I had to step
over him; he waked up, saw me, and told me that my
mother had again been very angry with me, and had
wished to send after me again, but that my father had
prevented her. (I had never gone to bed without saying
good-night to my mother, and asking her blessing. There
was no help for it now!)

I told my man that I would undress and go to bed by
myself, and I put out the candle. But I did not undress,
and did not go to bed.

I sat down on a chair, and sat a long while, as though
spell-bound. What I was feeling was so new and so sweet.
. . . I sat still, hardly looking round and not moving, drew
slow breaths, and only from time to time laughed silently
at some recollection, or turned cold within at the thought
that I was in love, that this was she, that this was love.
Zinaïda's face floated slowly before me in the darkness—
floated, and did not float away; her lips still wore the same

enigmatic smile, her eyes watched me, a little from one side, with a questioning, dreamy, tender look . . . as at the instant of parting from her. At last I got up, walked on tiptoe to my bed, and without undressing, laid my head carefully on the pillow, as though I were afraid by an abrupt movement to disturb what filled my soul. . . . I lay down, but did not even close my eyes. Soon I noticed that faint glimmers of light of some sort were thrown continually into the room. . . . I sat up and looked at the window. The window-frame could be clearly distinguished from the mysteriously and dimly-lighted panes. It is a storm, I thought; and a storm it really was, but it was raging so very far away that the thunder could not be heard; only blurred, long, as it were branching, gleams of lightning flashed continually over the sky; it was not flashing, though, so much as quivering and twitching like the wing of a dying bird. I got up, went to the window, and stood there till morning. . . . The lightning never ceased for an instant; it was what is called among the peasants a *sparrow night*. I gazed at the dumb sandy plain, at the dark mass of the Neskutchny gardens, at the yellowish façades of the distant buildings, which seemed to quiver too at each faint flash. . . . I gazed, and could not turn away; these silent lightning flashes, these gleams seemed in response to the secret silent fires which were aglow within me. Morning began to dawn; the sky was flushed in patches of crimson. As the sun came nearer, the lightning grew gradually paler, and ceased; the quivering gleams were fewer and fewer, and vanished at last, drowned in the sobering positive light of the coming day. . . .

And my lightning flashes vanished too. I felt great weariness and peace . . . but Zinaïda's image still floated triumphant over my soul. But it too, this image, seemed more tranquil: like a swan rising out of the reeds of a bog, it stood out from the other unbeautiful figures surrounding it, and as I fell asleep, I flung myself before it in farewell, trusting adoration. . . .

Oh, sweet emotions, gentle harmony, goodness and peace of the softened heart, melting bliss of the first raptures of love, where are they, were are they?

8

The next morning, when I came down to tea, my mother
scolded me—less severely, however, than I had expected
—and made me tell her how I had spent the previous evening. I answered her in few words, omitting many details, and trying to give the most innocent air to everything.

"Anyway, they're people who're not *comme il faut*," my
mother commented, "and you've no business to be hanging about there, instead of preparing yourself for the examination, and doing your work."

As I was well aware that my mother's anxiety about
my studies was confined to these few words, I did not feel
it necessary to make any rejoinder; but after morning tea
was over, my father took me by the arm, and turning into
the garden with me, forced me to tell him all I had seen
at the Zasyekins'.

A curious influence my father had over me, and curious
were the relations existing between us. He took hardly
any interest in my education, but he never hurt my feelings; he respected my freedom, he treated me—if I may
so express it—with courtesy, . . . only he never let me be
really close to him. I loved him, I admired him, he was
my ideal of a man—and Heavens! how passionately devoted I should have been to him, if I had not been continually conscious of his holding me off! But when he liked,
he could almost instantaneously, by a single word, a single gesture, call forth an unbounded confidence in him.
My soul expanded, I chattered away to him, as to a wise
friend, a kindly teacher . . . then he as suddenly got rid
of me, and again he was keeping me off, gently and affectionately, but still he kept me off.

Sometimes he was in high spirits, and then he was
ready to romp and frolic with me, like a boy (he was fond
of vigorous physical exercise of every sort); once—it never
happened a second time!—he caressed me with such ten-

derness that I almost shed tears. . . . But high spirits and
tenderness alike vanished completely, and what had
passed between us, gave me nothing to build on for the
future—it was as though I had dreamed it all. Sometimes
I would scrutinise his clever handsome bright face . . .
my heart would throb, and my whole being yearn to him
. . . he would seem to feel what was going on within me,
would give me a passing pat on the cheek, and go away,
or take up some work, or suddenly freeze all over as only
he knew how to freeze, and I shrank into myself at once,
and turned cold too. His rare fits of friendliness to me
were never called forth by my silent, but intelligible entreaties: they always occurred unexpectedly. Thinking
over my father's character later, I have come to the conclusion that he had no thoughts to spare for me and for
family life; his heart was in other things, and found complete satisfaction elsewhere. "Take for yourself what you
can, and don't be ruled by others; to belong to oneself—
the whole savour of life lies in that," he said to me one
day. Another time, I, as a young democrat, fell to airing
my views on liberty (he was 'kind,' as I used to call it, that
day; and at such times I could talk to him as I liked).
"Liberty," he repeated; "and do you know what can give
a man liberty?"

"What?"

"Will, his own will, and it gives power, which is better
than liberty. Know how to will, and you will be free, and
will lead."

My father, before all, and above all, desired to live, and
lived. . . . Perhaps he had a presentiment that he would
not have long to enjoy the "savour" of life: he died at
forty-two.

I described my evening at the Zasyekins' minutely to my
father. Half attentively, half carelessly, he listened to me,
sitting on a garden seat, drawing in the sand with his
cane. Now and then he laughed, shot bright, droll glances
at me, and spurred me on with short questions and as-
sents. At first I could not bring myself even to utter the
name of Zinaïda, but I could not restrain myself long,
and began singing her praises. My father still laughed;
then he grew thoughtful, stretched, and got up.

I remembered that as he came out of the house he had

ordered his horse to be saddled. He was a splendid horse-man, and, long before Rarey, had the secret of breaking in the most vicious horses.

"Shall I come with you, father?" I asked.

"No," he answered, and his face resumed its ordinary expression of friendly indifference. "Go alone, if you like; and tell the coachman I'm not going."

He turned his back on me and walked rapidly away. I looked after him; he disappeared through the gates. I saw his hat moving along beside the fence; he went into the Zasyekins'.

He stayed there not more than an hour, but then de-parted at once for the town, and did not return home till evening.

After dinner I went myself to the Zasyekins'. In the drawing-room I found only the old princess. On seeing me she scratched her head under her cap with a knitting-needle, and suddenly asked me, could I copy a petition for her.

"With pleasure," I replied, sitting down on the edge of a chair.

"Only mind and make the letters bigger," observed the princess, handing me a dirty sheet of paper; "and couldn't you do it to-day, my good sir?"

"Certainly, I will copy it to-day."

The door of the next room was just opened, and in the crack I saw the face of Zinaïda, pale and pensive, her hair flung carelessly back; she stared at me with big chilly eyes, and softly closed the door.

"Zina, Zina!" called the old lady. Zinaïda made no re-sponse. I took home the old lady's petition and spent the whole evening over it.

9

My "passion" dated from that day. I felt at that time, I recollect, something like what a man must feel on enter-ing the service: I had ceased now to be simply a young boy; I was in love. I have said that my passion dated from that day; I might have added that my sufferings too dated from the same day. Away from Zinaïda I pined; nothing was to my mind; everything went wrong with me; I spent whole days thinking intensely about her . . . I pined when away, . . . but in her presence I was no better off. I was jealous; I was conscious of my insignificance; I was stupidly sulky or stupidly abject, and, all the same, an invincible force drew me to her, and I could not help a shudder of delight whenever I stepped through the doorway of her room. Zinaïda guessed at once that I was in love with her, and indeed I never even thought of concealing it. She amused herself with my passion, made a fool of me, petted and tormented me. There is a sweetness in being the sole source, the autocratic and irresponsible cause of the greatest joy and profoundest pain to another, and I was like wax in Zinaïda's hands; though, indeed, I was not the only one in love with her. All the men who visited the house were crazy over her, and she kept them all in leading-strings at her feet. It amused her to arouse their hopes and then their fears, to turn them round her finger (she used to call it knocking their heads together), while they never dreamed of offering resistance and eagerly submitted to her. About her whole being, so full of life and beauty, there was a peculiarly bewitching mixture of slyness and carelessness, of artificiality and simplicity, of composure and frolicsomeness; about everything she did or said, about every action of hers, there clung a delicate, fine charm, in which an individual power was manifest at work. And her face was ever changing, working too; it expressed, almost at the same time, irony, dreaminess, and passion. Various emotions, delicate and quick-changing as the shadows of clouds on a sunny day of wind, chased one another continually over her lips and eyes.

Each of her adorers was necessary to her. Byelovzorov, whom she sometimes called "my wild beast," and sometimes simply "mine," would gladly have flung himself into the fire for her sake. With little confidence in his intellectual abilities and other qualities, he was for ever offering her marriage, hinting that the others were merely hanging about with no serious intention. Meidanov responded to the poetic fibres of her nature; a man of rather cold temperament, like almost all writers, he forced himself to convince her, and perhaps himself, that he adored her, sang her praises in endless verses, and read them to her with a peculiar enthusiasm, at once affected and sincere. She sympathised with him, and at the same time jeered at him a little; she had no great faith in him, and after listening to his outpourings, she would make him read Pushkin, as she said, to clear the air. Lushin, the ironical doctor, so cynical in words, knew her better than any of them, and loved her more than all, though he abused her to her face and behind her back. She could not help respecting him, but made him smart for it, and at times, with a peculiar, malignant pleasure, made him feel that he too was at her mercy. "I'm a flirt, I'm heartless, I'm an actress in my instincts," she said to him one day in my presence; "well and good! Give me your hand then; I'll stick this pin in it, you'll be ashamed of this young man's seeing it, it will hurt you, but you'll laugh for all that, you truthful person." Lushin crimsoned, turned away, bit his lips, but ended by submitting his hand. She pricked it, and he did in fact begin to laugh, . . . and she laughed, thrusting the pin in pretty deeply, and peeping into his eyes, which he vainly strove to keep in other directions. . . .

I understood least of all the relations existing between Zinaïda and Count Malevsky. He was handsome, clever, and adroit, but something equivocal, something false in him was apparent even to me, a boy of sixteen, and I marvelled that Zinaïda did not notice it. But possibly she did notice this element of falsity really and was not repelled by it. Her irregular education, strange acquaintances and habits, the constant presence of her mother, the poverty and disorder in their house, everything, from the very liberty the young girl enjoyed, with the consciousness of her superiority to the people around her, had developed in her a sort of half-contemptuous carelessness and lack of fastidiousness. At any time anything might happen; Vonifaty might announce that there was no sugar, or some revolting scandal would come to her ears, or her guests would fall to quarrelling among themselves —she would only shake her curls, and say, "What does it matter?" and care little enough about it.

But my blood, anyway, was sometimes on fire with indignation when Malevsky approached her, with a sly, fox-

like action, leaned gracefully on the back of her chair,
and began whispering in her ear with a self-satisfied and
ingratiating little smile, while she folded her arms across
her bosom, looked intently at him and smiled too, and
shook her head.

"What induces you to receive Count Malevsky?" I asked
her one day.

"He has such pretty moustaches," she answered. "But
that's rather beyond you."

"You needn't think I care for him," she said to me
another time. "No; I can't care for people I have to look
down upon. I must have some one who can master me,
. . . But, merciful heavens, I hope I may never come
across any one like that! I don't want to be caught in any
one's claws, not for anything."

"You'll never be in love, then?"

"And you? Don't I love you?" she said, and she flicked
me on the nose with the tip of her glove.

Yes, Zinaïda amused herself hugely at my expense. For
three weeks I saw her every day, and what didn't she do
with me! She rarely came to see us, and I was not sorry
for it; in our house she was transformed into a young
lady, a young princess, and I was a little overawed by her.
I was afraid of betraying myself before my mother; she
had taken a great dislike to Zinaïda, and kept a hostile
eye upon us. My father I was not so much afraid of; he
seemed not to notice me. He talked little to her, but always with special cleverness and significance. I gave up
working and reading; I even gave up walking about the
neighbourhood and riding my horse. Like a beetle tied
by the leg, I moved continually round and round my be-
loved little lodge. I would gladly have stopped there altogether, it seemed . . . but that was impossible. My
mother scolded me, and sometimes Zinaïda herself drove
me away. Then I used to shut myself up in my room, or
go down to the very end of the garden, and climbing
into what was left of a tall stone greenhouse, now in
ruins, sit for hours with my legs hanging over the wall
that looked on to the road, gazing and gazing and seeing
nothing. White butterflies flitted lazily by me, over the
dusty nettles; a saucy sparrow settled not far off on the
half crumbling red brickwork and twittered irritably, incessantly twisting and turning and preening his tail-

feathers; the still mistrustful rooks cawed now and then, sitting high, high up on the bare top of a birch-tree; the sun and wind played softly on its pliant branches; the tinkle of the bells of the Don monastery floated across to me from time to time, peaceful and dreary; while I sat, gazed, listened, and was filled full of a nameless sensation in which all was contained: sadness and joy and the fore-taste of the future, and the desire and dread of life. But at that time I understood nothing of it, and could have given a name to nothing of all that was passing at ran-dom within me, or should have called it all by one name —the name of Zinaïda.

Zinaïda continued to play cat and mouse with me. She flirted with me, and I was all agitation and rapture; then she would suddenly thrust me away, and I dared not go near her—dared not look at her.

I remember she was very cold to me for several days together; I was completely crushed, and creeping timidly to their lodge, tried to keep close to the old princess, re-gardless of the circumstance that she was particularly scolding and grumbling just at that time; her financial affairs had been going badly, and she had already had two "explanations" with the police officials.

One day I was walking in the garden beside the familiar fence, and I caught sight of Zinaïda; leaning on both arms, she was sitting on the grass, not stirring a muscle. I was about to make off cautiously, but she suddenly raised her head and beckoned me imperiously. My heart failed me; I did not understand her at first. She repeated her signal. I promptly jumped over the fence and ran joy-fully up to her, but she brought me to a halt with a look, and motioned me to the path two paces from her. In con-fusion, not knowing what to do, I fell on my knees at the edge of the path. She was so pale, such bitter suffering, such intense weariness, was expressed in every feature of her face, that it sent a pang to my heart, and I mut-tered unconsciously, "What is the matter?"

Zinaïda stretched out her hand, picked a blade of grass, bit it and flung it away from her.

"You love me very much?" she asked at last. "Yes."

I made no answer—indeed, what need was there to an-swer?

"Yes," she repeated, looking at me as before. "That's

so. The same eyes,"—she went on; sank into thought, and hid her face in her hands. "Everything's grown so loathsome to me," she whispered, "I would have gone to the other end of the world first—I can't bear it, I can't get over it. . . . And what is there before me! . . . Ah, I am wretched. . . . My God, how wretched I am!"

"What for?" I asked timidly.

Zinaïda made no answer, she simply shrugged her shoulders. I remained kneeling, gazing at her with intense sadness. Every word she had uttered simply cut me to the heart. At that instant I felt I would gladly have given my life, if only she should not grieve. I gazed at her—and though I could not understand why she was wretched, I vividly pictured to myself, how in a fit of insupportable anguish, she had suddenly come out into the garden, and sunk to the earth, as though mown down by a scythe. It was all bright and green about her; the wind was whispering in the leaves of the trees, and swinging now and then a long branch of a raspberry bush over Zinaïda's head. There was a sound of the cooing of doves, and the bees hummed, flying low over the scanty grass. Overhead the sun was radiantly blue—while I was so sorrowful. . . .

"Read me some poetry," said Zinaïda in an undertone, and she propped herself on her elbow; "I like your reading poetry. You read it in sing-song, but that's no matter, that comes of being young. Read me 'On the Hills of Georgia.' Only sit down first."

I sat down and read "On the Hills of Georgia."

" 'That the heart cannot choose but love,' " repeated Zinaïda. "That's where poetry's so fine; it tells us what is not, and what's not only better than what is, but much more like the truth, "cannot choose but love,"—it might want not to, but it can't help it." She was silent again, then all at once she started and got up. "Come along. Meidanov's indoors with mamma, he brought me his poem, but I deserted him. His feelings are hurt too now . . . I can't help it! you'll understand it all some day . . . only don't be angry with me!"

Zinaïda hurriedly pressed my hand and ran on ahead. We went back into the lodge. Meidanov set to reading us his "Manslayer," which had just appeared in print, but I did not hear him. He screamed and drawled his four-foot iambic lines, the alternating rhythms jingled like

little bells, noisy and meaningless, while I still watched
Zinaïda and tried to take in the import of her last words.

> "Perchance some unknown rival
> Has surprised and mastered thee?"

Meidanov bawled suddenly through his nose—and my
eyes and Zinaïda's met. She looked down and faintly
blushed. I saw her blush, and grew cold with terror. I had
been jealous before, but only at that instant the idea of
her being in love flashed upon my mind. "Good God! she
is in love!"

10

My real torments began from that instant. I racked my
brains, changed my mind, and changed it back again,
and kept an unremitting, though, as far as possible, secret watch on Zinaïda. A change had come over her, that
was obvious. She began going walks alone—and long
walks. Sometimes she would not see visitors; she would
sit for hours together in her room. This had never been a
habit of hers till now. I suddenly became—or fancied I
had become—extraordinarily penetrating.

"Isn't it he? or isn't it he?" I asked myself, passing in
inward agitation from one of her admirers to another.
Count Malevsky secretly struck me as more to be feared
than the others, though, for Zinaïda's sake, I was ashamed
to confess it to myself.

My watchfulness did not see beyond the end of my nose,
and its secrecy probably deceived no one; any way, Doctor
Lushin soon saw through me. But he, too, had changed of
late; he had grown thin, he laughed as often, but his
laugh seemed more hollow, more spiteful, shorter, an involuntary nervous irritability took the place of his former
light irony and assumed cynicism.

"Why are you incessantly hanging about here, young
man?" he said to me one day, when we were left alone
together in the Zasyekins' drawing-room. (The young
princess had not come home from a walk, and the shrill
voice of the old princess could be heard within; she was

scolding the maid.) "You ought to be studying, working—while you're young—and what are you doing?"

"You can't tell whether I work at home," I retorted with some haughtiness, but also with some hesitation.

"A great deal of work you do! that's not what you're thinking about! Well, I won't find fault with that . . . at your age that's in the natural order of things. But you've been awfully unlucky in your choice. Don't you see what this house is?"

"I don't understand you," I observed.

"You don't understand? so much the worse for you. I regard it as a duty to warn you. Old bachelors, like me, can come here, what harm can it do us! we're tough, nothing can hurt us, what harm can it do us; but your skin's tender yet—this air is bad for you—believe me, you may get harm from it."

"How so?"

"Why, are you well now? Are you in a normal condition? Is what you're feeling—beneficial to you—good for you?"

"Why, what am I feeling?" I said, while in my heart I knew the doctor was right.

"Ah, young man, young man," the doctor went on with an intonation that suggested that something highly insulting to me was contained in these two words, "what's the use of your prevaricating, when, thank God, what's in your heart is in your face, so far? But there, what's the use of talking? I shouldn't come here myself, if . . . (the doctor compressed his lips) . . . if I weren't such a queer fellow. Only this is what surprises me; how it is, you, with your intelligence, don't see what is going on around you?"

"And what is going on?" I put in, all on the alert.

The doctor looked at me with a sort of ironical compassion.

"Nice of me!" he said as though to himself, "as if he need know anything of it. In fact, I tell you again," he added, raising his voice, "the atmosphere here is not fit for you. You like being here, but what of that! it's nice and sweet-smelling in a greenhouse—but there's no living in it. Yes! do as I tell you, and go back to your Keidanov."

The old princess came in, and began complaining to the doctor of her toothache. Then Zinaïda appeared.

"Come," said the old princess, "you must scold her, doctor. She's drinking iced water all day long; is that good for her, pray, with her delicate chest?"

"Why do you do that?" asked Lushin.

"Why, what effect could it have?"

"What effect? You might get a chill and die."

"Truly? Do you mean it? Very well—so much the better."

"A fine idea!" muttered the doctor. The old princess had gone out.

"Yes, a fine idea," repeated Zinaïda. "Is life such a festive affair? Just look about you. . . . Is it nice, eh? Or do you imagine I don't understand it, and don't feel it? It gives me pleasure—drinking iced water; and can you seriously assure me that such a life is worth too much to be risked for an instant's pleasure—happiness I won't even talk about."

"Oh, very well," remarked Lushin, "caprice and irresponsibility. . . . Those two words sum you up; your whole nature's contained in those two words."

Zinaïda laughed nervously.

"You're late for the post, my dear doctor. You don't keep a good look-out; you're behind the times. Put on your spectacles. I'm in no capricious humour now. To make fools of you, to make a fool of myself . . . much fun there is in that!—and as for irresponsibility . . . M'sieu Voldemar," Zinaïda added suddenly, stamping, "don't make such a melancholy face. I can't endure people to pity me." She went quickly out of the room.

"It's bad for you, very bad for you, this atmosphere, young man," Lushin said to me once more.

11

On the evening of the same day the usual guests were assembled at the Zasyekins'. I was among them.

The conversation turned on Meidanov's poem. Zinaïda expressed genuine admiration of it. "But do you know what?" she said to him. "If I were a poet, I would choose quite different subjects. Perhaps it's all nonsense, but strange ideas sometimes come into my head, especially when I'm not asleep in the early morning, when the sky begins to turn rosy and grey both at once. I would, for instance . . . You won't laugh at me?"

"No, no!" we all cried, with one voice.

"I would describe," she went on, folding her arms across her bosom and looking away, "a whole company of young girls at night in a great boat, on a silent river. The moon is shining, and they are all in white, and wearing garlands of white flowers, and singing, you know, something in the nature of a hymn."

"I see—I see; go on," Meidanov commented with dreamy significance.

"All of a sudden, loud clamour, laughter, torches, tambourines on the bank. . . . It's a troop of Bacchantes dancing with songs and cries. It's your business to make a picture of it, Mr. Poet; . . . only I should like the torches to be red and to smoke a great deal, and the Bacchantes' eyes to gleam under their wreaths, and the wreaths to be dusky. Don't forget the tiger-skins, too, and goblets and gold—lots of gold. . . ."

"Where ought the gold to be?" asked Meidanov, tossing back his sleek hair and distending his nostrils.

"Where? on their shoulders and arms and legs—everywhere. They say in ancient times women wore gold rings on their ankles. The Bacchantes call the girls in the boat to them. The girls have ceased singing their hymn—they cannot go on with it, but they do not stir, the river carries them to the bank. And suddenly one of them slowly rises. . . . This you must describe nicely: how she slowly gets up in the moonlight, and how her companions are afraid. . . . She steps over the edge of the boat, the Bacchantes surround her, whirl her away into night and darkness. . . . Here put in smoke in clouds and everything in confusion. There is nothing but the sound of their shrill cry, and her wreath left lying on the bank."

Zinaïda ceased. ("Oh! she is in love!" I thought again.)

"And is that all?" asked Meidanov.

"That's all."

"That can't be the subject of a whole poem," he observed pompously, "but I will make use of your idea for a lyrical fragment."

"In the romantic style?" queried Malevsky.

"Of course, in the romantic style—Byronic."

"Well, to my mind, Hugo beats Byron," the young count observed negligently; "he's more interesting."

"Hugo is a writer of the first class," replied Meidanov; "and my friend, Tonkosheev, in his Spanish romance, *El Trovador* . . ."

"Ah! is that the book with the question-marks turned upside down?" Zinaïda interrupted.

"Yes. That's the custom with the Spanish. I was about to observe that Tonkosheev . . ."

"Come! you're going to argue about classicism and romanticism again," Zinaïda interrupted him a second time. "We'd much better play . . ."

"Forfeits?" put in Lushin.

"No, forfeits are a bore; at comparisons." (This game Zinaïda had invented herself. Some object was mentioned, every one tried to compare it with something, and the one who chose the best comparison got a prize.)

She went up to the window. The sun was just setting; high up in the sky were large red clouds.

"What are those clouds like?" questioned Zinaïda; and without waiting for our answer, she said, "I think they are like the purple sails on the golden ship of Cleopatra, when she sailed to meet Antony. Do you remember, Meidanov, you were telling me about it not long ago?"

All of us, like Polonius in *Hamlet,* opined that the clouds recalled nothing so much as those sails, and that not one of us could discover a better comparison.

"And how old was Antony then?" inquired Zinaïda.

"A young man, no doubt," observed Malevsky.

"Yes, a young man," Meidanov chimed in in confirmation.

"Excuse me," cried Lushin, "he was over forty."

"Over forty," repeated Zinaïda, giving him a rapid glance. . . .

I soon went home. "She is in love," my lips unconsciously repeated. . . . "But with whom?"

12

The days passed by. Zinaïda became stranger and stranger, and more and more incomprehensible. One day I went over to her, and saw her sitting in a basket-chair, her head pressed to the sharp edge of the table. She drew herself up . . . her whole face was wet with tears.

"Ah, you!" she said with a cruel smile. "Come here."

I went up to her. She put her hand on my head, and suddenly catching hold of my hair, began pulling it.

"It hurts me," I said at last.

"Ah! does it? And do you suppose nothing hurts me?" she replied.

"Ai!" she cried suddenly, seeing she had pulled a little tuft of hair out. "What have I done? Poor M'sieu Voldemar!"

She carefully smoothed the hair she had torn out, stroked it round her finger, and twisted it into a ring.

"I shall put your hair in a locket and wear it round my neck," she said, while the tears still glittered in her eyes. "That will be some small consolation to you, perhaps . . . and now good-bye."

I went home, and found an unpleasant state of things there. My mother was having a scene with my father; she was reproaching him with something, while he, as his habit was, maintained a polite and chilly silence, and soon left her. I could not hear what my mother was talking of, and indeed I had no thought to spare for the subject; I only remember that when the interview was over, she sent for me to her room, and referred with great displeasure to the frequent visits I paid the princess, who was, in her words, *une femme capable de tout*. I kissed her hand (this was what I always did when I wanted to cut short a conversation) and went off to my room. Zinaïda's tears had completely overwhelmed me; I positively did not know what to think, and was ready to cry myself; I was a child after all, in spite of my sixteen years. I had now given up thinking about Malevsky, though Byelovzorov looked more and more threatening every day, and glared at the wily count like a wolf at a sheep; but I thought of nothing and of no one. I was lost in imaginings, and was always seeking seclusion and solitude. I was particularly fond of the ruined greenhouse. I would climb up on the high wall, and perch myself, and sit there, such an unhappy, lonely, and melancholy youth, that I felt sorry for myself—and how consolatory where those mournful sensations, how I revelled in them! ...

One day I was sitting on the wall looking into the distance and listening to the ringing of the bells. . . . Suddenly something floated up to me—not a breath of wind and not a shiver, but as it were a whiff of fragrance—as it were, a sense of some one's being near. . . . I looked down. Below, on the path, in a light greyish gown, with a pink parasol on her shoulder, was Zinaïda, hurrying along. She caught sight of me, stopped, and pushing back the brim of her straw hat, she raised her velvety eyes to me.

"What are you doing up there at such a height?" she asked me with a rather queer smile. "Come," she went on, "you always declare you love me; jump down into the road to me if you really do love me."

Zinaïda had hardly uttered those words when I flew down, just as though some one had given me a violent push from behind. The wall was about fourteen feet high. I reached the ground on my feet, but the shock was so great that I could not keep my footing; I fell down, and for an instant fainted away. When I came to myself again, without opening my eyes, I felt Zinaïda beside me. "My dear boy," she was saying, bending over me, and there was a note of alarmed tenderness in her voice, "how could you do it, dear; how could you obey? . . . You know I love you. . . . Get up."

Her bosom was heaving close to me, her hands were caressing my head, and suddenly—what were my emotions at that moment—her soft, fresh lips began covering my face with kisses . . . they touched my lips. . . . But then Zinaïda probably guessed by the expression of my face that I had regained consciousness, though I still kept my eyes closed, and rising rapidly to her feet, she said: "Come, get up, naughty boy, silly, why are you lying in the dust?" I got up. "Give me my parasol," said Zinaïda,

"I threw it down somewhere, and don't stare at me like that . . . what ridiculous nonsense! you're not hurt, are you? stung by the nettles, I daresay? Don't stare at me, I tell you. . . . But he doesn't understand, he doesn't answer," she added, as though to herself. . . . "Go home, M'sieu Voldemar, brush yourself, and don't dare to follow me, or I shall be angry, and never again . . ."

She did not finish her sentence, but walked rapidly away, while I sat down by the side of the road . . . my legs would not support me. The nettles had stung my hands, my back ached, and my head was giddy; but the feeling of rapture I experienced then has never come a second time in my life. It turned to a sweet ache in all my limbs and found expression at last in joyful hops and skips and shouts. Yes, I was still a child.

13

I was so proud and light-hearted all that day, I so vividly retained on my face the feeling of Zinaïda's kisses, with such a shudder of delight I recalled every word she had uttered, I so hugged my unexpected happiness that I felt positively afraid, positively unwilling to see her, who had given rise to these new sensations. It seemed to me that now I could ask nothing more of fate, that now I ought to "go, and draw a deep last sigh and die." But, next day, when I went into the lodge, I felt great embarrassment, which I tried to conceal under a show of modest confidence, befitting a man who wishes to make it apparent that he knows how to keep a secret. Zinaïda received me very simply, without any emotion, she simply shook her finger at me and asked me, whether I wasn't black and blue? All my modest confidence and air of mystery vanished instantaneously and with them my embarrassment. Of course, I had not expected anything particular, but Zinaïda's composure was like a bucket of cold water thrown over me. I realised that in her eyes I was a child, and was extremely miserable! Zinaïda walked up and down the room, giving me a quick smile, whenever she caught my eye, but her thoughts were far away, I saw that clearly. . . . "Shall I begin about what happened yesterday myself," I pondered; "ask her, where she was hurrying off so fast, so as to find out once for all" . . . but with a gesture of despair, I merely went and sat down in a corner.

Byelovzorov came in; I felt relieved to see him.

"I've not been able to find you a quiet horse," he said in a sulky voice; "Freitag warrants one, but I don't feel any confidence in it, I am afraid."

"What are you afraid of?" said Zinaïda; "allow me to inquire?"

"What am I afraid of? Why, you don't know how to ride. Lord save us, what might happen! What whim is this has come over you all of a sudden?"

"Come, that's my business, Sir Wild Beast. In that case I will ask Piotr Vassilievitch." . . . (My father's name was Piotr Vassilievitch. I was surprised at her mentioning his name so lightly and freely, as though she were confident of his readiness to do her a service.)

"Oh, indeed," retorted Byelovzorov, "you mean to go out riding with him then?"

"With him or with some one else is nothing to do with you. Only not with you, anyway."

"Not with me," repeated Byelovzorov. "As you wish. Well, I shall find you a horse."

"Yes, only mind now, don't send some old cow. I warn you I want to gallop."

"Gallop away by all means . . . with whom is it, with Malevsky, you are going to ride?"

"And why not with him, Mr. Pugnacity? Come, be quiet," she added, "and don't glare. I'll take you too. You know that to my mind now Malevsky's—ugh!" She shook her head.

"You say that to console me," growled Byelovzorov.

Zinaïda half closed her eyes. "Does that console you? O . . . O . . . O . . . Mr. Pugnacity!" she said at last, as though she could find no other word. "And you, M'sieu Voldemar, would you come with us?"

"I don't care to . . . in a large party," I muttered, not raising my eyes.

"You prefer a *tête-à-tête*? . . . Well, freedom to the free, and heaven to the saints," she commented with a sigh. "Go

along, Byelovzorov, and bestir yourself. I must have a
horse for to-morrow."

"Oh, and where's the money to come from?" put in the
old princess.

Zinaïda scowled.

"I won't ask you for it; Byelovzorov will trust me."

"He'll trust you, will he?" . . . grumbled the old princess, and all of a sudden she screeched at the top of her
voice, "Duniashka!"

"Maman, I have given you a bell to ring," observed
Zinaïda.

"Duniashka!" repeated the old lady.

Byelovzorov took leave; I went away with him. Zinaïda
did not try to detain me.

14

The next day I got up early, cut myself a stick, and set
off beyond the town-gates. I thought I would walk off my
sorrow. It was a lovely day, bright and not too hot, a
fresh sportive breeze roved over the earth with temperate
rustle and frolic, setting all things a-flutter and harassing
nothing. I wandered a long while over hills and through
woods; I had not felt happy, I had left home with the intention of giving myself up to melancholy, but youth, the
exquisite weather, the fresh air, the pleasure of rapid
motion, the sweetness of repose, lying on the thick grass
in a solitary nook, gained the upper hand; the memory
of those never-to-be-forgotten words, those kisses, forced
itself once more upon my soul. It was sweet to me to think
that Zinaïda could not, anyway, fail to do justice to my
courage, my heroism. . . . "Others may seem better to her
than I," I mused, "let them! But others only say what they
would do, while I have done it. And what more would I
not do for her?" My fancy set to work. I began picturing
to myself how I would save her from the hands of enemies; how, covered with blood I would tear her by force
from prison, and expire at her feet. I remembered a picture hanging in our drawing-room—Malek-Adel bearing

away Matilda—but at that point my attention was absorbed by the appearance of a speckled woodpecker who climbed busily up the slender stem of a birch-tree and peeped out uneasily from behind it, first to the right, then to the left, like a musician behind the bass-viol.

Then I sang "Not the white snows," and passed from that to a song well known at that period: "I await thee, when the wanton zephyr," then I began reading aloud Yermak's address to the stars from Homyakov's tragedy. I made an attempt to compose something myself in a sentimental vein, and invented the line which was to conclude each verse: "Oh Zinaïda, Zinaïda!" but could get no further with it. Meanwhile it was getting on towards dinner-time. I went down into the valley; a narrow sandy path winding through it led to the town. I walked along this path. . . . The dull thud of horses' hoofs resounded behind me. I looked round instinctively, stood still and took off my cap. I saw my father and Zinaïda. They were riding side by side. My father was saying something to her, bending right over to her, his hand propped on the horse's neck, he was smiling. Zinaïda listened to him in silence, her eyes severely cast down, and her lips tightly pressed together. At first I saw them only; but a few instants later, Byelovzorov came into sight round a bend in the glade, he was wearing a hussar's uniform with a pelisse, and riding a foaming black horse. The gallant horse tossed its head, snorted and pranced from side to side, his rider was at once holding him in and spurring him on. I stood aside. My father gathered up the reins, moved away from Zinaïda, she slowly raised her eyes to him, and both galloped off. . . . Byelovzorov flew after them, his sabre clattering behind him. "He's as red as a crab," I reflected, "while she . . . why's she so pale? out riding the whole morning, and pale?"

I redoubled my pace, and got home just at dinner-time. My father was already sitting by my mother's chair, dressed for dinner, washed and fresh; he was reading an article from the *Journal des Débats* in his smooth musical voice; but my mother heard him without attention, and when she saw me, asked where I had been to all day long, and added that she didn't like this gadding about God knows where, and God knows in what company. "But I have been walking alone," I was on the point of replying, but I looked at my father, and for some reason or other held my peace.

15

For the next five or six days I hardly saw Zinaïda; she said she was ill, which did not, however, prevent the usual visitors from calling at the lodge to pay—as they expressed it, their duty—all, that is, except Meidanov, who promptly grew dejected and sulky when he had not an opportunity of being enthusiastic. Byelovzorov sat sullen and red-faced in a corner, buttoned up to the throat; on the refined face of Malevsky there flickered continually an evil smile; he had really fallen into disfavour with Zinaïda, and waited with special assiduity on the old princess, and even went with her in a hired coach to call on the Governor-General. This expedition turned out unsuccessful, however, and even led to an unpleasant experience for Malevsky; he was reminded of some scandal to do with certain officers of the engineers, and was forced in his explanations to plead his youth and inexperience at the time. Lushin came twice a day, but did not stay long; I was rather afraid of him after our last unreserved conversation, and at the same time felt a genuine attraction to him. He went a walk with me one day in the Neskutchny gardens, was very good-natured and nice, told me the names and properties of various plants and flowers, and suddenly, *à propos* of nothing at all, cried, hitting himself on his forehead, "And I, poor fool, thought her a flirt! it's clear self-sacrifice is sweet for some people!"

"What do you mean by that?" I inquired.

"I don't mean to tell you anything," Lushin replied abruptly.

Zinaïda avoided me; my presence—I could not help noticing it—affected her disagreeably. She involuntarily turned away from me . . . involuntarily; that was what was so bitter, that was what crushed me! But there was no help for it, and I tried not to cross her path, and only to watch her from a distance, in which I was not always successful. As before, something incomprehensible was happening to her; her face was different, she was different altogether. I was specially struck by the change that had taken place in her one warm still evening. I was sitting on a low garden bench under a spreading elderbush; I was fond of that nook; I could see from there the window of Zinaïda's room. I sat there; over my head a little bird was busily hopping about in the darkness of the leaves; a grey cat, stretching herself at full length, crept warily about the garden, and the first beetles were heavily droning in the air, which was still clear, though it was not light. I sat and gazed at the window, and waited to see if it would open; it did open, and Zinaïda appeared at it. She had on a white dress, and she herself, her face, shoulders, and arms, were pale to whiteness. She stayed a long while without moving, and looked out straight before her from under her knitted brows. I had never known such a look on her. Then she clasped her hands tightly, raised them to her lips, to her forehead, and suddenly pulling her fingers apart, she pushed back her hair behind her ears, tossed it, and with a sort of determination nodded her head, and slammed-to the window.

Three days later she met me in the garden. I was turning away, but she stopped me of herself.

"Give me your arm," she said to me with her old affectionateness, "it's a long while since we have had a talk together."

I stole a look at her; her eyes were full of a soft light, and her face seemed as it were smiling through a mist.

"Are you still not well?" I asked her.

"No, that's all over now," she answered, and she picked a small red rose. "I am a little tired, but that too will pass off."

"And will you be as you used to be again?" I asked.

Zinaïda put the rose up to her face, and I fancied the reflection of its bright petals had fallen on her cheeks. "Why, am I changed?" she questioned me.

"Yes, you are changed," I answered in a low voice.

"I have been cold to you, I know," began Zinaïda, "but you mustn't pay attention to that . . . I couldn't help it. . . . Come, why talk about it!"

"You don't want me to love you, that's what it is!" I cried gloomily, in an involuntary outburst.

"No, love me, but not as you did."

"How then?"

"Let us be friends—come now!" Zinaïda gave me the rose to smell. "Listen, you know I'm much older than you —I might be your aunt, really; well, not your aunt, but an older sister. And you . . ."

"You think me a child," I interrupted.

"Well, yes, a child, but a dear, good clever one, whom I love very much. Do you know what? From this day forth I confer on you the rank of page to me; and don't you forget that pages have to keep close to their ladies. Here is the token of your new dignity," she added, sticking the rose in the buttonhole of my jacket, "the token of my favour."

"I once received other favours from you," I muttered.

"Ah!" commented Zinaïda, and she gave me a sidelong look, "What a memory he has! Well? I'm quite ready now . . ." And stooping to me, she imprinted on my forehead a pure, tranquil kiss.

I only looked at her, while she turned away, and saying, "Follow me, my page," went into the lodge. I followed her—all in amazement. "Can this gentle, reasonable girl," I thought, "be the Zinaïda I used to know?" I fancied her very walk was quieter, her whole figure statelier and more graceful . . .

And, mercy! with what fresh force love burned within me!

16

After dinner the usual party assembled again at the lodge, and the young princess came out to them. All were there in full force, just as on that first evening which I never forgot; even Nirmatsky had limped to see her; Meidanov came this time earliest of all, he brought some new verses. The games of forfeits began again, but without the strange pranks, the practical jokes and noise—the gipsy element had vanished. Zinaïda gave a different tone to the proceedings. I sat beside her by virtue of my office as page. Among other things, she proposed that any one who had to pay a forfeit should tell his dream; but this was not successful. The dreams were either uninteresting (Byelovzorov had dreamed that he fed his mare on carp, and that she had a wooden head), or unnatural and invented. Meidanov regaled us with a regular romance; there were sepulchres in it, and angels with lyres, and talking flowers and music wafted from afar. Zinaïda did not let him finish. "If we are to have compositions," she said, "let every one tell something made up, and no pretence about it." The first who had to speak was again Byelovzorov.

The young hussar was confused. "I can't make up anything!" he cried.

"What nonsense!" said Zinaïda. "Well, imagine, for instance, you are married, and tell us how you would treat your wife. Would you lock her up?"

"Yes, I should lock her up."

"And would you stay with her yourself?"

"Yes, I should certainly stay with her myself."

"Very good. Well, but if she got sick of that, and she deceived you?"

"I should kill her."

"And if she ran away?"

"I should catch her up and kill her all the same."

"Oh. And suppose now I were your wife, what would you do then?"

Byelovzorov was silent a minute. "I should kill myself. . . ."

Zinaïda laughed. "I see yours is not a long story."

The next forfeit was Zinaïda's. She looked at the ceiling and considered. "Well, listen, she began at last, "what I have thought of. . . . Picture to yourselves a magnificent palace, a summer night, and a marvellous ball. This ball is given by a young queen. Everywhere gold and marble, crystal, silk, lights, diamonds, flowers, fragrant scents, every caprice of luxury."

"You love luxury?" Lushin interposed.

"Luxury is beautiful," she retorted; "I love everything beautiful."

"More than what is noble?" he asked.

"That's something clever, I don't understand it. Don't interrupt me. So the ball is magnificent. There are crowds of guests, all of them are young, handsome, and brave, all are frantically in love with the queen."

"Are there no women among the guests?" queried Malevsky.

"No—or wait a minute—yes, there are some."

"Are they all ugly?"

"No, charming. But the men are all in love with the queen. She is tall and graceful; she has a little gold diadem on her black hair."

I looked at Zinaïda, and at that instant she seemed to me so much above all of us, there was such bright intelligence, and such power about her unruffled brows, that I thought: "You are that queen!"

"They all throng about her," Zinaïda went on, "and all lavish the most flattering speeches upon her."

"And she likes flattery?" Lushin queried.

"What an intolerable person! he keeps interrupting . . . who doesn't like flattery?"

"One more last question," observed Malevsky, "has the queen a husband?"

"I hadn't thought about that. No, why should she have a husband?"

"To be sure," assented Malevsky, "why should she have a husband?"

"*Silence!*" cried Meidanov in French, which he spoke very badly.

"*Merci!*" Zinaïda said to him. "And so the queen hears their speeches, and hears the music, but does not look at one of the guests. Six windows are open from top to bottom, from floor to ceiling, and beyond them is a dark sky with big stars, a dark garden with big trees. The queen gazes out into the garden. Out there among the trees is a fountain; it is white in the darkness, and rises up tall, tall as an apparition. The queen hears, through the talk and the music, the soft splash of its waters. She gazes and thinks: you are all, gentlemen, noble, clever, and rich, you crowd round me, you treasure every word I utter, you are all ready to die at my feet, I hold you in my power . . . but out there, by the fountain, by that splashing water, stands and waits he whom I love, who holds me in his power. He has neither rich raiment nor precious stones, no one knows him, but he awaits me, and is certain I shall come—and I shall come—and there is no power that could stop me when I want to go out to him, and to stay with him, and be lost with him out there in the darkness of the garden, under the whispering of the trees, and the splash of the fountain . . ." Zinaïda ceased.

"Is that a made-up story?" Malevsky inquired slyly. Zinaïda did not even look at him.

"And what should we have done, gentlemen?" Lushin began suddenly, "if we had been among the guests, and had known of the lucky fellow at the fountain?"

"Stop a minute, stop a minute," interposed Zinaïda, "I will tell you myself what each of you would have done. You, Byelovzorov, would have challenged him to a duel; you, Meidanov, would have written an epigram on him. . . . No, though, you can't write epigrams, you would have made up a long poem on him in the style of Barbier, and would have inserted your production in the *Telegraph*. You, Nirmatsky, would have borrowed . . . no, you would have lent him money at high interest; you, doctor, . . ." she stopped. "There, I really don't know what you would have done. . . ."

"In the capacity of court physician," answered Lushin, "I would have advised the queen not to give balls when she was not in the humour for entertaining her guests. . . ."

"Perhaps you would have been right. And you, Count? . . ."

"And I?" repeated Malevsky with his evil smile. . . .

"You would offer him a poisoned sweetmeat."

Malevsky's face changed slightly, and assumed for an instant a Jewish expression, but he laughed directly.

"And as for you, Voldemar, . . ." Zinaïda went on, "but that's enough, though; let us play another game."

"M'sieu Voldemar, as the queen's page, would have held up her train when she ran into the garden," Malevsky remarked malignantly.

I was crimson with anger, but Zinaïda hurriedly laid a hand on my shoulder, and getting up, said in a rather shaky voice: "I have never given your excellency the right to be rude, and therefore I will ask you to leave us." She pointed to the door.

"Upon my word, princess," muttered Malevsky, and he turned quite pale.

"The princess is right," cried Byelovzorov, and he too rose.

"Good God, I'd not the least idea," Malevsky went on, "in my words there was nothing, I think, that could . . . I had no notion of offending you. . . . Forgive me."

Zinaïda looked him up and down coldly, and coldly smiled. "Stay, then, certainly," she pronounced with a careless gesture of her arm. "M'sieu Voldemar and I were needlessly incensed. It is your pleasure to sting . . . may it do you good."

"Forgive me," Malevsky repeated once more; while I, my thoughts dwelling on Zinaïda's gesture, said to myself again that no real queen could with greater dignity have shown a presumptuous subject to the door.

The game of forfeits went on for a short time after this little scene; every one felt rather ill at ease, not so much on account of this scene, as from another, not quite definite, but oppressive feeling. No one spoke of it, but every one was conscious of it in himself and in his neighbour. Meidanov read us his verses; and Malevsky praised them with exaggerated warmth. "He wants to show how good he is now," Lushin whispered to me. We soon broke up. A mood of reverie seemed to have come upon Zinaïda; the old princess sent word that she had a headache; Nirmatsky began to complain of his rheumatism. . . .

I could not for a long while get to sleep. I had been impressed by Zinaïda's story. "Can there have been a hint in it?" I asked myself: "and at whom and at what was she hinting? And if there really is anything to hint at . . . how is one to make up one's mind? No, no, it can't be," I whispered, turning over from one hot cheek on to the other. . . . But I remembered the expression of Zinaïda's face during her story. . . . I remembered the exclamation that had broken from Lushin in the Neskutchny gardens, the sudden change in her behaviour to me, and I was lost in conjectures. "Who is he?" These three words seemed to stand before my eyes traced upon the darkness; a lowering malignant cloud seemed hanging over me, and I felt its oppressiveness, and waited for it to break. I had grown used to many things of late; I had learned much from what I had seen at the Zasyekins; their disorderly ways, tallow candle-ends, broken knives and forks, grumpy Vonifaty, and shabby maid-servants, the manners of the old princess—all their strange mode of life no longer struck me. . . . But what I was dimly discerning now in Zinaïda, I could never get used to. . . . "An adventuress!" my mother had said of her one day. An adventuress—she, my idol, my divinity? This word stabbed me, I tried to get away from it into my pillow, I was indignant—and at the same time what would I not have agreed to, what would I not have given only to be that lucky fellow at the fountain! . . . My blood was on fire and boiling within me. "The garden . . . the fountain," I mused. . . . "I will go into the garden." I dressed quickly and slipped out of the house. The night was dark, the trees scarcely whispered, a soft chill air breathed down from the sky, a smell of fennel trailed across from the kitchen garden. I went through all the walks; the light sound of my own footsteps at once confused and emboldened me; I stood still, waited and heard my heart beating fast and loudly. At last I went up to the fence and leaned against the thin bar. Suddenly, or was it my fancy, a woman's figure flashed by, a few paces from me . . . I strained my eyes eagerly into the darkness, I held my breath. What was that? Did I hear steps, or was it my heart beating again? "Who is here?" I faltered, hardly audibly. What was that again, a smothered laugh . . . or a rustling in the leaves . . . or a sigh just at my ear? I felt afraid . . . "Who is here?" I repeated still more softly.

The air blew in a gust for an instant; a streak of fire flashed across the sky; it was a star falling. "Zinaïda?" I wanted to call, but the word died away on my lips. And all at once everything became profoundly still around, as is often the case in the middle of the night. . . . Even the grasshoppers ceased their churr in the trees—only a window rattled somewhere. I stood and stood, and then went back to my room, to my chilled bed. I felt a strange sensation; as though I had gone to a tryst, and had been left lonely, and had passed close by another's happiness.

17

The following day I only had a passing glimpse of Zinaïda: she was driving somewhere with the old princess in a cab. But I saw Lushin, who, however, barely vouchsafed me a greeting, and Malevsky. The young count grinned, and began affably talking to me. Of all those who visited at the lodge, he alone had succeeded in forcing his way into our house, and had favourably impressed my mother. My father did not take to him, and treated him with a civility almost insulting.

"Ah, *monsieur le page*," began Malevsky, "delighted to meet you. What is your lovely queen doing?"

His fresh handsome face was so detestable to me at that moment, and he looked at me with such contemptuous amusement that I did not answer him at all.

"Are you still angry?" he went on. "You've no reason to be. It wasn't I who called you a page, you know, and pages attend queens especially. But allow me to remark that you perform your duties very badly."

"How so?"

"Pages ought to be inseparable from their mistresses; pages ought to know everything they do, they ought, indeed, to watch over them," he added, lowering his voice, "day and night."

"What do you mean?"

"What do I mean? I express myself pretty clearly, I fancy. Day and night. By day it's not so much matter; it's light, and people are about in the daytime; but by night, then look out for misfortune. I advise you not to sleep at nights and to watch, watch with all your energies. You remember, in the garden, by night, at the fountain, that's where there's need to look out. You will thank me."

Malevsky laughed and turned his back on me. He, most likely, attached no great importance to what he had said to me, he had a reputation for mystifying, and was noted for his power of taking people in at masquerades, which was greatly augmented by the almost unconscious falsity

in which his whole nature was steeped. . . . He only
wanted to tease me; but every word he uttered was a poison that ran through my veins. The blood rushed to my
head, "Ah! so that's it!" I said to myself; "good! So there
was reason for me to feel drawn into the garden! That
shan't be so!" I cried aloud, and struck myself on the chest
with my fist, though precisely what should not be so I
could not have said. "Whether Malevsky himself goes into
the garden," I thought (he was bragging, perhaps; he has
insolence enough for that, "or some one else (the fence
of our garden was very low, and there was no difficulty in
getting over it), anyway, if any one falls into my hands,
it will be the worse for him! I don't advise any one to
meet me! I will prove to all the world and to her, the
traitress (I actually used the word "traitress") that I can
be revenged!"

I returned to my own room, took out of the writing-table
an English knife I had recently bought, felt its sharp edge,
and knitting my brows with an air of cold and concentrated determination, thrust it into my pocket, as though
doing such deeds was nothing out of the way for me, and
not the first time. My heart heaved angrily, and felt heavy
as a stone. All day long I kept a scowling brow and lips
tightly compressed, and was continually walking up and
down, clutching, with my hand in my pocket, the knife,
which was warm from my grasp, while I prepared myself
beforehand for something terrible. These new unknown
sensations so occupied and even delighted me, that I
hardly thought of Zinaïda herself. I was continually
haunted by Aleko, the young gipsy—"Where art thou
going, young handsome man? Lie there," and then, "thou
art all besprent with blood. . . . Oh, what hast thou done?
. . . Naught!" With what a cruel smile I repeated that
"Naught!" My father was not at home; but my mother,
who had for some time past been in an almost continual
state of dumb exasperation, noticed my gloomy and he-
roic aspect, and said to me at supper, "Why are you sulk-
ing like a mouse in a meal-tub?" I merely smiled condescendingly in reply, and thought, "If only they knew!" It
struck eleven; I went to my room, but did not undress; I
waited for midnight; at last it struck. "The time has
come!" I muttered between my teeth; and buttoning my-

self up to the throat, and even pulling my sleeves up, I went into the garden.

I had already fixed on the spot from which to keep watch. At the end of the garden, at the point where the fence, separating our domain from the Zasyekins', joined the common wall, grew a pine-tree, standing alone. Standing under its low thick branches, I could see well, as far as the darkness of the night permitted, what took place around. Close by, ran a winding path which had always seemed mysterious to me; it coiled like a snake under the fence, which at that point bore traces of having been climbed over, and led to a round arbour formed of thick acacias. I made my way to the pine-tree, leaned my back against its trunk, and began my watch.

The night was as still as the night before, but there were fewer clouds in the sky, and the outlines of bushes, even of tall flowers, could be more distinctly seen. The first moments of expectation were oppressive, almost terrible. I had made up my mind to everything. I only debated how to act; whether to thunder, "Where goest thou? Stand! show thyself—or death!" or simply to strike. . . . Every sound, every whisper and rustle, seemed to me portentous and extraordinary. . . . I prepared myself . . . I bent forward. . . . But half-an-hour passed, an hour passed; my blood had grown quieter, colder; the consciousness that I was doing all this for nothing, that I was even a little absurd, that Malevsky had been making fun of me, began to steal over me. I left my ambush, and walked all about the garden. As if to taunt me, there was not the smallest sound to be heard anywhere; everything was at rest. Even our dog was asleep, curled up into a ball at the gate. I climbed up into the ruins of the greenhouse, saw the open country far away before me, recalled my meeting with Zinaïda, and fell to dreaming. . . .

I started. . . . I fancied I heard the creak of a door opening, then the faint crack of a broken twig. In two bounds I got down from the ruin, and stood still, all aghast. Rapid, light, but cautious footsteps sounded distinctly in the garden. They were approaching me. "Here he is . . . here he is, at last!" flashed through my heart. With spasmodic haste, I pulled the knife out of my pocket; with spasmodic haste, I opened it. Flashes of red were whirling

before my eyes; my hair stood up on my head in my fear
and fury. . . . The steps were coming straight towards me;
I bent—I craned forward to meet him. . . . A man came
into view. . . . My God! it was my father!

I recognised him at once, though he was all muffled
up in a dark cloak, and his hat was pulled down over his
face. On tip-toe he walked by. He did not notice me,
though nothing concealed me; but I was so huddled up
and shrunk together that I fancy I was almost on the level
of the ground. The jealous Othello, ready for murder, was
suddenly transformed into a school-boy. . . . I was so taken
aback by my father's unexpected appearance that for the
first moment I did not notice where he had come from or
in what direction he disappeared. I only drew myself up,
and thought, "Why is it my father is walking about in
the garden at night?" when everything was still again. In
my horror I had dropped my knife in the grass, but I did
not even attempt to look for it; I was very much ashamed
of myself. I was completely sobered at once. On my way
to the house, however, I went up to my seat under the
elder-tree, and looked up at Zinaïda's window. The small
slightly-convex panes of the window shone dimly blue in
the faint light thrown on them by the night sky. All at
once—their colour began to change. . . . Behind them—I
saw this, saw it distinctly—softly and cautiously a white
blind was let down, let down right to the window-frame,
and so stayed.

"What is that for?" I said aloud almost involuntarily
when I found myself once more in my room. "A dream,
a chance, or . . ." The suppositions which suddenly rushed
into my head were so new and strange that I did not dare
to entertain them.

18

I got up in the morning with a headache. My emotion of
the previous day had vanished. It was replaced by a
dreary sense of blankness and a sort of sadness I had not
known till then, as though something had died in me.

"Why is it you're looking like a rabbit with half its brain removed?" said Lushin on meeting me. At lunch I stole a look first at my father, then at my mother: he was composed, as usual; she was, as usual, secretly irritated. I waited to see whether my father would make some friendly remarks to me, as he sometimes did. . . . But he did not even bestow his everyday cold greeting upon me. "Shall I tell Zinaïda all?" I wondered. . . . "It's all the same, anyway; all is at an end between us." I went to see her, but told her nothing, and, indeed, I could not even have managed to get a talk with her if I had wanted to. The old princess's son, a cadet of twelve years old, had come from Petersburg for his holidays; Zinaïda at once handed her brother over to me. "Here," she said, "my dear Volodya,"—it was the first time she had used this pet-name to me—"is a companion for you. His name is Volodya, too. Please, like him; he is still shy, but he has a good heart. Show him Neskutchny gardens, go walks with him, take him under your protection. You'll do that, won't you? you're so good, too!" She laid both her hands affectionately on my shoulders, and I was utterly bewildered. The presence of this boy transformed me, too, into a boy. I looked in silence at the cadet, who stared as silently at me. Zinaïda laughed, and pushed us towards each other. "Embrace each other, children!" We embraced each other. "Would you like me to show you the garden?" I inquired of the cadet. "If you please," he replied, in the regular cadet's hoarse voice. Zinaïda laughed again. . . . I had time to notice that she had never had such an exquisite colour in her face before. I set off with the cadet. There was an old-fashioned swing in our garden. I sat him down on the narrow plank seat, and began swinging him. He sat rigid in his new little uniform of stout cloth, with its broad gold braiding, and kept tight hold of the cords. "You'd better unbutton your collar," I said to him. "It's all right; we're used to it," he said, and cleared his throat. He was like his sister. The eyes especially recalled her. I liked being nice to him; and at the same time an aching sadness was gnawing at my heart. "Now I certainly am a child," I thought; "but yesterday. . . ." I remembered where I had dropped my knife the night before, and looked for it. The cadet asked me for it, picked a thick stalk of wild parsley, cut a pipe out of it, and began whistling. Othello whistled too.

But in the evening how he wept, this Othello, in Zinaïda's arms, when, seeking him out in a corner of the garden, she asked him why he was so depressed. My tears flowed with such violence that she was frightened. "What is wrong with you? What is it, Volodya?" she repeated; and seeing I made no answer, and did not cease weeping, she was about to kiss my wet cheek. But I turned away from her, and whispered through my sobs, "I know all. Why did you play with me? . . . What need had you of my love?"

"I am to blame, Volodya . . ." said Zinaïda. "I am very much to blame . . ." she added, wringing her hands. "How much there is bad and black and sinful in me! . . . But I am not playing with you now. I love you; you don't even suspect why and how. . . . But what is it you know?"

What could I say to her? She stood facing me, and looked at me; and I belonged to her altogether from head to foot directly she looked at me. . . . A quarter of an hour later I was running races with the cadet and Zinaïda. I was not crying, I was laughing, though my swollen eyelids dropped a tear or two as I laughed. I had Zinaïda's ribbon round my neck for a cravat, and I shouted with delight whenever I succeeded in catching her round the waist. She did just as she liked with me.

19

I should be in a great difficulty, if I were forced to describe exactly what passed within me in the course of the week after my unsuccessful midnight expedition. It was a strange feverish time, a sort of chaos, in which the most violently opposed feelings, thoughts, suspicions, hopes, joys, and sufferings, whirled together in a kind of hurricane. I was afraid to look into myself, if a boy of sixteen ever can look into himself; I was afraid to take stock of anything; I simply hastened to live through every day till evening; and at night I slept . . . the light-heart-

edness of childhood came to my aid. I did not want to
know whether I was loved, and I did not want to acknowl-
edge to myself that I was not loved; my father I avoided
—but Zinaïda I could not avoid. . . . I burnt as in a fire
in her presence . . . but what did I care to know what
the fire was in which I burned and melted—it was enough
that it was sweet to burn and melt. I gave myself up to
all my passing sensations, and cheated myself, turning
away from memories, and shutting my eyes to what I fore-
boded before me. . . . This weakness would not most likely
have lasted long in any case . . . a thunderbolt cut it all
short in a moment, and flung me into a new track altogether.

Coming in one day to dinner from a rather long walk,
I learnt with amazement that I was to dine alone, that
my father had gone away and my mother was unwell, did
not want any dinner, and had shut herself up in her bedroom. From the faces of the footmen, I surmised that
something extraordinary had taken place. . . . I did not
dare to cross-examine them, but I had a friend in the
young waiter Philip, who was passionately fond of poetry,
and a performer on the guitar. I addressed myself to him.
From him I learned that a terrible scene had taken place
between my father and mother (and every word had been
overheard in the maids' room; much of it had been in
French, but Masha the lady's-maid had lived five years
with a dressmaker from Paris, and she understood it all);
that my mother had reproached my father with infidelity,
with an intimacy with the young lady next door, that my
father at first had defended himself, but afterwards had
lost his temper, and he too had said something cruel, "reflecting on her age," which had made my mother cry; that
my mother too had alluded to some loan which it seemed
had been made to the old princess, and had spoken very
ill of her and of the young lady too, and that then my
father had threatened her. "And all the mischief," continued Philip, "came from an anonymous letter; and who
wrote it, no one knows, or else there'd have been no reason whatever for the matter to have come out at all."

"But was there really any ground?" I brought out with
difficulty, while my hands and feet went cold, and a sort
of shudder ran through my inmost being.

Philip winked meaningly. "There was. There's no hiding those things; for all that your father was careful this time—but there, you see, he'd, for instance, to hire a carriage or something . . . no getting on without servants, either."

I dismissed Philip, and fell on to my bed. I did not sob, I did not give myself up to despair; I did not ask myself when and how this had happened; I did not wonder how it was I had not guessed it before, long ago; I did not even upbraid my father. . . . What I had learnt was more than I could take in; this sudden revelation stunned me. . . . All was at an end. All the fair blossoms of my heart were roughly plucked at once, and lay about me, flung on the ground, and trampled underfoot.

20

My mother next day announced her intention of returning to the town. In the morning my father had gone into her bedroom, and stayed there a long while alone with her. No one had overheard what he said to her; but my mother wept no more; she regained her composure, and asked for food, but did not make her appearance nor change her plans. I remember I wandered about the whole day, but did not go into the garden, and never once glanced at the lodge, and in the evening I was the spectator of an amazing occurrence: my father conducted Count Malevsky by the arm through the dining-room into the hall, and, in the presence of a footman, said icily to him: "A few days ago your excellency was shown the door in our house; and now I am not going to enter into any kind of explanation with you, but I have the honour to announce to you that if you ever visit me again, I shall throw you out of the window. I don't like your handwriting." The count bowed, bit his lips, shrank away, and vanished.

Preparations were beginning for our removal to town, to Arbaty Street, where we had a house. My father himself probably no longer cared to remain at the country house; but clearly he had succeeded in persuading my mother not to make a public scandal. Everything was done quietly, without hurry; my mother even sent her compliments to the old princess, and expressed her regret that she was prevented by indisposition from seeing her again before her departure. I wandered about like one possessed, and only longed for one thing, for it all to be over as soon as possible. One thought I could not get out of my head: how could she, a young girl, and a princess too, after all, bring herself to such a step, knowing that my father was not a free man, and having an opportunity of marrying, for instance, Byelovzorov? What did she hope for? How was it she was not afraid of ruining her whole future? Yes, I thought, this is love, this is passion, this is devotion . . . and Lushin's words came back to me: to sacrifice oneself for some people is sweet. I chanced somehow to catch sight of something white in one of the windows of the lodge. . . . "Can it be Zinaïda's face?" I thought . . . yes, it really was her face. I could not restrain myself. I could not part from her without saying a last good-bye to her. I seized a favourable instant, and went into the lodge.

In the drawing-room the old princess met me with her usual slovenly and careless greetings.

"How's this, my good man, your folks are off in such a hurry?" she observed, thrusting snuff into her nose. I looked at her, and a load was taken off my heart. The word "loan," dropped by Philip, had been torturing me. She had no suspicion . . . at least I thought so then. Zinaïda came in from the next room, pale, and dressed in black, with her hair hanging loose; she took me by the hand without a word, and drew me away with her.

"I heard your voice," she began, "and came out at once. Is it so easy for you to leave us, bad boy?"

"I have come to say good-bye to you, princess," I answered, "probably for ever. You have heard, perhaps, we are going away."

Zinaïda looked intently at me.

"Yes, I have heard. Thanks for coming. I was beginning to think I should not see you again. Don't remember evil against me. I have sometimes tormented you, but all the same I am not what you imagine me."

She turned away, and leaned against the window.

"Really, I am not like that. I know you have a bad opinion of me."

"I?"

"Yes, you . . . you."

"I?" I repeated mournfully, and my heart throbbed as of old under the influence of her overpowering, indescribable fascination. "I? Believe me, Zinaïda Alexandrovna, whatever you did, however you tormented me, I should love and adore you to the end of my days."

She turned with a rapid motion to me, and flinging wide her arms, embraced my head, and gave me a warm and passionate kiss. God knows whom that long farewell kiss was seeking, but I eagerly tasted its sweetness. I knew that it would never be repeated. "Good-bye, good-bye," I kept saying . . .

She tore herself away, and went out. And I went away. I cannot describe the emotion with which I went away. I should not wish it ever to come again; but I should think myself unfortunate had I never experienced such an emotion.

We went back to town. I did not quickly shake off the past; I did not quickly get to work. My wound slowly began to heal; but I had no ill-feeling against my father. On the contrary he had, as it were, gained in my eyes . . . let psychologists explain the contradiction as best they can. One day I was walking along a boulevard, and to my indescribable delight, I came across Lushin. I liked him for his straightforward and unaffected character, and besides he was dear to me for the sake of the memories he aroused in me. I rushed up to him. "Aha!" he said, knitting his brows, "so it's you, young man. Let me have a look at you. You're still as yellow as ever, but yet there's not the same nonsense in your eyes. You look like a man, not a lap-dog. That's good. Well, what are you doing? working?"

I gave a sigh. I did not like to tell a lie, while I was ashamed to tell the truth.

"Well, never mind," Lushin went on, "don't be shy. The great thing is to lead a normal life, and not be the slave of your passions. What do you get if not? Wherever you are carried by the tide—it's all a bad look-out; a man must stand on his own feet, if he can get nothing but a rock to stand on. Here, I've got a cough . . . and Byelovzorov—have you heard anything of him?"

"No. What is it?"

"He's lost, and no news of him; they say he's gone away to the Caucasus. A lesson to you, young man. And it's all from not knowing how to part in time, to break out of the net. You seem to have got off very well. Mind you don't fall into the same snare again. Good-bye."

"I shan't," I thought. . . . "I shan't see her again." But I was destined to see Zinaïda once more.

21

My father used every day to ride out on horseback. He had a splendid English mare, a chestnut piebald, with a long slender neck and long legs, an inexhaustible and vicious beast. Her name was Electric. No one could ride her except my father. One day he came up to me in a good humour, a frame of mind in which I had not seen him for a long while; he was getting ready for his ride, and had already put on his spurs. I began entreating him to take me with him.

"We'd much better have a game of leap-frog," my father replied. "You'll never keep up with me on your cob."

"Yes, I will; I'll put on spurs too."

"All right, come along then."

We set off. I had a shaggy black horse, strong, and fairly spirited. It is true it had to gallop its utmost, when Electric went at full trot, still I was not left behind. I have never seen any one ride like my father; he had such a fine carelessly easy seat, that it seemed that the horse under him was conscious of it, and proud of its rider. We rode through all the boulevards, reached the "Maidens' Field," jumped several fences (at first I had been afraid to take a leap, but my father had a contempt for cowards, and I soon ceased to feel fear), twice crossed the river Moskva, and I was under the impression that we were on our way home, especially as my father of his own accord observed that my horse was tired, when suddenly he turned off away from me at the Crimean ford, and galloped along the river-bank. I rode after him. When he had reached a high stack of old timber, he slid quickly

off Electric, told me to dismount, and giving me his
horse's bridle, told me to wait for him there at the timber-stack, and, turning off into a small street, disappeared.
I began walking up and down the river-bank, leading the
horses, and scolding Electric, who kept pulling, shaking
her head, snorting and neighing as she went; and when
I stood still, never failed to paw the ground, and whining,
bite my cob on the neck; in fact she conducted herself altogether like a spoilt thorough-bred. My father did not
come back. A disagreeable damp mist rose from the river;
a fine rain began softly blowing up, and spotting with tiny
dark flecks the stupid grey timber-stack, which I kept
passing and repassing, and was deadly sick of by now. I
was terribly bored, and still my father did not come. A
sort of sentry-man, a Fin, grey all over like the timber,
and with a huge old-fashioned shako, like a pot, on his
head, and with a halberd (and how ever came a sentry,
if you think of it, on the banks of the Moskva!) drew near,
and turning his wrinkled face, like an old woman's, towards me, he observed, "What are you doing here with
the horses, young master? Let me hold them."

I made him no reply. He asked me for tobacco. To get
rid of him (I was in a fret of impatience, too), I took
a few steps in the direction in which my father had disappeared, then walked along the little street to the end,
turned the corner, and stood still. In the street, forty paces
from me, at the open window of a little wooden house,
stood my father, his back turned to me; he was leaning
forward over the window-sill, and in the house, half hidden by a curtain, sat a woman in a dark dress talking
to my father; this woman was Zinaïda.

I was petrified. This, I confess, I had never expected.
My first impulse was to run away. "My father will look
round," I thought, "and I am lost . . ." but a strange feeling—a feeling stronger than curiosity, stronger than
jealousy, stronger even than fear—held me there. I began
to watch; I strained my ears to listen. It seemed as though
my father were insisting on something. Zinaïda would
not consent. I seem to see her face now—mournful, serious, lovely, and with an inexpressible impress of devotion, grief, love, and a sort of despair—I can find no other
word for it. She uttered monosyllables, not raising her
eyes, simply smiling—submissively, but without yielding.

By that smile alone, I should have known my Zinaïda of old days. My father shrugged his shoulders, and straightened his hat on his head, which was always a sign of impatience with him. . . . Then I caught the words: *"Vous devez vous séparer de cette . . ."* Zinaïda sat up, and stretched out her arm. . . . Suddenly, before my very eyes, the impossible happened. My father suddenly lifted the whip, with which he had been switching the dust off his coat, and I heard a sharp blow on that arm, bare to the elbow. I could scarcely restrain myself from crying out; while Zinaïda shuddered, looked without a word at my father, and slowly raising her arm to her lips, kissed the streak of red upon it. My father flung away the whip, and running quickly up the steps, dashed into the house. . . . Zinaïda turned round, and with outstretched arms and downcast head, she too moved away from the window.

My heart sinking with panic, with a sort of awe-struck horror, I rushed back, and running down the lane, almost letting go my hold of Electric, went back to the bank of the river. I could not think clearly of anything. I knew that my cold and reserved father was sometimes seized by fits of fury; and all the same, I could never comprehend what I had just seen. . . . But I felt at the time that, however long I lived, I could never forget the gesture, the glance, the smile, of Zinaïda; that her image, this image so suddenly presented to me, was imprinted for ever on my memory. I stared vacantly at the river, and never noticed that my tears were streaming. "She is beaten," I was thinking, . . . "beaten . . . beaten. . . ."

"Hullo! what are you doing? Give me the mare!" I heard my father's voice saying behind me.

Mechanically I gave him the bridle. He leaped on to Electric . . . the mare, chill with standing, reared on her haunches, and leaped ten feet away . . . but my father soon subdued her; he drove the spurs into her sides, and gave her a blow on the neck with his fist. . . . "Ah, I've no whip," he muttered.

I remembered the swish and fall of the whip, heard so short a time before, and shuddered.

"Where did you put it?" I asked my father after a brief pause.

My father made no answer, and galloped on ahead. I overtook him. I felt that I must see his face.

"Were you bored waiting for me?" he muttered through his teeth.

"A little. Where did you drop your whip?" I asked again.

My father glanced quickly at me. "I didn't drop it," he replied; "I threw it away." He sank into thought, and dropped his head . . . and then, for the first, and almost for the last time, I saw how much tenderness and pity his stern features were capable of expressing.

He galloped on again, and this time I could not overtake him; I got home a quarter-of-an-hour after him.

"That's love," I said to myself again, as I sat at night before my writing-table, on which books and papers had begun to make their appearance; "that's passion! . . . To think of not revolting, of bearing a blow from any one whatever . . . even the dearest hand! But it seems one can, if one loves. . . . While I . . . I imagined . . ."

I had grown much older during the last month; and my love, with all its transports and sufferings, struck me myself as something small and childish and pitiful beside this other unimagined something, which I could hardly fully grasp, and which frightened me like an unknown, beautiful, but menacing face, which one strives in vain to make out clearly in the half-darkness. . . .

A strange and fearful dream came to me that same night. I dreamed I went into a low dark room. . . . My father was standing with a whip in his hand, stamping with anger; in the corner crouched Zinaïda, and not on her arm, but on her forehead, was a stripe of red . . . while behind them both towered Byelovzorov, covered with blood; he opened his white lips, and wrathfully threatened my father.

Two months later, I entered the university; and within six months my father died of a stroke in Petersburg, where he had just moved with my mother and me. A few days before his death he received a letter from Moscow which threw him into a violent agitation. . . . He went to my mother to beg some favour of her: and, I was told, he positively shed tears—he, my father! On the very morning of the day when he was stricken down, he had begun a letter to me in French. "My son," he wrote to me, "fear the love of woman; fear that bliss, that poison. . . ." After his death, my mother sent a considerable sum of money to Moscow.

22

Four years passed. I had just left the university, and did not know exactly what to do with myself, at what door to knock; I was hanging about for a time with nothing to do. One fine evening I met Meidanov at the theatre. He had got married, and had entered the civil service; but I found no change in him. He fell into ecstasies in just the same superfluous way, and just as suddenly grew depressed again.

"You know," he told me among other things, "Madame Dolsky's here."

"What Madame Dolsky?"

"Can you have forgotten her?—the young Princess Zasyekin whom we were all in love with, and you too. Do you remember at the country-house near Neskutchny gardens?"

"She married a Dolsky?"

"Yes."

"And is she here, in the theatre?"

"No: but she's in Petersburg. She came here a few days ago. She's going abroad."

"What sort of fellow is her husband?" I asked.

"A splendid fellow, with property. He's a colleague of mine in Moscow. You can well understand—after the scandal . . . you must know all about it . . ." (Meidanov smiled significantly) "it was no easy task for her to make a good marriage; there were consequences . . . but with her cleverness, everything is possible. Go and see her; she'll be delighted to see you. She's prettier than ever."

Meidanov gave me Zinaïda's address. She was staying at the Hotel Demut. Old memories were astir within me. . . . I determined next day to go to see my former "flame." But some business happened to turn up; a week passed, and then another, and when at last I went to the Hotel Demut and asked for Madame Dolsky, I learnt that four days before, she had died, almost suddenly, in childbirth.

I felt a sort of stab at my heart. The thought that I

might have seen her, and had not seen her, and should never see her—that bitter thought stung me with all the force of overwhelming reproach. "She is dead!" I repeated, staring stupidly at the hall-porter. I slowly made my way back to the street, and walked on without knowing myself where I was going. All the past swam up and rose at once before me. So this was the solution, this was the goal to which that young, ardent, brilliant life had striven, all haste and agitation! I mused on this; I fancied those dear features, those eyes, those curls—in the narrow box, in the damp underground darkness—lying here, not far from me—while I was still alive, and, maybe, a few paces from my father. . . . I thought all this; I strained my imagination, and yet all the while the lines:

> "From lips indifferent of her death I heard,
> Indifferently I listened to it, too,"

were echoing in my heart. O youth, youth! little dost thou care for anything; thou art master, as it were, of all the treasures of the universe—even sorrow gives thee pleasure, even grief thou canst turn to thy profit; thou art self-confident and insolent; thou sayest, "I alone am living—look you!" but thy days fly by all the while, and vanish without trace or reckoning; and everything in thee vanishes, like wax in the sun, like snow. . . . And, perhaps, the whole secret of thy charm lies, not in being able to do anything, but in being able to think thou wilt do anything; lies just in thy throwing to the winds, forces which thou couldst not make other use of; in each of us gravely regarding himself as a prodigal, gravely supposing that he is justified in saying, "Oh, what might I not have done if I had not wasted my time!"

I, now . . . what did I hope for, what did I expect, what rich future did I foresee, when the phantom of my first love, rising up for an instant, barely called forth one sigh, one mournful sentiment?

And what has come to pass of all I hoped for? And now, when the shades of evening begin to steal over my life, what have I left fresher, more precious, than the memories of the storm—so soon over—of early morning, of spring?

But I do myself injustice. Even then, in those light-hearted young days, I was not deaf to the voice of sorrow, when it called upon me, to the solemn strains floating to me from beyond the tomb. I remember, a few days after I heard of Zinaïda's death, I was present, through a peculiar, irresistible impulse, at the death of a poor old woman who lived in the same house as we. Covered with rags, lying on hard boards, with a sack under her head, she died hardly and painfully. Her whole life had been passed in the bitter struggle with daily want; she had known no joy, had not tasted the honey of happiness. One would have thought, surely she would rejoice at death, at her deliverance, her rest. But yet, as long as her decrepit body held out, as long as her breast still heaved in agony under the icy hand weighing upon it, until her last forces left her, the old woman crossed herself, and kept whispering, "Lord, forgive my sins"; and only with the last spark of consciousness, vanished from her eyes the look of fear, of horror of the end. And I remember that then, by the death-bed of that poor old woman, I felt aghast for Zinaïda, and longed to pray for her, for my father—and for myself.

1860

THE GAMBLER

THE GAMBLER
FROM THE DIARY OF A YOUNG MAN

by Fyodor Dostoyevsky

1

At last I have come back from my fortnight's absence.
Our friends have already been two days in Roulettenburg.
I imagined that they were expecting me with the greatest
eagerness; I was mistaken, however. The General had an
extremely independent air, he talked to me condescendingly and sent me away to his sister. I even fancied that
the General was a little ashamed to look at me. Marya
Filippovna was tremendously busy and scarcely spoke to
me; she took the money, however, counted it, and listened
to my whole report. They were expecting Mezentsov, the
little Frenchman, and some Englishman; as usual, as soon
as there was money there was a dinner-party; in the Moscow style. Polina Alexandrovna, seeing me, asked why I
had been away so long, and without waiting for an answer
went off somewhere. Of course, she did that on purpose.
We must have an explanation, though. Things have accu-
mulated.

They had assigned me a little room on the fourth storey
of the hotel. They know here that I belong to the *General's
suite*. It all looks as though they had managed to impress
the people. The General is looked upon by every one here
as a very rich Russian grandee. Even before dinner he
commissioned me, among other things, to change two
notes for a thousand francs each. I changed them at the
office of the hotel. Now we shall be looked upon as mil-
lionaires for a whole week, at least. I wanted to take
Misha and Nadya out for a walk, but on the stairs I was
summoned back to the General; he had graciously be-
thought him to inquire where I was taking them. The

man is absolutely unable to look me straight in the face;
he would like to very much, but every time I meet his eyes
with an intent, that is, disrespectful air, he seems overcome with embarrassment. In very bombastic language,
piling one sentence on another, and at last losing his
thread altogether, he gave me to understand that I was
to take the children for a walk in the park, as far as possible from the Casino. At last he lost his temper completely, and added sharply: "Or else maybe you'll be taking them into the gambling saloon. You must excuse me,"
he added, "but I know you are still rather thoughtless and
capable, perhaps, of gambling. In any case, though, I am
not your mentor and have no desire to be, yet I have the
right, at any rate, to desire that you will not compromise
me, so to speak. . . ."

"But I have no money," I said calmly; "one must have it
before one can lose it."

"You shall have it at once," answered the General, flushing a little; he rummaged in his bureau, looked up in an
account book, and it turned out that he had a hundred and
twenty roubles owing me.

"How are we to settle up?" he said. "We must change
it into thalers. Come, take a hundred thalers—the rest,
of course, won't be lost."

I took the money without a word.

"Please don't be offended by my words, you are so ready
to take offence. . . . If I did make an observation, it was
only, so to speak, by way of warning, and, of course, I
have some right to do so. . . ."

On my way home before dinner, with the children, I
met a perfect cavalcade. Our party had driven out to look
at some ruin. Two magnificent carriages, superb horses!
In one carriage was Mlle. Blanche with Marya Filippovna
and Polina; the Frenchman, the Englishman and our General were on horseback. The passers-by stopped and
stared; a sensation was created; but the General will have
a bad time, all the same. I calculated that with the four
thousand francs I had brought, added to what they had
evidently managed to get hold of, they had now seven or
eight thousand francs; but that is not enough for Mlle.
Blanche.

Mlle. Blanche, too, is staying at the hotel with her
mother; our Frenchman is somewhere in the house, too.

The footman calls him "Monsieur le Comte." Mlle. Blanche's mother is called "Madame la Comtesse"; well, who knows, they may be Comte and Comtesse.

I felt sure that M. le Comte would not recognize me when we assembled at dinner. The General, of course, would not have thought of introducing us or even saying a word to him on my behalf; and M. le Comte has been in Russia himself, and knows what is called an *outchitel* is very small fry. He knows me very well, however. But I must confess I made my appearance at dinner unbidden; I fancy the General forgot to give orders, or else he would certainly have sent me to dine at the *table d'hôte.* I came of my own accord, so that the General looked at me with astonishment. Kind-hearted Marya Filippovna immediately made a place for me; but my meeting with Mr. Astley saved the situation, and I could not help seeming to belong to the party.

I met this strange Englishman for the first time in the train in Prussia, where we sat opposite to one another, when I was travelling to join the family; then I came across him as I was going into France, and then again in Switzerland: in the course of that fortnight twice— and now I suddenly met him in Roulettenburg. I never met a man so shy in my life. He is stupidly shy and, of course, is aware of it himself, for he is by no means stupid. He is very sweet and gentle, however. I drew him into talk at our first meeting in Prussia. He told me that he had been that summer at North Cape, and that he was very anxious to visit the fair at Nizhni Novgorod. I don't know how he made acquaintance with the General; I believe that he is hopelessly in love with Polina. When she came in he glowed like a sunset. He was very glad that I was sitting beside him at the table and seemed already to look upon me as his bosom friend.

At dinner the Frenchman gave himself airs in an extraordinary way; he was nonchalant and majestic with every one. In Moscow, I remember, he used to blow soap bubbles. He talked a great deal about finance and Russian politics. The General sometimes ventured to contradict, but discreetly, and only so far as he could without too great loss of dignity.

I was in a strange mood; of course, before we were half through dinner I had asked myself my usual invariable question: "Why I went on dancing attendance on this General, and had not left them long ago?" From time to time I glanced at Polina Alexandrovna. She took no notice of me whatever. It ended by my flying into a rage and making up my mind to be rude.

I began by suddenly, apropos of nothing, breaking in on the conversation in a loud voice. What I longed to do above all things was to be abusive to the Frenchman. I turned round to the General and very loudly and distinctly, I believe, interrupted him. I observed that this summer it was utterly impossible for a Russian to dine at *table d'hôte*. The General turned upon me an astonished stare.

"If you are a self-respecting man," I went on, "you will certainly be inviting abuse and must put up with affronts to your dignity. In Paris, on the Rhine, even in Switzerland, there are so many little Poles, and French people who sympathize with them, that there's no chance for a Russian to utter a word."

I spoke in French. The General looked at me in amazement. I don't know whether he was angry or simply astonished at my so forgetting myself.

"It seems some one gave you a lesson," said the Frenchman, carelessly and contemptuously.

"I had a row for the first time with a Pole in Paris," I answered; "then with a French officer who took the Pole's part. And then some of the French came over to my side, when I told them how I tried to spit in Monseigneur's coffee."

"Spit?" asked the General, with dignified perplexity, and he even looked about him aghast.

The Frenchman scanned me mistrustfully.

"Just so," I answered. "After feeling convinced for two whole days that I might have to pay a brief visit to Rome about our business, I went to the office of the Papal Embassy to get my passport *viséed*. There I was met by a little abbé, a dried-up little man of about fifty, with a frost-bitten expression. After listening to me politely, but extremely drily, he asked me to wait a little. Though I was in a hurry, of course I sat down to wait, and took up *L'Opinion Nationale* and began reading a horribly abusive attack on Russia. Meanwhile, I heard some one in the next room ask to see Monseigneur; I saw my abbé bow to him. I addressed the same request to him again; he asked me to wait—more drily than ever. A little later some one else entered, a stranger, but on business, some Austrian; he was listened to and at once conducted upstairs. Then I felt very much vexed; I got up, went to the abbé and said resolutely, that as Monseigneur was receiving, he might settle my business, too. At once the abbé drew back in great surprise. It was beyond his comprehension that an insignificant Russian should dare to put himself on a level with Monseigneur's guests. As though delighted to have an opportunity of insulting me, he looked me up and down, and shouted in the most insolent tone: "Can you really suppose that Monseigneur is going to leave his coffee on your account?" Then I shouted, too, but more loudly than he: "Let me tell you I'm ready to spit in your Monseigneur's coffee! If you don't finish with my passport this minute, I'll go to him in person."

"'What! When the Cardinal is sitting with him!' cried the abbé, recoiling from me with horror, and, flinging wide his arms, he stood like a cross, with an air of being ready to die rather than let me pass.

"Then I answered him that 'I was a heretic and a barbarian, *que je suis hérétique et barbare,*' and that I cared nothing for all these Archbishops, Cardinals, Monseigneurs and all of them. In short, I showed I was not going to give way. The abbé looked at me with uneasy ill-humour, then snatched my passport and carried it upstairs. A minute later it had been *viséed.* Here, wouldn't you like to see it?" I took out the passport and showed the Roman *visé.*

"Well, I must say . . ." the General began.

"What saved you was saying that you were a heretic and barbarian," the Frenchman observed, with a smile. "*Cela n'était pas si bête.*"

"Why, am I to model myself upon our Russians here? They sit, not daring to open their lips, and almost ready to deny they are Russians. In Paris, anyway in my hotel, they began to treat me much more attentively when I told every one about my passage-at-arms with the abbé. The fat Polish *pan,* the person most antagonistic to me at *table d'hôte,* sank into the background. The Frenchmen did not even resent it when I told them that I had, two years previously, seen a man at whom, in 1812, a French *chasseur* had shot simply in order to discharge his gun. The man was at that time a child of ten, and his family had not succeeded in leaving Moscow."

"That's impossible," the Frenchman boiled up; "a French soldier would not fire at a child!"

"Yet it happened," I answered. "I was told it by a most respectable captain on the retired list, and I saw the scar on his cheek from the bullet myself."

The Frenchman began talking rapidly and at great length. The General began to support him, but I recommended him to read, for instance, passages in the "Notes" of General Perovsky, who was a prisoner in the hands of the French in 1812. At last Marya Filippovna began talking of something else to change the conversation. The General was very much displeased with me, for the Frenchman and I had almost begun shouting at one another. But I fancy my dispute with the Frenchman pleased Mr. Astley very much. Getting up from the table, he asked me to have a glass of wine with him.

In the evening I duly succeeded in getting a quarter of an hour's talk with Polina Alexandrovna. Our conversation took place when we were all out for a walk. We all went into the park by the Casino. Polina sat down on a seat facing the fountain, and let Nadenka play with some children not far from her. I, too, let Misha run off to the fountain, and we were at last left alone.

We began, of course, at first with business. Polina simply flew into a rage when I gave her only seven hundred guldens. She had reckoned positively on my pawning her diamonds in Paris for two thousand guldens, if not more.

"I must have money, come what may," she said. "I must get it or I am lost."

I began asking her what had happened during my absence.

"Nothing, but the arrival of two pieces of news from Petersburg: first that Granny was very ill, and then, two days later, that she seemed to be dying. The news came from Timofey Petrovitch," added Polina, "and he's a trustworthy man. We are expecting every day to hear news of the end."

"So you are all in suspense here?" I asked.

"Of course, all of us, and all the time; we've been hoping for nothing else for the last six months."

"And are *you* hoping for it?" I asked.

"Why, I'm no relation. I am only the General's step-daughter. But I am sure she will remember me in her will."

"I fancy you'll get a great deal," I said emphatically.

"Yes, she was fond of me; but what makes *you* think so?"

"Tell me," I answered with a question, "our *marquis* is initiated into all our secrets, it seems?"

"But why are you interested in that?" asked Polina, looking at me drily and austerely.

"I should think so; if I'm not mistaken, the General has already succeeded in borrowing from him."

"You guess very correctly."

"Well, would he have lent the money if he had not known about your 'granny'? Did you notice at dinner, three times speaking of her, he called her 'granny.' What intimate and friendly relations!"

"Yes, you are right. As soon as he knows that I have come into something by the will, he will pay his addresses to me at once. That is what you wanted to know, was it?"

"He will only begin to pay you his addresses? I thought he had been doing that a long time."

"You know perfectly well that he hasn't!" Polina said, with anger. "Where did you meet that Englishman?" she added, after a minute's silence.

"I knew you would ask about him directly."

I told her of my previous meetings with Mr. Astley on my journey.

"He is shy and given to falling in love, and, of course, he's fallen in love with you already."

"Yes, he's in love with me," answered Polina.

"And, of course, he's ten times as rich as the Frenchman. Why, is it certain that the Frenchman has anything? Isn't that open to doubt?"

"No, it is not. He has a château of some sort. The General has spoken of that positively. Well, are you satisfied?"

"If I were in your place I should certainly marry the Englishman."

"Why?" asked Polina.

"The Frenchman is better-looking, but he is nastier; and the Englishman, besides being honest, is ten times as rich," I snapped out.

"Yes, but on the other hand, the Frenchman is a *mar-*

quis and clever," she answered, in the most composed manner.

"But is it true?" I went on, in the same way.

"It certainly is."

Polina greatly disliked my questions, and I saw that she was trying to make me angry by her tone and the strangeness of her answers. I said as much to her at once.

"Well, it really amuses me to see you in such a rage. You must pay for the very fact of my allowing you to ask such questions and make such suppositions."

"I certainly consider myself entitled to ask you any sort of question," I answered calmly, "just because I am prepared to pay any price you like for it, and I set no value at all on my life now."

Polina laughed.

"You told me last time at the Schlangenberg, that you were prepared, at a word from me, to throw yourself head foremost from the rock, and it is a thousand feet high, I believe. Some day I shall utter that word, solely in order to see how you will pay the price, and trust me, I won't give way. You are hateful to me, just because I've allowed you to take such liberties, and even more hateful because you are so necessary to me. But so long as you are necessary to me, I must take care of you."

She began getting up. She spoke with irritation. Of late she had always ended every conversation with me in anger and irritation, real anger.

"Allow me to ask you, what about Mlle. Blanche?" I asked, not liking to let her go without explanation.

"You know all about Mlle. Blanche. Nothing more has happened since. Mlle. Blanche will, no doubt, be Madame la Générale, that is, if the rumour of Granny's death is confirmed, of course, for Mlle. Blanche and her mother and her cousin twice removed, the *marquis*—all know very well that we are ruined."

"And is the General hopelessly in love?"

"That's not the point now. Listen and remember: take these seven hundred florins and go and play. Win me as much as you can at roulette; I must have money now, come what may."

Saying this, she called Nadenka and went into the Casino, where she joined the rest of the party. I turned into the first path to the left, wondering and reflecting. I felt as though I had had a blow on the head after the command to go and play roulette. Strange to say, I had plenty to think about, but I was completely absorbed in analyzing the essential nature of my feeling towards Polina. It was true I had been more at ease during that fortnight's absence than I was now on the day of my return, though on the journey I had been as melancholy and restless as a madman, and at moments had even seen her in my dreams. Once, waking up in the train (in Switzerland), I began talking aloud, I believe, with Polina, which amused all the passengers in the carriage with me. And once more now I asked myself the question: "Do I love her?" And again I could not answer it, or, rather, I answered for the hundredth time that I hated her. Yes, she was hateful to me. There were moments (on every occasion at the end of our talks) when I would have given my life to strangle her! I swear if it had been possible on the spot to plunge a sharp knife in her bosom, I believe I should have snatched it up with relish. And yet I swear by all that's sacred that if at the Schlangenberg, at the fashionable peak, she really had said to me, "Throw yourself down," I should have thrown myself down at once, also with positive relish. I knew that. In one way or another it must be settled. All this she understood wonderfully well, and the idea that I knew, positively and distinctly, how utterly beyond my reach she was, how utterly impossible my mad dreams were of fulfilment, that thought, I am convinced, afforded her extraordinary satisfaction; if not, how could she, cautious and intelligent as she was, have been on such intimate and open terms with me? I believe she had hitherto looked on me as that empress of ancient times looked on the slave before whom she did not mind undressing because she did not regard him as a human being. Yes, often she did not regard me as a human being!

I had her commission, however, to win at roulette, at all costs. I had no time to consider why must I play, and why such haste, and what new scheme was hatching in that ever-calculating brain. Moreover, it was evident that during that fortnight new facts had arisen of which I had no idea yet. I must discover all that and get to the bottom of it and as quickly as possible. But there was no time now; I must go to roulette.

2

I confess it was disagreeable to me. Though I had made
up my mind that I would play, I had not proposed to play
for other people. It rather threw me out of my reckoning,
and I went into the gambling saloon with very disagreeable feelings. From the first glance I disliked everything in
it. I cannot endure the flunkeyishness of the newspapers
of the whole world, and especially our Russian papers, in
which, almost every spring, the journalists write articles
upon two things: first, on the extraordinary magnificence
and luxury of the gambling saloons on the Rhine, and secondly, on the heaps of gold which are said to lie on the
tables. They are not paid for it; it is simply done from disinterested obsequiousness. There was no sort of magnificence in these trashy rooms, and not only were there no
piles of gold lying on the table, but there was hardly any
gold at all. No doubt some time, in the course of the
season, some eccentric person, either an Englishman or
an Asiatic of some sort, a Turk, perhaps (as it was that
summer), would suddenly turn up and lose or win immense sums; all the others play for paltry guldens, and
on an average there is very little money lying on the tables.

As soon as I went into the gambling saloon (for the first
time in my life), I could not for some time make up my
mind to play. There was a crush besides. If I had been
alone, even then, I believe I should soon have gone away
and not have begun playing. I confess my heart was beating and I was not cool. I knew for certain, and had made
up my mind long before, that I should not leave Roulettenburg unchanged, that some radical and fundamental
change would take place in my destiny; so it must be and
so it would be. Ridiculous as it may be that I should expect so much for myself from roulette, yet I consider even
more ridiculous the conventional opinion accepted by all
that it is stupid and absurd to expect anything from gambling. And why should gambling be worse than any other
means of making money—for instance, commerce? It is

true that only one out of a hundred wins, but what is that to me?

In any case I determined to look about me first and not to begin anything in earnest that evening. If anything did happen that evening it would happen by chance and be something slight, and I staked my money accordingly. Besides, I had to study the game; for, in spite of the thousand descriptions of roulette which I had read so eagerly, I understood absolutely nothing of its working until I saw it myself.

In the first place it all struck me as so dirty, somehow, morally horrid and dirty. I am not speaking at all of the greedy, uneasy faces which by dozens, even by hundreds, crowd round the gambling tables. I see absolutely nothing dirty in the wish to win as quickly and as much as possible. I always thought very stupid the answer of that fat and prosperous moralist, who replied to some one's excuse "that he played for a very small stake," "So much the worse, it is such petty covetousness." As though covetousness were not exactly the same, whether on a big scale or a petty one. It is a matter of proportion. What is paltry to Rothschild is wealth to me, and as for profits and winnings, people, not only at roulette, but everywhere, do nothing but try to gain or squeeze something out of one another. Whether profits or gains are nasty is a different question. But I am not solving that question here. Since I was myself possessed by an intense desire of winning, I felt as I went into the hall all this covetousness, and all this covetous filth if you like, in a sense congenial and convenient. It is most charming when people do not stand on ceremony with one another, but act openly and above-board. And, indeed, why deceive oneself? Gambling is a most foolish and imprudent pursuit! What was particularly ugly at first sight, in all the rabble round the roulette table, was the respect they paid to that pursuit, the solemnity and even reverence with which they all crowded round the tables. That is why a sharp distinction is drawn here between the kind of game that is *mauvais genre* and the kind that is permissible to well-bred people. There are two sorts of gambling: one the gentlemanly sort: the other the plebeian, mercenary sort, the game played by all sorts of riff-raff. The distinction is sternly observed here, and how contemptible this distinction really is! A gentleman

may stake, for instance, five or ten louis d'or, rarely more;
he may, however, stake as much as a thousand francs if
he is very rich; but only for the sake of the play, simply for
amusement, that is, simply to look on at the process of
winning or of losing, but must on no account display an
interest in winning. If he wins, he may laugh aloud, for
instance; may make a remark to one of the bystanders; he
may even put down another stake, and may even double
it, but solely from curiosity, for the sake of watching and
calculating the chances, and not from the plebeian desire
to win. In fact, he must look on all gambling, roulette,
trente et quarante, as nothing else than a pastime got up
entirely for his amusement. He must not even suspect the
greed for gain and the shifty dodges on which the bank
depends.

It would be extremely good form, too, if he should imagine that all the other gamblers, all the rabble, trembling
over a gulden, were rich men and gentlemen like himself
and were playing simply for their diversion and amusement. This complete ignorance of reality and innocent view
of people would be, of course, extremely aristocratic. I
have seen many mammas push forward their daughters,
innocent and elegant misses of fifteen and sixteen, and,
giving them some gold coins, teach them how to play. The
young lady wins or loses, invariably smiles and walks
away, very well satisfied. Our General went up to the table
with solid dignity; a flunkey rushed to hand him a chair,
but he ignored the flunkey; he, very slowly and deliberately, took out his purse, very slowly and deliberately took
three hundred francs in gold from his purse, staked them
on the black, and won. He did not pick up his winnings, but
left them on the table. Black turned up again; he didn't pick
up his winnings that time either; and when, the third
time, red turned up, he lost at once twelve hundred francs.
He walked away with a smile and kept up his dignity. I am
positive he was raging inwardly, and if the stake had been
two or three times as much he would not have kept up his
dignity but would have betrayed his feelings. A Frenchman did, however, before my eyes, win and lose as much
as thirty thousand francs with perfect gaiety and no sign
of emotion. A real gentleman should not show excitement
even if he loses his whole fortune. Money ought to be so
much below his gentlemanly dignity as to be scarcely

worth noticing. Of course, it would have been extremely aristocratic not to notice the sordidness of all the rabble and all the surroundings. Sometimes, however, the opposite pose is no less aristocratic—to notice—that is, to look about one, even, perhaps, to stare through a lorgnette at the rabble; though always taking the rabble and the sordidness as nothing else but a diversion of a sort, as though it were a performance got up for the amusement of gentlemen. One may be jostled in that crowd, but one must look about one with complete conviction that one is oneself a spectator and that one is in no sense part of it. Though, again, to look very attentively is not quite the thing; that, again, would not be gentlemanly because, in any case, the spectacle does not deserve much, or close, attention. And, in fact, few spectacles do deserve a gentleman's close attention. And yet it seemed to me that all this was deserving of very close attention, especially for one who had come not only to observe it, but sincerely and genuinely reckoned himself as one of the rabble. As for my hidden moral convictions, there is no place for them, of course, in my present reasonings. Let that be enough for the present. I speak to relieve my conscience. But I notice one thing: that of late it has become horribly repugnant to me to test my thoughts and actions by any moral standard whatever. I was guided by something different. . . .

The rabble certainly did play very sordidly. I am ready to believe, indeed, that a great deal of the most ordinary thieving goes on at the gambling table. The croupiers who sit at each end of the table look at the stakes and reckon the winnings; they have a great deal to do. They are rabble, too! For the most part they are French. However, I was watching and observing, not with the object of describing roulette. I kept a sharp look-out for my own sake, so that I might know how to behave in the future. I noticed, for instance, that nothing was more common than for some one to stretch out his hand and snatch what one had won. A dispute would begin, often an uproar, and a nice job one would have to find witnesses and to prove that it was one's stake!

At first it was all an inexplicable puzzle to me. All I could guess and distinguish was that the stakes were on the numbers, on odd and even, and on the colours. I made up my mind to risk a hundred guldens of Polina Alexandrovna's money. The thought that I was not playing for myself seemed to throw me out of my reckoning. It was an extremely unpleasant feeling, and I wanted to be rid of it as soon as possible. I kept feeling that by beginning for Polina I should break my own luck. Is it impossible to approach the gambling table without becoming infected with superstition? I began by taking out five friedrichs d'or (fifty gulden) and putting them on the even. The wheel went round and thirteen turned up—I had lost. With a sickly feeling I staked another five friedrichs d'or on red, simply in order to settle the matter and go away. Red turned up again. I staked all the money again on the same, and again red turned up. On receiving forty friedrichs d'or I staked twenty upon the twelve middle figures, not knowing what would come of it. I was paid three times my stake. In this way from ten friedrichs d'or I had all at once eighty. I was overcome by a strange, unusual feeling which was so unbearable that I made up my mind to go away. It seemed to me that I should not have been playing at all like that if I had been playing for myself. I staked the whole eighty friedrichs d'or, however, on even. This time four turned up; another eighty friedrichs d'or was poured out to me; and, gathering up the whole heap of a hundred and sixty friedrichs d'or, I set off to find Polina Alexandrovna.

They were all walking somewhere in the park and I only succeeded in seeing her after supper. This time the Frenchman was not of the party, and the General unbosomed himself. Among other things he thought fit to observe to me that he would not wish to see me at the gambling tables. It seemed to him that it would compromise him if I were to lose too much: "But even if you were to win a very large sum I should be compromised, too," he added significantly. "Of course, I have no right to dictate your actions, but you must admit yourself . . ." At this point he broke off, as his habit was. I answered, drily, that I had very little money, and so I could not lose very conspicuously, even if I did play. Going upstairs to my room I succeeded in handing Polina her winnings, and told her that I would not play for her another time.

"Why not?" she asked, in a tremor.

"Because I want to play on my own account," I answered, looking at her with surprise; "and it hinders me."

"Then you still continue in your conviction that roulette is your only escape and salvation?" she asked ironically.

I answered very earnestly, that I did; that as for my confidence that I should win, it might be absurd; I was ready to admit it, but that I wanted to be let alone.

Polina Alexandrovna began insisting I should go halves with her in to-day's winnings, and was giving me eighty friedrichs d'or, suggesting that I should go on playing on those terms. I refused the half, positively and finally, and told her that I could not play for other people, not because I didn't want to, but because I should certainly lose.

"Yet I, too," she said, pondering, "stupid as it seems, am building all my hopes on roulette. And so you must go on playing, sharing with me, and—of course—you will."

At this point she walked away, without listening to further objections.

3

Yet all yesterday she did not say a single word to me about playing, and avoided speaking to me altogether. Her manner to me remained unchanged: the same absolute carelessness on meeting me; there was even a shade of contempt and dislike. Altogether she did not care to conceal her aversion; I noticed that. In spite of that she did not conceal from me, either, that I was in some way necessary to her and that she was keeping me for some purpose. A strange relation had grown up between us, incomprehensible to me in many ways when I considered her pride and haughtiness with every one. She knew, for instance, that I loved her madly, even allowed me to speak of my passion; and, of course, she could not have shown greater contempt for me than by allowing me to speak of my passion without hindrance or restriction. It was as much as to say that she thought so little of my feelings that she did not care in the least what I talked about to her and what I felt for her. She had talked a great deal about her own affairs before, but had never been completely open. What is more, there was this peculiar refinement in her contempt for me: she would know, for instance, that I was aware of

some circumstance in her life, or knew of some matter
that greatly concerned her, or she would tell me herself
something of her circumstances, if to forward her objects
she had to make use of me in some way, as a slave or an
errand-boy; but she would always tell me only so much as
a man employed on her errands need know, and if I did
not know the whole chain of events, if she saw herself
how worried and anxious I was over her worries and anxieties, she never deigned to comfort me by giving me her full
confidence as a friend; though she often made use of me
for commissions that were not only troublesome, but dangerous, so that to my thinking she was bound to be open
with me. Was it worth her while, indeed, to trouble herself about my feelings, about my being worried, and perhaps three times as much worried and tormented by her
anxieties and failures as she was herself?

I knew of her intention to play roulette three weeks before. She had even warned me that I should have to play
for her, and it would be improper for her to play herself.
From the tone of her words, I noticed even then that she
had serious anxieties, and was not actuated simply by a
desire for money. What is money to her for its own sake?
She must have some object, there must be some circumstance at which I can only guess, but of which so far I
have no knowledge. Of course, the humiliation and the
slavery in which she held me might have made it possible
for me (it often does) to question her coarsely and bluntly.
Seeing that in her eyes I was a slave and utterly insignificant, there was nothing for her to be offended at in my
coarse curiosity. But the fact is, that though she allowed
me to ask questions, she did not answer them, and sometimes did not notice them at all. That was the position
between us.

A great deal was said yesterday about a telegram which
had been sent off four days before, and to which no answer had been received. The General was evidently upset
and preoccupied. It had, of course, something to do with
Granny. The Frenchman was troubled, too. Yesterday, for
instance, after dinner, they had a long, serious talk. The
Frenchman's tone to all of us was unusually high and
mighty, quite in the spirit of the saying: "Seat a pig at
table and it will put its feet on it." Even with Polina he

was casual to the point of rudeness; at the same time he gladly took part in the walks in the public gardens and in the rides and drives into the country. I had long known some of the circumstances that bound the Frenchman to the General: they had made plans for establishing a factory together in Russia; I don't know whether their project had fallen through, or whether it was being discussed. Moreover, I had by chance come to know part of a family secret. The Frenchman had actually, in the previous year, come to the General's rescue, and had given him thirty thousand roubles to make up a deficit of Government monies missing when he resigned his duties. And, of course, the General is in his grip; but now the principal person in the whole business is Mlle. Blanche; about that I am sure I'm not mistaken.

What is Mlle. Blanche? Here among us it is said that she is a distinguished Frenchwoman, with a colossal fortune and a mother accompanying her. It is known, too, that she is some sort of relation of our *marquis,* but a very distant one: a cousin, or something of the sort. I am told that before I went to Paris, the Frenchman and Mlle. Blanche were on much more ceremonious, were, so to speak, on a more delicate and refined footing; now their acquaintance, their friendship and relationship, was of a rather coarse and more intimate character. Perhaps our prospects seemed to them so poor that they did not think it very necessary to stand on ceremony and keep up appearances with us. I noticed even the day before yesterday how Mr. Astley looked at Mlle. Blanche and her mother. It seemed to me that he knew them. It even seemed to me that our Frenchman had met Mr. Astley before. Mr. Astley, however, is so shy, so reserved and silent, that one can be almost certain of him—he won't wash dirty linen in public. Anyway, the Frenchman barely bows to him and scarcely looks at him, so he is not afraid of him. One can understand that, perhaps, but why does Mlle. Blanche not look at him either? Especially when the *marquis* let slip yesterday in the course of conversation—I don't remember in what connection—that Mr. Astley had a colossal fortune and that he—the *marquis*—knew this for a fact; at that point Mlle. Blanche might well have looked at Mr. Astley. Altogether the General was uneasy. One can understand what a telegram announcing his aunt's death would mean!

Though I felt sure Polina was, apparently for some object, avoiding a conversation with me, I assumed a cold and indifferent air: I kept thinking that before long she would come to me of herself. But both to-day and yesterday I concentrated my attention principally on Mlle. Blanche. Poor General! He is completely done for! To fall in love at fifty-five with such a violent passion is a calamity, of course! When one takes into consideration the fact that he is a widower, his children, the ruin of his estate, his debts, and, finally, the woman it is his lot to fall in love with. Mlle. Blanche is handsome. But I don't know if I shall be understood if I say that she has a face of the type of which one might feel frightened. I, anyway, have always been afraid of women of that sort. She is probably five-and-twenty. She is well grown and broad, with sloping shoulders; she has a magnificent throat and bosom; her complexion is swarthy yellow. Her hair is as black as Indian ink, and she has a tremendous lot of it, enough to make two ordinary coiffures. Her eyes are black with yellowish whites; she has an insolent look in her eyes; her teeth are very white; her lips are always painted; she smells of musk. She dresses effectively, richly and with *chic,* but with much taste. Her hands and feet are exquisite. Her voice is a husky contralto. Sometimes she laughs, showing all her teeth, but her usual expression is a silent and impudent stare—before Polina and Marya Filippovna, anyway (there is a strange rumour that Marya Filippovna is going back to Russia). I fancy that Mlle. Blanche has had no sort of education. Possibly she is not even intelligent; but, on the other hand, she is striking and she is artful. I fancy her life has not passed without adventures. If one is to tell the whole truth, it is quite possible that the *marquis* is no relation of hers at all, and that her mother is not her mother. But there is evidence that in Berlin, where we went with them, her mother and she had some decent acquaintances. As for the *marquis* himself, though I still doubt his being a *marquis,* yet the fact that he is received in decent society—among Russians, for instance, in Moscow, and in some places in Germany—is not open to doubt. I don't know what he is in France. They say he has a château.

I thought that a great deal would have happened during

this fortnight, and yet I don't know if anything decisive has been said between Mlle. Blanche and the General. Everything depends on our fortune, however; that is, whether the General can show them plenty of money. If, for instance, news were to come that Granny were not dead, I am convinced that Mlle. Blanche would vanish at once. It surprises and amuses me to see what a gossip I've become. Oh! how I loathe it all! How delighted I should be to drop it all, and them all! But can I leave Polina, can I give up spying round her? Spying, of course, is low, but what do I care about that?

I was interested in Mr. Astley, too, to-day and yesterday. Yes, I am convinced he's in love with Polina. It is curious and absurd how much may be expressed by the eyes of a modest and painfully chaste man, moved by love, at the very time when the man would gladly sink into the earth rather than express or betray anything by word or glance. Mr. Astley very often meets us on our walks. He takes off his hat and passes by, though, of course, he is dying to join us. If he is invited to do so, he immediately refuses. At places where we rest—at the Casino, by the bandstand, or before the fountain—he always stands somewhere not far from our seat; and wherever we may be—in the park, in the wood, or on the Schlangenberg—one has only to glance round, to look about one, and somewhere, either in the nearest path or behind the bushes, Mr. Astley's head appears. I fancy he is looking for an opportunity to have a conversation with me apart. This morning we met and exchanged a couple of words. He sometimes speaks very abruptly. Without saying "good-morning," he began by blurting out—

"Oh, Mlle. Blanche! . . . I have seen a great many women like Mlle. Blanche!"

He paused, looking at me significantly. What he meant to say by that I don't know. For on my asking what he meant, he shook his head with a sly smile, and added, "Oh, well, that's how it is. Is Mlle. Pauline very fond of flowers?"

"I don't know; I don't know at all," I answered.

"What? You don't even know that!" he cried, with the utmost amazement.

"I don't know; I haven't noticed at all," I repeated, laughing.

"H'm! That gives me a queer idea."

Then he shook his head and walked away. He looked pleased, though. We talked the most awful French together.

4

To-day has been an absurd, grotesque, ridiculous day. Now it is eleven o'clock at night. I am sitting in my little cupboard of a room, recalling it. It began with my having to go to roulette to play for Polina Alexandrovna. I took the hundred and sixty friedrichs d'or, but on two conditions: first, that I would not go halves—that is, if I won I would take nothing for myself; and secondly, that in the evening Polina should explain to me why she needed to win, and how much money. I can't, in any case, suppose that it is simply for the sake of money. Evidently the money is needed, and as quickly as possible, for some particular object. She promised to explain, and I set off. In the gambling hall the crowd was awful. How insolent and how greedy they all were! I forced my way into the middle and stood near the croupier; then I began timidly experimenting, staking two or three coins at a time. Meanwhile, I kept quiet and looked on; it seemed to me that calculation meant very little, and had by no means the importance attributed to it by some players. They sit with papers before them scrawled over in pencil, note the strokes, reckon, deduce the chances, calculate, finally stake and—lose exactly as we simple mortals who play without calculations. On the other hand, I drew one conclusion which I believe to be correct: that is, though there is no system, there really is a sort of order in the sequence of casual chances —and that, of course, is very strange. For instance, it happens that after the twelve middle numbers come the twelve later numbers; twice, for instance, it turns up on the twelve last numbers and passes to the twelve first numbers. After falling on the twelve first numbers, it passes again to numbers in the middle third, turns up three or four times in succession on numbers between thirteen and twenty-four, and again passes to numbers in the last third; then, after turning up two numbers between twenty-five and thirty-six, it passes to a number among the first twelve, turns up once again on a number among the first third, and again passes for three strokes in succession to the middle numbers; and in that way goes on for an hour and a half or two hours. One, three and two—one, three and two. It's very amusing. One day or one morning, for instance, red will be followed by black and back again almost without any order, shifting every minute, so that it never turns up red or black for more than two or three strokes in succession. Another day, or another evening, there will be nothing but red over and over again, turning up, for instance, more than twenty-two times in succession, and so for a whole day. A great deal of this was explained to me by Mr. Astley, who spent the whole morning at the tables, but did not once put down a stake,

As for me, I lost every farthing very quickly. I staked straight off twenty friedrichs d'or on even and won, staked again and again won, and went on like that two or three times. I imagine I must have had about four hundred friedrichs d'or in my hands in about five minutes. At that point I ought to have gone away, but a strange sensation rose up in me, a sort of defiance of fate, a desire to challenge it, to put out my tongue at it. I laid down the largest stake allowed—four thousand gulden—and lost it. Then, getting hot, I pulled out all I had left, staked it on the same number, and lost again, after which I walked away from the table as though I were stunned. I could not even grasp what had happened to me, and did not tell Polina Alexandrovna of my losing till just before dinner. I spent the rest of the day sauntering in the park.

At dinner I was again in an excited state, just as I had been three days before. The Frenchman and Mlle. Blanche were dining with us again. It appeared that Mlle. Blanche had been in the gambling hall that morning and had witnessed my exploits. This time she addressed me, it seemed, somewhat attentively. The Frenchman set to work more directly, and asked me: Was it my own money I had lost? I fancy he suspects Polina. In fact, there is something behind it. I lied at once and said it was.

The General was extremely surprised. Where had I got such a sum? I explained that I had begun with ten fried-

richs d'or, that after six or seven times staking successfully on equal chances I had five or six hundred gulden,
and that afterwards I had lost it all in two turns.

All that, of course, sounded probable. As I explained
this I looked at Polina, but I could distinguish nothing
from her face. She let me lie, however, and did not set it
right; from this I concluded that I had to lie and conceal
that I was in collaboration with her. In any case, I thought
to myself, she is bound to give me an explanation, and
promised me this morning to reveal something.

I expected the General would have made some remark
to me, but he remained mute; I noticed, however, signs of
disturbance and uneasiness in his face. Possibly in his
straitened circumstances it was simply painful to him to
hear that such a pile of gold had come into, and within a
quarter of an hour had passed out of, the hands of such
a reckless fool as me.

I suspect that he had a rather hot encounter with the
Frenchman yesterday. They were shut up together talking
for a long time. The Frenchman went away seeming irritated, and came to see the General again early this morning—probably to continue the conversation of the previous day.

Hearing what I had lost, the Frenchman observed bit-
ingly, even spitefully, that one ought to have more sense.
He added—I don't know why—that though a great many
Russians gamble, Russians were not, in his opinion, well
qualified even for gambling.

"In my mind," said I, "roulette is simply made for Russians."

And when at my challenge the Frenchman laughed contemptuously, I observed that I was, of course, right, for
to speak of the Russians as gamblers was abusing them far
more than praising them, and so I might be believed.

"On what do you base your opinion?" asked the Frenchman.

"On the fact that the faculty of amassing capital has,
with the progress of history, taken a place—and almost
the foremost place—among the virtues and merits of the
civilized man of the West. The Russian is not only incapable of amassing capital, but dissipates it in a reckless
and unseemly way. Nevertheless we Russians need money,
too," I added, "and consequently we are very glad and very

eager to make use of such means as roulette, for instance, in which one can grow rich all at once, in two hours, without work. That's very fascinating to us; and since we play badly, recklessly, without taking trouble, we usually lose!"

"That's partly true," observed the Frenchman complacently.

"No, it is not true, and you ought to be ashamed to speak like that of your country," observed the General, sternly and impressively.

"Allow me," I answered. "I really don't know which is more disgusting: Russian unseemliness or the German faculty of accumulation by honest toil."

"What an unseemly idea!" exclaimed the General.

"What a Russian idea!" exclaimed the Frenchman.

I laughed; I had an intense desire to provoke them.

"Well, I should prefer to dwell all my life in a Kirgiz tent," I cried, "than bow down to the German idol."

"What idol?" cried the General, beginning to be angry in earnest.

"The German faculty for accumulating wealth. I've not been here long, but yet all I have been able to observe and verify revolts my Tatar blood. My God! I don't want any such virtue! I succeeded yesterday in making a round of eight miles, and it's all exactly as in the edifying German picture-books: there is here in every house a *vater* horribly virtuous and extraordinarily honest—so honest that you are afraid to go near him. I can't endure honest people whom one is afraid to go near. Every such German *vater* has a family, and in the evening they read improving books aloud. Elms and chestnut trees rustle over the house. The sun is setting; there is a stork on the roof, and everything is extraordinarily practical and touching. . . . Don't be angry, General; let me tell it in a touching style. I remember how my father used to read similar books to my mother and me under the lime-trees in the garden. . . . So I am in a position to judge. And in what complete bondage and submission every such family is here. They all work like oxen and all save money like Jews. Suppose the *vater* has saved up so many gulden and is reckoning on giving his son on a trade or a bit of land; to do so, he gives his daughter no dowry, and she becomes an old maid. To do so, the youngest son is sold into bondage or into the army, and the money is added to the family capital. This is actually done here; I've been making inquiries. All this is done from nothing but honesty, from such intense honesty that the younger son who is sold believes that he is sold from nothing but honesty: and that is the ideal when the victim himself rejoices at being led to the sacrifice. What more? Why, the elder son is no better off: he has an Amalia and their hearts are united, but they can't be married because the pile of gulden is not large enough. They, too, wait with perfect morality and good faith, and go to the sacrifice with a smile. Amalia's cheeks grow thin and hollow. At last, in twenty years, their prosperity is increased; the gulden have been honestly and virtuously accumulating. The *vater* gives his blessing to the forty-year-old son and his Amalia of thirty-five, whose chest has grown hollow and whose nose has turned red. . . . With that he weeps, reads them a moral sermon, and dies. The eldest son becomes himself a virtuous *vater* and begins the same story over again. In that way, in fifty or seventy years, the grandson of the first *vater* really has a considerable capital, and he leaves it to his son, and he to his, and he to his, till in five or six generations one of them is a Baron Rothschild or goodness knows who. Come, isn't that a majestic spectacle? A hundred or two hundred years of continuous toil, patience, intelligence, honesty, character, determination, prudence, the stork on the roof! What more do you want? Why, there's nothing loftier than that; and from that standpoint they are beginning to judge the whole world and to punish the guilty; that is, any who are ever so little unlike them. Well, so that's the point: I would rather waste my substance in the Russian style or grow rich at roulette. I don't care to be Goppe and Co. in five generations. I want money for myself, and I don't look upon myself as something subordinate to capital and necessary to it. I know that I have been talking awful nonsense, but, never mind, such are my convictions."

"I don't know whether there is much truth in what you have been saying," said the General thoughtfully, "but I do know you begin to give yourself insufferable airs as soon are you are permitted to forget yourself in the least . . ."

As his habit was, he broke off without finishing. If our General began to speak of anything in the slightest degree more important than his ordinary everyday conversation, he never finished his sentences. The Frenchman listened carelessly with rather wide-open eyes; he had scarcely understood anything of what I had said. Polina gazed with haughty indifference. She seemed not to hear my words, or anything else that was said that day at table.

5

She was unusually thoughtful, but directly we got up from table she bade me escort her for a walk. We took the children and went into the park towards the fountain.

As I felt particularly excited, I blurted out the crude and stupid question: why the Marquis de Grieux, our Frenchman, no longer escorted her when she went out anywhere, and did not even speak to her for days together.

"Because he is a rascal," she answered me strangely.

I had never heard her speak like that of De Grieux, and I received it in silence, afraid to interpret her irritability.

"Have you noticed that he is not on good terms with the General to-day?"

"You want to know what is the matter?" she answered drily and irritably. "You know that the General is completely mortgaged to him; all his property is his, and if Granny doesn't die, the Frenchman will come into possession of everything that is mortgaged to him."

"And is it true that everything is mortgaged? I had heard it, but I did not know that everything was."

"To be sure it is."

"Then farewell to Mlle. Blanche," said I. "She won't be the General's wife, then! Do you know, it strikes me the General is so much in love that he may shoot himself if Mlle. Blanche throws him over. It is dangerous to be so much in love at his age."

"I fancy that something will happen to him, too," Polina Alexandrovna observed musingly.

"And how splendid that would be!" I cried. "They couldn't have shown more coarsely that she was only marrying him for his money! There's no regard for decency, even; there's no ceremony about it whatever. That's wonderful! And about Granny—could there be anything more comic and sordid than to be continually sending telegram after telegram: 'Is she dead, is she dead?' How do you like it, Polina Alexandrovna?"

"That's all nonsense," she said, interrupting me with an air of disgust. "I wonder at your being in such good spirits. What are you so pleased about? Surely not at having lost my money?"

"Why did you give it to me to lose? I told you I could not play for other people—especially for you! I obey you, whatever you order me to do, but I can't answer for the result. I warned you that nothing would come of it. Are you very much upset at losing so much money? What do you want so much for?"

"Why these questions?"

"Why, you promised to explain to me . . . Listen: I am absolutely convinced that when I begin playing for myself (and I've got twelve friedrichs d'or) I shall win. Then you can borrow as much from me as you like."

She made a contemptuous grimace.

"Don't be angry with me for such a suggestion," I went on. "I am so deeply conscious that I am nothing beside you—that is, in your eyes—that you may even borrow money from me. Presents from me cannot insult you. Besides, I lost yours."

She looked at me quickly, and seeing that I was speaking irritably and sarcastically, interrupted the conversation again.

"There's nothing of interest to you in my circumstances. If you want to know, I'm simply in debt. I've borrowed money and I wanted to repay it. I had the strange and mad idea that I should be sure to win here at the gambling table. Why I had the idea I can't understand, but I believed in it. Who knows, perhaps I believed it because no other alternative was left me."

"Or because it was quite *necessary* you should win. It's exactly like a drowning man clutching at a straw. You will admit that if he were not drowning he would not look at a straw as a branch of a tree."

Polina was surprised.

"Why," she said, "you were reckoning on the same thing yourself! A fortnight ago you said a great deal to me about your being absolutely convinced that you would win here at roulette, and tried to persuade me not to look upon you as mad; or were you joking then? But I remember you spoke so seriously that it was impossible to take it as a joke."

"That's true," I answered thoughtfully. "I am convinced to this moment that I shall win. I confess you have led me now to wonder why my senseless and unseemly failure to-day has not left the slightest doubt in me. I am still fully convinced that as soon as I begin playing for myself I shall be certain to win."

"Why are you so positive?"

"If you will have it—I don't know. I only know that I *must* win, that it is the only resource left me. Well, that's why, perhaps, I fancy I am bound to win."

"Then you, too, absolutely *must* have it, since you are so fanatically certain?"

"I wager you think I'm not capable of feeling that I *must* have anything?"

"That's nothing to me," Polina answered quietly and indifferently. "Yes, if you like. I doubt whether anything troubles you in earnest. You may be troubled, but not in earnest. You are an unstable person, not to be relied on. What do you want money for? I could see nothing serious in the reasons you brought forward the other day."

"By the way," I interrupted, "you said that you had to repay a debt. A fine debt it must be! To the Frenchman, I suppose?"

"What questions! You're particularly impertinent to-day. Are you drunk, perhaps?"

"You know that I consider myself at liberty to say anything to you, and sometimes ask you very candid questions. I repeat, I'm your slave, and one does not mind what one says to a slave, and cannot take offence at anything he says."

"And I can't endure that 'slave' theory of yours."

"Observe that I don't speak of my slavery because I want to be your slave. I simply speak of it as a fact which doesn't depend on me in the least."

"Tell me plainly, what do you want money for?"

"What do you want to know that for?"

"As you please," she replied, with a proud movement of her head.

"You can't endure the 'slave' theory, but insist on slavishness: 'Answer and don't argue.' So be it. Why do I want money? you ask. How can you ask? Money is everything!"

"I understand that, but not falling into such madness from wanting it! You, too, are growing frenzied, fatalistic. There must be something behind it, some special object. Speak without beating about the bush; I wish it."

She seemed beginning to get angry, and I was awfully pleased at her questioning me with such heat.

"Of course there is an object," I answered, "but I don't know how to explain what it is. Nothing else but that with money I should become to you a different man, not a slave."

"What? How will you manage that?"

"How shall I manage it? What, you don't even understand how I could manage to make you look at me as anything but a slave? Well, that's just what I don't care for, such surprise and incredulity!"

"You said this slavery was a pleasure to you. I thought it was myself."

"You thought so!" I cried, with a strange enjoyment. "Oh, how delightful such naïveté is from you! Oh, yes, yes, slavery to you is a pleasure. There is—there is a pleasure in the utmost limit of humiliation and insignificance!" I went on maundering. "Goodness knows, perhaps there is in the knout when the knout lies in the back and tears the flesh. . . . But I should perhaps like to enjoy another kind of enjoyment. Yesterday, in your presence, the General thought fit to read me a lecture for the seven hundred roubles a year which perhaps I may not receive from him after all. The Marquis de Grieux raises his eyebrows and stares at me without noticing me. And I, perhaps, have a passionate desire to pull the Marquis de Grieux by the nose in your presence!"

"That's the speech of a milksop. One can behave with dignity in any position. If there is a struggle, it is elevating, not humiliating."

"That's straight out of a copybook. You simply take for granted that I don't know how to behave with dignity; that is, that perhaps I am a man of moral dignity, but that I don't know how to behave with dignity. You understand that that perhaps may be so. Yes, all Russians are like that; and do you know why? Because Russians are too richly endowed and many-sided to be able readily to evolve

a code of manners. It is a question of good form. For the
most part we Russians are so richly endowed that we need
genius to evolve our code of manners. And genius is most
often absent, for, indeed, it is a rarity at all times. It's
only among the French, and perhaps some other Europeans, that the code of manners is so well defined that
one may have an air of the utmost dignity and yet be a
man of no moral dignity whatever. That's why good form
means so much with them. A Frenchman will put up with
an insult, a real, moral insult, without blinking, but he
wouldn't endure a flip on the nose for anything, because
that is a breach of the received code, sanctified for ages.
That's why our Russian young ladies have such a weakness for Frenchmen, that their manners are so good.
Though, to my thinking, they have no manners at all; it's
simply the cock in them, *le coq gaulois*. I can't understand
it, though; I'm not a woman. Perhaps cocks are nice. And,
in fact, I've been talking nonsense, and you don't stop me.
You must stop me more often. When I talk to you I long to
tell you everything, everything, everything. I am oblivious
of all good manners. I'll even admit that I have no manners, no moral qualities either. I tell you that. I don't even
worry my head about moral qualities of any sort; everything has come to a standstill in me now; you know why.
I have not one human idea in my head. For a long time
past I've known nothing that has gone on in the world,
either in Russia or here. Here I've been through Dresden,
and I don't remember what Dresden was like. You know
what has swallowed me up. As I have no hope whatever
and am nothing in your eyes, I speak openly: I see nothing but you everywhere, and all the rest is naught to me.
Why and how I love you I don't know. Perhaps you are not
at all nice really, you know. Fancy! I don't know whether
you are good or not, even to look at. You certainly have not
a good heart; your mind may very well be ignoble."

"Perhaps that's how it is you reckon on buying me with
money," she said, "because you don't believe in my sense of
honour."

"When did I reckon on buying you with money?" I cried.

"You have been talking till you don't know what you are
saying. If you don't think of buying me, you think of buying my respect with your money."

"Oh no, that's not it at all. I told you it was difficult for me to explain. You are overwhelming me. Don't be angry with my chatter. You know why you can't be angry with me: I'm simply mad. Though I really don't care, even if you are angry. When I am upstairs in my little garret I have only to remember and imagine the rustle of your dress, and I am ready to bite off my hands. And what are you angry with me for? For calling myself your slave? Make use of my being your slave, make use of it, make use of it! Do you know that I shall kill you one day? I shall kill you not because I shall cease to love you or be jealous, I shall simply kill you because I have an impulse to devour you. You laugh. . . ."

"I'm not laughing," she answered wrathfully. "I order you to be silent."

She stood still, almost breathless with anger. Upon my word, I don't know whether she was handsome, but I always liked to look at her when she stood facing me like that, and so I often liked to provoke her anger. Perhaps she had noticed this and was angry on purpose. I said as much to her.

"How disgusting!" she said, with an air of repulsion.

"I don't care," I went on. "Do you know, too, that it is dangerous for us to walk together? I often have an irresistible longing to beat you, to disfigure you, to strangle you. And what do you think—won't it come to that? You are driving me into brain fever. Do you suppose I am afraid of a scandal? Your anger—why, what is your anger to me? I love you without hope, and I know that after this I shall love you a thousand times more than ever. If ever I do kill you I shall have to kill myself, too. Oh, well, I shall put off killing myself as long as possible, so as to go on feeling this insufferable pain of being without you. Do you know something incredible? I love you *more* every day, and yet that is almost impossible. And how can I help being a fatalist? Do you remember the day before yesterday, on the Schlangenberg, I whispered at your provocation, 'Say the word, and I will leap into that abyss?' If you had said that word I should have jumped in then. Don't you believe that I would have leapt down?"

"What stupid talk!" she cried.

"I don't care whether it is stupid or clever!" I cried. "I know that in your presence I must talk, and talk, and talk—and I do talk. I lose all self-respect in your presence, and I don't care."

"What use would it be for me to order you to jump off the Schlangenberg?" she said in a dry and peculiarly insulting manner. "It would be absolutely useless to me."

"Splendid," I cried; "you said that splendid 'useless' on purpose to overwhelm me. I see through you. Useless, you say? But pleasure is always of use, and savage, unbounded power—if only over a fly—is a pleasure in its way, too. Man is a despot by nature, and loves to be a torturer. You like it awfully."

I remember she looked at me with peculiar fixed attention. My face must have expressed my incoherent and absurd sensations. I remember to this moment that our conversation actually was almost word for word exactly as I have described it here. My eyes were bloodshot. There were flecks of foam on my lips. And as for the Schlangenberg, I swear on my word of honour even now, if she had told me to fling myself down I should have flung myself down! If only for a joke she had said it, with contempt, if with a jeer at me she had said it, I should even then have leapt down!

"No, why? I believe you," she pronounced, as only she knows how to speak, with such contempt and venom, with such scorn that, by God, I could have killed her at the moment.

She risked it. I was not lying about that, too, in what I said to her.

"You are not a coward?" she asked me suddenly.

"Perhaps I am a coward. I don't know. . . . I have not thought about it for a long time."

"If I were to say to you, 'Kill this man,' would you kill him?"

"Whom?"

"Whom I choose."

"The Frenchman?"

"Don't ask questions, but answer. Whom I tell you. I want to know whether you spoke seriously just now?"

She waited for my answer so gravely and impatiently that it struck me as strange.

"Come, do tell me, what has been happening here?" I cried. "What are you afraid of—me, or what? I see all the muddle here for myself. You are the stepdaughter of a mad and ruined man possessed by a passion for that devil —Blanche. Then there is this Frenchman, with his mysterious influence over you, and—here you ask me now so gravely . . . such a question. At any rate let me know, or I shall go mad on the spot and do something. Are you ashamed to deign to be open with me? Surely you can't care what I think of you?"

"I am not speaking to you of that at all. I asked you a question and I'm waiting for the answer."

"Of course I will kill any one you tell me to," I cried. "But can you possibly . . . could you tell me to do it?"

"Do you suppose I should spare you? I shall tell you to, and stand aside and look on. Can you endure that? Why, no, as though you could! You would kill him, perhaps, if you were told, and then you would come and kill me for having dared to send you."

I felt as though I were stunned at these words. Of course, even then I looked upon her question as half a joke, a challenge; yet she had spoken very earnestly. I was struck, nevertheless, at her speaking out so frankly, at her maintaining such rights over me, at her accepting such power over me and saying so bluntly: "Go to ruin, and I'll stand aside and look on." In those words there was something so open and cynical that to my mind it was going too far. That, then, was how she looked at me. This was something more than slavery or insignificance. If one looks at a man like that, one exalts him to one's own level, and absurd and incredible as all our conversation was, yet there was a throb at my heart.

Suddenly she laughed. We were sitting on a bench, before the playing children, facing the place where the carriages used to stop and people used to get out in the avenue before the Casino.

"Do you see that stout baroness?" she cried. "That is Baroness Burmerhelm. She has only been here three days. Do you see her husband—a tall, lean Prussian with a stick? Do you remember how he looked at us the day before yesterday? Go up to the Baroness at once, take off your hat, and say something to her in French."

"Why?"

"You swore that you would jump down the Schlangen- you swear you are ready to kill any one if I tell you.

Instead of these murders and tragedies I only want to laugh. Go without discussing it. I want to see the Baron thrash you with his stick."

"You challenge me; you think I won't do it?"

"Yes, I do challenge you. Go; I want you to!"

"By all means, I am going, though it's a wild freak. Only, I say, I hope it won't be unpleasant for the General, and through him for you. Upon my honour, I am not thinking of myself, but of you and the General. And what a mad idea to insult a woman!"

"Yes, you are only a chatterer, as I see," she said contemptuously. "Your eyes were fierce and bloodshot, but perhaps that was only because you had too much wine at dinner. Do you suppose that I don't understand that it is stupid and vulgar, and that the General would be angry? I simply want to laugh; I want to, and that's all about it! And what should you insult a woman for? Why, just to be thrashed."

I turned and went in silence to carry out her commission. Of course it was stupid, and of course I did not know how to get out of it, but as I began to get closer to the Baroness I remember, as it were, something within myself urging me on; it was an impulse of schoolboyish mischief. Besides, I was horribly overwrought, and felt just as though I were drunk.

6

Now two days have passed since that stupid day. And what a noise and fuss and talk and uproar there was! And how unseemly and disgraceful, how stupid and vulgar, it was! And I was the cause of it all. Yet at times it's laughable— to me, at any rate. I can't make up my mind what happened to me, whether I really was in a state of frenzy, or whether it was a momentary aberration and I behaved disgracefully till I was pulled up. At times it seemed to me that my mind was giving way. And at times it seems to me that I have not outgrown childhood and schoolboyishness, and that it was simply a crude schoolboy's prank.

It was Polina, it was all Polina! Perhaps I shouldn't have behaved like a schoolboy if it hadn't been for her. Who knows? perhaps I did it out of despair (stupid as it seems, though, to reason like that). And I don't understand, I don't understand what there is fine in her! She is fine, though; she is; I believe she's fine. She drives other men off their heads, too. She's tall and graceful, only very slender. It seems to me you could tie her in a knot or bend her double. Her foot is long and narrow—tormenting. Tormenting is just what it is. Her hair has a reddish tint. Her eyes are regular cat's eyes, but how proudly and disdainfully she can look with them. Four months ago, when I had only just come, she was talking hotly for a long while one evening with De Grieux in the drawing-room, and looked at him in such a way . . . that afterwards, when I went up to my room to go to bed, I imagined that she must have just given him a slap in the face. She stood facing him and looked at him. It was from that evening that I loved her.

To come to the point, however.

I stepped off the path into the avenue, and stood waiting for the Baron and the Baroness. When they were five paces from me I took off my hat and bowed.

I remember the Baroness was wearing a light grey dress of immense circumference, with flounces, a crinoline, and a train. She was short and exceptionally stout, with such a fearful double chin that she seemed to have no neck. Her face was crimson. Her eyes were small, spiteful and insolent. She walked as though she were doing an honour to all beholders. The Baron was lean and tall. Like most Germans, he had a wry face covered with thousands of fine wrinkles, and wore spectacles; he was about forty-five. His legs seemed to start from his chest: that's a sign of race. He was as proud as a peacock. He was rather clumsy. There was something like a sheep in the expression of his face that would pass with them for profundity.

All this flashed upon my sight in three seconds.

My bow and the hat in my hand gradually arrested their attention. The Baron slightly knitted his brows. The Baroness simply sailed straight at me.

"*Madame la baronne,*" I articulated distinctly, emphasizing each word, "*j'ai l'honneur d'être votre esclave.*"

Then I bowed, replaced my hat, and walked past the

Baron, turning my face towards him with a polite smile.

She had told me to take off my hat, but I had bowed and behaved like an impudent schoolboy on my own account. Goodness knows what impelled me to! I felt as though I were plunging into space.

"*Hein!*" cried, or rather croaked, the Baron, turning towards me with angry surprise.

I turned and remained in respectful expectation, still gazing at him with a smile. He was evidently perplexed, and raised his eyebrows as high as they would go. His face grew darker and darker. The Baroness, too, turned towards me, and she, too, stared in wrathful surprise. The passersby began to look on. Some even stopped.

"*Hein!*" the Baron croaked again, with redoubled gutturalness and redoubled anger.

"*Ja wohl!*" I drawled, still looking him straight in the face.

"*Sind Sie rasend?*" he cried, waving his stick and beginning, I think, to be a little nervous. He was perhaps perplexed by my appearance. I was very well, even foppishly, dressed, like a man belonging to the best society.

"*Ja wo-o-ohl!*" I shouted suddenly at the top of my voice, drawling the *o* like the Berliners, who use the expression *Ja wohl* in every sentence, and drawl the letter *o* more or less according to the shade of their thought or feeling.

The Baron and Baroness turned away quickly and almost ran away from me in terror. Of the spectators, some were talking, others were gazing at me in amazement. I don't remember very clearly, though.

I turned and walked at my ordinary pace to Polina Alexandrovna.

But when I was within a hundred paces of her seat, I saw her get up and walk with the children towards the hotel.

I overtook her at the door.

"I have performed . . . the foolery," I said, when I reached her.

"Well, what of it? Now you can get out of the scrape," she answered. She walked upstairs without even glancing at me.

I spent the whole evening walking about the park. I crossed the park and then the wood beyond and walked into another state. In a cottage I had an omelette and some wine; for that idyllic repast they extorted a whole thaler and a half.

It was eleven o'clock before I returned home. I was at once summoned before the General.

Our party occupied two suites in the hotel; they have four rooms. The first is a big room—a drawing-room with a piano in it. The next, also a large room, is the General's study. Here he was awaiting me, standing in the middle of the room in a majestic pose. De Grieux sat lolling on the sofa.

"Allow me to ask you, sir, what have you been about?" began the General, addressing me.

"I should be glad if you would go straight to the point, General," said I. "You probably mean to refer to my encounter with a German this morning?"

"A German? That German was Baron Burmerhelm, a very important personage! You insulted him and the Baroness."

"Not in the least."

"You alarmed them, sir!" cried the General.

"Not a bit of it. When I was in Berlin the sound was for ever in my ears of that *Ja wohl*, continually repeated at every word and disgustingly drawled out by them. When I met them in the avenue that *Ja wohl* suddenly came into my mind, I don't know why, and—well, it had an irritating effect on me. . . . Besides, the Baroness, who has met me three times, has the habit of walking straight at me as though I were a worm who might be trampled underfoot. You must admit that I, too, may have my proper pride. I took off my hat and said politely (I assure you I said it politely): '*Madame, j'ai l'honneur d'être votre esclave.*' When the Baron turned round and said, '*Hein!*' I felt an impulse to shout, '*Ja wohl!*' I shouted it twice: the first time in an ordinary tone, and the second—I drawled it as much as I could. That was all."

I must own I was intensely delighted at this extremely schoolboyish explanation. I had a strange desire to make the story as absurd as possible in the telling.

And as I went on, I got more and more to relish it.

"Are you laughing at me?" cried the General. He turned to the Frenchman and explained to him in French that I was positively going out of my way to provoke a scandal!

De Grieux laughed contemptuously and shrugged his shoulders.

"Oh, don't imagine that; it was not so at all!" I cried. "My conduct was wrong, of course; I confess that with the utmost candour. My behaviour may even be called a stupid and improper schoolboy prank, but—nothing more. And do you know, General, I heartily regret it. But there is one circumstance which, to my mind at least, almost saves me from repentance. Lately, for the last fortnight, indeed, I've not been feeling well: I have felt ill, nervous, irritable, moody, and on some occasions I lose all control of myself. Really, I've sometimes had an intense impulse to attack the Marquis de Grieux and . . . However, there's no need to say, he might be offended. In short, it's the sign of illness. I don't know whether the Baroness Burmerhelm will take this fact into consideration when I beg her pardon (for I intend to apologize). I imagine she will not consider it, especially as that line of excuse has been somewhat abused in legal circles of late. Lawyers have taken to arguing in criminal cases that their clients were not responsible at the moment of their crime, and that it was a form of disease. 'He killed him,' they say, 'and has no memory of it.' And only imagine, General, the medical authorities support them—and actually maintain that there are illnesses, temporary aberrations, in which a man scarcely remembers anything, or has only a half or a quarter of his memory. But the Baron and Baroness are people of the older generation; besides, they are Prussian *junkers* and landowners, and so are probably unaware of this advance in the world of medical jurisprudence, and will not accept my explanation. What do you think, General?"

"Enough, sir," the General pronounced sharply, with surprised indignation; "enough! I will try once for all to rid myself of your mischievous pranks. You are not going to apologize to the Baron and Baroness. Any communication with you, even though it were to consist solely of your request for forgiveness, would be beneath their dignity. The Baron has learnt that you are a member of my household; he has already had an explanation with me at the Casino, and I assure you that he was within an ace of asking me to give him satisfaction. Do you understand what you have exposed me to—me, sir? I—I was forced to ask the Baron's pardon, and gave him my word that immediately, this very day, you would cease to be a member of my household."

"Allow me, allow me, General; then did he insist on that himself, that I should cease to belong to your household, as you were pleased to express it?"

"No, but I considered myself bound to give him that satisfaction, and, of course, the Baron was satisfied. We must part, sir. There is what is owing to you, four friedrichs d'or and three florins, according to the reckoning here. Here is the money, and here is the note of the account; you can verify it. Good-bye. From this time forth we are strangers. I've had nothing but trouble and unpleasantness from you. I will call the *kellner* and inform him from this day forth that I am not responsible for your hotel expenses. I have the honour to remain your obedient servant."

I took the money and the paper upon which the account was written in pencil, bowed to the General, and said to him very seriously—

"General, the matter cannot end like this. I am very sorry that you were put into an unpleasant position with the Baron, but, excuse me, you were to blame for it yourself. Why did you take it upon yourself to be responsible for me to the Baron? What is the meaning of the expression that I am a member of your household? I am simply a teacher in your house, that is all. I am neither your son nor your ward, and you cannot be responsible for my actions. I am a legally responsible person, I am twenty-five, I am a graduate of the university, I am a nobleman, I am not connected with you in any way. Nothing but my unbounded respect for your dignity prevents me now from demanding from you the fullest explanation and satisfaction for taking upon yourself the right to answer for me."

The General was so much amazed that he flung up his hands, then turned suddenly to the Frenchman and hurriedly informed him that I had just all but challenged him to a duel.

The Frenchman laughed aloud.

"But I am not going to let the Baron off," I said, with complete composure, not in the least embarrassed by M. de Grieux's laughter; "and as, General, you consented to listen to the Baron's complaint to-day and have taken up his cause, and have made yourself, as it were, a party in the whole affair, I have the honour to inform you that no later than to-morrow morning I shall ask the Baron on my own account for a formal explanation of the reasons which led him to apply to other persons—as though I were unable or unfit to answer for myself."

What I foresaw happened. The General, hearing of this new absurdity, became horribly nervous.

"What, do you mean to keep up this damnable business?" he shouted. "What a position you are putting me in —good heavens! Don't dare, don't dare, sir, or, I swear! . . . There are police here, too, and I . . . I . . . in fact, by my rank . . . and the Baron's, too . . . in fact, you shall be arrested and turned out of the state by the police, to teach you not to make a disturbance. Do you understand that, sir?" And although he was breathless with anger, he was also horribly frightened.

"General," I answered, with a composure that was insufferable to him, "you can't arrest any one for making a disturbance before they have made a disturbance. I have not yet begun to make my explanations to the Baron, and you don't know in the least in what form or on what grounds I intend to proceed. I only wish to have an explanation of a position insulting to me, *i. e.* that I am under the control of a person who has authority over my freedom of action. There is no need for you to be so anxious and uneasy."

"For goodness' sake, for goodness' sake, Alexey Ivanovitch, drop this insane intention!" muttered the General, suddenly changing his wrathful tone for one of entreaty, and even clutching me by the hand. "Fancy what it will lead to! Fresh unpleasantness! You must see for yourself that I must be particular here . . . particularly now! particularly now! . . . Oh, you don't know, you don't know all my circumstances! . . . When we leave this place I shall be willing to take you back again; I was only speaking of now, in fact—of course, you understand there are reasons!" he cried in despair. "Alexey Ivanovitch, Alexey Ivanovitch . . ."

Retreating to the door, I begged him more earnestly not to worry himself, promised him that everything should go off well and with propriety, and hastily withdrew.

The Russian abroad is sometimes too easily cowed, and is horribly afraid of what people will say, how they will look at him, and whether this or that will be the proper thing. In short, they behave as though they were in corsets, especially those who have pretensions to consequence. The thing that pleases them most is a certain established traditional etiquette, which they follow slavishly in hotels, on their walks, in assemblies, on a journey. . . . But the General had let slip that, apart from this, there was a particular circumstance, that he must be "particular." That was why he so weakly showed the white feather and changed his tone with me. I took this as evidence and made a note of it; and, of course, he might have brought my folly to the notice of the authorities, so that I really had to be careful.

I did not particularly want to anger the General, however; but I did want to anger Polina. Polina had treated me so badly, and had thrust me into such a stupid position, that I could not help wanting to force her to beg me to stop. My schoolboyish prank might compromise her, too. Moreover, another feeling and desire was taking shape in me: though I might be reduced to a nonentity in her presence, that did not prove that I could not hold my own before other people, or that the Baron could thrash me. I longed to have the laugh against them all, and to come off with flying colours. Let them see! She would be frightened by the scandal and call me back again, or, even if she didn't, at least she would see that I could hold my own.

(A wonderful piece of news! I have just heard from the nurse, whom I met on the stairs, that Marya Filippovna set off to-day, entirely alone, by the evening train to Karlsbad to see her cousin. What's the meaning of that? Nurse says that she has long been meaning to go; but how was it no one knew of it? Though perhaps I was the only one who did not know it. The nurse let slip that Marya Filippovna had words with the General the day before yesterday. I understand. No doubt that is Mlle. Blanche. Yes, something decisive is coming.)

7

In the morning I called for the *kellner* and told him to make out a separate bill for me. My room was not such an expensive one as to make me feel alarmed and anxious to leave the hotel. I had sixteen friedrichs d'or, and there . . . there perhaps was wealth! Strange to say, I have not won yet, but I behave, I feel and think, like a rich man, and cannot imagine anything else.

In spite of the early hour I intended to go at once to see Mr. Astley at the Hôtel d'Angleterre, which was quite close by, when suddenly De Grieux came in to me. That had never happened before, and, what is more, that gentleman and I had for some time past been on very queer and strained terms. He openly displayed his contempt for me, even tried not to conceal it; and I—I had my own reasons for disliking him. In short, I hated him. His visit greatly surprised me. I at once detected that something special was brewing.

He came in very politely and complimented me on my room. Seeing that I had my hat in my hand, he inquired whether I could be going out for a walk so early. When he heard that I was going to see Mr. Astley on business, he pondered, he reflected, and his face assumed an exceedingly careworn expression.

De Grieux was like all Frenchmen; that is, gay and polite when necessary and profitable to be so, and insufferably tedious when the necessity to be gay and polite was over. A Frenchman is not often naturally polite. He is always polite, as it were, to order, with a motive. If he sees the necessity for being fantastic, original, a little out of the ordinary, then his freakishness is most stupid and unnatural, and is made up of accepted and long-vulgarized traditions. The natural Frenchman is composed of the most plebeian, petty, ordinary practical sense—in fact, he is one of the most wearisome creatures in the world. In my opinion, only the innocent and inexperienced—especially Russian young ladies—are fascinated by Frenchmen. To every decent person the conventionalism of the established traditions of drawing-room politeness, ease and gaiety are at once evident and intolerable.

"I have come to see you on business," he began, with marked directness, though with courtesy, "and I will not disguise that I have come as an ambassador, or rather as a mediator, from the General. As I know Russian very imperfectly I understood very little of what passed yesterday, but the General explained it to me in detail, and I confess . . ."

"But, listen, M. de Grieux," I interrupted; "here you have undertaken to be a mediator in this affair. I am, of course, an *outchitel,* and have never laid claim to the honour of being a great friend of this family, nor of being on particularly intimate terms with it, and so I don't know all the circumstances; but explain: are you now entirely a member of the family? You take such an interest in everything and are certain at once to be a mediator . . ."

This question did not please him. It was too transparent for him, and he did not want to speak out.

"I am connected with the General partly by business, partly by *certain special* circumstances," he said drily. "The General has sent me to ask you to abandon the intentions you expressed yesterday. All you thought of doing was no doubt very clever; but he begged me to represent to you that you would be utterly unsuccessful; what's more, the Baron will not receive you, and in any case is in a position to rid himself of any further unpleasantness on your part. You must see that yourself. Tell me, what is the object of going on with it? The General promises to take you back into his home at the first convenient opportunity, and until that time will continue your salary, *vos appointements.* That will be fairly profitable, won't it?"

I retorted very calmly that he was rather mistaken; that perhaps I shouldn't be kicked out at the Baron's, but, on the contrary, should be listened to; and I asked him to admit that he had probably come to find out what steps I was going to take in the matter.

"Oh, heavens! Since the General is so interested, he will, of course, be glad to know how you are going to behave, and what you are going to do."

I proceeded to explain, and he began listening, stretching himself at his ease and inclining his head on one side towards me, with an obvious, undisguised expression of irony on his face. Altogether he behaved very loftily. I tried with all my might to pretend that I took a very serious view of the matter. I explained that since the Baron had addressed a complaint of me to the General as though I were the latter's servant, he had, in the first place, deprived me thereby of my position; and secondly, had treated me as a person who was incapable of answering for himself and who was not worth speaking to. Of course, I said, I felt with justice that I had been insulted; however, considering the difference of age, position in society, and so on, and so on (I could scarcely restrain my laughter at this point), I did not want to rush into fresh indiscretion by directly insisting on satisfaction from the Baron, or even proposing a duel to him; nevertheless, I considered myself fully entitled to offer the Baron, and still more the Baroness, my apologies, especially since of late I had really felt ill, overwrought, and, so to say, fanciful, and so on, and so on. However, the Baron had, by his applying to the General, which was a slight to me, and by his insisting that the General should deprive me of my post, put me in such a position that now I could not offer him and the Baroness my apologies, because he and the Baroness and all the world would certainly suppose that I came to apologize because I was frightened and in order to be reinstated in my post. From all this it followed that I found myself now compelled to beg the Baron first of all to apologize to me in the most formal terms; for instance, to say that he had no desire to insult me. And when the Baron said this I should feel that my hands were set free, and with perfect candour and sincerity I should offer him my apologies. In brief, I concluded, I could only beg the Baron to untie my hands.

"Fie! how petty and how far-fetched! And why do you want to apologize? Come, admit, *monsieur . . . monsieur . . .* that you are doing all this on purpose to vex the General . . . and perhaps you have some special object . . . *mon cher monsieur . . . pardon, j'ai oublié votre nom, M. Alexis? . . . N'est-ce pas?*"

"But, excuse me, *mon cher marquis,* what has it to do with you?"

"*Mais le général . . .*"

"But what about the General? He said something last

night, that he had to be particularly careful . . . and was so upset . . . but I did not understand it."

"There is, there certainly is a particular circumstance," De Grieux caught me up in an insistent voice, in which a note of vexation was more and more marked. "You know Mlle. de Cominges . . .?"

"That is, Mlle. Blanche?"

"Why, yes, Mlle. Blanche de Cominges . . . *et madame sa mère.* You see for yourself, the General . . . in short, the General is in love; in fact . . . in fact, the marriage may be celebrated here. And fancy, scandal, gossip . . ."

"I see no scandal or gossip connected with the marriage in this."

"But *le baron est si irascible, un caractère Prussien, vous savez, enfin il fera une querelle d'Allemand.*"

"With me, then, and not with you, for I no longer belong to the household. . . ." (I tried to be as irrational as possible on purpose.) "But, excuse me, is it settled, then, that Mlle. Blanche is to marry the General? What are they waiting for? I mean, why conceal this from us, at any rate from the members of the household?"

"I cannot . . . however, it is not quite . . . besides . . . you know, they are expecting news from Russia; the General has to make arrangements . . ."

"*Ah! ah! La baboulinka!*"

De Grieux looked at me with hatred.

"In short," he interrupted, "I fully rely on your innate courtesy, on your intelligence, on your tact. . . . You will certainly do this for the family in which you have been received like one of themselves, in which you have been liked and respected . . ."

"Excuse me, I've been dismissed! You maintain now that that is only in appearance; but you must admit, if you were told: 'I won't send you packing, but, for the look of the thing, kindly take yourself off' . . . You see, it comes almost to the same thing."

"Well, if that's how it is, if no request will have any influence on you," he began sternly and haughtily, "allow me to assure you that steps will be taken. There are authorities here; you'll be turned out to-day—*que diable! Un blanc-bec comme vous* wants to challenge a personage like the Baron! And do you think that you will not be interfered with? And, let me assure you, nobody is afraid of you here! I have approached you on my own account, because you have been worrying the General. And do you imagine that the Baron will not order his flunkeys to turn you out of the house?"

"But, you see, I'm not going myself," I answered, with the utmost composure. "You are mistaken, M. de Grieux; all this will be done much more decorously than you imagine. I am just setting off to Mr. Astley, and I am going to ask him to be my intermediary; in fact, to be my second. The man likes me, and certainly will not refuse. He will go to the Baron, and the Baron will receive him. Even if I am an *outchitel* and seem to be something subordinate and, well, defenceless, Mr. Astley is a nephew of a lord, of a real lord; every one knows that—Lord Pibroch—and that lord is here. Believe me, the Baron will be courteous to Mr. Astley and will listen to him. And if he won't listen, Mr. Astley will look upon it as a personal affront (you know how persistent Englishmen are), and will send a friend to call on the Baron; he has powerful friends. You may reckon, now, upon things not turning out quite as you expect."

The Frenchman was certainly scared; all this was really very much like the truth, and so it seemed that I really might be able to get up a scandal.

"Come, I beg you," he said in a voice of actual entreaty, "do drop the whole business! It seems to please you that it will cause a scandal! It is not satisfaction you want, but a scandal! As I have told you, it is very amusing and even witty—which is perhaps what you are aiming at. But, in short," he concluded, seeing that I had got up and was taking my hat, "I've come to give you these few lines from a certain person; read them; I was charged to wait for an answer."

Saying this, he took out of his pocket a little note, folded and sealed with a wafer, and handed it to me.

It was in Polina's handwriting.

"I fancy that you intend to go on with this affair, but there are special circumstances which I will explain to you perhaps later; please leave off and give way. It is all such silliness! I need you, and you promised yourself to obey me. Remember the Schlangenberg; I beg you to be obedient, and, if necessary, I command you.—Your P.

"P.S.—If you are angry with me for what happened yesterday, forgive me."

Everything seemed to be heaving before my eyes when I read these lines. My lips turned white and I began to tremble. The accursed Frenchman watched me with an exaggerated air of discretion, with his eyes turned away as though to avoid noticing my confusion. He had better have laughed at me outright.

"Very good," I answered; "tell Mademoiselle that she may set her mind at rest. Allow me to ask you," I added sharply, "why you have been so long giving me this letter. Instead of chattering about all sorts of nonsense, I think you ought to have begun with that . . . if you came expressly with that object."

"Oh, I wanted . . . all this is so strange that you must excuse my natural impatience. I was in haste to learn from you in person what you intended to do. Besides, I don't know what is in that note, and I thought there was no hurry for me to give it you."

"I understand: the long and the short of it is you were told only to give me the letter in case of the utmost necessity, and if you could settle it by word of mouth you were not to give it to me. Is that right? Tell me plainly, M. de Grieux."

"*Peut-être*," he said, assuming an air of peculiar reserve, and looking at me with a peculiar glance.

I took off my hat; he took off his hat and went out. It seemed to me that there was an ironical smile on his lips. And, indeed, what else could one expect?

"We'll be quits yet, Frenchy; we'll settle our accounts," I muttered as I went down the stairs. I could not think clearly; I felt as though I had had a blow on my head. The air revived me a little.

Two minutes later, as soon as ever I was able to reflect clearly, two thoughts stood out vividly before me: the *first* was that such trivial incidents, that a few mischievous and far-fetched threats from a mere boy, had caused such *universal* consternation! The second thought was: what sort of influence had this Frenchman over Polina? A mere word from him and she does anything he wants—writes a note and even *begs* me. Of course, their relations have always been a mystery to me from the very beginning, ever since I began to know them; but of late I have noticed in her a positive aversion and even contempt for him, while he did not even look at her, was absolutely rude to her. I had noticed it. Polina herself had spoken of him to me with aversion; she had dropped some extremely significant admissions . . . so he simply had her in his power. She was in some sort of bondage to him.

8

On the promenade, as it is called here, that is, in the chestnut avenue, I met my Englishman.

"Oh, oh!" he began, as soon as he saw me. "I was coming to see you, and you are on your way to me. So you have parted from your people?"

"Tell me, first, how it is that you know all this?" I asked in amazement. "Is it possible that everybody knows of it?"

"Oh, no, every one doesn't; and, indeed, it's not worth their knowing. No one is talking about it."

"Then how do you know it?"

"I know, that is, I chanced to learn it. Now, where are you going when you leave here? I like you and that is why I was coming to see you."

"You are a splendid man, Mr. Astley," said I (I was very much interested, however, to know where he could have learnt it), "and since I have not yet had my coffee, and most likely you have not had a good cup, come to the café in the Casino. Let us sit down and have a smoke there, and I will tell you all about it, and . . . you tell me, too . . ."

The café was a hundred steps away. They brought us some coffee. We sat down and I lighted a cigarette. Mr. Astley did not light one and, gazing at me, prepared to listen.

"I am not going anywhere. I am staying here," I began.

"And I was sure you would," observed Mr. Astley approvingly.

On my way to Mr. Astley I had not meant to tell him anything of my love for Polina, and, in fact, I expressly intended to say nothing to him about it. All that time I had hardly said one word to him about it. He was, besides, very reserved. From the first I noticed that Polina had made a great impression upon him, but he never uttered her name. But, strange to say, now no sooner had he sat down and turned upon me his fixed, pewtery eyes, I felt, I don't know why, a desire to tell him everything, that is, all about my love in all its aspects. I was talking to him for half an hour and it was very pleasant to me; it was the first time I had talked of it! Noticing that at certain ardent sentences he was embarrassed, I purposely exaggerated my ardour. Only one thing I regret: I said, perhaps, more than I should about the Frenchman. . . .

Mr. Astley listened, sitting facing me without moving, looking straight into my eyes, not uttering a word, a sound; but when I spoke of the Frenchman, he suddenly pulled me up and asked me, severely, whether I had the right to refer to this circumstance which did not concern me? Mr. Astley always asked questions very strangely.

"You are right. I am afraid not," I answered.

"You can say nothing definite, nothing that is not supposition about that *marquis* and Miss Polina?"

I was surprised again at such a point-blank question from a man so reserved as Mr. Astley.

"No, nothing definite," I answered; "of course not."

"If so, you have done wrong, not only in speaking of it to me, but even in thinking of it yourself."

"Very good, very good; I admit it, but that is not the point now," I interrupted, wondering at myself. At this point I told him the whole of yesterday's story in full detail: Polina's prank, my adventure with the Baron, my dismissal, the General's extraordinary dismay, and, finally, I described in detail De Grieux's visit that morning. Lastly I showed him the note.

"What do you deduce from all this?" I asked. "I came on purpose to find out what you think. For my part, I could kill that Frenchman, and perhaps I shall."

"So could I," said Mr. Astley. "As regards Miss Polina, you know . . . we may enter into relations even with people who are detestable to us if we are compelled by necessity. There may be relations of which you know nothing, dependent upon outside circumstances. I think you may set your mind at rest—to some extent, of course. As for her action yesterday, it was strange, of course; not that she wanted to get rid of you and expose you to the Baron's walking-stick (I don't understand why he did not use it, since he had it in his hand), but because such a prank is improper . . . for such an . . . exquisite young lady. Of course, she couldn't have expected that you would carry out her jesting wish so literally . . ."

"Do you know what?" I cried suddenly, looking intently at Mr. Astley. "It strikes me that you have heard about this already—do you know from whom? From Miss Polina herself!"

Mr. Astley looked at me with surprise.

"Your eyes are sparkling and I can read your suspicion in them," he said, regaining his former composure; "but you have no right whatever to express your suspicions. I cannot recognize the right, and I absolutely refuse to answer your question."

"Enough! There's no need," I cried, strangely perturbed, and not knowing why it had come into my head. And when, where and how could Mr. Astley have been chosen by Polina to confide in? Though, of late, indeed, I had, to some extent, lost sight of Mr. Astley, and Polina was always an enigma to me, such an enigma that now, for instance, after launching into an account of my passion to Mr. Astley, I was suddenly struck while I was speaking by the fact that there was scarcely anything positive and definite I could say about our relations. Everything was, on the contrary, strange, unstable, and, in fact, quite unique.

"Oh, very well, very well. I am utterly perplexed and there is a great deal I can't understand at present," I answered, gasping as though I were breathless. "You are a good man, though. And now, another matter, and I ask not your advice, but your opinion."

After a brief pause I began.

"What do you think? Why was the General so scared? Why did he make such a to-do over my stupid practical joke? Such a fuss that even De Grieux thought it necessary to interfere (and he interferes only in the most important matters); visited me (think of that!), begged and besought me—he, De Grieux—begged and besought me!

Note, finally, he came at nine o'clock, and by that time Miss Polina's letter was in his hands. One wonders when it was written. Perhaps they waked Miss Polina up on purpose! Apart from what I see clearly from this, that Miss Polina is his slave (for she even begs my forgiveness!)—apart from that, how is she concerned in all this, she personally; why is she so much interested? Why are they frightened of some Baron? And what if the General is marrying Mlle. Blanche de Cominges? They say that, owing to that circumstance, they must be *particular,* but you must admit that this is somewhat too particular! What do you think? I am sure from your eyes you know more about it than I do!"

Mr. Astley laughed and nodded.

"Certainly. I believe I know much more about it than you," he said. "Mlle. Blanche is the only person concerned, and I am sure that is the absolute truth."

"Well, what about Mlle. Blanche?" I cried impatiently. (I suddenly had a hope that something would be disclosed about Mlle. Polina.)

"I fancy that Mlle. Blanche has at the moment special reasons for avoiding a meeting with the Baron and Baroness, even more an unpleasant meeting, worse still, a scandalous one."

"Well, well . . ."

"Two years ago Mlle. Blanche was here at Roulettenburg in the season. I was here, too. Mlle. Blanche was not called Mlle. de Cominges then, and her mother, Madame *la maman* Cominges, was non-existent then. Anyway, she was never mentioned. De Grieux—De Grieux was not here either. I cherish the conviction that, far from being relations, they have only very recently become acquainted. He—De Grieux—has only become a marquis very recently, too—I am sure of that from one circumstance. One may assume, in fact, that his name has not been De Grieux very long either. I know a man here who has met him passing under another name."

"But he really has a very respectable circle of acquaintances."

"That may be. Even Mlle. Blanche may have. But two years ago, at the request of that very Baroness, Mlle. Blanche was invited by the police to leave the town, and she did leave it."

"How was that?"

"She made her appearance here first with an Italian, a prince of some sort, with an historical name—Barberini, or something like it—a man covered with rings and diamonds, not false ones either. They used to drive about in a magnificent carriage. Mlle. Blanche used to play *trente et quarante,* at first winning, though her luck changed later on, as far as I remember. I remember one evening she lost a considerable sum. But, worse still, *un beau matin* her prince vanished; the horses and the carriage vanished too, everything vanished. The bills owing at the hotels were immense. Mlle. Selma (she suddenly ceased to be Barberini, and became Mlle. Selma) was in the utmost despair. She was shrieking and wailing all over the hotel, and rent her clothes in her fury. There was a Polish count staying here at the hotel (all Polish travellers are counts), and Mlle. Selma, rending her garments and scratching her face like a cat with her beautiful perfumed fingers, made some impression on him. They talked things over, and by dinner-time she was consoled. In the evening he made his appearance at the Casino with the lady on his arm. As usual, Mlle. Selma laughed very loudly, and her manner was somewhat more free and easy than before. She definitely showed that she belonged to the class of ladies who, when they go up to the roulette table, shoulder the other players aside to clear a space for themselves. That's particularly *chic* among such ladies. You must have noticed it?"

"Oh, yes."

"It's not worth noticing. To the annoyance of the decent public they are not moved on here—at least, not those of them who can change a thousand-rouble note every day, at the roulette table. As soon as they cease to produce a note to change they are asked to withdraw, however. Mlle. Selma still went on changing notes, but her play became more unlucky than ever. Note that such ladies are very often lucky in their play; they have a wonderful self-control. However, my story is finished. One day the count vanished just as the prince had done. However, Mlle. Selma made her appearance at the roulette table alone; this time no one came forward to offer her his arm. In two days she had lost everything. After laying down her last louis d'or and losing it, she looked round, and saw, close by her, Baron Burmerhelm, who was scrutinizing her intently and with profound indignation. But Mlle. Selma, not noticing his indignation, accosted the Baron with that smile we all know so well, and asked him to put down ten louis d'or on the red for her. In consequence of a complaint from the Baroness she received that evening an invitation not to show herself at the Casino again. If you are surprised at my knowing all these petty and extremely improper details, it is because I have heard them from Mr. Fider, one of my relations, who carried off Mlle. Selma in his carriage from Roulettenburg to Spa that very evening. Now, remember, Mlle. Blanche wishes to become the General's wife; probably in order in future not to receive such invitations as that one from the police at the Casino, the year before last. Now she does not play; but that is because, as it seems, she has capital of her own which she lends out at a percentage to gamblers here. That's a much safer speculation. I even suspect that the luckless General is in debt to her. Perhaps De Grieux is, too. Perhaps De Grieux is associated with her. You will admit that, till the wedding, at any rate, she can hardly be anxious to attract the attention of the Baron and Baroness in any way. In short, in her position, nothing could be more disadvantageous than a scandal. You are connected with their party and your conduct might cause a scandal, especially as she appears in public every day either arm-in-arm with the General or in company with Miss Polina. Now do you understand?"

"No, I don't!" I cried, thumping the table so violently that the garçon ran up in alarm.

"Tell me, Mr. Astley," I said furiously. "If you knew all this story and, therefore, know positively what Mlle. Blanche de Cominges is, why didn't you warn me at least, the General, or, most of all, most of all, Miss Polina, who has shown herself here at the Casino in public, arm-in-arm with Mlle. Blanche? Can such a thing be allowed?"

"I had no reason to warn you, for you could have done nothing," Mr. Astley answered calmly. "Besides, warn them of what? The General knows about Mlle. Blanche perhaps more than I do, yet he still goes about with her and Miss Polina. The General is an unlucky man. I saw Mlle. Blanche yesterday, galloping on a splendid horse with M. de Grieux and that little Russian Prince, and the

General was galloping after them on a chestnut. He told me in the morning that his legs ached, but he sat his horse well. And it struck me at that moment that he was an utterly ruined man. Besides, all this is no business of mine, and I have only lately had the honour of making Miss Polina's acquaintance. However" (Mr. Astley caught himself up), "I've told you already that I do not recognize your right to ask certain questions, though I have a genuine liking for you . . ."

"Enough," I said, getting up. "It is clear as daylight to me now, that Miss Polina knows all about Mlle. Blanche, but that she cannot part from her Frenchman, and so she brings herself to going about with Mlle. Blanche. Believe me, no other influence would compel her to go about with Mlle. Blanche and to beg me in her letter not to interfere with the Baron! Damn it all, there's no understanding it!"

"You forget, in the first place, that Mlle. de Cominges is the General's *fiancée*, and in the second place that Miss Polina is the General's stepdaughter, that she has a little brother and sister, the General's own children, who are utterly neglected by that insane man and have, I believe, been robbed by him."

"Yes, yes, that is so! To leave the children would mean abandoning them altogether; to remain means protecting their interests and, perhaps, saving some fragments of their property. Yes, yes, all that is true. But still, still! . . . Ah, now I understand why they are all so concerned about Granny!"

"About whom?" asked Mr. Astley.

"That old witch in Moscow who won't die, and about whom they are expecting a telegram that she is dying."

"Yes, of course, all interest is concentrated on her. Everything depends on what she leaves them! If he comes in for a fortune the General will marry, Miss Polina will be set free, and De Grieux . . ."

"Well, and De Grieux?"

"And De Grieux will be paid; that is all he is waiting for here."

"Is that all, do you think that is all he's waiting for?"

"I know nothing more." Mr. Astley was obstinately silent.

"But I do, I do!" I repeated fiercely. "He's waiting for the inheritance too, because Polina will get a dowry, and as soon as she gets the money will throw herself on his neck. All women are like that! Even the proudest of them turn into the meanest slaves! Polina is only capable of loving passionately: nothing else. That's my opinion of her! Look at her, particularly when she is sitting alone, thinking; it's something predestined, doomed, fated! She is capable of all the horrors of life, and passion . . . she . . . she . . . but who is that calling me?" I exclaimed suddenly. "Who is shouting? I heard some one shout in Russian: Alexey Ivanovitch! A woman's voice. Listen, listen!"

At this moment we were approaching the hotel. We had left the café long ago, almost without noticing it.

"I did hear a woman calling, but I don't know who was being called; it is Russian. Now I see where the shouts come from," said Mr. Astley. "It is that woman sitting in a big armchair who has just been carried up the steps by so many flunkeys. They are carrying trunks after her, so the train must have just come in."

"But why is she calling me? She is shouting again; look, she is waving to us."

"I see she is waving," said Mr. Astley.

"Alexey Ivanovitch! Alexey Ivanovitch! Mercy on us, what a dolt he is!" came desperate shouts from the hotel steps.

We almost ran to the entrance. I ran up the steps and . . . my hands dropped at my sides with amazement and my feet seemed rooted to the ground.

9

At the top of the broad steps at the hotel entrance, surrounded by footmen and maids and the many obsequious servants of the hotel, in the presence of the *ober-kellner* himself, eager to receive the exalted visitor, who had arrived with her own servants and with so many trunks and boxes, and had been carried up the steps in an invalid-chair, was seated—*Granny!* Yes, it was she herself, the terrible old Moscow lady and wealthy landowner, An-

tonida Vassilyevna Tarasyevitchev, the *Granny* about
whom telegrams had been sent and received, who had
been dying and was not dead, and who had suddenly
dropped upon us in person, like snow on our heads.
Though she was seventy-five and had for the last five years
lost the use of her legs and had to be carried about everywhere in a chair, yet she had arrived and was, as always,
alert, captious, self-satisfied, sitting upright in her chair,
shouting in a loud, peremptory voice and scolding every
one. In fact, she was exactly the same as she had been on
the only two occasions that I had the honour of seeing her
during the time I had been tutor in the General's family.
Naturally I stood rooted to the spot with amazement. As
she was being carried up the steps, she had detected me
a hundred paces away, with her lynx-like eyes, had recognized me and called me by my name, which she had made
a note of, once for all, as she always did. And this was the
woman they had expected to be in her coffin, buried, and
leaving them her property. That was the thought that
flashed into my mind. "Why, she will outlive all of us and
every one in the hotel! But, my goodness! what will our
friends do now, what will the General do? She will turn
the whole hotel upside down!"

"Well, my good man, why are you standing with your
eyes starting out of your head?" Granny went on shouting
to me. "Can't you welcome me? Can't you say 'How do
you do'? Or have you grown proud and won't? Or, perhaps, you don't recognize me? Potapitch, do you hear?"
She turned to her butler, an old man with grey hair and a
pink bald patch on his head, wearing a dress-coat and
white tie. "Do you hear? he doesn't recognize me. They
had buried me! They sent telegram upon telegram to ask
whether I was dead or not! You see, I know all about it!
Here, you see, I am quite alive."

"Upon my word, Antonida Vassilyevna, why should I
wish you harm?" I answered gaily, recovering myself. "I
was only surprised. ... . And how could I help being surprised at such an unexpected . . ."

"What is there to surprise you? I just got into the train
and came. The train was comfortable and not jolting.
Have you been for a walk?"

"Yes, I've been a walk to the Casino."

"It's pleasant here," said Granny, looking about her. "It's warm and the trees are magnificent. I like that! Are the family at home? The General?"

"Oh, yes, at this time they are sure to be all at home."

"So they have fixed hours here, and everything in style? They set the tone. I am told they keep their carriage, *les seigneurs russes!* They spend all their money and then they go abroad. And is Praskovya with them?"

"Yes, Polina Alexandrovna, too."

"And the Frenchy? Oh, well, I shall see them all for myself. Alexey Ivanovitch, show me the way straight to him. Are you comfortable here?"

"Fairly so, Antonida Vassilyevna."

"Potapitch, tell that dolt, the *kellner,* to give me a nice convenient set of rooms, not too high up, and take my things there at once. Why are they all so eager to carry me? Why do they put themselves forward? Ech, the slavish creatures! Who is this with you?" she asked, addressing me again.

"This is Mr. Astley," I answered.

"What Mr. Astley?"

"A traveller, a good friend of mine; an acquaintance of the General's, too."

"An Englishman. To be sure he stares at me and keeps his mouth shut. I like Englishmen, though. Well, carry me upstairs, straight to their rooms. Where are they?"

They carried Granny up; I walked up the broad staircase in front. Our procession was very striking. Every one we met stopped and stared. Our hotel is considered the best, the most expensive, and the most aristocratic in the place. Magnificent ladies and dignified Englishmen were always to be met on the staircase and in the corridors. Many people were making inquiries below of the *ober-kellner,* who was greatly impressed. He answered, of course, that this was a distinguished foreign lady, *une russe, une comtesse, grande dame,* and that she was taking the very apartments that had been occupied the week before by *la grande duchesse de* N. Granny's commanding and authoritative appearance as she was carried up in the chair was chiefly responsible for the sensation she caused. Whenever she met any one fresh she scrutinized him inquisitively and questioned me about him in a loud voice.

Granny was powerfully built, and though she did not get up from her chair, it could be seen that she was very tall. Her back was as straight as a board and she did not lean back in her chair. Her big grey head with its large, bold features was held erect; she had a positively haughty and defiant expression; and it was evident that her air and gestures were perfectly natural. In spite of her seventy-five years there was still a certain vigour in her face: and even her teeth were almost perfect. She was wearing a black silk dress and a white cap.

"She interests me very much," Mr. Astley, who was going up beside me, whispered to me.

"She knows about the telegrams," I thought. "She knows about De Grieux, too, but I fancy she does not know much about Mlle. Blanche as yet." I communicated this thought to Mr. Astley.

Sinful man that I was, after the first surprise was over, I was immensely delighted at the thunderbolt that we were launching at the General. I was elated; and I walked in front feeling very gay.

Our apartments were on the third floor. Without announcing her arrival or even knocking at the door, I simply flung it wide-open and Granny was carried in, in triumph. All of them were, as by design, assembled in the General's study. It was twelve o'clock and, I believe, some excursion was being planned for the whole party. Some were to drive, others were to ride on horseback, some acquaintances had been asked to join the party. Besides the General and Polina, with the children and their nurse, there were sitting in the study De Grieux, Mlle. Blanche, again wearing her riding-habit, her mother, the little Prince, and a learned German traveller whom I had not seen before.

Granny's chair was set down in the middle of the room, three paces from the General. My goodness! I shall never forget the sensation! As we went in the General was describing something, while De Grieux was correcting him. I must observe that Mlle. Blanche and De Grieux had for the last few days been particularly attentive to the little Prince, *à la barbe du pauvre général,* and the tone of the party was extremely gay and genially intimate, though, perhaps, it was artificial. Seeing Granny, the General was

struck dumb. His mouth dropped open and he broke off
in the middle of a word. He gazed at her open-eyed, as
though spellbound by the eye of a basilisk. Granny looked
at him in silence, too, immovably, but what a triumphant,
challenging and ironical look it was! They gazed at each
other for ten full seconds in the midst of profound silence
on the part of all around them. For the first moment De
Grieux was petrified, but immediately afterwards a look
of extreme uneasiness flitted over his face. Mlle. Blanche
raised her eyebrows, opened her mouth and gazed wildly
at Granny. The Prince and the learned German stared at
the whole scene in great astonishment. Polina's eyes expressed the utmost wonder and perplexity, and she suddenly turned white as a handkerchief; a minute later the
blood rushed rapidly into her face, flushing her cheeks.
Yes, this was a catastrophe for all of them! I kept turning
my eyes from Granny to all surrounding her and back
again. Mr. Astley stood on one side, calm and polite as
usual.

"Well, here I am! Instead of a telegram!" Granny broke
the silence by going off into a peal of laughter. "Well,
you didn't expect me?"

"Antonida Vassilyevna . . . Auntie . . . But how on
earth . . ." muttered the unhappy General.

If Granny had remained silent for a few seconds longer,
he would, perhaps, have had a stroke.

"How on earth what? I got into the train and came.
What's the railway for? You all thought that I had been
laid out, and had left you a fortune? You see, I know
how you sent telegrams from here. What a lot of money
you must have wasted on them! They cost a good bit from
here. I simply threw my legs over my shoulders and came
off here. Is this the Frenchman? M. de Grieux, I fancy?"

"Oui, madame," De Grieux responded; "et croyez, je
suis si enchanté . . . votre santé . . . c'est un miracle . . .
vous voir ici . . . une surprise charmante. . . ."

"Charmante, I daresay; I know you, you mummer. I
haven't this much faith in you," and she pointed her little
finger at him. "Who is this?" she asked, indicating Mlle.
Blanche. The striking-looking Frenchwoman, in a riding-
habit with a whip in her hand, evidently impressed her.
"Some one living here?"

"This is Mlle. Blanche de Cominges, and this is her

mamma, Madame de Cominges; they are staying in this hotel," I explained.

"Is the daughter married?" Granny questioned me without ceremony.

"Mlle. de Cominges is an unmarried lady," I answered, purposely speaking in a low voice and as respectfully as possible.

"Lively?"

"I do not understand the question."

"You are not dull with her? Does she understand Russian? De Grieux picked it up in Moscow. He had a smattering of it."

I explained that Mlle. de Cominges had never been in Russia.

"*Bonjour*," said Granny, turning abruptly to Mlle. Blanche.

"*Bonjour, madame.*" Mlle. Blanche made an elegant and ceremonious curtsey, hastening, under the cover of modesty and politeness, to express by her whole face and figure her extreme astonishment at such a strange question and manner of address.

"Oh, she casts down her eyes, she is giving herself airs and graces; you can see the sort she is at once; an actress of some kind. I'm stopping here below in the hotel," she said, turning suddenly to the General. "I shall be your neighbour. Are you glad or sorry?"

"Oh, Auntie! do believe in my sincere feelings . . . of pleasure," the General responded. He had by now recovered himself to some extent, and as, upon occasion, he could speak appropriately and with dignity, and even with some pretension to effectiveness, he began displaying his gifts now. "We have been so alarmed and upset by the news of your illness. . . . We received such despairing telegrams, and all at once . . ."

"Come, you are lying, you are lying," Granny interrupted at once.

"But how could you"—the General, too, made haste to interrupt, raising his voice and trying not to notice the word "lying"—how could you bring yourself to undertake such a journey? You must admit that at your age and in your state of health . . . at any rate it is all so unexpected that our surprise is very natural. But I am so pleased . . . and we all" (he began smiling with an ingratiating and delighted air) "will try our utmost that you shall spend your season here as agreeably as possible. . . ."

"Come, that's enough; that's idle chatter; you are talking nonsense, as usual. I can dispose of my time for myself. Though I've nothing against you, I don't bear a grudge. You ask how I could come? What is there surprising about it? It was the simplest thing. And why are you so surprised? How are you, Praskovya? What do you do here?"

"How do you do, Granny?" said Polina, going up to her. "Have you been long on the journey?"

"Well, she's asked a sensible question—the others could say nothing but oh and ah! Why, you see, I lay in bed and lay in bed and was doctored and doctored, so I sent the doctors away and called in the sexton from St. Nicolas. He had cured a peasant woman of the same disease by means of hayseed. And he did me good, too. On the third day I was in a perspiration all day and I got up. Then my Germans gathered round again, put on their spectacles and began to argue. 'If you were to go abroad now,' said they, 'and take a course of the waters, all your symptoms would disappear.' And why shouldn't I? I thought. The fools of Zazhigins began sighing and moaning: 'Where are you off to?' they said. Well, so here I am! It took me a day to get ready, and the following week, on a Friday, I took a maid, and Potapitch, and the footman, Fyodor, but I sent Fyodor back from Berlin, because I saw he was not wanted, and I could have come quite alone. I took a special compartment and there are porters at all the stations, and for twenty kopecks they will carry you wherever you like. I say, what rooms he has taken!" she said in conclusion, looking about her. "How do you get the money, my good man? Why, everything you've got is mortgaged. What a lot of money you must owe to this Frenchman alone! I know all about it; you see, I know all about it!"

"Oh, Auntie . . ." said the General, all confusion. "I am surprised, Auntie . . . I imagine that I am free to act . . . Besides, my expenses are not beyond my means, and we are here . . ."

"They are not? You say so! Then you must have robbed your children of their last farthing—you, their trustee!"

"After that, after such words," began the General, indignant, "I really don't know . . ."

"To be sure you don't! I'll be bound you are always at roulette here? Have you whistled it all away?"

The General was so overwhelmed that he almost spluttered in the rush of his feelings.

"Roulette! I? In my position . . . I? Think what you are saying, Auntie; you must still be unwell . . ."

"Come, you are lying, you are lying. I'll be bound they can't tear you away; it's all lies! I'll have a look to-day what this roulette is like. You, Praskovya, tell me where to go and what to see, and Alexey Ivanovitch here will show me, and you, Potapitch, make a note of all the places to go to. What is there to see here?" she said, addressing Polina again.

"Close by are the ruins of the castle; then there is the Schlangenberg."

"What is it, the Schlangenberg? A wood or what?"

"No, not a wood, it's a mountain; there is a peak there . . ."

"What do you mean by a peak?"

"The very highest point on the mountain. It is an enclosed place—the view from it is unique."

"What about carrying my chair up the mountain? They wouldn't be able to drag it up, would they?"

"Oh, we can find porters," I answered.

At this moment, Fedosya, the nurse, came up to greet Granny and brought the General's children to her.

"Come, there's no need for kissing! I cannot bear kissing children, they always have dirty noses. Well, how do you get on here, Fedosya?"

"It's very, very nice here, Antonida Vassilyevna," answered Fedosya. "How have you been, ma'am? We've been so worried about you."

"I know, you are a good soul. Do you always have visitors?"—she turned to Polina again. "Who is that wretched little rascal in spectacles?"

"Prince Nilsky," Polina whispered.

"Ah, a Russian. And I thought he wouldn't understand! Perhaps he didn't hear. I have seen Mr. Astley already. Here he is again," said Granny, catching sight of him. "How do you do?"—she turned to him suddenly.

Mr. Astley bowed to her in silence.

"Have you no good news to tell me? Say something! Translate that to him, Polina."

Polina translated it.

"Yes. That with great pleasure and delight I am looking at you, and very glad that you are in good health," Mr. Astley answered seriously, but with perfect readiness. It was translated to Granny and it was evident she was pleased.

"How well Englishmen always answer," she observed. "That's why I always like Englishmen. There's no comparison between them and Frenchmen! Come and see me," she said, addressing Mr. Astley again. "I'll try not to worry you too much. Translate that to him, and tell him that I am here below—here below—do you hear? Below, below," she repeated to Mr. Astley, pointing downwards.

Mr. Astley was extremely pleased at the invitation.

Granny looked Polina up and down attentively and with a satisfied air.

"I was fond of you, Praskovya," she said suddenly. "You're a fine wench, the best of the lot, and as for will—my goodness! Well, I have will too; turn round. That's not a false chignon, is it?"

"No, Granny, it's my own."

"To be sure. I don't care for the silly fashion of the day. You look very nice. I should fall in love with you if I were a young gentleman. Why don't you get married? But it is time for me to go. And I want to go out, for I've had nothing but the train and the train . . . Well, are you still cross?" she added, turning to the General.

"Upon my word, Auntie, what nonsense!" cried the General, delighted. "I understand at your age . . ."

"*Cette vieille est tombée en enfance*," De Grieux whispered to me.

"I want to see everything here. Will you let me have Alexey Ivanovitch?" Granny went on to the General.

"Oh, as much as you like, but I will myself . . . and Polina, M. de Grieux . . . we shall all think it a pleasure to accompany you."

"*Mais, madame, cela sera un plaisir*" . . . De Grieux addressed her with a bewitching smile.

"A *plaisir*, to be sure; you are absurd, my good sir. I am not going to give you any money, though," she added suddenly. "But now to my rooms; I must have a look at

them, and then we'll go the round of everything. Come,
lift me up." Granny was lifted up again and we all flocked
downstairs behind her chair. The General walked as
though stunned by a blow on the head. De Grieux was
considering something. Mlle. Blanche seemed about to remain, but for some reason she made up her mind to come
with the rest. The Prince followed her at once, and no
one was left in the General's study but Madame de Cominges and the German.

10

At watering-places and, I believe, in Europe generally,
hotelkeepers and *ober-kellners,* in assigning rooms to
their visitors, are guided not so much by the demands
and desires of the latter as by their own personal opinion
of them, and, one must add, they are rarely mistaken. But
for some reason I cannot explain, they had assigned
Granny such a splendid suite that they had quite overshot
the mark. It consisted of four splendidly furnished rooms
with a bathroom, quarters for the servants and a special
room for the maid, and so on. Some *grande duchesse* really
had been staying in those rooms the week before, a fact
of which the new occupant was informed at once, in order
to enhance the value of the apartments. Granny was carried, or rather wheeled, through all the rooms, and she
looked at them attentively and severely. The *ober-kellner,*
an elderly man with a bald head, followed her respectfully at this first survey.

I don't know what they all took Granny to be, but apparently for a very important and, above all, wealthy lady.
They put down in the book at once: *"Madame la générale,
princesse de Tarasyevitchev,"* though Granny had never
been a princess. Her servants, her special compartment in
the train, the mass of useless bags, portmanteaus, and
even chests that had come with Granny, probably laid the
foundation of her prestige; while her invalid-chair, her
abrupt tone and voice, her eccentric questions, which
were made with the most unconstrained air that would

tolerate no contradiction—in short, Granny's whole figure, erect, brisk, imperious—increased the awe in which she was held by all. As she looked at the rooms, Granny sometimes told them to stop her chair, pointed to some object in the furniture and addressed unexpected questions to the *ober-kellner*, who still smiled respectfully, though he was beginning to feel nervous. Granny put her questions in French, which she spoke, however, rather badly, so that I usually translated. The *ober-kellner's* answers for the most part did not please her and seemed unsatisfactory. And, indeed, she kept asking about all sorts of things quite irrelevant. Suddenly, for instance, stopping before a picture, a rather feeble copy of some well-known picture of a mythological subject, she would ask—

"Whose portrait is that?"

The *ober-kellner* replied that no doubt it was some countess.

"How is it you don't know? You live here and don't know. Why is it here? Why is she squinting?"

The *ober-kellner* could not answer these questions satisfactorily, and positively lost his head.

"Oh, what a blockhead!" commented Granny, in Russian.

She was wheeled on. The same performance was repeated with a Dresden statuette, which Granny looked at for a long time, and then ordered them to remove, no one knew why. Finally, she worried the *ober-kellner* about what the carpets in the bedroom cost, and where they had been woven! The *ober-kellner* promised to make inquiries.

"What asses," Granny grumbled, and concentrated her whole attention on the bed. "What a gorgeous canopy! Open the bed."

They opened the bed.

"More, more, turn it all over. Take off the pillows, the pillows, lift up the feather-bed."

Everything was turned over. Granny examined it attentively.

"It's a good thing there are no bugs. Take away all the linen! Make it up with my linen and my pillows. But all this is too gorgeous. Such rooms are not for an old woman like me. I shall be dreary all alone. Alexey Ivanovitch, you must come and see me very often when your lessons with the children are over."

"I left the General's service yesterday," I answered, "and am living in the hotel quite independently."

"How is that?"

"A German of high rank, a Baron, with his Baroness, came here from Berlin the other day. I addressed him yesterday in German without keeping to the Berlin accent."

"Well, what then?"

"He thought it an impertinence and complained to the General, and yesterday the General discharged me."

"Why, did you swear at the Baron, or what? (though if you had it wouldn't have mattered!)"

"Oh, no. On the contrary, the Baron raised his stick to thrash me."

"And did you, sniveller, allow your tutor to be treated like that?" she said suddenly, addressing the General; "and turned him out of his place too! Noodles! you're all a set of noodles, as I see."

"Don't disturb yourself, Auntie," said the General, with a shade of condescending familiarity; "I can manage my own business. Besides, Alexey Ivanovitch has not given you quite a correct account of it."

"And you just put up with it?"—she turned to me.

"I meant to challenge the Baron to a duel," I answered, as calmly and as modestly as I could, "but the General opposed it."

"Why did you oppose it?"—Granny turned to the General again. ("And you can go, my good man; you can come when you are called," she said, addressing the *ober-kellner;* "no need to stand about gaping. I can't endure this Nürnberg rabble!")

The man bowed and went out, not, of course, understanding Granny's compliments.

"Upon my word, Auntie, surely a duel was out of the question."

"Why out of the question? Men are all cocks; so they should fight. You are all noodles, I see, you don't know how to stand up for your country. Come, take me up, Potapitch; see that there are always two porters: engage them. I don't want more than two. I shall only want them to carry me up and down stairs, and to wheel me on the levels in the street. Explain that to them; and pay them beforehand—they will be more respectful. You will always be with me yourself, and you, Alexey Ivanovitch, point out that Baron to me when we are out: that I may have a look at the von Baron. Well, where is the roulette?"

I explained that the roulette tables were in rooms in the Casino. Then followed questions: Were there many of them? Did many people play? Did they play all day long? How was it arranged? I answered at last, that she had much better see all this with her own eyes, and that it was rather difficult to describe it.

"Well, then, take me straight there! You go first, Alexey Ivanovitch!"

"Why, Auntie, don't you really mean to rest after your journey?" the General asked anxiously. He seemed rather flurried and, indeed, they all seemed embarrassed and were exchanging glances. Probably they all felt it rather risky and, indeed, humiliating to accompany Granny to the Casino, where, of course, she might do something eccentric, and in public; at the same time, they all proposed to accompany her.

"Why should I rest? I am not tired and, besides, I've been sitting still for three days. And then we will go and see the springs and medicinal waters; where are they? And then . . . we'll go and see, what was it you said, Praskovya?—peak, wasn't it?"

"Yes, Granny."

"Well, peak, then, if it is a peak. And what else is there here?"

"There are a great many objects of interest, Granny," Polina exerted herself to say.

"Why don't you know them! Marfa, you shall come with me, too," she said, addressing her maid.

"But why should she come?" the General said fussily; "and in fact it's out of the question, and I doubt whether Potapitch will be admitted into the Casino."

"What nonsense! Am I to abandon her because she is a servant? She's a human being, too; here we have been on our travels for a week; she wants to have a look at things, too. With whom could she go except me? She wouldn't dare show her nose in the street by herself."

"But, Granny . . ."

"Why, are you ashamed to be with me? Then stay at home; you are not asked. Why, what a General! I am a General's widow myself. And why should you all come trailing after me? I can look at it all with Alexey Ivano-vitch."

But De Grieux insisted that we should all accompany her, and launched out into the most polite phrases about the pleasure of accompanying her, and so on. We all started.

"Elle est tombée en enfance," De Grieux repeated to the General; *"seule, elle fera des bêtises . . ."* I heard nothing more, but he evidently had some design, and, possibly, his hopes had revived.

It was half a mile to the Casino. The way was through an avenue of chestnuts to a square, going round which, they came out straight on the Casino. The General was to some extent reassured, for our procession, though some-what eccentric, was, nevertheless, decorous and present-able. And there was nothing surprising in the fact of an invalid who could not walk putting in an appearance at the Casino; but, anyway, the General was afraid of the Casino; why should an invalid unable to walk, and an old lady, too, go into the gambling saloon? Polina and Mlle. Blanche walked on each side of the bath-chair. Mlle. Blanche laughed, was modestly animated and even some-times jested very politely with Granny, so much so that the latter spoke of her approvingly at last. Polina, on the other side, was obliged to be continually answering Granny's innumerable questions, such as: "Who was that passed? Who was that woman driving past? Is it a big town? Is it a big garden? What are those trees? What's that hill? Do eagles fly here? What is that absurd-looking roof?" Mr. Astley walked beside me and whispered that he expected a great deal from that morning. Potapitch and Marfa walked in the background close behind the bath-chair, Potapitch in his swallow-tailed coat and white tie, but with a cap on his head, and Marfa (a red-faced maidservant, forty years old and beginning to turn grey) in a cap, cotton gown, and creaking goatskin slippers. Granny turned to them very often and addressed remarks to them. De Grieux was talking with an air of determina-tion. Probably he was reassuring the General, evidently he was giving him some advice. But Granny had already pronounced the fatal phrase: "I am not going to give you money." Perhaps to De Grieux this announcement sounded incredible, but the General knew his aunt. I noticed that De Grieux and Mlle. Blanche were continually exchanging glances. I could distinguish the Prince and the German traveller at the further end of the avenue; they had stopped, and were walking away from us.

Our visit to the Casino was a triumph. The porters and attendants displayed the same deference as in the hotel. They looked at us, however, with curiosity. Granny began by giving orders that she should be wheeled through all the rooms. Some she admired, others made no impression on her; she asked questions about them all. At last we came to the roulette room. The lackeys, who stood like sentinels at closed doors, flung the doors wide open as though they were impressed.

Granny's appearance at the roulette table made a profound impression on the public. At the roulette tables and at the other end of the room, where there was a table with *trente et quarante,* there was a crowd of a hundred and fifty or two hundred players, several rows deep. Those who had succeeded in squeezing their way right up to the table, held fast, as they always do, and would not give up their places to any one until they had lost; for simple spectators were not allowed to stand at the tables and occupy the space. Though there were chairs set round the table, few of the players sat down, especially when there was a great crowd, because standing one could get closer and consequently pick out one's place and put down one's stake more conveniently. The second and the third rows pressed up upon the first, waiting and watching for their turn; but sometimes a hand would be impatiently thrust forward through the first row to put down a stake. Even from the third row people managed to seize chances of poking forward their stakes; consequently every ten or even five minutes there was some "scene" over disputed stakes at one end of the hall or another. The police of the Casino were, however, fairly good. It was, of course, impossible to prevent crowding; on the contrary, the owners were glad of the rush of people because it was profitable, but eight croupiers sitting round the table kept a vigilant watch on the stakes: they even kept count of them, and when disputes arose they could settle them. In extreme cases they called in the police, and the trouble was over in an instant. There were police officers in plain clothes stationed here and there among the players, so that they could not be recognized. They were especially on the lookout for thieves and professional pick-pockets, who are very numerous at the roulette tables, as it affords them excellent opportunity for exercising their skill. The fact is, elsewhere thieves must pick pockets or break locks, and such enterprises, when unsuccessful, have a very troublesome ending. But in this case the thief has only to go up to the roulette table, begin playing, and all at once, openly and publicly, take another person's winnings and put them in his pocket. If a dispute arises, the cheat insists loudly that the stake was his. If the trick is played cleverly and the witnesses hesitate, the thief may often succeed in carrying off the money, if the sum is not a very large one, of course. In that case the croupiers or some one of the other players are almost certain to have been keeping an eye on it. But if the sum is not a large one, the real owner sometimes actually declines to keep up the dispute, and goes away shrinking from the scandal. But if they succeed in detecting a thief, they turn him out at once with contumely.

All this Granny watched from a distance with wild curiosity. She was much delighted at a thief's being turned out. *Trente et quarante* did not interest her very much; she was more pleased at roulette and the rolling of the little ball. She evinced a desire at last to get a closer view of the game. I don't know how it happened, but the attendants and other officious persons (principally Poles who had lost, and who pressed their services on lucky players and foreigners of all sorts) at once, and in spite of the crowd, cleared a place for Granny in the very middle of the table beside the chief croupier, and wheeled her chair to it. A number of visitors who were not playing, but watching the play (chiefly Englishmen with their families), at once crowded round the table to watch Granny from behind the players. Numbers of lorgnettes were turned in her direction. The coupier's expectations rose. Such an eccentric person certainly seemed to promise something out of the ordinary. An old woman of over seventy, who could not walk, yet wished to play, was, of course, not a sight to be seen ever day. I squeezed my way up to the table too, and took my stand beside Granny. Potapitch and Marfa were left somewhere in the distance

among the crowd. The General, Polina, De Grieux, and
Mlle. Blanche stood aside, too, among the spectators.

At first Granny began looking about at the players. She
began in a half whisper asking me abrupt, jerky questions. Who was that man and who was this woman? She
was particularly delighted by a young man at the end
of the table, who was playing for very high stakes, putting
down thousands and had, as people whispered around,
already won as much as forty thousand francs, which lay
before him in heaps of gold and banknotes. He was pale;
his eyes glittered and his hands were shaking; he was
staking now without counting, by handfuls, and yet he
kept on winning and winning, kept raking in and raking
in the money. The attendants hung about him solicitously,
set a chair for him, cleared a place round him that he
might have more room, that he might not be crowded—
all this in expectation of a liberal tip. Some players, after
they have won, tip the attendants without counting a
handful of coins in their joy. A Pole had already established himself at his side, and was deferentially but continually whispering to him, probably telling him what to
stake on, advising and directing his play—of course, he,
too, expecting a tip later on! But the player scarcely looked
at him. He staked at random and kept winning. He evidently did not know what he was doing.

Granny watched him for some minutes.

"Tell him," Granny said suddenly, growing excited and
giving me a poke, "tell him to give it up, to take his money
quickly and go away. He'll lose it all directly, he'll lose it
all!" she urged, almost breathless with agitation. "Where's
Potapitch? Send Potapitch to him. Come, tell him, tell
him," she went on, poking me. "Where is Potapitch?
Sortez! Sortez!"—she began herself shouting to the young
man.

I bent down to her and whispered resolutely that she
must not shout like this here, that even talking aloud was
forbidden, because it hindered counting, and that we
should be turned out directly.

"How vexatious! The man's lost! I suppose it's his own
doing. . . . I can't look at him, it quite upsets me. What a
dolt!" and Granny made haste to turn in another direction.

On the left, on the other side of the table, there was con-
spicuous among the players a young lady, and beside her

a sort of dwarf. Who this dwarf was, and whether he was
a relation or brought by her for the sake of effect, I don't
know. I had noticed the lady before; she made her appearance at the gambling table every day, at one o'clock in the
afternoon, and went away exactly at two; she always
played for an hour. She was already known, and a chair
was set for her at once. She took out of her pocket some
gold, some thousand-franc notes, and began staking
quietly, coolly, prudently, making pencil notes on a bit of
paper of the numbers about which the chances grouped
themselves, and trying to work out a system. She staked
considerable sums. She used to win every day—one, two,
or at the most three thousand francs—not more, and instantly went away. Granny scrutinized her for a long time.

"Well, that one won't lose! That one there won't lose!
Of what class is she! Do you know? Who is she?"

"She must be a Frenchwoman, of a certain class, you
know," I whispered.

"Ah, one can tell the bird by its flight. One can see she
has a sharp claw. Explain to me now what every turn
means and how one has to bet!"

I explained as far as I could to Granny all the various
points on which one could stake: *rouge et noir, pair et impair, manque et passe,* and finally the various subtleties
in the system of the numbers. Granny listened attentively,
remembered, asked questions, and began to master it. One
could point to examples of every kind, so that she very
quickly and readily picked up a great deal.

"But what is *zéro?* You see that croupier, the curly-
headed one, the chief one, showed *zéro* just now? And
why did he scoop up everything that was on the table?
Such a heap, he took it all for himself. What is the meaning of it?"

"*Zéro,* Granny, means that the bank wins all. If the little ball falls on *zéro,* everything on the table goes to the
bank. It is true you can stake your money so as to keep
it, but the bank pays nothing."

"You don't say so! And shall I get nothing?"

"No, Granny, if before this you had staked on *zéro* you
would have got thirty-five times what you staked."

"What! thirty-five times, and does it often turn up?
Why don't they stake on it, the fools."

"There are thirty-six chances against it, Granny."

"What nonsense. Potapitch! Potapitch! Stay, I've money with me—here." She took out of her pocket a tightly packed purse, and picked out of it a friedrich d'or. "Stake it on the *zéro* at once."

"Granny, *zéro* has only just turned up," I said; "so now it won't turn up for a long time. You will lose a great deal; wait a little, anyway."

"Oh, nonsense; put it down!"

"As you please, but it may not turn up again till the evening. You may go on staking thousands; it has happened."

"Oh, nonsense, nonsense. If you are afraid of the wolf you shouldn't go into the forest. What? Have I lost? Stake again!"

A second friedrich d'or was lost: she staked a third. Granny could scarcely sit still in her seat. She stared with feverish eyes at the little ball dancing on the spokes of the turning wheel. She lost a third, too. Granny was beside herself, she could not sit still, she even thumped on the table with her fist when the croupier announced, "*trente-six*" instead of the *zéro* she was expecting.

"There, look at it," said Granny angrily; "isn't that cursed little *zéro* coming soon? As sure as I'm alive, I'll sit here till *zéro* does come! It's that cursed curly-headed croupier's doing; he'll never let it come! Alexey Ivanovitch, stake two gold pieces at once! Staking as much as you do, even if *zéro* does come you'll get nothing by it."

"Granny!"

"Stake, stake! it is not your money."

I staked two friedrichs d'or. The ball flew about the wheel for a long time, at last it began dancing about the spokes. Granny was numb with excitement, and squeezed my fingers, and all at once—

"*Zéro!*" boomed the croupier.

"You see, you see!"—Granny turned to me quickly, beaming and delighted. "I told you so. The Lord Himself put it into my head to stake those two gold pieces! Well, how much do I get now? Why don't they give it me? Potapitch, Marfa, where are they? Where have all our people got to? Potapitch, Potapitch!"

"Granny, afterwards," I whispered; "Potapitch is at the door, they won't let him in. Look, Granny, they are giving you the money, take it!" A heavy roll of printed blue notes, worth fifty friedrichs d'or, was thrust towards Granny and twenty friedrichs d'or were counted out to her. I scooped it all up in a shovel and handed it to Granny.

"Faites le jeu, messieurs! Faites le jeu, messieurs! Rien ne va plus?" called the croupier, inviting the public to stake, and preparing to turn the wheel.

"Heavens! we are too late. They're just going to turn it. Put it down, put it down!" Granny urged me in a flurry. "Don't dawdle, make haste!" She was beside herself and poked me with all her might.

"What am I to stake it on, Granny?"

"On *zéro*, on *zéro*! On *zéro* again! Stake as much as possible! How much have we got altogether? Seventy friedrichs d'or. There's no need to spare it. Stake twenty friedrichs d'or at once."

"Think what you are doing, Granny! Sometimes it does not turn up for two hundred times running! I assure you, you may go on staking your whole fortune."

"Oh, nonsense, nonsense! Put it down! How your tongue does wag! I know what I'm about." Granny was positively quivering with excitement.

"By the regulations it's not allowed to stake more than twelve roubles on *zéro* at once, Granny; here I have staked that."

"Why is it not allowed? Aren't you lying? Monsieur! Monsieur!"—she nudged the croupier, who was sitting near her on the left, and was about to set the wheel turning. *"Combien zéro? Douze? Douze?"*

I immediately interpreted the question in French.

"Oui, madame," the croupier confirmed politely; "as the winnings from no single stake must exceed four thousand florins by the regulations," he added in explanation.

"Well, there's no help for it, stake twelve."

"Le jeu est fait," cried the croupier. The wheel rotated, and thirty turned up. She had lost.

"Again, again, again! Stake again!" cried Granny. I no longer resisted, and, shrugging my shoulders, staked another twelve friedrichs d'or. The wheel turned a long time. Granny was simply quivering as she watched the wheel. "Can she really imagine that *zéro* will win again?" I thought, looking at her with wonder. Her face was beaming with a firm conviction of winning, an unhesitating expectation that in another minute they would shout *"Zéro!"* The ball jumped into the cage.

"Zéro!" cried the croupier.

"What!!!" Granny turned to me with intense triumph.

I was a gambler myself, I felt that at the moment my arms and legs were trembling, there was a throbbing in my head. Of course, this was a rare chance that *zéro* should have come up three times in some dozen turns; but there was nothing particularly wonderful about it. I had myself seen *zéro* turn up three times *running* two days before, and a gambler who had been zealously noting down the lucky numbers, observed aloud that, only the day before, *zéro* had turned up only once in twenty-four hours.

Granny's winnings were counted out to her with particular attention and deference as she had won such a large sum. She received four hundred and twenty fried-richs d'or, that is, four thousand florins and seventy fried-richs d'or. She was given twenty friedrichs d'or in gold, and four thousand florins in banknotes.

This time Granny did not call Potapitch; she had other preoccupations. She did not even babble or quiver outwardly! She was, if one may so express it, quivering inwardly. She was entirely concentrated on something, absorbed in one aim.

"Alexey Ivanovitch, he said that one could only stake four thousand florins at once, didn't he? Come, take it, stake the whole four thousand on the red," Granny commanded.

It was useless to protest; the wheel began rotating.

"Rouge," the croupier proclaimed.

Again she had won four thousand florins, making eight in all.

"Give me four, and stake four again on red," Granny commanded. Again I staked four thousand.

"Rouge," the croupier pronounced again.

"Twelve thousand altogether! Give it me all here. Pour the gold here into the purse and put away the notes. That's enough! Home! Wheel my chair out."

11

The chair was wheeled to the door at the other end of the room. Granny was radiant. All our party immediately thronged round her with congratulations. However eccentric Granny's behaviour might be, her triumph covered a multitude of sins, and the General was no longer afraid of compromising himself in public by his relationship with such a strange woman. With a condescending and familiarly good-humoured smile, as though humouring a child, he congratulated Granny. He was, however, evidently impressed, like all the other spectators. People talked all round and pointed at Granny. Many passed by to get a closer view of her! Mr. Astley was talking of her aside, with two English acquaintances. Some majestic ladies gazed at her with majestic amazement, as though at a marvel. . . . De Grieux positively showered congratulations and smiles upon her.

"*Quelle victoire!*" he said.

"*Mais, madame, c'était du feu,*" Mlle. Blanche commented, with an ingratiating smile.

"Yes, I just went and won twelve thousand florins! Twelve, indeed; what about the gold? With the gold it makes almost thirteen. What is that in our money? Will it be six thousand?"

I explained that it made more than seven, and in the present state of exchange might even amount to eight.

"Well, that's something worth having, eight thousand! And you stay here, you noodles, and do nothing! Potapitch, Marfa, did you see?"

"My goodness! how did you do it, ma'am? Eight thousand!" exclaimed Marfa, wriggling.

"There! there's five gold pieces for you, here!"

Potapitch and Marfa flew to kiss her hand.

"And give the porters, too, a friedrich d'or each. Give it them in gold, Alexey Ivanovitch. Why is that flunkey bowing and the other one too? Are they congratulating me? Give them a friedrich d'or too."

"*Madame la princesse . . . un pauvre expatrié . . . mal-*

heur continuel . . . les princes russes sont si généreux . . ."
A person with moustaches and an obsequious smile, in a
threadbare coat and gay-coloured waistcoat, came cringing
about Granny's chair, waving his hat in his hand.

"Give him a friedrich d'or too. . . . No, give him two;
that's enough, or there will be no end to them. Lift me
up and carry me out. Praskovya"—she turned to Polina
Alexandrovna—"I'll buy you a dress to-morrow, and I'll
buy Mlle. . . . what's her name, Mlle. Blanche, isn't it?
I'll buy her a dress too. Translate that to her, Praskovya!"

"Merci, madame." Mlle. Blanche made a grateful curtsey
while she exchanged an ironical smile with De Grieux and
the General. The General was rather embarrassed and
was greatly relieved when we reached the avenue.

"Fedosya—won't Fedosya be surprised," said Granny,
thinking of the General's nurse. "I must make her a
present of a dress. Hey, Alexey Ivanovitch, Alexey Ivanovitch, give this to the poor man."

A man in rags, with bent back, passed us on the road,
and looked at us.

"And perhaps he is not a poor man, but a rogue,
Granny."

"Give him a gulden, give it him!"

I went up to the man and gave it him. He looked at
me in wild amazement, but took the gulden, however.
He smelt of spirits.

"And you, Alexey Ivanovitch. Have you not tried your
luck yet?"

"No, Granny."

"But your eyes were burning, I saw them."

"I shall try, Granny, I certainly shall later."

"And stake on *zéro* straight away. You will see! How
much have you in hand?"

"Only twenty friedrichs d'or, Granny."

"That's not much. I will give you fifty friedrich's d'or.
I will lend it if you like. Here, take this roll—but don't
you expect anything, all the same, my good man, I am
not going to give you anything," she said, suddenly addressing the General.

The latter winced, but he said nothing. De Grieux
frowned.

"Que diable, c'est une terrible vieille!" he muttered to
the General through his teeth.

"A beggar, a beggar, another beggar!" cried Granny. "Give him a gulden, too, Alexey Ivanovitch."

This time it was a grey-headed old man with a wooden leg, in a long-skirted blue coat and with a long stick in his hand. He looked like an old soldier. But when I held out a gulden to him he stepped back and looked at me angrily.

"Was ist's der Teufel," he shouted, following up with a dozen oaths.

"Oh, he's a fool," cried Granny, dismissing him with a wave of her hand. "Go on! I'm hungry! Now we'll have dinner directly; then I'll rest a little, and back here again."

"You want to play again, Granny!" I cried.

"What do you expect? That you should all sit here and sulk while I watch you?"

"Mais, madame—" De Grieux drew near—*"les chances peuvent tourner, une seule mauvaise chance et vous perdrez tout . . . surtout avec votre jeu . . . C'est terrible!"*

"Vous perdrez absolument," chirped Mlle. Blanche.

"But what is it to do with all of you? I shouldn't lose your money, but my own! And where is that Mr. Astley?" she asked me.

"He stayed in the Casino, Granny."

"I'm sorry, he's such a nice man."

On reaching home Granny met the *ober-kellner* on the stairs, called him and began bragging of her winnings; then she sent for Fedosya, made her a present of three friedrichs d'or and ordered dinner to be served. Fedosya and Marfa hovered over her at dinner.

"I watched you, ma'am," Marfa cackled, "and said to Potapitch, 'What does our lady want to do?' And the money on the table—saints alive! the money! I haven't seen so much money in the whole of my life, and all round were gentlefolk—nothing but gentlefolk sitting. 'And wherever do all these gentlefolk come from, Potapitch?' said I. May our Lady Herself help her, I thought. I was praying for you, ma'am, and my heart was simply sinking, simply sinking; I was all of a tremble. Lord help her, I thought, and here the Lord has sent you luck. I've been trembling ever since, ma'am. I'm all of a tremble now."

"Alexey Ivanovitch, after dinner, at four o'clock, get ready and we'll go. Now good-bye for a time; don't forget to send for a doctor for me. I must drink the waters, too. Go, or maybe you'll forget."

As I left Granny I was in a sort of stupor. I tried to imagine what would happen now to all our people and what turn things would take. I saw clearly that they (epecially the General) had not yet succeeded in recovering from the first shock. The fact of Granny's arrival instead of the telegram which they were expecting from hour to hour to announce her death (and consequently the inheritance of her fortune) had so completely shattered the whole fabric of their plans and intentions that Granny's further exploits at roulette threw them into positive bewilderment and a sort of stupefaction seemed to have come over all of them.

Meanwhile this second fact was almost more important than the first; for though Granny had repeated twice that she would not give the General any money, yet, who knows?—there was no need to give up all hope yet. De Grieux, who was involved in all the General's affairs, had not lost hope. I am convinced that Mlle. Blanche, also much involved in the General's affairs (I should think so: to marry a General and with a considerable fortune!), would not have given up hope, and would have tried all her fascinating arts upon Granny—in contrast with the proud and incomprehensible Polina, who did not know how to curry favour with any one. But now, now that Granny had had such success at roulette, now that Granny's personality had shown itself so clearly and so typically (a refractory and imperious old lady, *et tombée en enfance*), now, perhaps, all was lost. Why, she was as pleased as a child, so pleased that she would go on till she was ruined and had lost everything. Heavens! I thought (and, God forgive me, with a malignant laugh), why, every friedrich d'or Granny staked just now must have been a fresh sore in the General's heart, must have maddened De Grieux and infuriated Mlle. de Cominges, who saw the cup slipping from her lips. Another fact: even in her triumph and joy of winning, when Granny was giving money away to every one, and taking every passer-by for a beggar, even then she had let fall to the General, "I'm not going to give you anything, though!" That meant that she had fastened upon that idea, was sticking to it, had made up her mind about it. There was danger! danger!

All these reflections were revolving in my mind as I mounted the front stairs from Granny's apartments to my garret in the very top storey. All this interested me strongly. Though, of course, I could before have divined the strongest leading motives prompting the actors before me, yet I did not know for certain all the mysteries and intrigues of the drama. Polina had never been fully open with me. Though it did happen at times that she revealed her feelings to me, yet I noticed that almost always after such confidences she would make fun of all she had said, or would try to obscure the matter and put it in a different light. Oh, she had hidden a great deal! In any case, I foresaw that the *dénouement* of this mysterious and constrained position was at hand. One more shock—and everything would be ended and revealed. About my fortunes, which were also involved in all this, I scarcely troubled. I was in a strange mood: I had only twenty friedrichs d'or in my pocket; I was in a foreign land without a job or means of livelihood, without hope, without prospects, and —I did not trouble my head about it! If it had not been for the thought of Polina, I should have abandoned myself to the comic interest of the approaching catastrophe, and should have been shouting with laughter. But I was troubled about Polina; her fate was being decided, I divined that; but I regret to say that it was not altogether her fate that troubled me. I wanted to fathom her secrets; I wanted her to come to me and say: "I love you," and if not that, if that was senseless insanity, then . . . well, what was there to care about? Did I know what I wanted? I was like one demented: all I wanted was to be near her, in the halo of her glory, in her radiance, always, for ever, all my life. I knew nothing more! And could I leave her?

In their passage on the third storey I felt as though something nudged me. I turned round and, twenty paces or more from me, I saw coming out of a door Polina. She seemed waiting: and as soon as she saw me beckoned to me.

"Polina Alexandrovna . . ."

"Hush!" she said.

"Imagine," I whispered to her, "I felt as though some one had nudged me just now; I looked round—you! It seems as though there were a sort of electricity from you!"

"Take this letter," Polina articulated anxiously with a

frown, probably not hearing what I had said, "and give it into Mr. Astley's own hands at once. Make haste, I beg you. There is no need of an answer. He will . . ."

She did not finish.

"Mr. Astley?" I repeated in surprise.

But Polina had already disappeared behind the door.

"Aha, so they are in correspondence!" I ran at once, of course, to Mr. Astley; first to his hotel, where I did not find him, then to the Casino, where I hurried through all the rooms: and at last, as I was returning home in vexation, almost in despair, I met him by chance, with a party of Englishmen and Englishwomen on horseback. I beckoned to him, stopped him and gave him the letter: we had not time even to exchange a glance. But I suspect that Mr. Astley purposely gave rein to his horse.

Was I tortured by jealousy? Anyway, I was in an utterly shattered condition. I did not even want to find out what they were writing to one another about. And so he was trusted by her! "Her friend, her friend," I thought, "and that is clear (and when has he had time to become her friend), but is there love in the case? Of course not," common-sense whispered to me. But common-sense alone counts for little in such cases; anyway, this, too, had to be cleared up. Things were growing unpleasantly complicated.

Before I had time to go into the hotel, first the porter and then the *ober-kellner*, coming out of his room, informed me that I was wanted, that I had been asked for, three times they had sent to ask: where was I?—that I was asked to go as quickly as possible to the General's rooms. I was in the most disagreeable frame of mind. In the General's room I found, besides the General himself, De Grieux and Mlle. Blanche—alone, without her mother. The mother was evidently an official one, only used for show. But when it came to real *business* she acted for herself. And probably the woman knew little of her so-called daughter's affairs.

They were, however, consulting warmly about something, and the doors of the study were actually locked— which had never happened before. Coming to the door, I heard loud voices—De Grieux's insolent and malignant voice, Blanche's shrill fury, and the General's pitiful tones, evidently defending himself about something. Upon my entrance they all, as it were, pulled themselves up and restrained themselves. De Grieux smoothed his hair and forced a smile into his angry face—that horrid official French smile which I so detest. The crushed and desperate General tried to assume an air of dignity, but it was a mechanical effort. Only Mlle. Blanche's countenance, blazing with anger, scarcely changed. She only ceased speaking while she fixed her eyes upon me in impatient expectation. I may mention that hitherto she had treated me with extraordinary casualness, had even refused to respond to my bows, and had simply declined to see me.

"Alexey Ivanovitch," the General began in a soft mollifying tone, "allow me to tell you that it is strange, exceedingly strange . . . in fact, your conduct in regard to me and my family . . . in fact, it is exceedingly strange . . ."

"*Eh! ce n'est pas ça,*" De Grieux interposed, with vexation and contempt. (There's no doubt he was the leading spirit.) "*Mon cher monsieur, notre cher général se trompe,* in taking up this tone" (I translate the rest of his speech in Russian), "but he meant to say . . . that is to warn you, or rather to beg you most earnestly not to ruin him— yes, indeed, not to ruin him! I make use of that expression."

"But how, how?" I interrupted.

"Why, you are undertaking to be the guide (or how shall I express it?) of this old woman, *cette pauvre terrible vieille*"—De Grieux himself hesitated—"but you know she'll lose everything; she will gamble away her whole fortune! You know yourself, you have seen yourself, how she plays! If she begins to lose, she will never leave off from obstinacy, from anger, and will lose everything, she will gamble away everything, and in such cases one can never regain one's losses and then . . . then . . ."

"And then," the General put in, "then you will ruin the whole family! I and my family are her heirs, she has no nearer relations. I tell you openly: my affairs are in a bad way, a very bad way. You know my position to some extent. . . . If she loses a considerable sum or even (Lord help us!) her whole fortune, what will become of me, of my children!" (The General looked round at De Grieux.) "Of me." (He looked round at Mlle. Blanche, who turned away from him with contempt.) "Alexey Ivanovitch, save us, save us! . . ."

"But how, General, how, how can I? . . . What influence have I in the matter?"

"Refuse, refuse, give her up! . . ."

"Then some one else will turn up," I said.

"*Ce n'est pas ça, ce n'est pas ça,*" De Grieux interrupted again, "*que diable!* No, don't desert her, but at least advise her, dissuade her, draw her away . . . don't let her play too much, distract her in some way."

"But how can I do that? If you would undertake the task yourself, M. de Grieux," I added, as naïvely as I could.

Here I caught a rapid, fiery, questioning glance from Mlle. Blanche at M. de Grieux. And in De Grieux's own face there was something peculiar, something he could not himself disguise.

"The point is, she won't accept me now!" De Grieux cried, with a wave of his hand. "If only . . . later on . . ."

De Grieux looked rapidly and meaningly at Mlle. Blanche.

"*O, mon cher M. Alexis, soyez si bon.*" Mlle. Blanche herself took a step towards me with a most fascinating smile, she seized me by both hands and pressed them warmly. Damn it all! That diabolical face knew how to change completely in one moment. At that instant her face was so imploring, so sweet, it was such a child-like and even mischievous smile; at the end of the phrase she gave me such a sly wink, unseen by all the rest; she meant to do for me completely, and it was successfully done; only it was horribly coarse.

Then the General leapt up, positively leapt up. "Alexey Ivanovitch, forgive me for beginning as I did just now. I did not mean that at all. . . . I beg you, I beseech you, I bow down before you in Russian style—you alone, you alone can save us. Mlle. de Cominges and I implore you—you understand, you understand, of course." He besought me, indicating Mlle. Blanche with his eyes. He was a very pitiful figure.

At that instant there came three subdued and respectful knocks at the door; it was opened—the corridor attendant was knocking and a few steps behind him stood Potapitch. They came with messages from Granny; they were charged to find and bring me at once. "She is angry," Potapitch informed me.

"But it is only half-past three."

"She could not get to sleep; she kept tossing about, and then at last she got up, sent for her chair and for you. She's at the front door now."

"Quelle mégère," cried De Grieux.

I did, in fact, find Granny on the steps, out of all patience at my not being there. She could not wait till four o'clock.

"Come," she cried, and we set off again to roulette.

12

Granny was in an impatient and irritable mood; it was evident that roulette had made a deep impression on her mind. She took no notice of anything else and was altogether absent-minded. For instance, she asked me no questions on the road as she had done before. Seeing a luxurious carriage whirling by, she was on the point of raising her hand and asking: What is it? Whose is it?— but I believe she did not hear what I answered: her absorption was continually interrupted by abrupt and impatient gesticulations. When I pointed out to her Baron and Baroness Burmerhelm, who were approaching the Casino, she looked absent-mindedly at them and said, quite indifferently, "Ah!" and, turning round quickly to Potapitch and Marfa, who were walking behind her, snapped out to them—

"Why are you hanging upon us? We can't take you every time! Go home! You and I are enough," she added, when they had hurriedly turned and gone home.

They were already expecting Granny at the Casino. They immediately made room for her in the same place, next to the croupier. I fancy that these croupiers, who are always so strictly decorous and appear to be ordinary officials who are absolutely indifferent as to whether the bank wins or loses, are by no means so unconcerned at the bank's losses and, of course, receive instructions for attracting players and for augmenting the profits—for which they doubtless receive prizes and bonuses. They looked upon Granny, anyway, as their prey.

Then just what we had expected happened.

This was how it was.

Granny pounced at once on *zéro* and immediately ordered me to stake twelve friedrichs d'or. She staked once, twice, three times—*zéro* never turned up.

"Put it down! Put it down!" Granny nudged me, impatiently. I obeyed.

"How many times have we staked?" she asked at last, grinding her teeth with impatience.

"I have staked twelve times, Granny. I have put down a hundred and forty-four friedrichs d'or. I tell you, Granny, very likely till evening . . ."

"Hold your tongue!" Granny interrupted. "Stake on *zéro*, and stake at once a thousand gulden on red. Here, take the note."

Red won, and *zéro* failed once more; a thousand gulden was gained.

"You see, you see!" whispered Granny, "we have gained almost all that we have lost. Stake again on *zéro*; we'll stake ten times more and then give it up."

But the fifth time Granny was thoroughly sick of it.

"The devil take that filthy *zéro*. Come, stake the whole four thousand gulden on the red," she commanded me.

"Granny! it will be so much; why, what if red does not turn up?" I besought her; but Granny almost beat me. (Indeed, she nudged me so violently that she might almost be said to have attacked me.) There was no help for it, I staked on red the whole four thousand won that morning. The wheel turned. Granny sat calmly and proudly erect, never doubting that she would certainly win.

"*Zéro!*" boomed the croupier.

At first Granny did not understand, but when she saw the croupier scoop up her four thousand gulden together with everything on the table, and learned that *zéro*, which had not turned up for so long and on which we had staked in vain almost two hundred friedrichs d'or, had, as though to spite her, turned up just as Granny was abusing it, she groaned and flung up her hands in view of the whole hall. People around actually laughed.

"Holy saints! The cursed thing has turned up!" Granny wailed, "the hateful, hateful thing! That's your doing! It's all your doing"—she pounced upon me furiously, pushing me. "It was you persuaded me."

"Granny, I talked sense to you; how can I answer for chance?"

"I'll chance you," she whispered angrily. "Go away."

"Good-bye, Granny." I turned to go away.

"Alexey Ivanovitch, Alexey Ivanovitch! stop. Where are you off to? Come, what's the matter, what's the matter? Ach, he's in a rage! Stupid, come, stay, stay; come, don't be angry; I am a fool myself! Come, tell me what are we to do now!"

"I won't undertake to tell you, Granny, because you will blame me. Play for yourself, tell me and I'll put down the stakes."

"Well, well! Come, stake another four thousand gulden on red! Here, take my pocket-book." She took it out of her pocket and gave it me. "Come, make haste and take it, there's twenty thousand roubles sterling in it."

"Granny," I murmured, "such stakes . . ."

"As sure as I am alive, I'll win it back. . . . Stake."

We staked and lost.

"Stake, stake the whole eight!"

"You can't, Granny, four is the highest stake! . . ."

"Well, stake four!"

This time we won. Granny cheered up.

"You see, you see," she nudged me; "stake four again!" She staked—she lost; then we lost again and again.

"Granny, the whole twelve thousand is gone," I told her.

"I see it's all gone," she answered with the calm of fury, if I may so express it. "I see, my good friend, I see," she muttered, with a fixed, as it were, absent-minded stare. "Ech, as sure I am alive, stake another four thousand gulden!"

"But there's no money, Granny; there are some of our Russian five per cents. and some bills of exchange of some sort, but no money."

"And in the purse?"

"There's some small change, Granny."

"Are there any money-changers here? I was told one could change any of our notes," Granny inquired resolutely.

"Oh, as much as you like, but what you'll lose on the exchange . . . would horrify a Jew!"

"Nonsense! I'll win it all back. Take me! Call those blockheads!"

I wheeled away the chair; the porters appeared and we went out of the Casino.

"Make haste, make haste, make haste," Granny commanded. "Show us the way, Alexey Ivanovitch, and take us the nearest . . . Is it far?"

"Two steps, Granny."

But at the turning from the square into the avenue we were met by our whole party: the General, De Grieux, Mlle. Blanche and her mamma. Polina Alexandrovna was not with them, nor Mr. Astley either.

"Well! Don't stop us!" cried Granny. "Well, what do you want? I have no time to spare for you now!"

I walked behind; De Grieux ran up to me.

"She's lost all she gained this morning and twelve thousand gulden as well. We are going to change some five per cents.," I whispered to him quickly.

De Grieux stamped and ran to tell the General. We went on wheeling Granny.

"Stop, stop!" the General whispered to me frantically.

"You try stopping her," I whispered.

"Auntie!" said the General, approaching, "Auntie . . . we are just . . . we are just . . ." his voice quivered and failed him, "hiring a horse and driving into the country . . . a most exquisite view . . . the peak . . . We were coming to invite you."

"Oh, bother you and your peak." Granny waved him off irritably.

"There are trees there . . . we will have tea . . ." the General went on, utterly desperate.

"*Nous boirons du lait, sur l'herbe fraîche,*" added De Grieux, with ferocious fury.

Du lait, de l'herbe fraîche, that is the Paris bourgeois notion of the ideally idyllic; that is, as we all know, his conception of *nature et la vérité!*

"Oh, go on with you and your milk! Lap it up yourself; it gives me the bellyache. And why do you pester me?" cried Granny. "I tell you I've no time to waste."

"It's here, Granny," I said; "it's here!"

We had reached the house where the bank was. I went in to change the notes; Granny was left waiting at the entrance; De Grieux, the General and Blanche stood apart waiting, not knowing what to do. Granny looked wrathfully at them, and they walked away in the direction of the Casino.

They offered me such ruinous terms that I did not accept them, and went back to Granny for instructions.

"Ah, the brigands!" she cried, flinging up her hands. "Well, never mind! Change it," she cried resolutely; "stay, call the banker out to me!"

"One of the clerks, Granny, do you mean?"

"Yes, a clerk, it's all the same. Ach, the brigands!"

The clerk consented to come when he learned that it was an invalid and aged countess, unable to come in, who was asking for him. Granny spent a long time loudly and angrily reproaching him for swindling her, and haggled with him in a mixture of Russian, French and German, while I came to the rescue in translating. The grave clerk listened to us in silence and shook his head. He looked at Granny with an intent stare that was hardly respectful; at last he began smiling.

"Well, get along with you," cried Granny. "Choke yourself with the money! Change it with him, Alexey Ivanovitch; there's no time to waste, or we would go elsewhere. . . ."

"The clerk says that other banks give even less."

I don't remember the sums exactly, but the banker's charges were terrible. I received close upon twelve thousand florins in gold and notes, took the account and carried it to Granny.

"Well, well, well, it's no use counting it," she said, with a wave of her hand. "Make haste, make haste, make haste!

"I'll never stake again on that damned *zéro* nor on the red either," she pronounced, as she was wheeled up to the Casino.

This time I did my very utmost to impress upon her the necessity of staking smaller sums, trying to persuade her that with the change of luck she would always be able to increase her stake. But she was so impatient that, though she agreed at first, it was impossible to restrain her when the play had begun; as soon as she had won a stake of ten, of twenty friedrichs d'or—

"There, you see, there, you see," she would begin nudging me; "there, you see, we've won; if only we had staked four thousand instead of ten, we should have won four thousand, but as it is what's the good? It's all your doing, all your doing!"

And, vexed as I felt, watching her play, I made up my mind at last to keep quiet and to give no more advice.

Suddenly De Grieux skipped up.

The other two were close by; I noticed Mlle. Blanche standing on one side with her mother, exchanging amenities with the Prince. The General was obviously out of favour, almost banished. Blanche would not even look at him, though he was doing his utmost to cajole her! The poor General! He flushed and grew pale by turns, trembled and could not even follow Granny's play. Blanche and the Prince finally went away; the General ran after them.

"Madame, madame," De Grieux whispered in a honeyed voice to Granny, squeezing his way close up to her ear. "Madame, such stakes do not answer. . . . No, no, it's impossible . . ." he said, in broken Russian. "No!"

"How, then? Come, show me!" said Granny, turning to him.

De Grieux babbled something rapidly in French, began excitedly advising, said she must wait for a chance, began reckoning some numbers. . . . Granny did not understand a word. He kept turning to me, for me to translate; tapped the table with his fingers, pointed; finally took a pencil and was about to reckon something on paper. At last Granny lost patience.

"Come, get away, get away! You keep talking nonsense! 'Madame, madame,' he doesn't understand it himself; go away."

"*Mais, madame,*" De Grieux murmured, and he began once more showing and explaining.

"Well, stake once as he says," Granny said to me; "let us see: perhaps it really will answer."

All De Grieux wanted was to dissuade her from staking large sums; he suggested that she should stake on numbers, either individually or collectively. I staked as he directed, a friedrich d'or on each of the odd numbers in the first twelve and five friedrichs d'or respectively on the groups of numbers from twelve to eighteen and from eighteen to twenty-four, staking in all sixteen friedrich d'or.

The wheel turned.

"*Zéro!*" cried the croupier.

We had lost everything.

"You blockhead!" cried Granny, addressing De Grieux. "You scoundrelly Frenchman! So this is how he advises, the monster. Go away, go away! He knows nothing about it and comes fussing round!"

Fearfully offended, De Grieux shrugged his shoulders, looked contemptuously at Granny, and walked away. He felt ashamed of having interfered; he had been in too great a hurry.

An hour later, in spite of all our efforts, we had lost everything.

"Home," said Granny.

She did not utter a single word till we got into the avenue. In the avenue and approaching the hotel she began to break into exclamations—

"What a fool! What a silly fool! You're an old fool, you are!"

As soon as we got to her apartments—

"Tea!" cried Granny. "And pack up at once! We are going!"

"Where does your honour mean to go?" Marfa was beginning.

"What has it to do with you? Mind your own business! Potapitch, pack up everything: all the luggage. We are going back to Moscow. I have thrown away fifteen thousand roubles!"

"Fifteen thousand, madame! My God!" Potapitch cried, flinging up his hands with deep feeling, probably meaning to humour her.

"Come, come, you fool! He is beginning to whimper! Hold your tongue! Pack up! The bill, make haste, make haste!"

"The next train goes at half-past nine, Granny," I said, to check her furore.

"And what is it now?"

"Half-past seven."

"How annoying! Well, it doesn't matter! Alexey Ivanovitch, I haven't a farthing. Here are two more notes. Run there and change these for me too. Or I have nothing for the journey."

I set off. Returning to the hotel half an hour later, I found our whole party at Granny's. Learning that Granny was going off to Moscow, they seemed to be even more upset than by her losses. Even though her going might save her property, what was to become of the General? Who would pay De Grieux? Mlle. Blanche would, of course, decline to wait for Granny to die and would certainly now make up to the Prince or to somebody else. They were all standing before Granny, trying to console her and persuade her. Again Polina was not there. Granny was shouting at them furiously.

"Let me alone, you devils! What business is it of yours? Why does that goat's beard come forcing himself upon me?" she cried at De Grieux; "and you, my fine bird?" she cried, addressing Mlle. Blanche, "what are you after?"

"*Diantre!*" whispered Mlle. Blanche, with an angry flash of her eyes, but suddenly she burst out laughing and went out of the room.

"*Elle vivra cent ans!*" she called to the General, as she went out of the door.

"Ah, so you are reckoning on my death?" Granny yelled to the General. "Get away! Turn them all out, Alexey Ivanovitch! What business is it of yours? I've fooled away my own money, not yours!"

The General shrugged his shoulders, bowed and went out. De Grieux followed him.

"Call Praskovya," Granny told Marfa.

Five minutes later Marfa returned with Polina. All this time Polina had been sitting in her own room with the children, and I fancy had purposely made up her mind not to go out all day. Her face was serious, sad and anxious.

"Praskovya," began Granny, "is it true, as I learned by accident just now, that that fool, your stepfather, means to marry that silly feather-head of a Frenchwoman—an actress is she, or, something worse? Tell me, is it true?"

"I don't know anything about it for certain, Granny," answered Polina, "but from the words of Mlle. Blanche herself, who does not feel it necessary to conceal anything, I conclude . . ."

"Enough," Granny broke in vigorously, "I understand! I always reckoned that he was capable of it and I have always thought him a most foolish and feather-headed man. He thinks no end of himself, because he is a General (he was promoted from a Colonel on retiring), and he gives himself airs. I know, my good girl, how you kept sending telegram after telegram to Moscow, to ask if your old Granny would soon be laid out. They were on the look-out for my money; without money that nasty hussy, what's her name—De Cominges—wouldn't take him for her footman, especially with his false teeth. She has a lot of money herself, they say, lends at interest, has made a lot. I am not blaming you, Praskovya, it wasn't you who sent the telegrams; and I don't want to remember the past, either. I know you've got a bad temper—a wasp! You can sting to hurt; but I'm sorry for you because I was fond of your mother, Katerina. Well, you throw up everything here and come with me. You've nowhere to go, you know; and it's not fitting for you to be with them now. Stop!" cried Granny, as Polina was about to speak; "I've not finished. I ask nothing of you. As you know, I have in Moscow a palace; you can have a whole storey to yourself and not come and see me for weeks at a time if my temper does not suit you! Well, will you or not?"

"Let me ask you first: do you really mean to set off at once?"

"Do you suppose I'm joking, my good girl! I've said I'm going and I'm going. I've wasted fifteen thousand roubles to-day over your damned roulette. Five years ago I promised to rebuild a wooden church with stone on my estate near Moscow, and instead of that I've thrown away my money here. Now, my girl, I'm going home to build the church."

"And the waters, Granny? You came to drink the waters?"

"Bother you and the waters, too. Don't irritate me, Praskovya; are you doing it on purpose? Tell me, will you come or not?"

"I thank you very, very much," Polina began, with feeling, "for the home you offer me. You have guessed my position to some extent. I am so grateful to you that I shall perhaps come to you soon; but now there are reasons . . . important reasons . . . and I can't decide at once, on the spur of the moment. If you were staying only a fortnight . . ."

"You mean you won't?"

"I mean I can't. Besides, in any case I can't leave my brother and sister, as . . . as . . . as it may actually happen that they may be left abandoned, so . . . if you would take me with the children, Granny, I certainly would come, and, believe me, I would repay you for it!" she added warmly; "but without the children I can't come, Granny."

"Well, don't whimper." (Polina had no intention of whimpering—indeed, I had never seen her cry.) "Some place will be found for the chickens, my henhouse is big enough. Besides, it is time they were at school. Well, so you are not coming now! Well, Praskovya, mind! I wished for your good, but I know why you won't come! I know all about it, Praskovya. That Frenchman will bring you no good."

Polina flushed crimson. I positively shuddered. (Every one knows all about it. I am the only one to know nothing!)

"Come, come, don't frown. I am not going to say anything more. Only take care no harm comes of it, understand. You are a clever wench; I shall be sorry for you. Well, that's enough. I should not like to look on you as on the others! Go along, good-bye!"

"I'll come to see you off," said Polina.

"There's no need, don't you interfere; I am sick of you all."

Polina was kissing Granny's hand, but the latter pulled it away and kissed her on the cheek.

As she passed me, Polina looked at me quickly and immediately turned away her eyes.

"Well, good-bye to you, too, Alexey Ivanovitch, there's only an hour before the train starts, and I think you must be tired out with me. Here, take these fifty pieces of gold."

"I thank you very much, Granny; I'm ashamed . . ."

"Come, come!" cried Granny, but so vigorously and angrily that I dared say no more and took it.

"When you are running about Moscow without a job come to me: I will give you some introductions. Now, get along with you!"

I went to my room and lay down on my bed. I lay there for half an hour on my back, with my hands clasped behind my head. The catastrophe had come at last, I had something to think about. I made up my mind to talk earnestly to Polina. The nasty Frenchman! So it was true then! But what could there be at the bottom of it? Polina and De Grieux! Heavens! what a pair!

It was all simply incredible. I suddenly jumped up, beside myself, to look for Mr. Astley, and at all costs to make him speak out. No doubt in this matter, too, he knew more than I did. Mr. Astley? He was another riddle to me!

But suddenly there was a tap at my door. I looked up. It was Potapitch.

"Alexey Ivanovitch, you are wanted to come to my lady!"

"What's the matter? Is she setting off? The train does not start for twenty minutes."

"She's uneasy, she can't sit still. 'Make haste, make haste!' she says, meaning to fetch you, sir. For Christ's sake, don't delay."

I ran downstairs at once. Granny was being wheeled out into the passage, her pocket-book was in her hand.

"Alexey Ivanovitch, go on ahead; we're coming."

"Where, Granny?"

"As sure as I'm alive, I'll win it back. Come, march, don't ask questions! Does the play go on there till midnight?"

I was thunderstruck. I thought a moment, but at once made up my mind.

"Do as you please, Antonida Vassilyevna, I'm not coming."

"What's that for? What now? Have you all eaten too many pancakes, or what?"

"Do as you please, I should blame myself for it afterwards; I won't. I won't take part in it or look on it; spare me, Antonida Vassilyevna. Here are your fifty friedrichs d'or back; good-bye!" And, laying the fifty friedrichs d'or on the little table near which Granny's chair was standing, I bowed and went out.

"What nonsense!" Granny shouted after me. "Don't come if you don't want to, I can find the way by myself! Potapitch, come with me! Come, lift me up, carry me!"

I did not find Mr. Astley and returned home. It was late, after midnight, when I learned from Potapitch how Granny's day ended. She lost all that I had changed for her that evening—that is, in Russian money, another ten thousand roubles. The little Pole, to whom she had given two friedrichs d'or the day before, had attached himself to her and had directed her play the whole time. At first, before the Pole came, she had made Potapitch put down the stakes, but soon she dismissed him; it was at that moment the Pole turned up. As ill-luck would have it, he understood Russian and babbled away in a mixture of three

languages, so that they understood each other after a
fashion. Granny abused him mercilessly the whole time;
and though he incessantly "laid himself at his lady's feet,"
"yet he couldn't be compared with you, Alexey Ivanovitch,"
said Potapitch. "She treated you *like a gentleman,* while
the other—I saw it with my own eyes, God strike me dead
—stole her money off the table. She caught him at it herself twice. She did give it to him with all sorts of names,
sir, even pulled his hair once, upon my word she did, so
that folks were laughing round about. She's lost everything, sir, everything, all you changed for her; we brought
her back here—she only asked for a drink of water,
crossed herself and went to bed. She's worn out, to be sure;
she fell asleep at once. God send her heavenly dreams.
Och! these foreign parts!" Potapitch wound up. "I said it
would lead to no good. If only we could soon be back in
Moscow! We'd everything we wanted at home in Moscow:
a garden, flowers such as you don't have here, fragrance,
the apples are swelling, plenty of room everywhere. No,
we had to come abroad. Oh, oh, oh . . ."

13

Now almost a whole month has passed since I touched
these notes of mine, which were begun under the influence
of confused but intense impressions. The catastrophe
which I felt to be approaching has actually come, but in
a form a hundred times more violent and startling than I
had expected. It has all been something strange, grotesque
and even tragic—at least for me. Several things have happened to me that were almost miraculous; that is, at least,
how I look upon them to this day—though from another
point of view, particularly in the whirl of events in which
I was involved at that time, they were only somewhat out
of the common. But what is most marvellous to me is my
own attitude to all these events. To this day I cannot understand myself, and it has all floated by like a dream—
even my passion—it was violent and sincere, but . . . what
has become of it now? It is true that sometimes the
thought flashes through my brain: "Wasn't I out of my

mind then, and wasn't I all that time somewhere in a madhouse and perhaps I'm there now, so that was all my fancy and still is my fancy . . ." I put my notes together and read them over. (Who knows—perhaps to convince myself that I did not write them in a madhouse.) Now I am entirely alone. Autumn is coming on and the leaves are turning yellow. I'm still in this dismal little town (oh! how dismal the little German towns are!), and instead of considering what to do next, I go on living under the influence of the sensations I have just passed through, under the influence of memories still fresh, under the influence of the whirl of events which caught me up and flung me aside again. At times I fancy that I am still caught up in that whirlwind, that that storm is still raging, carrying me along with it, and again I lose sight of all order and measure and I whirl round and round again. . . .

However, I may, perhaps, leave off whirling and settle down in a way if, so far as I can, I put clearly before my mind all the incidents of the past month. I feel drawn to my pen again. Besides, I have sometimes nothing at all to do in the evenings. I am so hard up for something to do that, odd as it seems, I even take from the scurvy lending library here the novels of Paul de Kock (in a German translation), though I can't endure them; yet I read them and wonder at myself. It is as though I were afraid of breaking the spell of the recent past by a serious book or any serious occupation. It is as though that grotesque dream, with all the impressions left by it, was so precious to me that I am afraid to let anything new touch upon it for fear it should all vanish in smoke. Is it all so precious to me? Yes, of course it is precious. Perhaps I shall remember it for forty years. . . .

And so I take up my writing again. I can give a brief account of it to some extent now: the impressions are not at all the same.

In the first place, to finish with Granny. The following day she lost everything. It was what was bound to happen. When once any one is started upon that road, it is like a man in a sledge flying down a snow mountain more and more swiftly. She played all day till eight o'clock in the evening; I was not present and only know what happened from what I was told.

Potapitch was in attendance on her at the Casino all day. Several Poles in succession guided Granny's operations in the course of the day. She began by dismissing the Pole whose hair she had pulled the day before and taking on another, but he turned out almost worse. After dismissing the second, and accepting again the first, who had never left her side, but had been squeezing himself in behind her chair and continually poking his head in during the whole period of his disgrace, she sank at last into complete despair. The second Pole also refused to move away; one stationed himself on her right and the other on her left. They were abusing one another the whole time and quarrelling over the stakes and the game, calling each other *"laidak"* and other Polish civilities, making it up again, putting down money recklessly and playing at random. When they quarrelled they put the money down regardless of each other—one, for instance, on the red and the other on the black. It ended in their completely bewildering and overwhelming Granny, so that at last, almost in tears, she appealed to the old croupier, begging him to protect her and to send them away. They were, in fact, immediately turned out in spite of their outcries and protests; they both shouted out at once and tried to prove that Granny owed them something, that she had deceived them about something and had treated them basely and dishonourably. The luckless Potapitch told me all this the same evening almost with tears, and complained that they stuffed their pockets with money, that he himself had seen them shamelessly steal and continually thrust the money in their pockets. One, for instance, would beg five friedrichs d'or for his trouble and begin putting them down on the spot side by side with Granny's stakes. Granny won, but the man shouted that his stake was the winning one and that Granny's had lost. When they were dismissed Potapitch came forward and said that their pockets were full of gold. Granny at once bade the croupier to look into it and, in spite of the outcries of the Poles (they cackled like two cocks caught in the hand), the police came forward and their pockets were immediately emptied for Granny's benefit. Granny enjoyed unmistakable prestige among the croupiers and the whole staff of the Casino all that day, until she had lost everything. By degrees her fame spread all over the town. All the visitors at the watering-place, of all nations, small and great, streamed to look on at *"une vieille comtesse russe tombée en enfance,"* who had already lost "some millions."

But Granny gained very, very little by being rescued from the two Poles. They were at once replaced by a third, who spoke perfectly pure Russian and was dressed like a gentleman, though he did look like a flunkey with a huge moustache and a sense of his own importance. He, too "laid himself at his lady's feet and kissed them," but behaved haughtily to those about him, was despotic over the play; in fact, immediately behaved like Granny's master rather than her servant. Every minute, at every turn in the game, he turned to her and swore with awful oaths that he was himself a *"pan* of good position," and that he wouldn't take a kopeck of Granny's money. He repeated this oath so many times that Granny was completely intimidated. But as this *pan* certainly seemed at first to improve her luck, Granny was not willing to abandon him on her own account. An hour later the two Poles who had been turned out of the Casino turned up behind Granny's chair again, and again proffered their services if only to run errands for her. Potapitch swore that the *"pan* of good position" winked at them and even put something in their hands. As Granny had no dinner and could not leave her chair, one of the Poles certainly was of use: he ran off once to the dining-room of the Casino and brought her a cup of broth and afterwards some tea. They both ran about, however. But towards the end of the day, when it became evident to everyone that she would stake her last banknote, there were behind her chair as many as six Poles who had never been seen or heard of before. When Granny was playing her last coin, they not only ceased to obey her, but took no notice of her whatever, squeezed their way up to the table in front of her, snatched the money themselves, put down the stakes and made their own play, shouted and quarrelled, talked to the *"pan* of good position" as to one of themselves, while the *"pan* of good position" himself seemed almost oblivious of Granny's existence. Even when Granny, after losing everything, was returning after eight o'clock to the hotel, three or four Poles ran at the side of her bath-chair, still unable to bring themselves to leave her; they kept shouting at the top of their voices, declaring in a hurried gabble that Granny had cheated them in some way and must give them something. They followed her in this way right up to the hotel, from which they were at last driven away with blows.

By Potapitch's reckoning Granny had lost in all ninety thousand roubles that day, apart from what she had lost the day before. All her notes, her exchequer bonds, all the shares she had with her, she had changed, one after another. I marvelled how she could have stood those seven or eight hours sitting there in her chair and scarcely leaving the table, but Potapitch told me that three or four times she had begun winning considerably; and, carried on by fresh hope, she could not tear herself away. But gamblers know how a man can sit for almost twenty-four hours at cards, without looking to right or to left.

Meanwhile, very critical events were taking place all that day at the hotel. In the morning, before eleven o'clock, when Granny was still at home, our people—that is, the General and De Grieux—made up their minds to take the final step. Learning that Granny had given up all idea of setting off, but was going back to the Casino, they went in full conclave (all but Polina) to talk things over with her finally and even *openly*. The General, trembling and with a sinking heart in view of the awful possibilities for himself, overdid it. After spending half an hour in prayers and in entreaties and making a clean breast of everything— that is, of all his debts and even his passion for Mlle. Blanche (he quite lost his head), the General suddenly adopted a menacing tone and even began shouting and stamping at Granny; cried that she was disgracing their name, had become a scandal to the whole town, and finally . . . finally: "You are shaming the Russian name," cried the General, and he told her that the police would be called in! Granny finally drove him from her with a stick (an actual stick). The General and De Grieux consulted once or twice that morning, and the question that agitated them was whether it were not possible in some way to bring in the police, on the plea that an unfortunate but venerable old lady, sinking into her dotage, was gambling away her whole fortune, and so on; whether, in fact, it would be possible to put her under any sort of supervision or restraint. . . . But De Grieux only shrugged his shoulders and laughed in the General's face, as the latter pranced up and down his study talking excitedly. Finally, De Grieux went off with a wave of his hand. In the evening we learned that he had left the hotel altogether, after having been in very earnest and mysterious confabulation with Mlle. Blanche. As for Mlle. Blanche, she had taken her measures early in the morning: she threw the General over completely and would not even admit him to her presence. When the General ran to the Casino in search of her and met her arm-in-arm with the Prince, neither she nor Madame de Cominges deigned to notice him. The Prince did not bow to him either. Mlle. Blanche spent that whole day hard at work upon the Prince, trying to force from him a definite declaration. But alas! she was cruelly deceived in her reckoning! This little catastrophe took place in the evening. It suddenly came out that he was as poor as a church mouse, and, what is more, was himself reckoning on borrowing from her on an I O U to try his luck at roulette. Blanche turned him out indignantly and locked herself up in her room.

On the morning of that day I went to Mr. Astley—or, to be more exact, I went in search of Mr. Astley, but could find him nowhere. He was not at home, or in the park, or in the Casino. He was not dining at his hotel that day. It was past four o'clock when I suddenly saw him walking from the railway station towards the Hôtel d'Angleterre. He was in a hurry and was very much preoccupied, though it was hard to trace any anxiety or any perturbation whatever in his face. He held out his hand to me cordially, with his habitual exclamation "Ah!" but without stopping walked on with rather a rapid step. I attached myself to him, but he managed to answer me in such a way that I did not succeed in even asking him about anything. Moreover, I felt, for some reason, ashamed to begin speaking of Polina; he did not ask a word about her. I told him about Granny. He listened attentively and seriously and shrugged his shoulders.

"She will gamble away everything," I observed.

"Oh, yes," he answered; "she went in to play just as I was going away, and afterwards I learnt for a fact that she had lost everything. If there were time I would look in at the Casino, for it is curious."

"Where have you been?" I cried, wondering that I had not asked before.

"I've been in Frankfurt."

"On business?"

"Yes, on business."

Well, what more was there for me to ask? I did, how-ever, continue walking beside him, but he suddenly turned into the Hôtel des Quatre Saisons, nodded to me and van-ished. As I walked home I gradually realized that if I had talked to him for a couple of hours I should have learnt absolutely nothing, because . . . I had nothing to ask him! Yes, that was so, of course! I could not possibly formulate my question.

All that day Polina spent walking with the children and their nurse in the park, or sitting at home. She had for a long time past avoided the General, and scarcely spoke to him about anything—about anything serious, at any rate. I had noticed that for a long time past. But knowing what a position the General was in to-day, I imagined that he could hardly pass her over—that is, there could not but be an important conversation about family affairs between them. When, however, I returned to the hotel, after my conversation with Mr. Astley, I met Polina with the chil-dren. There was an expression of the most unruffled calm on her face, as though she alone had remained untouched by the family tempest. She nodded in response to my bow. I returned home feeling quite malignant.

I had, of course, avoided seeing her and had seen noth-ing of her since the incident with the Burmerhelms. There was some affectation and pose in this; but as time went on, I felt more and more genuinely indignant. Even if she did not care for me in the least, she should not, I thought, have trampled on my feelings like that and have received my declarations so contemptuously. She knew that I really loved her; she admitted me, she allowed me to speak like that! It is true that it had begun rather strangely. Some time before, long ago, in fact, two months before, I began to notice that she wanted to make me her friend, her con-fidant, and indeed was in a way testing me. But somehow this did not come off then; instead of that there remained the strange relations that existed between us; that is how it was I began to speak to her like that. But if my love re-pelled her, why did she not directly forbid me to speak of it?

She did not forbid me; indeed she sometimes provoked me to talk of it and . . . and, of course, she did this for fun. I know for certain. I noticed it unmistakably—it was agreeable to her to listen and to work me up to a state of misery, to wound me by some display of the utmost contempt and disregard. And, of course, she knew that I could not exist without her. It was three days since the affair with the Baron and I could not endure our separation any longer. When I met her just now near the Casino, my heart throbbed so that I turned pale. But she could not get on without me, either! She needed me and—surely, surely not as a buffoon, a clown?

She had a secret—that was clear! Her conversation with Granny had stabbed my heart. Why, I had urged her a thousand times to be open with me, and she knew that I was ready to give my life for her. But she always put me off, almost with contempt, or had asked of me, instead of the sacrifice of my life, such pranks as the one with the Baron!

Was not that enough to make one indignant? Could that Frenchman be all the world to her? And Mr. Astley? But at that point the position became utterly incomprehensible—and meanwhile, my God! what agonies I went through!

On getting home, in an access of fury I snatched up my pen and scribbled the following letter to her—

"Polina Alexandrovna, I see clearly that the *dénouement* is at hand which will affect you also. I repeat for the last time: do you need my life or not? If I can be of use in *any way whatever*, dispose of me as you think fit, and I will meanwhile remain in my room and not go out at all. If you need me, write to me or send for me."

I sealed up this note and sent if off by the corridor attendant, instructing him to give it into her hands. I expected no answer, but three minutes later the attendant returned with the message that "she sent her greetings."

It was past six when I was summoned to the General.

He was in his study, dressed as though he were on the point of going out. His hat and coat were lying on the sofa. It seemed to me as I went in that he was standing in the middle of the room with his legs wide apart and his head hanging, talking aloud to himself. But as soon as he saw me, he rushed at me almost crying out, so that I involuntarily stepped back and was almost running away, but he seized me by both hands and drew me to the sofa; sat

down on the sofa himself, made me sit down in an arm-
chair just opposite himself, and, keeping tight hold of my
hand, with trembling lips and with tears suddenly glistening on his eyelashes, began speaking in an imploring voice.

"Alexey Ivanovitch, save, save me, spare me."

It was a long while before I could understand. He kept
talking and talking and talking, continually repeating,
"Spare me, spare me!" At last I guessed that he expected
something in the way of advice from me; or, rather, abandoned by all in his misery and anxiety, he had thought of
me and had sent for me, simply to talk and talk and talk
to me.

He was mad, or at any rate utterly distraught. He
clasped his hands and was on the point of dropping on his
knees before me to implore me (what do you suppose?) to
go at once to Mlle. Blanche and to beseech, to urge her to
return to him and marry him.

"Upon my word, General," I cried; "why, Mlle. Blanche
is perhaps scarcely aware of my existence. What can I
do?"

But it was vain to protest; he didn't understand what
was said to him. He fell to talking about Granny, too, but
with terrible incoherence; he was still harping on the idea
of sending for the police.

"Among us, among us," he began, suddenly boiling over
with indignation; "among us, in a well-ordered state, in
fact, where there is a Government in control of things,
such old women would have been put under guardianship
at once! Yes, my dear sir, yes," he went on, suddenly dropping into a scolding tone, jumping up from his chair and
pacing about the room; "you may not be aware of the fact,
honoured sir," he said, addressing some imaginary "honoured sir" in the corner, "so let me tell you . . . yes . . .
among us such old women are kept in order, kept in order;
yes, indeed. . . . Oh, damn it all!"

And he flung himself on the sofa again, and a minute
later, almost sobbing, gasping for breath, hastened to tell
me that Mlle. Blanche would not marry him because
Granny had come instead of the telegram, and that now it
was clear he would not come into the inheritance. He
imagined that I knew nothing of this till then. I began to
speak of De Grieux; he waved his hand: "He has gone
away! Everything of mine he has in pawn; I'm stripped of

everything! That money you brought . . . that money—I don't know how much there is, I think seven hundred francs are left and that's enough, that's all and what's to come—I don't know, I don't know! . . .".

"How will you pay your hotel bill?" I cried in alarm; "and . . . afterwards what will you do?"

He looked at me pensively, but I fancy he did not understand and perhaps did not hear what I said. I tried to speak of Polina Alexandrovna, of the children; he hurriedly answered: "Yes! yes!" but at once fell to talking of the Prince again, saying that Blanche would go away with him now and "then . . . then, what am I to do, Alexey Ivanovitch?" he asked, addressing me suddenly. "I vow, by God! I don't know what to do; tell me, isn't this ingratitude? Isn't this ingratitude?"

Finally he dissolved into floods of tears.

There was no doing anything with such a man; it would be dangerous to leave him alone, too—something might happen to him. I got rid of him somehow, but let nurse know she must look in upon him pretty frequently, and also spoke to the corridor attendant, a very sensible fellow; he, too, promised me to keep an eye on the General.

I had hardly left the General when Potapitch came to summon me to Granny. It was eight o'clock and she had only just come back from the Casino after losing everything. I went to her; the old lady was sitting in an armchair, utterly worn out and evidently ill. Marfa was giving her a cup of tea and almost forcing her to drink it. And Granny's tone and voice were utterly changed.

"Good-day, Alexey Ivanovitch, my good sir," she said, bending her head slowly, and with dignity; "excuse me for troubling you once more, you must excuse an old woman. I have left everything behind there, my friend, nearly a hundred thousand roubles. You did well not to come with me yesterday. Now I have no money, not a farthing. I don't want to delay a moment, at half-past nine I'm setting off. I have sent to that Englishman of yours—what's his name, Astley—I want to ask him to lend me three thousand francs for a week. So you must persuade him not to take it amiss and refuse. I am still fairly well off, my friend. I have still three villages and two houses. And there is still some money. I didn't bring it all with me. I tell you this that he may not feel any doubts . . . Ah, here he is! One can see he is a nice man."

Mr. Astley had hastened to come at Granny's first summons. With no hesitation and without wasting words he promptly counted out three thousand francs for an I O U which Granny signed. When this business was settled he made haste to take his leave and go away.

"And now you can go, too, Alexey Ivanovitch. I have only a little over an hour left. I want to lie down: my bones ache. Don't be hard on an old fool like me. Henceforward I won't blame young people for being flighty, and it would be a sin for me now to blame that luckless fellow, your General, either. I won't give him any money, though, as he wants me to, because—to my thinking he is utterly silly; only, old fool as I am, I've no more sense than he. Verily God seeks out and punishes pride, even in old age. Well, good-bye. Marfa, lift me up!"

I wanted to see Granny off, however. What's more, I was in a state of suspense; I kept expecting that in another minute something would happen. I could not sit quietly in my room. I went out into the corridor, even for a moment went out for a saunter along the avenue. My letter to her had been clear and decisive and the present catastrophe was, of course, a final one. I heard in the hotel that De Grieux had left. If she rejected me as a friend, perhaps she would not reject me as a servant. I was necessary to her, I was of use to her, if only to run her errands, it was bound to be so!

When the train was due to start I ran to the station and saw Granny into the train. Her whole party were together, in a special reserved compartment. "Thank you, my good friend, for your disinterested sympathy," she said, at parting from me; "and tell Praskovya, in reference to what we were discussing yesterday, I shall expect her."

I went home. Passing the General's rooms I met the old nurse and inquired after the General. "Oh, he's all right, sir," she answered me dolefully. I went in, however, but stood still in positive amazement. Mlle. Blanche and the General were both laughing heartily. Madame de Cominges was sitting on the sofa close by. The General was evidently beside himself with delight. He was murmuring incoherently and going off into prolonged fits of nervous laughter, during which his face was puckered with innu-

merable wrinkles and his eyes disappeared from sight.
Afterwards I learnt from Blanche herself that, having dismissed the Prince and having heard how the General was
weeping, she had taken it into her head to comfort him by
going to see him for a minute. But the poor General did
not know that at that time his fate was decided, and that
Mlle. Blanche had already packed to set off for Paris by
the first train next morning.

Stopping in the doorway of the General's study, I
changed my mind and went away unnoticed. Going up to
my own room and opening the door, I suddenly noticed a
figure in the half-darkness sitting on a chair in the corner
by the window. She did not get up when I went in. I
went up quickly, looked, and—my heart stood still: it was
Polina.

14

I positively cried out aloud.

"What is it? What is it?" she asked me strangely. She
was pale and looked gloomy.

"You ask what is it? You? Here in my room!"

"If I come, then I come *altogether*. That's my way. You'll
see that directly; light the candle."

I lighted a candle. She got up, went up to the table, and
put before me an open letter.

"Read it," she ordered me.

"It's—it's De Grieux's handwriting," I cried, taking the
letter. My hands trembled and the lines danced before my
eyes. I have forgotten the exact wording of the letter, but
here is the main drift of it, if not the actual words:

"Mademoiselle," wrote De Grieux, "an unfortunate circumstance compels me to go away at once. You have, no
doubt, observed that I have purposely avoided a final explanation with you until such time as the whole position
might be cleared up. The arrival of your old relation (*de la
vieille dame*) and her absurd behaviour have put an end to
my doubts. The unsettled state of my own affairs forbids

me to cherish further the sweet hopes which I permitted
myself to indulge for some time. I regret the past, but I
trust that you will not detect in my behaviour anything unworthy of a gentleman and an honest man (*gentilhomme
et honnête homme*). Having lost almost all my money in
loans to your stepfather, I find myself compelled to make
the utmost use of what is left to me; I have already sent
word to my friend in Petersburg to arrange at once for the
sale of the estates he has mortgaged to me; knowing, however, that your frivolous stepfather has squandered your
private fortune I have determined to forgive him fifty
thousand francs, and I am returning him part of my
claims on his property equivalent to that sum, so that you
are now put in a position to regain all that you have lost by
demanding the property from him by legal process. I hope,
Mademoiselle, that in the present position of affairs my
action will be very advantageous to you. I hope, too, that
by this action I am fully performing the duty of a man and
a gentleman. Rest assured that your memory is imprinted
upon my heart for ever."

"Well, that's all clear," I said, turning to Polina; "surely
you could have expected nothing else," I added, with indignation.

"I expected nothing," she answered, with apparent composure, though there was a tremor in her voice. "I had
made up my mind long ago; I read his mind and knew
what he was thinking. He thought that I was trying—that
I should insist . . ." (She broke off without finishing her
sentence, bit her lips and was silent.) "I purposely doubled
my scorn towards him," she began again. "I waited to see
what was coming from him. If a telegram had come telling of the inheritance I'd have flung him the money borrowed from that idiot, my stepfather, and would have sent
him about his business. He has been hateful to me for
ages and ages. Oh! he was not the same man! a thousand
times over, I tell you, he was different! but now, now . . .
Oh, with what happiness I could fling that fifty thousand
in his nasty face and spit and stamp . . ."

"But the security, the I O U for that fifty thousand, is in
the General's hands. Take it and return it to De Grieux."

"Oh, that's not the same thing, that's not the same
thing . . ."

"Yes, that's true, it's not the same thing. Besides, what is the General capable of now? And Granny!" I cried suddenly.

Polina looked at me, as it were absent-mindedly and impatiently.

"Why Granny?" asked Polina, with vexation. "I can't go to her . . . And I don't want to ask any one's pardon," she added irritably.

"What's to be done!" I cried, "and how, oh, how could you love De Grieux! Oh, the scoundrel, the scoundrel! If you like I will kill him in a duel! Where is he now?"

"He's at Frankfurt, and will be there three days."

"One word from you and I'll set off to-morrow by the first train," I said, with stupid enthusiasm.

She laughed.

"Why, he'll say, maybe: 'Give me back the fifty thousand francs first.' Besides, what should you fight him for? . . . What nonsense it is!"

"But where, where is one to get that fifty thousand francs?" I repeated, grinding my teeth as though it had been possible to pick them up from the floor. "I say—Mr. Astley," I suggested, turning to her with a strange idea dawning upon me. Her eyes flashed.

"What, do you mean to say *you yourself* want me to turn from you to that Englishman!" she said, looking in my face with a searching glance and smiling bitterly. For the first time in her life she addressed me in the second person singular.

I believe she was giddy with emotion at the moment, and all at once she sat down on the sofa as though she were exhausted.

It was as though I had been struck by a flash of lightning. I stood up and could not believe my eyes, could not believe my ears! Why, then she loved me! She had come to me and not to Mr. Astley!

She, she, a young girl, had come to my room in a hotel, so she had utterly compromised herself by her own act, and I, I was standing before her and still did not understand.

One wild idea flashed through my mind.

"Polina, give me only one hour. Stay here only one hour and . . . I'll come back. That's . . . that's essential! You shall see! Be here, be here!"

And I ran out of the room, not responding to her amazed and questioning look; she called something after me but I did not turn back.

Sometimes the wildest idea, the most apparently impossible thought, takes possession of one's mind so strongly that one accepts it at last as something substantial . . . more than that, if the idea is associated with a strong passionate desire, then sometimes one will accept it at last as something fated, inevitable, predestined—as something bound to be, and bound to happen. Perhaps there is something else in it, some combination of presentiments, some extraordinary effort of will, self-poisoning by one's own fancy—or something else—I don't know what, but on that evening (which I shall never in my life forget) something marvellous happened to me. Though it is quite justified by the laws of arithmetic, nevertheless it is a marvel to me to this day. And why, why had that conviction so long before taken such firm and deep root in my mind? I had certainly thought about it—I repeat—not as a chance among others which might or might not come to pass, but as something which was absolutely bound to happen!

It was a quarter past ten. I went into the Casino with a confident expectation and at the same time with an excitement I had never experienced before. There were still a good many people in the gambling hall, though not half as many as in the morning.

Between ten and eleven there are still to be found in the gambling halls the genuine desperate gamblers for whom nothing exists at a spa but roulette, who have come for that alone, who scarcely notice what is going on around them and take no interest in anything during the whole season, but play from morning till night and would be ready perhaps to play all night till dawn, too, if it were possible. And they always disperse with annoyance when at twelve o'clock the roulette hall is closed. And when the senior croupier announces, just before midnight. "*Les trois derniers coups, messieurs*," they are ready to stake on those last three strokes all they have in their pockets—and do, in fact, lose most at that time. I went up to the very table where Granny had sat that day. It was not crowded, and so I soon took my place at the table standing. Exactly before me was the word *Passe* scrawled on the green cloth.

Passe is the series of numbers from nineteen inclusive to thirty-six.

The first series of numbers from one to eighteen inclusive is called *manque;* but what was that to me? I was not calculating, I had not even heard what had been the winning number last, and I did not ask about it when I began to play—as every player of any prudence would do. I pulled out all my twenty friedrichs d'or and staked them on *Passe,* the word which lay before me.

"*Vingt-deux,*" cried the croupier.

I had won and again staked all: including my winnings.

"*Trente-et-un,*" cried the croupier.

I had won again. I had in all eighty friedrichs d'or. I staked the whole of that sum on the twelve middle numbers (my winnings would be three to one, but the chances were two to one against me). The wheel rotated and stopped at twenty-four. I was passed three rolls each of fifty friedrichs d'or in paper and ten gold coins; I had now two hundred friedrichs d'or.

I was as though in delirium and I moved the whole heap of gold to red—and suddenly thought better of it. And for the only time that whole evening, all the time I was playing, I felt chilled with terror and a shudder made my arms and legs tremble, I felt with horror and instantly realized what losing would mean for me now! My whole life was at stake.

"*Rouge,*" cried the croupier, and I drew a breath; fiery pins and needles were tingling all over my body. I was paid in banknotes. It came to four thousand florins and eighty friedrichs d'or (I could still keep count at that stage).

Then, I remember, I staked two thousand florins on the twelve middle numbers, and lost: I staked my gold, the eighty friedrichs d'or, and lost. I was seized with fury: I snatched up the two hundred florins I had left and staked them on the first twelve numbers—haphazard, at random, without thinking! There was, however, an instant of suspense, like, perhaps, the feeling experienced by Madame Blanchard when she flew from a balloon in Paris to the earth.

"*Quatre!*" cried the croupier.

Now with my stake I had six thousand florins. I looked triumphant already. I was afraid of nothing—nothing, and staked four thousand florins on black. Nine people followed my example and staked on black. The croupiers exchanged glances and said something to one another. People were talking all round in suspense.

Black won. I don't remember my winnings after, nor what I staked on. I only remember as though in a dream that I won, I believe, sixteen thousand florins; suddenly three unlucky turns took twelve thousand from it; then I staked the last four thousand on *Passe* (but I scarcely felt anything as I did so; I simply waited in a mechanical, senseless way)—and again I won; then I won four times running. I only remember that I gathered up money in thousands; I remember, too, that the middle twelve won most often and I kept to it. It turned up with a sort of regularity, certainly three or four times in succession, then it did not turn up twice running and then it followed three or four times in succession. Such astonishing regularity is sometimes met with in streaks, and that is what throws inveterate gamblers who calculate with a pencil in their hands out of their reckoning. And what horrible ironies of fate happen sometimes in such cases!

I believe not more than half an hour had passed since I came into the room, when suddenly the croupier informed me that I had won thirty thousand florins, and as the bank did not meet claims for a larger sum at one time the roulette would be closed till next morning. I snatched up all my gold, dropped it into my pockets, snatched up all my notes, and at once went into the other room where there was another roulette table; the whole crowd streamed after me; there at once a place was cleared for me and I fell to staking again haphazard without reckoning. I don't understand what saved me!

At times, however, a glimmer of prudence began to dawn upon my mind. I clung to certain numbers and combinations, but soon abandoned them and staked almost unconsciously. I must have been very absent-minded; I remember the croupiers several times corrected me. I made several gross mistakes. My temples were soaked with sweat and my hands were shaking. The Poles ran up, too, with offers of their services, but I listened to no one. My luck was unbroken! Suddenly there were sounds of loud talk and laughter, and every one cried "Bravo, bravo!" some even clapped their hands. Here, too, I collected three hundred thousand florins, and the bank closed till next day.

"Go away, go away," a voice whispered on my right.

It was a Frankfurt Jew; he was standing beside me all the time, and I believe sometimes helped me in my play.

"For goodness' sake go," another voice whispered in my left ear.

I took a hurried glance. It was a lady about thirty, very soberly and quietly dressed, with a tired, pale, sickly face which yet bore traces of having once been beautiful. At that moment I was stuffing my pockets with the notes, which I crumpled up anyhow, and gathering up the gold that lay on the table. Snatching up the last roll of notes, I succeeded in putting it into the pale lady's hands quite without attracting notice; I had an intense desire to do so at the time, and I remember her pale slim fingers pressed my hand warmly in token of gratitude. All that took place in one instant.

Having collected quickly all my winnings I went quickly to the *trente et quarante*.

Trente et quarante is frequented by the aristocratic public. Unlike roulette, it is a game of cards. Here the bank will pay up to a hundred thousand thalers at once. The largest stake is here also four thousand florins. I knew nothing of the game, and scarcely knew how to bet on it, except the red and the black upon which one can bet in this game too. And I stuck to red and black. The whole Casino crowded round. I don't remember whether I once thought of Polina all this time. I was experiencing an overwhelming enjoyment in scooping up and taking away the notes which grew up in a heap before me.

It seemed as though fate were urging me on. This time, as luck would have it, a circumstance occurred which, however, is fairly frequent in the game. Chance favours red, for instance, ten or even fifteen times in succession. I had heard two days before that in the previous week red had turned up twenty-two times in succession; it was something which had never been remembered in roulette, and it was talked of with amazement. Every one, of course, abandoned red at once, and after the tenth time, for instance, scarcely any one dared to stake on it. But none of the experienced players staked on black either. The experienced gambler knows what is meant by this "freak of chance." It would mean that after red had won sixteen

times, at the seventeenth time the luck would infallibly
fall on black. Novices at play rush to this conclusion in
crowds, double and treble their stakes, and lose terribly.

But, noticing that red had turned up seven times running, by strange perversity I staked on it. I am convinced
that vanity was half responsible for it; I wanted to impress
the spectators by taking a mad risk, and—oh, the strange
sensation—I remember distinctly that, quite apart from
the promptings of vanity, I was possessed by an intense
craving for risk. Perhaps passing through so many sensations my soul was not satisfied but only irritated by them
and craved still more sensation—and stronger and
stronger ones—till utterly exhausted. And, truly I am not
lying, if the regulations had allowed me to stake fifty thousand florins at once, I should certainly have staked them.
People around shouted that it was madness—that red had
won fourteen times already!

"Monsieur a gagné déjá cent mille florins," I heard a
voice say near me.

I suddenly came to myself. What? I had won during
that evening a hundred thousand florins! And what more
did I want? I fell on my banknotes, crumpled them up in
my pockets without counting them, scooped up all my
gold, all my rolls of notes, and ran out of the Casino.
Every one was laughing as I went through the room, looking at my bulging pockets and at the way I staggered
under the weight of gold. I think it weighed over twenty
pounds. Several hands were held out to me; I gave it away
in handfuls as I snatched it up. Two Jews stopped me at
the outer door.

"You are bold—you are very bold," they said to me, "but
be sure to go away to-morrow as soon as possible, or else
you will lose it all—you will lose it all. . . ."

I didn't listen to them. The avenue was so dark that I
could not see my hand before my face. It was half a mile
to the hotel. I had never been afraid of thieves or robbers
even as a small boy; I did not think of them now either. I
don't remember what I thought of on the road; I had no
thoughts. I was only aware of an immense enjoyment—
success, victory, power—I don't know how to express it.
Polina's image hovered before my mind too; I remembered
her and was conscious I was going to her; I should be with
her in a moment, should be telling her and showing her

. . . But I hardly remembered what she had said to me earlier, and why I had gone, and all the sensations I had felt, not more than an hour and a half before, seemed to me something long past, transformed, grown old—something of which we should say no more because everything now would begin anew. Almost at the end of the avenue a sudden panic came upon me. What if I were robbed and murdered at this instant? At every step my panic grew greater. I almost ran. Suddenly, at the end of the avenue there was the glare of our hotel with its many windows lighted up—thank God, home!

I ran up to my storey and rapidly opened the door. Polina was there, sitting on the sofa with her arms crossed, with a lighted candle before her. She looked at me with amazement, and no doubt at that moment I must have looked rather strange. I stood before her and began flinging down all my piles of money on the table.

15

I remember she fixed a very intent look on my face, but without even moving from her seat or changing her position.

"I've won two hundred thousand francs!" I cried, as I flung down the last roll of notes.

The huge bundles of notes and piles of gold filled up the whole table; I could not take my eyes off it. At moments I completely forgot Polina. At one moment I began arranging the heap of banknotes, folding them up together, at the next I began undoing the rolls of gold and heaping them up in one pile; then I abandoned it all and strode rapidly up and down the room, lost in thought, then went up to the table, counting the money again. Suddenly, as though coming to myself, I ran to the door and locked it with two turns of the key. Then I stood pondering before my little portmanteau.

"Shall I put it in the portmanteau till to-morrow?" I said, suddenly remembering Polina and turning towards her.

She was still sitting in the same place without stirring, but watching me attentively. Her expression was somehow strange; I did not like that expression. I am not mistaken if I say that there was hatred in it.

I went up to her quickly.

"Polina, here are twenty-five thousand florins—that's fifty thousand francs—more, in fact. Take it, throw it in his face to-morrow."

She did not answer me.

"If you like I will take you away early in the morning. Shall I?"

She suddenly burst out laughing. She laughed for a long time.

I looked at her with wonder and a mortified feeling. That laugh was very much like sarcastic laughter at my expense, which had always been so frequent at the times of my most passionate declarations.

At last she ceased laughing and frowned; she looked at me sternly from under her brows.

"I won't take your money," she declared contemptuously.

"How? What's this?" I cried. "Polina, why?"

"I won't take money for nothing."

"I offer it you as a friend; I offer you my life."

She looked at me with a long, penetrating look, as though she would pierce me through with it.

"You give too much," she said, with a laugh; "De Grieux's mistress is not worth fifty thousand francs."

"Polina, how can you talk to me like that!" I cried, reproachfully. "Am I a De Grieux?"

"I hate you! Yes . . . yes! . . . I love you no more than De Grieux," she cried, her eyes suddenly flashing.

Then she suddenly covered her face with her hands and went into hysterics. I rushed to her.

I realized that something had happened to her while I was away. She seemed quite out of her mind.

"Buy me! Do you want to? Do you want to? For fifty thousand francs, like De Grieux?" broke from her with convulsive sobs.

I held her in my arms, kissed her hands, her feet, fell on my knees before her.

Her hysterics passed off. She put both hands on my shoulders, and looked at me intently; she seemed trying to read something in my face. She listened to me, but evidently did not hear what I was saying to her. Some doubt and anxiety betrayed itself in her face. I was anxious about her; it seemed to me that her brain was giving way. Then she began softly drawing me to her; a trustful smile began straying over her face; but she suddenly pushed me away, and again fell to scanning me with a darkened look.

Suddenly she fell to embracing me.

"You love me, you love me, don't you?" she said. "Why, you . . . why, you . . . wanted to fight the Baron for my sake!"

And suddenly she burst out laughing—as though she had recalled something sweet and funny. She cried and laughed all at once. Well, what was I to do? I was in a fever myself. I remember she began saying something to me—but I could scarcely understand anything. It was a sort of delirium—a sort of babble—as though she wanted to tell me something as rapidly as possible—a delirium which was interrupted from time to time with the merriest laughter, which at last frightened me. "No, no; you are sweet, sweet," she repeated. "You are my faithful one!" And again she put her hands on my shoulders, again she looked at me and repeated, "You love me . . . love me . . . will love me?" I could not take my eyes off her; I had never seen her before in such a mood of love and tenderness; it is true this, of course, was delirium, but . . . noticing my passionate expression, she suddenly began smiling slyly; apropos of nothing she began suddenly talking of Mr. Astley.

She talked incessantly of Mr. Astley, however (she talked of him particularly when she had been trying to tell me of something that evening), but what she meant exactly I could not quite grasp; she seemed to be actually laughing at him. She repeated continually that he was waiting and that, did I know, he was certainly standing under the window?

"Yes, yes, under the window; come open it: look out: look out: he certainly is here! She pushed me to the window, but as soon as I made a movement to go she went off into peals of laughter and I remained with her, and she fell to embracing me.

"Shall we go away? shall we go away to-morrow?" The question suddenly came into her mind uneasily. "Well . . ."

(and she sank into thought). "Well, shall we overtake Granny; what do you think? I think we might overtake her at Berlin. What do you think she will say when she sees us? And Mr. Astley? . . . Well, he won't leap off the Schlangenberg—what do you think?" (She burst out laughing.) "Come, listen, do you know where he is going next summer? He wants to go to the North Pole for scientific investigations, and he has asked me to go with him, ha-ha-ha! He says that we Russians can do nothing without Europeans and are incapable of anything. . . . But he is good-natured, too! Do you know he makes excuses for the General? He says that Blanche . . . that passion—oh, I don't know, I don't know," she repeated, as though she didn't know what she was talking about. "They are poor— how sorry I am for them, and Granny . . . Come, listen, listen, how could you kill De Grieux? And did you really imagine you could kill him? Oh, silly fellow! Can you really think I would let you fight with De Grieux? Why, you did not even kill the Baron," she added, suddenly laughing. "Oh, how funny you were then with the Baron. I looked at you both from the seat; and how unwilling you were to go then, when I sent you. How I laughed then, how I laughed," she added, laughing.

And suddenly she kissed and embraced me again. Again she pressed her face to mine passionately and tenderly. I heard nothing and thought of nothing more. My head was in a whirl. . . .

I think it was about seven o'clock in the morning when I woke up. The sun was shining into the room. Polina was sitting beside me and looking about her strangely, as though she were waking from some darkness and trying to collect her thoughts. She, too, had only just woken up and was gazing at the table and the money. My head ached and was heavy. I tried to take Polina by the hand: she pushed me away and jumped up from the sofa. The dawning day was overcast. Rain had fallen before sunrise. She went to the window, she opened it, put out her head and shoulders and with her face in her hands and her elbows on the window-sill, stayed for three minutes looking out without turning to me or hearing what I said to her. I wondered with dread what would happen now and how it would end. All at once she got up from the window, went up to the table and, looking at me with infinite hatred, with lips trembling with anger, she said to me—

"Well, give me my fifty thousand francs now?"

"Polina, again, again?" I was beginning.

"Or have you changed your mind? Ha-ha-ha! Perhaps you regret it now."

Twenty-five thousand florins, counted out the evening before, were lying on the table; I took the money and gave it to her.

"It's mine now, isn't it? That's so, isn't it? Isn't it?" she asked me, spitefully holding the money in her hand.

"Yes, it was always yours," I answered.

"Well, there are your fifty thousand francs for you!"

With a swing of her arm she flung the money at me. It hit me a stinging blow in the face and the coins flew all over the table. After doing this Polina ran out of the room.

I know that at that moment she was certainly not in her right mind, though I don't understand such temporary insanity. It is true that she is still ill, even now, a month later. What was the cause of her condition, and, above all, of this whim? Was it wounded pride? Despair at having brought herself to come to me? Had I shown any sign of priding myself on my happiness, and did I, like De Grieux, want to get rid of her by giving her fifty thousand francs? But that was not so; I know that, on my conscience. I believe that her vanity was partly responsible; her vanity prompted her to distrust and insult me, although all that perhaps was not clear, even to herself. In that case, of course, I was punished for De Grieux and was made responsible, though I was not much to blame. It is true that all this was almost only delirium; it is true, too, that I knew she was in delirium and . . . did not take that fact into consideration; perhaps she cannot forgive me for that now. Yes, but that is now; but then, then? Why, she was not in such a delirium and so ill then as to be utterly oblivious of what she was doing; when she came to me with De Grieux's letter she knew what she was doing.

I made haste to thrust all my notes and my heap of gold into the bed, covered it over and went out ten minutes after Polina. I made sure she would run home, and I thought I would slip in to them on the sly, and in the hall ask the nurse how the young lady was. What was my astonishment when I learnt from Nurse, whom I met on the stairs, that Polina had not yet returned home and that Nurse was coming to me for her.

"She only just left my room about ten minutes ago; where can she have gone?"

Nurse looked at me reproachfully.

And meanwhile it had caused a regular scandal, which by now was all over the hotel. In the porter's room and at the *ober-kellner's* it was whispered that Fräulein had run out of the hotel in the rain at six o'clock in the morning in the direction of the Hôtel d'Angleterre. From what they said and hinted, I noticed that they all knew already that she had spent the night in my room. However, stories were being told of the whole family: it had become known all through the hotel that the General had gone out of his mind and was crying. The story was that Granny was his mother, who had come expressly from Russia to prevent her son's marriage with Mlle. de Cominges, and was going to cut him out of her will if he disobeyed her, and, as he certainly would disobey her, the Countess had purposely thrown away all her money at roulette before his eyes, so that he should get nothing. "*Diese Russen!*" repeated the *ober-kellner*, shaking his head indignantly. The others laughed. The *ober-kellner* was making out his bill. My winning was known about already. Karl, my corridor attendant, was the first to congratulate me. But I had no thought for any of them. I rushed to the Hôtel d'Angleterre.

It was early; Mr. Astley was seeing no one; learning that it was I, he came out into the corridor to me and stopped before me, turning his pewtery eyes upon me in silence, waiting to hear what I should say. I inquired about Polina.

"She is ill," answered Mr. Astley, looking at me as fixedly as before.

"Then she really is with you?"

"Yes, she is."

"Then, what do you . . . do you mean to keep her?"

"Yes."

"Mr. Astley, it will make a scandal; it's impossible. Besides, she is quite ill; perhaps you don't see it?"

"Oh, yes, I notice it, and I've just told you she is ill. If she had not been ill she would not have spent the night with you."

"Then you know that?"

"Yes, I know it. She came here yesterday and I would have taken her to a relation of mine, but as she was ill, she made a mistake and went to you."

"Fancy that! Well, I congratulate you, Mr. Astley. By the way, you've given me an idea: weren't you standing all night under our window? Miss Polina was making me open the window and look out all night to see whether you were standing under the window; she kept laughing about it."

"Really? No, I didn't stand under the window; but I was waiting in the corridor and walking round."

"But she must be looked after, Mr. Astley."

"Oh, yes, I've sent for the doctor, and, if she dies, you will answer to me for her death."

I was amazed.

"Upon my word, Mr. Astley, what do you want?"

"And is it true that you won two hundred thousand thalers yesterday?"

"Only a hundred thousand florins."

"Well, do you see, you had better go off to Paris this morning!"

"What for?"

"All Russians who have money go to Paris," Mr. Astley explained, in a tone of voice as though he had read this in a book.

"What could I do now in Paris, in the summer? I love her, Mr. Astley, you know it yourself."

"Really? I am convinced you don't. If you remain here you will certainly lose all you have won and you will have nothing left to go to Paris with. But, good-bye, I am perfectly certain you will go to Paris to-day."

"Very well, good-bye, only I shan't go to Paris. Think, Mr. Astley, what will be happening here? The General . . . and now this adventure with Miss Polina—why, that will be all over the town."

"Yes, all over the town; I believe the General is not thinking about that: he has no thoughts to spare for that. Besides, Miss Polina has a perfect right to live where she likes. In regard to that family, one may say quite correctly that the family no longer exists."

I walked away laughing at this Englishman's strange conviction that I was going to Paris. "He wants to shoot me in a duel, though," I thought, "if Mlle. Polina dies—what a complication!" I swear I was sorry for Polina, but, strange to say, from the very moment when I reached the gambling tables the previous evening and began winning a pile of money, my love had retreated, so to speak, into the background. I say this now; but at the time I did not realize all this clearly. Can I really be a gambler? Can I really . . . have loved Polina so strangely? No, I love her to this day. God is my witness! And then, when I left Mr. Astley and went home, I was genuinely miserable and blaming myself. But . . . at this point a very strange and silly thing happened to me.

I was hurrying to see the General, when suddenly not far from his rooms, a door was opened and some one called me. It was Madame *la veuve* Cominges, and she called me at the bidding of Mlle. Blanche. I went in to see Mlle. Blanche.

They had a small suite of apartments, consisting of two rooms. I could hear Mlle. Blanche laugh and call out from the bedroom.

She was getting up.

"*Ah, c'est lui! Viens donc, bête!* Is it true, *que tu as gagné une montagne d'or et d'argent? J'aimerais mieux l'or.*"

"Yes, I did win," I answered, laughing.

"How much?"

"A hundred thousand florins."

"*Bibi, comme tu es bête.* Why, come in here. I can't hear anything. *Nous ferons bombance, n'est-ce pas?*"

I went in to her. She was lying under a pink satin quilt, above which her robust, swarthy, wonderfully swarthy, shoulders were visible, shoulders such as one only sees in one's dreams, covered to some extent by a batiste night-gown bordered with white lace which was wonderfully becoming to her dark skin.

"*Mon fils, as-tu du cœur?*" she cried, seeing me, and burst out laughing. She laughed very good-humouredly, and sometimes quite genuinely.

"*Tout autre,*" I began, paraphrasing Corneille.

"Here you see, *vois-tu,*" she began babbling; "to begin with, find my stockings, help me to put them on; and then, *si tu n'es pas trop bête, je te prends à Paris.* You know I am just going."

"Just going?"

"In half an hour."

All her things were indeed packed. All her portmanteaus and things were ready. Coffee had been served some time before.

"*Eh bien,* if you like, *tu verras Paris. Dis donc qu'est-ce que c'est qu'un outchitel? Tu étais bien bête, quand tu étais outchitel.* Where are my stockings? Put them on for me?"

She thrust out some positively fascinating feet, little dark-skinned feet, not in the least misshapen, as feet that look so small in shoes always are. I laughed and began drawing her silk stockings on for her. Meanwhile Mlle. Blanche sat up in bed, prattling away.

"*Eh bien, que feras-tu, si je te prends avec?* To begin with, I want fifty thousand francs. You'll give them to me at Frankfurt. *Nous allons à Paris:* there we'll play together: *et je te ferai voir des étoiles en plein jour.* You will see women such as you have never seen before. Listen . . ."

"Wait a minute, so if I give you fifty thousand francs, what will be left for me?"

"*Et cent cinquante mille francs,* you have forgotten: and what's more, I consent to live with you a month, two months: *que sais-je!* In those two months we shall certainly get through that hundred and fifty thousand francs, you see, *je suis bonne enfant,* and I tell you beforehand, *mais tu verras des étoiles.*"

"What! all in two months!"

"Why! does that horrify you? *Ah, vil esclave!* But, do you know? one month of such a life is worth your whole existence. One month—*et après, le déluge! Mais tu ne peux comprendre; va!* Go along, go along, you are not worth it! *Aie, que fais-tu?*"

At that moment I was putting a stocking on the other leg, but could not resist kissing it. She pulled it away and began hitting me on the head with the tip of her foot. At last, she turned me out altogether.

"*Eh bien! mon outchitel, je t'attends, si tu veux;* I am starting in a quarter of an hour!" she called after me.

On returning home I felt as though my head were going

round. Well, it was not my fault that Mlle. Polina had thrown the whole pile of money in my face, and had even yesterday preferred Mr. Astley to me. Some of the bank-notes that had been scattered about were still lying on the floor; I picked them up. At that moment the door opened and the *ober-kellner* himself made his appearance (he had never deigned to look into my room before) with a suggestion that I might like to move downstairs to a magnificent suite of apartments which had just been vacated by Count V.

I stood still and thought a little.

"My bill—I am just leaving, in ten minutes," I cried. "If it's to be Paris, let it be Paris," I thought to myself; "it seems it was fated at my birth!"

A quarter of an hour later we were actually sitting in a reserved compartment, Mlle. Blanche, Madame *la veuve* Cominges and I. Mlle. Blanche, looking at me, laughed till she was almost hysterical. Madame de Cominges followed suit; I cannot say that I felt cheerful. My life had broken in two, but since the previous day I had grown used to staking everything on a card. Perhaps it is really the truth that my sudden wealth was too much for me and had turned my head. *Peut-être, je ne demandais pas mieux.* It seemed to me for a time—but only for a time, the scenes were shifted. "But in a month I shall be here, and then . . . and then we will try our strength, Mr. Astley!" No, as I recall it now, I was awfully sad then, though I did laugh as loudly as that idiot, Blanche.

"But what is the matter with you? How silly you are! Oh! how silly you are!" Blanche kept exclaiming, interrupting her laughter to scold me in earnest. "Oh well, oh well, we'll spend your two hundred thousand francs: but in exchange *mais tu seras heureux comme un petit roi;* I will tie your cravat myself and introduce you to Hortense. And when we have spent all our money, you will come back here and break the bank again. What did the Jews tell you? The great thing is—boldness, and you have it, and you will bring me money to Paris more than once again. *Quant à moi je veux cinquante mille francs de rentes et alors . . ."*

"And the General?" I asked her.

"Why, the General, as you know, comes to see me every day with a bouquet. This time I purposely asked him to get me some very rare flowers. The poor fellow will come back and will find the bird has flown. He'll fly after us, you will see. Ha-ha-ha! I shall be awfully pleased to see him. He'll be of use to me in Paris; Mr. Astley will pay his bill here. . . ."

And so that was the way in which I went to Paris.

16

What shall I say about Paris? It was madness, of course, and foolery. I only spent a little over three weeks in Paris, and by the end of that time my hundred thousand francs was finished. I speak only of a hundred thousand. The other hundred thousand I gave to Mlle. Blanche in hard cash—fifty thousand at Frankfurt and three days later in Paris I gave her an I O U for another fifty thousand francs, though a week later she exchanged this for cash from me. *"Et les cent mille francs, qui nous restent, tu les mangeras avec moi, mon outchitel."* She always called me an *outchitel*, *i.e.*, a tutor. It is difficult to imagine anything in the world meaner, stingier and more niggardly than the class of creatures to which Mlle. Blanche belonged. But that was in the spending of her own money. As regards my hundred thousand francs, she openly informed me, later on, that she needed them to establish herself in Paris, "as now I am going to settle in decent style once for all, and now no one shall turn me aside for a long time; at least, that is my plan," she added. I hardly saw that hundred thousand, however; she kept the money the whole time, and in my purse, into which she looked every day, there was never more than a hundred francs, and always less and less.

"What do you want money for?" she would say, sometimes, in the simplest way, and I did not dispute with her. But she furnished and decorated her flat very nicely with that money, and afterwards, when she took me to her new abode, as she showed me the rooms, she said: "You see what care and taste can do even with the scantiest means." These "scanty means" amounted to fifty thousand francs, however. With the second fifty thousand she provided herself with a carriage and horses. Moreover, we gave two balls, that is, two evening parties at which were present Hortense, Lizette and Cléopatra, women remarkable in very many respects and even quite good-looking. At those two evenings I had to play the very foolish part of host, to receive and entertain the stupidest rich tradesmen, incredibly ignorant and shameless, various army lieutenants and miserable little authors and journalistic insects, who appeared in the most fashionable swallow-tails and straw-coloured gloves, and displayed a vanity and affectation whose proportions were beyond anything conceivable in Petersburg—and that is saying a great deal. Many of them thought fit to jeer at me; but I got drunk with champagne and lolled at full length in a back room. To me it was all loathsome to the last degree. "C'est un outchitel," Blanche kept saying about me, "il a gagné deux cent mille francs. Without me he wouldn't have known how to spend it. And afterwards he will be an outchitel again; don't you know of a place for one? we ought to do something for him."

I had recourse to champagne very often, because I was often sad and dreadfully bored. I lived in the most bourgeois, in the most mercenary surroundings in which every sou was reckoned and accounted for. Blanche disliked me for the first fortnight: I noticed that; it is true, she dressed me like a dandy, and tied my cravat for me every day, but in her soul she genuinely despised me. I did not pay the slightest attention to that. Bored and dispirited, I used to go usually to the Château de Fleurs, where regularly every evening I got drunk and practised the cancan (which they dance so disgustingly there), and acquired in the end a kind of celebrity.

At last Blanche gauged my true character. She had for some reason conceived the idea that I should spend all the time we were together walking after her with a pencil and paper in my hand, and should always be reckoning how much she had spent, how much she had stolen, how much she would spend and how much more she would steal. And she was, of course, convinced that we should have a regular battle over every ten-franc piece. She had an answer in readiness for every attack that she anticipated from me; but when she found I did not attack her, she could not at first refrain from defending herself, unprovoked. Sometimes she would begin with great heat, but seeing that I remained silent as a rule, lying on a sofa gazing at the ceiling—at last, she was surprised. At first she thought I was simply stupid, *"un outchitel,"* and merely cut short her explanations, probably thinking to herself: "Why, he's a fool. There's no need to lay it on for him, since he doesn't understand." She would go away but come back again ten minutes later (this happened at a time when she was spending most ferociously, spending on a scale quite out of proportion to our means: she had, for instance, got rid of the horses first bought and bought another pair for sixteen thousand francs).

"Well, so you are not cross, *bibi*?" she said, coming up to me.

"N—n—n—no! You weary me!" I said, removing her hands from me, but this seemed to her so curious, that she immediately sat down beside me.

"You see, I only decided to pay so much because they could be sold later on if need be. They can be sold again for twenty thousand francs."

"No doubt, no doubt; they are splendid horses, and you have a fine turnout now; it suits you; well, that's enough."

"Then you are not cross?"

"Why should I be? You are sensible to provide yourself with things that are necessary to you. All that will be of use to you afterwards. I see that it is quite necessary for you to establish yourself in such a style; otherwise you will never save up your million. Our hundred thousand francs is only a beginning; a drop in the ocean."

Blanche had expected from me anything but such reflections (instead of outcries and reproaches). She seemed to drop from the clouds.

"So that's what you are like! *Mais tu as l'esprit pour comprendre. Sais-tu, mon garçon,* though you are an *outchitel* you ought to have been born a prince. So you don't grudge the money's going so quickly?"

"Bother the money! The quicker the better!"

"*Mais sais-tu . . . mais dis donc,* are you rich? *Mais sais-tu,* you really despise money too much. *Qu'est ce que tu feras après, dis donc?*"

"*Après,* I shall go to Homburg and win another hundred thousand francs."

"Oui, oui, c'est ça, c'est magnifique! And I know you
will certainly win it and bring it here. *Dis donc,* why you
will make me really love you. *Eh bien,* I will love you all
the time for being like that, and won't once be unfaithful
to you. You see, I have not loved you all this time, *parceque je croyais que tu n'étais qu'un outchitel (quelque
chose comme un laquais, n'est-ce pas?),* but I have been
faithful to you all the same, *parceque je suis bonne fille."*

"Come, you are lying! How about Albert, that swarthy-
faced little officer; do you suppose I didn't see last time?"

"Oh, oh, *mais tu es . . ."*

"Come, you are lying, you are lying; why, do you suppose I should be angry? Why, it's no matter; *il faut que
la jeunesse se passe.* And there's no need for you to send
him away if you had him before me and are fond of him.
Only don't give him money, do you hear?"

"So you are not angry about it? *Mais tu es un vrai philosophe, sais-tu? Un vrai philosophe!"* she cried enthusiastically.

*"Eh bien! je t'aimerai, je t'aimerai—tu verras, tu seras
content!"*

And from that time she really did seem to be attached
to me, to be really affectionate; and so our last ten days
passed. The "stars" promised me I did not see. But in
some respects she really did keep her word. What is more,
she introduced me to Hortense, who really was a remarkable woman in her own way, and in our circle was
called *Thérèse philosophe. . . .*

However, there is no need to enlarge upon that; all that
might make a separate story, in a different tone, which I
do not want to introduce into this story. The fact is, I
longed above everything for all this episode to be over.
But our hundred thousand francs lasted, as I have mentioned already, almost a month—at which I was genuinely surprised; eighty thousand of that, at least, Blanche
spent on things for herself, and we lived on no more than
twenty thousand francs, and—yet it was enough. Blanche,
who was in the end almost open with me (or, at any rate,
did not lie to me about some things), declared that, anyway, the debts she had been obliged to make would not
fall upon me: "I have never given you bills or I O U's to
sign," she said, "because I was sorry for you; but any other
girl would have certainly done it and got you into prison.

You see, you see how I loved you and how good I am!
Think of what that devil of a wedding alone is going to
cost me!"

We really were going to have a wedding. It took place
at the very end of my month, and it may be assumed that
the last remains of my hundred thousand francs went
upon it; that was how the thing ended; that is, my month
ended with that, and after it I received my formal dismissal.

This was how it happened: a week after our arrival in
Paris the General suddenly turned up. He came straight
to Blanche, and from his first call almost lived with us.
He had a lodging of his own, it is true. Blanche received
him joyfully, with shrieks of laughter, and even flew to
embrace him; as things had turned out, she was unwilling to let him go: and he had to follow her about everywhere, on the boulevards, and to the theatres, and to call
on her acquaintances, and to take her for drives. The
General was still of use for such purposes; he was of rather
imposing and decorous appearance—he was above the
average in height, with dyed whiskers and moustaches
(he had once served in the Cuirassiers); he was still pre-
sentable-looking, though his face was puffy. His manners
were superb; he looked well in evening dress. In Paris
he began wearing his decorations. The promenade on the
boulevard with a man like this was not only possible, but
advantageous. The good-natured and senseless General
was immensely delighted with all this; he had not reckoned upon it at all when he came to see us on arriving
in Paris. He had come, then, almost trembling with terror; he was afraid that Blanche would make an uproar
and order him to be turned out; and so he was highly delighted at the changed aspect of the position, and spent
the whole month in a sort of senseless rapture: and he
was in the same state when I left him. I learnt that on the
morning of our sudden departure from Roulettenburg he
had had some sort of a fit. He had fallen insensible, and
had been all that week almost like a madman, talking
incessantly. He was being nursed and doctored, but he
suddenly threw up everything, got into the train and flew
off to Paris. Of course, Blanche's reception was the best
cure for him; but the traces of his illness remained long
after, in spite of his joy and his enthusiastic condition.

He was utterly incapable of reflection or even of carrying on a conversation on any serious subject; when any such topic was brought forward, he confined himself to nodding his head and ejaculating, "H'm!" at every word. He often laughed, but it was a nervous, sickly laugh, as though he were giggling; another time he would sit for hours looking as black as night, knitting his bushy brows. Of many things he had no recollection whatever; he had become absent-minded to an unseemly degree, and had acquired the habit of talking to himself. Blanche was the only person who could rouse him; and, indeed, his attacks of gloom and depression, when he hid himself in a corner, meant nothing but that he hadn't seen Blanche for a long time, or that Blanche had gone off somewhere without taking him, or had not been nice to him before going. At the same time he could not say what he wanted, and did not know why he was depressed and miserable. After sitting for two or three hours (I noticed this on two or three occasions when Blanche had gone out for the whole day, probably to see Albert), he would suddenly begin to look about him in a nervous fluster, to stare round, to recollect himself, and seem to be looking for something; but seeing no one and not remembering the question he meant to ask, he sank into forgetfulness again till Blanche reappeared, gay, frisky, gorgeously dressed, with her ringing laugh; she would run up to him, begin teasing him, and even kissing him—a favour which she did not often, however, bestow upon him. Once the General was so delighted to see her that he even burst into tears—I really marvelled at him.

From the very first, Blanche began to plead his cause before me. Indeed, she waxed eloquent in his behalf; reminded me that she had betrayed the General for my sake, that she was almost engaged to him, had given him her word; that he had abandoned his family on her account, and, lastly, that I had been in his service and ought to remember that, and that I ought to be ashamed. . . . I said nothing while she rattled away at a terrific pace. At last I laughed: and with that the matter ended, that is, at first, she thought I was a fool: but at last came to the conclusion that I was a very nice and accommodating man. In fact, I had the good fortune to win in the end the complete approval of that excellent young woman.

(Blanche really was, though, a very good-natured girl—in her own way, of course; I had not such a high opinion of her at first.) "You're a kind and clever man," she used to say to me towards the end, "and . . . and . . . it's only a pity you are such a fool! You never, never, save anything!"

"Un vrai russe, un calmouk!" Several times she sent me to take the General for a walk about the streets, exactly as she might send her lapdog out with her footman. I took him, however, to the theatre, and to the Bal-Mabille, and to the restaurants. Blanche gave me the money for this, though the General had some of his own, and he was very fond of taking out his pocket-book before people. But I had almost to use force to prevent him from buying a brooch for seven hundred francs, by which he was fascinated in the Palais Royal and of which he wanted, at all costs, to make Blanche a present. But what was a brooch of seven hundred francs to her? The General hadn't more than a thousand francs altogether. I could never find out where he had got that money from. I imagine it was from Mr. Astley, especially as the latter had paid their bill at the hotel. As for the General's attitude to me all this time, I believe that he did not even guess at my relations with Blanche. Though he had heard vaguely that I had won a fortune, yet he probably supposed that I was with Blanche in the capacity of a private secretary or even a servant. Anyway, he always, as before, spoke to me condescendingly, authoritatively, and even sometimes fell to scolding me. One morning he amused Blanche and me immensely at breakfast. He was not at all ready to take offence, but suddenly he was huffy with me—why?—I don't know to this day. No doubt he did not know himself. In fact, he made a speech without a beginning or an end, *à bâtons rompus*, shouted that I was an impudent boy, that he would give me a lesson . . . that he would let me know it . . . and so on. But no one could make out anything from it. Blanche went off into peals of laughter. At last he was somehow appeased and taken out for a walk. I noticed sometimes, however, that he grew sad, that he was regretting some one and something, he was missing something, in spite of Blanche's presence. On two such occasions he began talking to me of himself, but could not express himself clearly, alluded to his times in the army, to his deceased wife, to his family affairs, to his property. He would

stumble upon some phrase—and was delighted with it and would repeat it a hundred times a day, though perhaps it expressed neither his feelings nor his thoughts. I tried to talk to him about his children: but he turned off the subject with incoherent babble, and passed hurriedly to another topic: "Yes, yes, my children, you are right, my children!" Only once he grew sentimental—we were with him at the theatre: "Those unhappy children!" he began suddenly. "Yes, sir, those un—happy children!" And several times afterwards that evening he repeated the same words: "unhappy children!" Once, when I began to speak of Polina, he flew into a frenzy. "She's an ungrateful girl," he cried. "She's wicked and ungrateful! She has disgraced her family. If there were laws here I would make her mind her p's and q's. Yes, indeed, yes, indeed!" As for De Grieux, he could not bear even to hear his name: "He has been the ruin of me," he would say, "he has robbed me, he has destroyed me! He has been my nightmare for the last two years! He has haunted my dreams for whole months! It's, it's, it's . . . Oh, never speak to me of him!"

I saw there was an understanding between them, but, as usual, I said nothing. Blanche announced the news to me, first—it was just a week before we parted: *"Il a du chance,"* she babbled. "Granny really is ill this time, and certainly will die. Mr. Astley has sent a telegram. You must admit that the General is her heir, anyway, and even if he were not, he would not interfere with me in anything. In the first place, he has his pension, and in the second place, he will live in a back room and will be perfectly happy. I shall be 'Madame la Générale.' I shall get into a good set" (Blanche was continually dreaming of this), "in the end I shall be a Russian landowner, *j'aurai un château, des moujiks, et puis j'aurai toujours mon million.*"

"Well, what if he begins to be jealous, begins to insist . . . on goodness knows what—do you understand?"

"Oh, no, *non, non, non!* How dare he! I have taken precautions, you needn't be afraid. I have even made him sign some I O U's for Albert. The least thing—and he will be arrested; and he won't dare!"

"Well, marry him. . . ."

The marriage was celebrated without any great pomp;

it was a quiet family affair. Albert was invited and a few other intimate friends. Hortense, Cléopatra and company were studiously excluded. The bridegroom was extremely interested in his position. Blanche herself tied his cravat with her own hands, and pomaded his head: and in his swallow-tailed coat with his white tie he looked *très comme il faut*.

"*Il est pourtant très comme il faut*," Blanche herself observed to me, coming out of the General's room, as though the idea that the General was *très comme il faut* was a surprise even to her. Though I assisted at the whole affair as an idle spectator, yet I took so little interest in the details that I have to a great extent forgotten the course of events. I only remember that Blanche turned out not to be called "De Cominges," and her mamma not to be *la veuve* "Cominges," but "Du Placet." Why they had been both "De Cominges" till then, I don't know. But the General remained very much pleased with that, and "Du Placet" pleased him, in fact, better than "De Cominges," On the morning of the wedding, fully dressed for the part, he kept walking to and fro in the drawing-room, repeating to himself with a grave and important air, "Mlle. Blanche du Placet! Blanche du Placet, du Placet!" . . . and his countenance beamed with a certain complacency. At church, before the *maire*, and at the wedding breakfast at home, he was not only joyful but proud. There was a change in both of them. Blanche, too, had an air of peculiar dignity.

"I shall have to behave myself quite differently now," she said to me, perfectly seriously: "*mais vois-tu*, I never thought of one very horrid thing: I even fancy, to this day, I can't learn my surname. Zagoryansky, Zagozyansky, Madame la Générale de Sago—Sago, *ces diables de noms russes, enfin madame la générale a quatorze consonnes! Comme c'est agréable, n'est-ce pas?*"

At last we parted, and Blanche, that silly Blanche, positively shed tears when she said good-bye to me. "*Tu étais bon enfant*," she said, whimpering. "*Je te croyais bête et tu en avais l'air*, but it suits you." And, pressing my hand at parting, she suddenly cried, "*Attends!*" rushed to her boudoir and, two minutes later, brought me a banknote for two thousand francs. That I should never have believed possible! "It may be of use to you. You may be a

very learned *outchitel,* but you are an awfully stupid man.
I am not going to give you more than two thousand, for
you'll lose it gambling, anyway. Well, good-bye! *Nous
serons toujours bon amis,* and if you win, be sure to come
to me again, *et tu seras heureux!"*

I had five hundred francs left of my own. I had besides
a splendid watch that cost a thousand francs, some dia-
mond studs, and so on, so that I could go on a good time
longer without anxiety. I am staying in this little town on
purpose to collect myself, and, above all, I am waiting for
Mr. Astley. I have learnt for a fact that he will pass
through the town and stay here for twenty-four hours on
business. I shall find out about everything; and then—
then I shall go straight to Homburg. I am not going to
Roulettenburg; not till next year anyway. They say it is a
bad omen to try your luck twice running at the same
tables; and Homburg is the real place for play.

17

It is a year and eight months since I looked at these notes,
and only now in sadness and dejection it has occurred to
me to read them through. So I stopped then at my going
to Homburg. My God! With what a light heart, compara-
tively speaking, I wrote those last lines! Though not with
a light heart exactly, but with a sort of self-confidence,
with undaunted hopes! Had I any doubt of myself? And
now more than a year and a half has passed, and I am,
to my own mind, far worse than a beggar! Yes, what is
being a beggar? A beggar is nothing! I have simply ruined
myself! However, there is nothing I can compare myself
with, and there is no need to give myself a moral lecture!
Nothing could be stupider than moral reflections at this
date! O, self-satisfied people, with what proud satisfaction
these prattlers prepare to deliver their lectures! If only
they knew how thoroughly I understand the loathsome-
ness of my present position, they would not be able to
bring their tongues to reprimand me. Why, what, what
can they tell me that I do not know? And is that the

point? The point is that—one turn of the wheel, and all
will be changed, and those very moralists will be the first
(I am convinced of that) to come up to congratulate me
with friendly jests. And they will not all turn away from
me as they do now. But, hang them all! What am I now?
Zero. What may I be to-morrow? To-morrow I may rise
from the dead and begin to live again! There are still the
makings of a man in me.

I did, in fact, go to Homburg then, but . . . afterwards
I went to Roulettenburg again, and to Spa. I have even
been in Baden, where I went as valet to the councillor
Gintse, a scoundrel, who was my master here. Yes, I was
a lackey for five whole months! I got a place immediately
after coming out of prison. (I was sent to prison in Roulettenburg for a debt I made here.) Some one, I don't
know who, paid my debt—who was it? Was it Mr. Astley?
Polina? I don't know, but the debt was paid; two hundred thalers in all, and I was set free. What could I do?
I entered the service of this Gintse. He is a young man
and frivolous, he liked to be idle, and I could read and
write in three languages. At first I went into his service
as a sort of secretary at thirty guldens a month; but I
ended by becoming a regular valet: he had not the means
to keep a secretary; and he lowered my wages; I had nowhere to go, I remained—and in that way became a lackey
by my own doing. I had not enough to eat or to drink in
his service, but on the other hand, in five months I saved
up seventy gulden. One evening in Baden, however, I announced to him that I intended parting from him; the
same evening I went to roulette. Oh, how my heart beat!
No, it was not money that I wanted. All that I wanted
then was that next day all these Gintses, all these *ober-
kellners*, all these magnificent Baden ladies—that they
might be all talking about me, repeating my story, wondering at me, admiring me, praising me, and doing hom-
age to my new success. All these are childish dreams and
desires, but . . . who knows, perhaps I should meet Polina
again, too, I should tell her, and she would see that I was
above all these stupid ups and downs of fate. . . . Oh, it
was not money that was dear to me! I knew I should fling
it away to some Blanche again and should drive in Paris
again for three weeks with a pair of my own horses, cost-
ing sixteen thousand francs. I know for certain that I am

not mean; I believe that I am not even a spendthrift—and yet with what a tremor, with what a thrill at my heart, I hear the croupier's cry: *trente-et-un, rouge, impair et passe*, or: *quatre, noir, pair et manque!* With what avidity I look at the gambling table on which louis d'or, friedrichs d'or and thalers lie scattered: on the piles of gold when they are scattered from the croupier's shovel like glowing embers, or at the piles of silver a yard high that lie round the wheel. Even on my way to the gambling hall, as soon as I hear, two rooms away, the clink of the scattered money I almost go into convulsions.

Oh! that evening, when I took my seventy gulden to the gambling table, was remarkable too. I began with ten gulden, staking them again on *passe*. I have a prejudice in favour of *passe*. I lost. I had sixty gulden left in silver money; I thought a little and chose *zéro*. I began staking five gulden at a time on *zéro*; at the third turn the wheel stopped at *zéro*; I almost died of joy when I received one hundred and seventy-five gulden; I had not been so delighted when I won a hundred thousand gulden. I immediately staked a hundred gulden on *rouge*—it won; the two hundred on *rouge*—it won; the whole of the four hundred on *noir*—it won; the whole eight hundred on *manque*—it won; altogether with what I had before it made one thousand seven hundred gulden and that—in less than five minutes! Yes, at moments like that one forgets all one's former failures! Why, I had gained this by risking more than life itself, I dared to risk it, and—there I was again, a man among men.

I took a room at the hotel, locked myself in and sat till three o'clock counting over my money. In the morning I woke up, no longer a lackey. I determined the same day to go to Homburg: I had not been a lackey or been in prison there. Half an hour before my train left, I set off to stake on two hazards, no more, and lost fifteen hundred florins. Yet I went to Homburg all the same, and I have been here for a month. . . .

I am living, of course, in continual anxiety. I play for the tiniest stakes, and I keep waiting for something, calculating, standing for whole days at the gambling table and watching the play; I even dream of playing—but I feel that in all this, I have, as it were, grown stiff and wooden, as though I had sunk into a muddy swamp. I gather this from my feeling when I met Mr. Astley. We had not seen each other since that time, and we met by accident. This was how it happened: I was walking in the gardens and reckoning that now I was almost without money, but that I had fifty gulden—and that I had, moreover, three days before paid all I owed at the hotel. And so it was possible for me to go once more to roulette—if I were to win anything, I might be able to go on playing; if I lost I should have to get a lackey's place again, if I did not come across Russians in want of a tutor. Absorbed in these thoughts, I went my daily walk, across the park and the forest in the adjoining principality.

Sometimes I used to walk like this for four hours at a time, and go back to Homburg hungry and tired. I had scarcely gone out of the gardens into the park, when suddenly I saw on one of the seats Mr. Astley. He saw me before I saw him, and called to me. I sat down beside him. Detecting in him a certain dignity of manner, I instantly moderated my delight; though I was awfully delighted to see him.

"And so you are here! I thought I should meet you," he said to me. "Don't trouble yourself to tell me your story; I know, I know all about it; I know every detail of your life during this last year and eight months."

"Bah! What a watch you keep on your old friends!" I answered. "It is very creditable in you not to forget. . . . Stay, though, you have given me an idea. Wasn't it you bought me out of prison at Roulettenburg where I was imprisoned for debt for two hundred gulden? Some unknown person paid it for me."

"No, oh, no; it was not I who bought you out when you were in prison at Roulettenburg for a debt of two hundred gulden. But I knew that you were imprisoned for a debt of two hundred gulden."

"Then you know who did pay my debt?"

"Oh, no, I can't say that I know who bought you out."

"Strange; I don't know any of our Russians; besides, the Russians here, I imagine, would not do it; at home in Russia the Orthodox may buy out other Orthodox Christians. I thought it must have been some eccentric Englishman who did it as a freak."

Mr. Astley listened to me with some surprise. I believe he had expected to find me dejected and crushed.

"I am very glad, however, to find that you have quite maintained your independence of spirit and even your cheerfulness," he pronounced, with a rather disagreeable air.

"That is, you are chafing inwardly with vexation at my not being crushed and humiliated," I said, laughing.

He did not at once understand, but when he understood, he smiled.

"I like your observations: I recognize in those words my clever, enthusiastic and, at the same time, cynical old friend; only Russians can combine in themselves so many opposites at the same time. It is true, a man likes to see even his best friend humiliated; a great part of friendship rests on humiliation. But in the present case I assure you that I am genuinely glad that you are not dejected. Tell me, do you intend to give up gambling?"

"Oh, damn! I shall give it up at once as soon as I . . ."

"As soon as you have won back what you have lost! Just what I thought; you needn't say any more—I know—you have spoken unawares, and so you have spoken the truth. Tell me, have you any occupation except gambling?"

"No, none. . . ."

He began cross-examining me. I knew nothing. I scarcely looked into the newspapers, and had literally not opened a single book all that time.

"You've grown rusty," he observed. "You have not only given up life, all your interests, private and public, the duties of a man and a citizen, your friends (and you really had friends)—you have not only given up your objects, such as they were, all but gambling—you have even given up your memories. I remember you at an intense and ardent moment of your life; but I am sure you have forgotten all the best feelings you had then; your dreams, your most genuine desires now do not rise above *pair, impair, rouge, noir,* the twelve middle numbers, and so on, I am sure!"

"Enough, Mr. Astley, please, please don't remind me," I cried with vexation, almost with anger, "let me tell you, I've forgotten absolutely nothing; but I've only for a time put everything out of my mind, even my memories, until I can make a radical improvement in my circumstances; then . . . then you will see, I shall rise again from the dead!"

"You will be here still in ten years' time," he said. "I bet you I shall remind you of this on this very seat, if I'm alive."

"Well, that's enough," I interrupted impatiently; "and to prove to you that I am not so forgetful of the past, let me ask: where is Miss Polina now? If it was not you who got me out of prison, it must have been her doing. I have had no news of her of any sort since that time."

"No, oh no, I don't believe she did buy you out. She's in Switzerland now, and you'll do me a great favour if you leave off asking about Miss Polina," he said resolutely, and even with some anger.

"That means that she has wounded you very much!" I laughed with displeasure.

"Miss Polina is of all people deserving of respect the very best, but I repeat—you will do me a great favour if you cease questioning me concerning Miss Polina. You never knew her: and her name on your lips I regard as an insult to my moral feelings."

"You don't say so! you are wrong, however; besides, what have I to talk to you about except that, tell me that? Why, all our memories really amount to that! Don't be uneasy, though; I don't want to know your private secret affairs. . . . I am only interested, so to say, in Miss Polina's external affairs. That you could tell me in a couple of words."

"Certainly, on condition that with those two words all is over. Miss Polina was ill for a long time; she's ill even now. For some time she stayed with my mother and sister in the north of England. Six months ago, her grandmother—you remember that madwoman?—died and left her, personally, a fortune of seven thousand pounds. At the present time Miss Polina is travelling with the family of my married sister. Her little brother and sister, too, were provided for by their grandmother's will, and are at school in London. The General, her stepfather, died a month ago in Paris of a stroke. Mlle. Blanche treated him well, but succeeded in getting possession of all he received from the grandmother. . . . I believe that's all."

"And De Grieux? Is not he travelling in Switzerland, too?"

"No, De Grieux is not travelling in Switzerland: and I don't know where De Grieux is; besides, once for all, I warn you to avoid such insinuations and ungentlemanly coupling of names, or you will certainly have to answer for it to me."

"What! in spite of our friendly relations in the past?"

"Yes, in spite of our friendly relations in the past."

"I beg a thousand pardons, Mr. Astley. But allow me, though: there is nothing insulting or ungentlemanly about it; I am not blaming Miss Polina for anything. Besides— a Frenchman and a Russian young lady, speaking generally—it's a combination, Mr. Astley, which is beyond your or my explaining or fully comprehending."

"If you will not mention the name of De Grieux in company with another name, I should like you to explain what you mean by the expression of 'the Frenchman and the Russian young lady.' What do you mean by that 'combination'? Why the Frenchman exactly and why the Russian young lady?"

"You see you are interested. But that's a long story, Mr. Astley. You need to understand many things first. But it is an important question, however absurd it may seem at first sight. The Frenchman, Mr. Astley, is the product of a finished beautiful tradition. You, as a Briton, may not agree with this; I, as a Russian, do not either, from envy maybe; but our young ladies may be of a different opinion. You may think Racine artificial, affected and perfumed; probably you won't even read him. I, too, think him artificial, affected and perfumed—from one point of view even absurd; but he is charming, Mr. Astley, and, what is more, he is a great poet, whether we like it or not. The national type of Frenchman, or, rather, of Parisian, had been moulded into elegant forms while we were still bears. The revolution inherited the traditions of the aristocracy. Now even the vulgarest Frenchman has manners, modes of address, expressions and even thoughts, of perfectly elegant form, though his own initiative, his own soul and heart, have had no part in the creation of that form; it has all come to him through inheritance. Well, Mr. Astley, I must inform you now that there is not a creature on the earth more confiding, and more candid, than a good, clean and not too sophisticated Russian girl. De Grieux, appearing in a peculiar rôle, masquerading, can conquer her heart with extraordinary ease; he has elegance of form, Mr. Astley, and the young lady takes this form for his individual soul, as the natural form of his soul and his heart, and not as an external garment, which has come to him by inheritance. Though it will greatly displease you, I must tell you that Englishmen are for the most part awkward and inelegant, and Russians are rather quick to detect beauty, and are eager for it. But to detect beauty of soul and originality of character needs incomparably more independence and freedom than is to be found in our women, above all in our young ladies—and of course ever so much more experience. Miss Polina—forgive me, the word is spoken and one can't take it back—needs a long, long time to bring herself to prefer you to the scoundrel De Grieux. She thinks highly of you, becomes your friend, opens all her heart to you; but yet the hateful scoundrel, the base and petty money-grubber, De Grieux, will still dominate her heart. Mere obstinacy and vanity, so to say, will maintain his supremacy, because at one time this De Grieux appeared to her with the halo of an elegant marquis, a disillusioned liberal, who is supposed to have ruined himself to help her family and her frivolous stepfather. All these shams have been discovered later on. But the fact that they have been discovered makes no difference: anyway, what she wants is the original De Grieux —that's what she wants! And the more she hates the present De Grieux the more she pines for the original one, though he existed only in her imagination. You are a sugarboiler, Mr. Astley."

"Yes, I am a partner in the well-known firm, Lovel & Co."

"Well, you see, Mr. Astley, on one side—a sugar-boiler, and on the other—Apollo Belvedere; it is somewhat incongruous. And I am not even a sugar-boiler; I am simply a paltry gambler at roulette, and have even been a lackey, which I think Miss Polina knows very well, as I fancy she has good detectives."

"You are exasperated, and that is why you talk all this nonsense," Mr. Astley said coolly, after a moment's thought. "Besides, there is nothing original in what you say."

"I admit that! But the awful thing is, my noble friend, that however stale, however hackneyed, however farcical my statements may be—they are nevertheless true! Anyway, you and I have made no way at all!"

"That's disgusting nonsense . . . because, because . . . let me tell you!" Mr. Astley, with flashing eyes, pronounced in a quivering voice, "let me tell you, you ungrateful, unworthy, shallow and unhappy man, that I am come to Homburg expressly at her wish, to see you, to have a long and open conversation with you and to tell her everything—what you are feeling, thinking, hoping, and . . . what you remember!"

"Is it possible? Is it possible?" I cried, and tears rushed in streams from my eyes.

I could not restrain them. I believe it was the first time it happened in my life.

"Yes, unhappy man, she loved you, and I can tell you that, because you are—a lost man! What is more, if I were to tell you that she loves you to this day—you would stay here just the same! Yes, you have destroyed yourself. You had some abilities, a lively disposition, and were not a bad fellow; you might have even been of service to your country, which is in such need of men, but—you will remain here, and your life is over. I don't blame you. To my mind all Russians are like that, or disposed to be like that. If it is not roulette it is something similar. The exceptions are very rare. You are not the first who does not understand the meaning of work (I am not talking of your peasantry). Roulette is a game pre-eminently for the Russians. So far you've been honest and preferred serving as a lackey to stealing. . . . But I dread to think what may come in the future. Enough, good-bye! No doubt you are in want of money? Here are ten louis d'or from me. I won't give you more, for you'll gamble it away in any case. Take it and good-bye! Take it!"

"No, Mr. Astley, after all you have said."

"Ta—ake it!" he cried. "I believe that you are still an honourable man, and I give it as a true friend gives to another friend. If I were sure that you would throw up gambling, leave Homburg and would return to your own country, I would be ready to give you at once a thousand pounds to begin a new career. But I don't give you a thousand pounds: I give you only ten louis d'or just because a thousand pounds and ten louis d'or are just the same to you now; it's all the same—you'll gamble it away. Take it and good-bye."

"I will take it if you will let me embrace you at parting."

"Oh, with pleasure!"

We embraced with sincere feeling, and Mr. Astley went away.

No, he is wrong! If I was crude and silly about Polina and De Grieux, he was crude and hasty about Russians. I say nothing of myself. However . . . however, all that is not the point for the time: that is all words, words, and words, deeds are what are wanted! Switzerland is the great thing now! To-morrow . . . Oh, if only it were possible to set off to-morrow! To begin anew, to rise again. I must show them. . . . Let Polina know that I still can be a man. I have only to . . . But now it's too late—but to-morrow . . . oh, I have a presentiment and it cannot fail to be! I have now fifteen louis d'or, and I have begun with fifteen gulden! If one begins carefully . . . and can I, can I be such a baby! Can I fail to understand that I am a lost man, but—can I not rise again! Yes! I have only for once in my life to be prudent and patient and—that is all! I have only for once to show will power and in one hour I can transform my destiny! The great thing is will power. Only remember what happened to me seven months ago at Roulettenburg just before my final failure. Oh! it was a remarkable instance of determination: I had lost everything then, everything. . . . I was going out of the Casino, I looked, there was still one gulden in my waistcoat pocket: "Then I shall have something for dinner," I thought. But after I had gone a hundred paces I changed my mind and went back. I staked that gulden on *manque* (that time it was on *manque*), and there really is something peculiar in the feeling when, alone in a strange land, far from home and from friends, not knowing whether you will have anything to eat that day—you stake your last gulden, your very last! I won, and twenty minutes later I went out of the Casino, having a hundred and seventy gulden in my pocket. That's a fact! That's what the last gulden can sometimes do! And what if I had lost heart then? What if I had not dared to risk it? . . .

To-morrow, to-morrow it will all be over!

1 8 6 6

MASTER AND MAN

MASTER AND MAN

by Leo Tolstoy

1

It happened in the seventies, in winter, on the day after
St. Nicholas' Day.[1] There was a holiday in the parish, and
the village landowner and second-guild merchant, Vasili
Andreyitch Brekhunof, could not be absent, as he had to
attend church—he was a churchwarden—and receive and
entertain friends and acquaintances at home.

But at last all the guests were gone, and Vasili Andreyitch began preparations for a drive over to see a neighboring landed proprietor about buying from him the forest
for which they had been bargaining this long while. He
was in great haste to go, so as to forestall the town merchants, who might snatch away this profitable purchase.

The youthful landowner asked ten thousand rubles for
the forest, simply because Vasili Andreyitch offered seven
thousand. In reality, seven thousand was but a third of the
real worth of the forest. Vasili Andreyitch might, perhaps,
even now make the bargain, because the forest stood in
his district, and by an old standing agreement between
him and the other village merchants, no one of them
competed in another's territory. But Vasili Andreyitch
had learned that the timber-merchants from the capital
town of the province intended to bid for the Goryatchkin
forest, and he decided to go at once and conclude the bargain. Accordingly, as soon as the feast was over, he took
seven hundred rubles of his own from the strong box,
added to them twenty-three hundred belonging to the
church, so as to make three thousand, and, after carefully
counting the whole, he put the money into his pocket-book
and made haste to be gone.

[1] Winter St. Nicholas' Day is December 6 (O.S.).

Nikita, the laborer, the only one of Vasili Andreyitch's men who was not drunk that day, ran to harness the horse. He was not drunk on this occasion, because he had been a drunkard, and now since the last day before the fast, when he spent his coat and leather boots in drink, he had sworn off and for two months had not tasted liquor. He was not drinking even now, in spite of the temptation arising from the universal consumption of alcohol during the first two days of the holiday.

Nikita was a fifty-year-old muzhik from a neighboring village; no manager,[1] as folk said of him, but one who lived most of his life with other people, and not at his own home. He was esteemed everywhere for his industry, dexterity, and strength, and still more for his kindliness and pleasantness. But he never lived long in one place, because twice a year, or even oftener, he took to drinking; and at such times, besides spending all he had, he became turbulent and quarrelsome. Vasili Andreyitch had dismissed him several times, and afterward engaged him again; valuing his honesty and kindness to animals, but chiefly his cheapness. The merchant did not pay Nikita eighty rubles, the worth of such a man, but forty; and even that he paid without regular account, in small instalments, and mostly not in cash, but in high-priced goods from his own shop.

Nikita's wife, Marfa, a vigorous and once beautiful woman, carried on the home, with a boy almost fully grown and two girls. She never urged Nikita to live at home: first, because she had lived for about twenty years with a cooper, a muzhik from another village, who lodged with them; and secondly, because, although she treated her husband as she pleased when he was sober, she feared him like fire when he was drinking.

Once, when drunk at home, Nikita, apparently to revenge himself for all the submissiveness he had shown his wife when sober, broke open her box, took her best clothes, and, seizing an ax, cut to shreds all her sarafans and garments. All the wages Nikita earned went to his wife, and he made no objection to this arrangement. Thus it was that Marfa, two days before the holiday, came to Vasili Andreyitch, and got from him wheat flour, tea, sugar, and a pint of vodka,—about three rubles' worth in

[1] *Nye khozyaïn.*

all,—and five rubles in cash; and she thanked him as for a special favor, although, at the lowest figure, Vasili Andreyitch owed twenty rubles.

"What agreement did I make with you?" said Vasili Andreyitch to Nikita. "If you want anything, take it; you will work it out. I am not like other folks, with their delays, and accounts, and fines. We are dealing straightforwardly. You work for me, and I'll stand by you."

Talking in this way, Vasili Andreyitch was honestly convinced of his beneficence to Nikita; and he was so plausible that all those who depended on him for their money, beginning with Nikita, confirmed him in this conviction that he was not only not cheating them, but was doing them a service.

"I understand, Vasili Andreyitch; I do my best, I try to do as I would for my own father. I understand all right," answered Nikita, though he understood very well that Vasili Andreyitch was cheating him; at the same time he felt that it was useless to try to get the accounts cleared up. While there was nowhere else to go, he must stay where he was, and take what he could get.

Now, on receiving his master's orders to put the horse in, Nikita, willingly and cheerfully as always, and with a firm and easy stride, stepped to the cart-shed, took down from the nail the heavy, tasseled leather bridle, and, jingling the rings of the bit, went to the closed stable where by himself stood the horse which Vasili Andreyitch had ordered harnessed.

"Well, silly,[1] were you lonely, lonely?" said Nikita, in answer to the soft, welcoming whinny which greeted him from the stallion, a fairly good dark bay of medium height, with sloping quarters, who stood solitary in his stall. "No, no! Quiet, quiet, there's plenty of time! Let me give you a drink first," he went on, addressing the horse as if he were speaking to a creature which could understand human speech. With the skirt of his coat he swept down the horse's broad, double-ridged back, rough and dusty as it was; then he put the bridle on the handsome young head, arranged his ears and mane, and, throwing off the rope, led him away to drink.

Picking his way out of the dung-cumbered stall, Mukhortui began to plunge, making play with his hind foot,

[1] *Durachok*, diminutive of *dura*, a fool.

pretending that he wanted to kick Nikita, who was hurrying him to the well.

"Now, then, behave yourself, you rogue," said Nikita, knowing how careful Mukhortui was that the hind foot should only just touch his greasy sheepskin coat, but do no hurt; and Nikita himself especially enjoyed this sport.

After drinking the cold water, the horse drew a deep sigh, and moved his wet, strong lips, from which transparent drops fell into the trough; then, after standing a moment as if in thought, he suddenly gave a loud neigh.

"If you want no more, you needn't take it. Well, let it be at that; but don't ask again for more," said Nikita, with perfect seriousness, emphasizing to Mukhortui the consequences of his behavior. Then he briskly ran back to the shed, pulling the rein on the gay young horse, who lashed out all the way along the yard.

No other men were about, except a stranger to the place, the husband of the cook, who had come for the holiday.

"Go and ask, there's a good fellow, which sledge is wanted, the wide one or the little one," said Nikita to him.

The cook's husband went into the high-perched, iron-roofed house, and soon returned with the answer that the small one was ordered. By this time Nikita had put on the brass-studded saddle, and, carrying in one hand the light, painted yoke, with the other hand he led the horse toward the two sledges which stood under the shed.

"All right, the small one it is," said he, backing into the shafts the intelligent horse, which all the time pretended to bite at him; and, with the help of the cook's husband, he began to harness.

When all was nearly ready, and only the reins needed attention, Nikita sent the cook's husband to the shed for straw and to the storehouse for some sacking.

"That's capital! There, there; don't bristle up so!" said Nikita, squeezing into the sledge the freshly thrashed oat straw which the cook's husband had brought. "Now give me the sacking, while we spread it out, and put the cloth over it. That's all right, just the thing, comfortable to sit on," said he, doing that which he was talking about, and making the cloth tight over the straw all round.

"Thanks, my dear fellow," said Nikita to the cook's husband. "When two work, it's done quicker."

Then, disentangling the leather reins, the ends of which

were brought together and tied on a ring, he took the driver's seat on the sledge, and shook up the good horse, who
stirred himself, eager to make across the frozen refuse
that littered the yard, toward the gate.

"Uncle Mikit, eh, uncle!" [1] came a shout behind him,
from a seven-year-old boy in a black fur cloak, new white
felt boots, and warm cap, who came hurrying out from
the entrance-hall toward the yard. "Put me in?" he asked
in a shrill voice, buttoning his little coat as he ran.

"All right, come, my dove," said Nikita; and, stopping
the sledge, he put in the master's son, whose face grew
radiant with joy, and drove out into the road.

It was three o'clock, and cold—about ten degrees of
frost—gloomy and windy. Half the sky was shrouded by
a low-hanging dark cloud. In the yard it seemed quiet,
but in the street the wind was more noticeable. The snow
blew down from the roof of the barn close by, and at the
corner by the baths flew whirling round. Nikita had
scarcely driven out and turned round by the front door,
when Vasili Andreyitch, too, with a cigarette in his mouth,
wearing a sheepskin overcoat tightly fastened by a girdle
placed low, came out from the entrance-hall. He strode
down the trampled snow of the high steps, which creaked
under his leather-trimmed felt boots, and stopped. Drawing in one final puff of smoke, he flung down his cigarette
and trampled it underfoot; then, breathing out the smoke
through his mustaches and critically surveying the horse,
he began to turn in the corners of his overcoat collar on
both sides of his ruddy face, clean-shaven, except for a
mustache, so as to keep the fur clear from the moisture
of his breath.

"See there! What a funny little rascal! He's all ready!"
said he, as he caught sight of his little pale, thin son in
the sledge. Vasili Andreyitch was excited by the wine he
had taken with his guests, and was therefore more than
usually satisfied with everything which belonged to him,
and with everything he did. The sight of his son, whom
he always in his own mind thought of as his heir, now
caused him great satisfaction. He looked at him, and as
he did so he smirked and showed his long teeth.

His wife, a pale and meager woman, about to become
a mother, stood behind him in the entrance-hall with a

[1] *Dyadya Mikit, dyadyushka; dyadyushka* is diminutive of *dyadya.*

woolen shawl so wrapped about her head and shoulders that only her eyes could be seen.

"Would it not be better to take Nikita with you?" she asked, timidly stepping out from the door.

Vasili Andreyitch made no reply, but merely spat, scowling angrily at her words, which evidently were disagreeable to him.

"You have money with you," the wife continued, in the same plaintive voice. "What if the weather should get worse! Be careful, for God's sake."

"Do you think I don't know the road, that I need a guide?" retorted Vasili Andreyitch, with that affected compression of the lips with which he ordinarily addressed dealers in the market, and bringing out every syllable with extraordinary precision, as if he valued his own speech.

"Really, I would take him. I beg of you, for God's sake!" repeated his wife, folding her shawl closer.

"Just listen! She sticks to it like a leaf in the bath! . . . Why, where must I take him to?"

"Well, Vasili Andreyitch, I'm ready," said Nikita, cheerfully. "If I'm away, there are only the horses to be fed," he added, turning to his mistress.

"I'll look after that, Nikitushka; I'll tell Semyon," answered the mistress.

"Well, then, shall I come, Vasili Andreyitch?" asked Nikita, waiting.

"It seems we must have some regard for the old woman. But if you come, go and put on something warmer," said Vasili Andreyitch, smiling once more, and winking at Nikita's sheepskin coat, which was torn under the arms and down the back, and soiled and patched and frayed into fringes round the skirts.

"Hey, dear soul, come and hold the horse awhile!" shouted Nikita to the cook's husband, in the yard.

"I'll hold him myself," said the little boy, taking his half-frozen red hands out of his pockets, and seizing the cold leather reins.

"Only don't be too long putting your best coat [1] on! Be quick!" shouted Vasili Andreyitch, grinning at Nikita.

"In a breath, batyushka, Vasili Andreyitch!" said Nikita, and, with his trousers stuffed into his old patched

[1] He calls it a *diplomat*.

felt boots, he swiftly ran down the yard to the laborers' quarters.

"Here, Arinushka,[1] give me my khalat off the oven. I have to go with the master!" said Nikita, hastening into the room, and taking his girdle down from the nail.

The cook, who had just finished her after-dinner nap, and was about to get ready the samovar for her husband, turned cheerily to Nikita, and, catching his haste, moved about quickly, just as he was doing, took the well-worn woolen khalat off the oven, where it was drying, and shook and rubbed it.

"There now, you'll have a chance to spread and have a good time with your husband here," said Nikita to the cook; always, as part of his good-natured politeness, ready to say something to any one whom he came across.

Then, putting round himself the narrow shrunken girdle, he drew in his breath and tightened it about his spare body as much as he could.

"There," he said afterward, addressing himself, not to the cook, but to the girdle, while tucking the ends under his belt, "this way, you won't jump out." Then, working his shoulders up and down to get his arms loose, he put on the khalat, again stretching his back to free his arms, and poked up under his sleeves and took his mittens from the shelf. "Now, we're all right."

"You ought to change your boots," said the cook; "those boots are very bad."

Nikita stopped, as if remembering something.

"Yes, I ought. . . . But it will go as it is; it's not far." And he ran out into the yard.

"Won't you be cold, Nikitushka?" said his mistress, as he came up to the sledge.

"Why should I be cold? It is quite warm," answered Nikita, arranging the straw in the fore part of the sledge, so as to bring it over his legs, and stowing under it the whip which the good horse would not need.

Vasili Andreyitch had already taken his place in the sledge, almost filling up the whole of the curved back with the bulk of his body wrapped in two shubas; and, taking up the reins, he started at once. Nikita jumped in, seating himself in front, to the left, and hanging one leg over the side.

[1] Diminutive of Arina, popular form of Irina, Irene.

2

The good stallion took the sledge along at a brisk pace, over the smooth frozen road through the village; the runners creaking faintly as they went.

"Look at him there, hanging on! Give me the whip, Nikita," shouted Vasili Andreyitch, evidently enjoying the sight of his boy holding to the sledge-runners, behind. "I'll give it to you! Run to your mamma, you young dog!"

The boy jumped off. Mukhortui began to pace and then, getting his breath, broke into a trot.

Krestui, the village where Vasili Andreyitch lived, consisted of six houses. Scarcely had they passed the blacksmith's izba, the last in the village, when they suddenly remarked that the wind was much stronger than they had thought. The road was by this time scarcely visible. The tracks of the sledge were instantly covered with snow, and the road was to be distinguished only by the fact that it was higher than anything else. There was a whirl of snow over the fields, and the line where the earth and sky join could not be distinguished. The Telyatin forest, always plainly in sight, loomed dimly through the driving snow-dust. The wind came from the left hand, persistently blowing to one side the mane on Mukhortui's powerful neck, turning away even his knotted tail, and pressing Nikita's high collar—he sat on the windward side— against his face and nose.

"There is no chance of showing his speed, with this snow," said Vasili Andreyitch, proud of his good horse. "I once went to Pashutino with him, and we got there in half an hour."

"What?" said Nikita, who could not hear on account of his collar.

"Pashutino, I said; and he did it in half an hour," shouted Vasili Andreyitch.

"A good horse that, no question," said Nikita.

They became silent. But Vasili Andreyitch wanted to talk.

"Say, I suppose you tell your wife [1] not to give any drink to the cooper?" said Vasili Andreyitch in the same loud voice, being perfectly convinced that Nikita must feel flattered, talking with such an important and sensible man as himself, and he was so pleased with his jest that it never entered his head that the subject might be unpleasant to Nikita.

Again the man failed to catch his master's words, the voice being carried away by the wind.

Vasili Andreyitch, in his loud clear voice, repeated the jest about the cooper.

"God help them, Vasili Andreyitch, I don't meddle in these matters. I only hope that she does no harm to the lad; if she does—then God help her!"

"That is right," said Vasili Andreyitch. "Well, are you going to buy a horse in the spring?" Thus he began a new topic of conversation.

"Yes, I must buy one," answered Nikita, turning aside the collar of his kaftan, and leaning toward his master. Now the conversation became interesting to him, and he did not wish to lose a word.

"My lad is grown up, he must plow for himself, but now he is hired out all the time," said he.

"Well, then, take the horse with the thin loins; the price will not be high," shouted Vasili Andreyitch, feeling himself excited and consequently eagerly entering into his favorite business of horse-dealing, to which he gave all his intellectual powers.

"You give me fifteen rubles, and I'll buy in the market," said Nikita, who knew that at the highest price the horse which Vasili Andreyitch called "Bezkostretchnui" and wanted to sell him, was not worth more than seven rubles, but would cost him at his master's hands twenty-five; and that meant half a year's wages gone.

"The horse is a good one. I treat you as I would myself. Conscientiously. Brekhunof injures no man. Let me stand the loss, and me only. Honestly," he shouted in the voice which he used in cheating [2] his customers, "a genuine horse."

"As you think," said Nikita, sighing, and convinced

[1] *Khozyaïka.*
[2] *Zagovarivat' zubui,* "talk the teeth out."

that it was useless to listen further; and he again drew the collar over his ear and face.

They drove in silence for about half an hour. The wind cut sharply into Nikita's side and arm, where his shuba was torn. He huddled himself up and breathed into his coat-collar, which covered his mouth; and so he was not wholly cold!

"What do you think; shall we go through Karamuishevo, or keep the straight road?" said Vasili Andreyitch.

The road through Karamuishevo was more frequented, and staked on both sides; but it was longer. The straight road was nearer, but it was little used, and either there were no stakes, or they were poor ones left standing covered with snow.

Nikita thought awhile.

"Through Karamuishevo is farther, but it is better going," he said.

"But straight on, we have only to be careful not to lose the road in passing the little valley, and then the way is fairly good, sheltered by the forest," said Vasili Andreyitch, who favored the direct road.

"As you wish," replied Nikita, and again he rolled up his collar.

So Vasili Andreyitch took this way, and after driving about half a verst, he came to a place where there was a long oak branch which shook in the wind, and to which a few dry leaves were clinging, and there he turned to the left.

On turning, the wind blew almost directly against them, and the snow showered from on high. Vasili Andreyitch stirred up his horse, and inflated his cheeks, blowing his breath upon his mustaches. Nikita dozed.

They drove thus silently for about ten minutes. Suddenly Vasili Andreyitch began to say something.

"What?" asked Nikita, opening his eyes.

Vasili Andreyitch did not answer, but bent himself about, looking behind them, and then ahead of the horse. The sweat had curled the animal's coat on the groin and neck, and he was going at a walk.

"I say, what's the watter?" repeated Nikita.

"What is the matter?" mocked Vasili Andreyitch, irritated. "I see no stakes. We must be off the road."

"Well, pull up then, and I will find the road," said Nikita, and lightly jumping down, he drew out the whip from the straw and started off to the left, from his own side of the sledge.

The snow was not deep that season, so that one could travel anywhere, but in places it was up to one's knee, and got into Nikita's boots. He walked about, feeling with his feet and the whip, but no road was to be found.

"Well?" said Vasili Andreyitch, when Nikita returned to the sledge.

"There is no road on this side. I must try the other."

"There's something dark there in front. Go and see what it is," said Vasili Andreyitch.

Nikita walked ahead; got near the dark patch; and found it was black earth which the wind had strewn over the snow, from some fields of winter wheat. After searching to the right also, he returned to the sledge, shook the snow off himself, cleared his boots, and took his seat.

"We must go to the right," he said decidedly. "The wind was on our left before, now it is straight in my face. To the right," he repeated, with the same decision.

Vasili Andreyitch heeded him and turned to the right. But yet no road was found. He drove on in this direction for some time. The wind did not diminish, and the snow still fell.

"We seem to be astray altogether, Vasili Andreyitch," suddenly exclaimed Nikita, as if he were announcing some pleasant news. "What is that?" he said, pointing to some black potato-leaves, which thrust themselves through the snow.

Vasili Andreyitch stopped the horse, which by this time was in a heavy perspiration and stood with its deep sides heaving.

"What can it mean?" asked he.

"It means that we are on the Zakharovsky lands. Why, we are ever so far astray!"

"You lie!" remarked Vasili Andreyitch.

"I am not lying, Vasili Andreyitch; it is the truth," said Nikita. "You can feel that the sledge is moving over a potato-field, and there are the heaps of old leaves. It is the Zakharovsky factory-land."

"What a long way we are out!" said Vasili Andreyitch. "What are we to do?"

"Go straight ahead, that's all. We shall reach some

place," said Nikita. "If we do not get to Zakharovka, we shall come out at the owner's farm."

Vasili Andreyitch assented, and let the horse go as Nikita had said. They drove in this way for a long while. At times they passed over winter wheat fields all bare, and the sledge creaked over the humps of frozen soil. Sometimes they passed a stubble-field, sometimes a corn-field, where they could see the upstanding wormwood and straw beaten by the wind; sometimes they drove into deep and even white snow on all sides, with nothing visible above it.

The snow whirled down from on high, and sometimes seemed to rise up from below. The horse was evidently tiring; his coat grew crisp and white with frozen sweat, and he walked. Suddenly he stumbled in some ditch or water-course, and went down. Vasili Andreyitch wanted to halt, but Nikita cried to him: —

"Why should we stop? We have gone astray, and we must find our road. Hey, old fellow, hey," he shouted in an encouraging voice to the horse; and he jumped from the sledge, sinking into the ditch.

The horse dashed forward, and quickly landed upon a frozen heap. Obviously it was a made ditch.

"Where are we, then?" said Vasili Andreyitch.

"We shall see," answered Nikita. "Go ahead, we shall get to somewhere."

"Is not that the Goryatchkin forest?" asked Vasili Andreyitch, pointing out a dark mass which showed across the snow in front of them.

"When we get nearer, we shall see what forest it is," said Nikita.

He noticed that from the side of the dark mass, long, dry willow leaves were fluttering toward them; and so he knew that it was no forest, but a settlement; yet he chose not to say so. And, in fact, they had scarcely gone twenty-five yards beyond the ditch, when they distinctly made out the trees, and heard a new and melancholy sound. Nikita was right; it was not a forest but a row of tall willow trees, whereon a few scattered leaves still shivered. The willows were evidently ranged along the ditch of a threshing-floor. Coming up to the trees, through which the wind moaned and sighed, the horse suddenly planted his forefeet above the height of the sledge, then drew up his hind legs after him, turned to the left and leaped, sinking up to his knees in the snow. It was a road.

"Here we are," said Nikita, "but I don't know where."

The horse without erring ran along the snow-covered road, and they had not gone eighty yards when they saw the straight strip of a wattled fence, from which the snow was flying in the wind. Passing under a deeply drifted roof of a granary, the road turned in the direction of the wind, and brought them upon a snowdrift. But ahead of them was a passage between two houses; the drift was merely blown across the road, and had to be crossed. Indeed, after passing the drift, they came into a village street. In front of the end house of the village, the wind was shaking desperately the frozen linen which hung there: shirts, one red, one white, some leg-cloths, and a skirt. The white shirt especially shook frantically, tugging at the sleeves.

"Look there, either a lazy woman or a dead one left her linen out over the holiday," said Nikita, seeing the fluttering shirts.

3

At the beginning of the street, the wind was still fierce, and the road was snow-covered; but well within the village, it was calm, warm, and cheerful. At one house a dog was barking; at another, a woman, with a sleeveless coat over her head, came running out from somewhere, and stopped at the door of an izba to see who was driving past. In the middle of the village could be heard the sound of girls singing.

Here, in the village, the wind and the snow and the frost seemed subdued.

"Why, this is Grishkino," said Vasili Andreyitch.

"It is," said Nikita.

Grishkino it was. So they had strayed eight versts too far to the left, and traveled out of their proper direction; still, they had got somewhat nearer to their destination. From Grishkino to Goryatchkino was about five versts more.

In the middle of the village they almost ran into a tall man, walking in the center of the road.

"Who is driving?" said this man, and he held the horse. Then, recognizing Vasili Andreyitch, he took hold of the shaft, and reached the sledge, where he sat himself on the driver's seat.

It was the muzhik Isaï, well known to Vasili Andreyitch, and known throughout the district as the most notorious horse-thief.

"Ah, Vasili Andreyitch, where is God sending you?" said Isaï, from whom Nikita caught the smell of vodka.

"We are going to Goryatchkino."

"You've come a long way round! You should have gone through Malakhovo."

"'Should have' is good, but we got astray," said Vasili Andreyitch, pulling up.

"A good horse," said Isaï, examining him, and dexterously tightening the loosened knot in his thick tail. "Are you going to stay the night here?"

"No, friend, we must go on."

"Your business must be pressing. And who is that? Ah, Nikita Stepanuich!"

"Who else?" answered Nikita. "Look here, good friend, can you tell us how not to miss the road again?"

"How can you possibly miss it? Just turn back straight along the street, and then outside the houses; keep straight ahead. Don't go to the left. When you reach the highroad, then turn to the right."

"And which turning do we take out of the highroad— the summer or the winter road?" asked Nikita.

"The winter road. As soon as you get clear of the village there are some bushes, and opposite them is a way-mark, an oaken one, all branches. There is the road."

Vasili Andreyitch turned the horse back, and drove through the village.

"You had better stay the night," Isaï shouted after them. But Vasili Andreyitch did not answer, and started up the horse; five versts of smooth road, two versts of it through the forest, was easy enough to drive over, especially as the wind seemed quieter and the snow had apparently ceased falling.

After once more passing along the street, darkened and trodden with fresh horse-tracks, and after passing the house where the linen was hung out,—the white shirt was by this time torn, and hung by one frozen sleeve,—they came to the weirdly moaning and sighing willows, and then were again in the open country.

Not only had the snow-storm not ceased, but it seemed to have gained strength. The whole road was under snow, and only the stakes proved that they were keeping right. But even these signs of the road were difficult to make out, for the wind blew straight into their faces.

Vasili Andreyitch screwed up his eyes, and bent his head, examining the way-marks; but for the most part, he left the horse alone, trusting to his sagacity. And, in fact, the creature went truly, turning now to the left, now to the right, along the windings of the road which he sensed under his feet. So that in spite of the thickening snow and strengthening wind, the way-marks were still to be seen, now on the left, now on the right.

They had driven thus for ten minutes, when suddenly, straight in front of their horse, appeared a black object moving through the obliquely flying whirlwind of snow. It was a party of travelers. Mukhortui had overtaken them, and he struck his forefeet against the cross-bar of their sledge.

"Drive round! . . . a-a-i! . . . Go ahead!" cried voices from the sledge.

Vasili Andreyitch started to go round them. In the sledge were four peasants, three men and a woman, evidently returning from a festival visit. One of the men was whipping the snow-plastered rump of their little horse with a switch, while two of them, waving their arms from the fore part of the sledge, shouted out something. The woman, muffled up and covered with snow, sat quiet and rigid at the back.

"Where are you from?" asked Vasili Andreyitch.

"A-a-a-skiye!" was all that could be heard.

"I say, where are you from?"

"A-a-a-skiye!" shouted one of the peasants, with all his strength; but nevertheless it was impossible to make out the name.

"Go on! don't give up!" cried another, the one who kept beating his poor little horse.

"So you have come from the festival, have you?"

"Get on! get on! Up, Semka! drive round! Up, up!"

The sledges struck together, almost locked their sides, then fell apart, and the peasants' sledge began to drop behind.

The shaggy, snow-covered, big-bellied pony, laboriously breathing under the duga-bow, and evidently at the end of his strength in his vain efforts to escape from the switch belaboring him, staggered along on his short legs through the deep snow, which he trod down with difficulty. With distended nostrils, and ears set back in distress, and with his lower lip stuck out like a fish's, he kept his muzzle near Nikita's shoulder for a moment; then he began to fall behind.

"See what drink does," said Nikita. "They have tired that horse to death. What heathens!" [1]

For a few minutes, the pantings of the tired-out horse could be heard, with the drunken shouts of the peasants. Then the pantings became inaudible, and the shouts, also. Again nothing could be heard round about except the wind whistling in their ears, and the occasional scrape of the sledge-runners on a bare spot of road.

This encounter enlivened and encouraged Vasili Andreyitch, and he drove more boldly, not examining the way-marks, and again trusting to his horse.

Nikita had nothing to occupy him, and dozed just as he always did in such circumstances, thus wasting much good daylight. Suddenly the horse stopped, and Nikita was jerked forward, knocking his nose against the front.

"It seems we are going wrong again," said Vasili Andreyitch.

"What is the matter?"

"The way-marks are not to be seen. We must be out of the road."

"Well, if we've lost the road, we must look for it," said Nikita, laconically; and again stepping easily in his great bark overshoes, he started out to explore the snow.

He walked for a long time, now out of sight, now reappearing, then disappearing; at last, he returned.

"There is no road here; it may be farther on," said he, sitting down in the sledge.

It was already beginning to grow dark. The storm was neither increasing, nor did it diminish.

[1] *Aziatui kak yest'*, like Asiatics.

"I should like to hear those peasants again," said Vasili Andreyitch.

"Yes, but they won't pass near us; we must be a good distance off the road. Maybe they are astray, too," said Nikita.

"Where shall we make for, then?"

"Leave the horse to himself. He will find his way. Give me the reins."

Vasili Andreyitch handed over the reins; the more willingly because his hands, in spite of his warm gloves, were beginning to freeze.

Nikita took the reins, and held them lightly, trying to give no pressure; he was glad to prove the good sense of his favorite. And in fact, the intelligent horse, turning one ear and then the other, first in this and then in that direction, presently began to wheel round.

"He just doesn't speak," said Nikita. "Look how he manages it! Go on, go on, that's good."

The wind was now at their backs; they felt warmer.

"Is he not wise?" continued Nikita, delighted with his horse. "A Kirghiz beast is strong, but stupid. But this one,—see what he does with his ears. There is no need of a telegraph-wire; he can feel through a mile."

Hardly half an hour had gone, when a forest, or a village, or something, loomed up in front; and, to their right, the way-marks again showed. Evidently they were on the road again. "We are back at Grishkino, are we not?" exclaimed Nikita, suddenly.

Indeed, on the left hand rose the same granary, with the snow flying from it; and farther on was the same line with the frozen washing—the shirts and drawers, so fiercely shaken by the wind.

Again they drove through the street, again felt the quiet, warmth, and cheerfulness, again saw the road with the horse-tracks; heard voices, songs, the barking of a dog. It was now so dark that a few windows were lighted.

Halfway down the street, Vasili Andreyitch turned the horse toward a large two-storied brick house, and drew up at the steps.

Nikita went to the snow-dimmed window, in the light from which glittered the flitting flakes, and knocked with the handle of the whip.

"Who is there?" a voice answered to his knock.

"The Brekhunofs, from Krestui, my good man," answered Nikita. "Come out for a minute."

Some one moved from the window, and in about two minutes the door in the entrance-hall was heard to open, the latch of the front door clicked, and holding the door against the wind, there peeped out a tall, old, white-bearded muzhik, who had thrown a sheepskin coat over his white holiday shirt. Behind him was a young fellow in a red shirt and leather boots.

"What, is it you, Andreyitch?" said the old man.

"We have lost our road, friend," said Vasili Andreyitch. "We set out for Goryatchkino, and found ourselves here. Then we went on, but lost the road again."

"Why, how you've wandered!" answered the old man. "Petrushka, go, open the gates," he said to the young man in the red shirt.

"Of course I will," said the young fellow, cheerfully, as he ran off through the entrance-hall.

"We are not stopping for the night, friend," said Vasili Andreyitch.

"Where can you go in the night-time? You had better stop."

"Should be very glad to spend the night, but I must go on business, friend; it's impossible!"

"Well, then, at least warm yourself a little; the samovar is just ready," said the old man.

"Warm ourselves? We can do that," said Vasili Andreyitch. "It cannot get darker, and when the moon is up, it will be still lighter. Come, Mikit, let us go in and warm up a bit."

"Why, yes, let us warm ourselves," said Nikita, who was very cold, and whose great desire was to thaw out his benumbed limbs in a well-heated room.

Vasili Andreyitch went with the old man into the house. Nikita drove through the gates opened by Petrushka, by whose advice he stood the horse under the pent-roof of the shed, the floor of which was strewn with stable-litter. The high duga-bow caught the roof-beam, and the hens and a cock, already gone to roost up there, began to cackle angrily and scratch on the wood. Some startled sheep, pattering their feet on the frozen dung-heap, huddled themselves out of the way. A dog yelped desperately in fright, after the manner of young hounds, and barked fiercely at the stranger.

Nikita held conversation with them all. He begged pardon of the fowls, and calmed them with assurances that he would give them no more trouble; he reproved the sheep for being needlessly frightened; and while fastening up the horse, he kept on exhorting the little dog.

"That will do," said he, shaking the snow from himself. "Hear, how he is barking!" added he, for the dog's benefit. "That's quite enough for you, quite enough, stupid! That will do! Why do you bother yourself? There are no thieves or strangers about."

"It is like the tale of the Three Domestic Counselors," said the young man, thrusting the sledge under the shed with his strong arms.

"What about the counselors?"

"The tale is in P'ulson. A thief sneaks up to a house; the dog barks,—that means 'Be on your guard;' the cock crows,—that means 'Get up;' the cat washes itself,—that means 'A welcome guest is coming, be ready for him,'" said the young man, with a smile.

Petrukha could read and write, and knew, almost by heart, the only book he possessed, which was Paulson's primer; and he liked, especially when, as now, he had been drinking a little too much, to quote from the book some saying which seemed appropriate to the occasion.

"Quite true," said Nikita.

"I suppose you are cold, uncle," said Petrukha.

"Yes, something that way," said Nikita. They both crossed the yard and entered the house.

4

The house at which Vasili Andreyitch had drawn up was one of the richest in the village. The family had five allotments of land, and hired still more outside. Their establishment owned six horses, three cows, two yearling heifers, and twenty head of sheep. In the house lived twenty-two souls; four married sons, six grandchildren (of whom one, Petrukha, was married), two great-grand-children, three orphans, and four daughters-in-law with their children. It was one of the few families, living together in one household; yet even here was that indefinable interior work of disintegration,—beginning, as usual, among the women,—infallibly bound to bring about speedy separation. Two sons were water-carriers in Moscow; one was in the army. At present, those at home were the old man, his wife, the second son who was manager [1] of the house, the oldest son who had come from Moscow on a holiday, and all the women and children. Besides the family there was a guest, a neighbor, who was an intimate friend.

Over the table in the living-room hung a shaded lamp, which threw a bright light down on the tea-service, a bottle of vodka, and some eatables, and on the brick walls, where, in the "red corner," hung the ikons with pictures on each side of them.

At the head of the table sat Vasili Andreyitch, in his black fur coat, sucking his frozen mustaches, and scrutinizing the people and the room with his bulging, hawk-like eyes. Beside him at the table sat the white-bearded, bald, old father of the house, in a white homespun shirt; next him sat the son from Moscow, with his sturdy back and shoulders, clad in a thin cotton shirt; then the other son, the broad-shouldered eldest brother, who acted as head of the house; then a lean and red-haired muzhik—the visiting neighbor.

The mushiks, having drunk and eaten, prepared to take tea, and the samovar was already boiling as it stood on the floor near the oven. The children were to be seen on the oven and on sleeping-shelves. On the wall bench sat a woman with a cradle beside her. The aged mother of the house, whose face was covered with a network of fine wrinkles even to the lips, waited on Vasili Andreyitch.

As Nikita entered the room, she was just filling a coarse glass with vodka, and handing it to Vasili Andreyitch.

"No harm done, Vasili Andreyitch, but you must wish our good health," said she. "Have a drink, dear!"

The sight and smell of vodka, especially in his cold and tired condition, greatly disturbed Nikita's mind. He frowned, and after shaking the snow from his kaftan and

[1] *Khozyaïn.*

hat, stood before the holy images: without apparently seeing any one, he made the sign of the cross thrice, and bowed to the images; then, turning to the old man, he bowed to him first, afterward to all who sat at table, and again to the women beside the oven; and saying, "Good fortune to your feast," he began to take off his overcoat without looking at the table.

"Why, you are all over frost, uncle" said the eldest brother, looking at the snow which crowned Nikita's face, eyes, and beard.

Nikita took off his kaftan, shook it again, hung it near the oven, and came to the table. They offered him vodka also. There was a moment's bitter struggle; he came very near taking the glass and pouring the fragrant, transparent liquid into his mouth, but he looked at Vasili Andreyitch, remembered his vow, remembered the lost boots, the cooper, his son for whom he had promised to buy a horse when the spring came; he sighed, and refused.

"I don't drink, thank you humbly," he said gloomily, and sat down on the bench, near the second window.

"Why not?" asked the eldest brother.

"I don't drink, that's all," said Nikita, not daring to raise his eyes, and looking at his thin beard and mustache, and at the thawing icicles clinging to them.

"It is not good for him," said Vasili Andreyitch, munching a biscuit after emptying his glass.

"Then have some tea," said the kindly old woman. "I dare say you are quite benumbed, good soul. How lazy you women are with the samovar!"

"It is ready," answered the youngest, and wiping round the samovar with an apron, she bore it heavily to the table, and set it down with a thud.

Meanwhile, Vasili Andreyitch told how they had gone astray and worked back twice to the same village; what mistakes they had made, and how they had met the drunken peasants. Their hosts expressed surprise, showed why and where they had missed the road, told them the names of the revelers they had met, and made plain how they ought to go.

"From here to Molchanovka, a child might go; the only thing is to make sure where to turn out of the high-road; you'll see a bush there. But yet you did not get there," said the neighbor.

"You ought to stop here. The women will make up a bed," said the old woman, persuasively.

"You would make a better start in the morning; much pleasanter, that," said the old man, affirming what his wife had said.

"Impossible, friend! Business!" said Vasili Andreyitch. "If you let an hour go, you may not be able to make it up in a year," added he, remembering the forest and the dealers who might do him out of his purchase. "We shall get there, shan't we?" he said, turning to Nikita.

"We may lose ourselves again," said Nikita, gloomily. He was gloomy, because of the intense longing he felt for the vodka; and the tea, the only thing which could quench that longing, had not yet been offered to him.

"We have only to reach the turning, and there is no more danger of losing the road, as it goes straight through the forest," said Vasili Andreyitch.

"Just as you say, Vasili Andreyitch; if you want to go, let us go," said Nikita, taking the glass of tea offered to him.

"Well, let us drink up our tea, and then forward march!"

Nikita said nothing, but shook his head; and carefully pouring the tea into the saucer, began to warm his hands and his swollen fingers over the steam. Then, taking a small bite of sugar in his mouth, he turned to their hosts, said, "Your health," and drank down the warming liquid.

"Couldn't some one come with us to the turning?" asked Vasili Andreyitch.

"Why not? Certainly," said the eldest son. "Petrukha will put in the horse, and go with you as far as the turning."

"Then put in your horse, and I shall be in your debt."

"My dear man," said the kindly old woman, "we are right glad to do it."

"Petrukha, go and put in the mare," said the eldest son.

"All right," said Petrukha, smiling; and, without delay, taking his cap from the nail, he hurried away to harness up.

While the harnessing was in progress, the talk turned back to the point where it stood when Vasili Andreyitch arrived. The old man had complained to his neighbor, the village-elder, about the conduct of his third son, who had sent him no present this holiday-time, though he had sent a French shawl to his wife.

"These young folk are getting worse and worse," said the old man.

"Very much worse!" said the neighbor. "They are unmanageable. They know too much. There's Demotchkin, now, who broke his father's arm. It all comes from too much learning."

Nikita listened, watched the faces, and it was evident that he, too, would like to have a share in the conversation, had he not been so busy with his tea; as it was, he only nodded his head approvingly. He emptied glass after glass, growing warmer and warmer, and more and more comfortable. The talk continued in one strain, all about the harm that comes from family division; and it was clearly no theoretical discussion, but concerned with a rupture in this very house, arising through the second son, who sat there in his place, morosely silent. The question was a painful one, and absorbed the whole family; but out of politeness they refrained from discussing their private affairs before strangers.

At last, however, the old man could endure it no longer. In a tearful voice, he began to say that there should be no break-up of the family while he lived; that the house had much to thank God for, but if they fell apart—they must become beggars.

"Just like the Matveyefs," said the neighbor. "There was plenty among them all, but when they broke up the family, there was nothing for any of them."

"That's just what you want to do," said the old man to his son.

The son answered nothing, and there was a painful pause. The silence was broken by Petrukha, who had by this time harnessed the horse and returned to the room, where he had been standing for a few minutes, smiling all the time.

"There is a tale in P'ulson, just like this," said he. "A father gave his sons a broom to break. They could not break it while it was bound together, but they broke it easily by taking every switch by itself. That's the way here," he said, with his broad smile. "All's ready!" he added.

"Well, if we're ready, let us start," said Vasili Andreyitch. "As to this quarrel, don't you give in, grandfather. You got everything together, and you are the master. Apply to the magistrate; he will show you how to keep your authority."

"And he gives himself such airs, such airs," continued the old man, in his complaining voice. "There is no ordering him! It is as if Satan lived in him."

Meanwhile, Nikita, having drunk his fifth glass of tea, did not stand it upside down, in sign that he had finished, but laid it on its side, hoping they might fill it a sixth time. But there was no longer any water in the samovar, and the hostess did not fill up for him again, and then Vasili Andreyitch began to put on his things. There was no help; Nikita also rose, put back into the sugar-basin the little lump of sugar, which he had nibbled on all sides, wiped the moisture from his face with the skirt of his coat, and went to put on his khalat.

After getting into the garment, he sighed heavily; then, having thanked their hosts and said good-by, he went out from the warm, bright room, and through the dark, cold entrance-hall, where the wind creaked the doors and drove the snow in at the chinks, into the dark yard.

Petrukha, in his shuba, stood in the center of the yard with the horse, and smiling recited verses from Paulson: —

> *Storm-clouds veil the sky with darkness,*
> *Swiftly whirl the snowblasts wild,*
> *Now the storm roars like a wild beast,*
> *Now it waileth like a child.*[1]

Nikita nodded appreciatively, and arranged the reins.

The old man, coming out with Vasili Andreyitch, brought a lantern into the entry, and was going to show the way; but the wind put it out at once. Even in the inclosed yard, one could see that the storm had become much more violent.

"What weather!" thought Vasili Andreyitch. "I'm afraid we shall not get there. But it must be! Business! And then, I have put our friend to the trouble of harnessing his horse. God helping, we shall get there."

[1] This is rendered in rude fashion by Petrukha. The Russian poem given in Paulson is by Pushkin.

Their aged host also thought it better not to go; but he had offered his arguments already, and they had not lis- tened to him. It was useless to ask them again.

"Maybe it is old age makes me overcautious; they will get there all right," thought he. "And we can all go to bed at the proper time. It will be less bother."

As for Petrukha, he had no thought of danger: he knew the way so well and the whole region, and then besides, the lines about "the snowblasts wild" encouraged him, be- cause they were a quite true description of what was going on out-of-doors. Nikita had no wish to go at all; but he was long used to follow other people's wishes, and to give up his own. Therefore no one withheld the travelers.

5

Vasili Andreyitch went over to his sledge, found it with some difficulty in the darkness, got in, and took the reins.

"Go ahead!" he shouted.

Petrukha, kneeling in his sledge, started the horse. Mukhortui, who had before been whinnying, aware of the mare's nearness, now dashed after her, and they drove out into the street. They rode once more through the vil- lage, down the same road, past the space where the frozen linen had hung, but was no longer to be seen; past the same barn, now snowed-up almost as high as the roof, from which the snow flew incessantly; past the moaning, whistling, and bending willows; and again they came to where the sea of snow raged from above and below. The wind was so violent that, taking the travelers sidewise when they were crossing its direction, it heeled the sledge over and pushed the horse aside. Petrukha drove his good mare in front, at an easy trot, giving her an occasional lively shout of encouragement. Mukhortui pressed after her.

After driving thus for about ten minutes, Petrukha turned around and called out something. But neither Vasili Andreyitch nor Nikita could hear for the wind, but they guessed that they had reached the turning. In fact, Petrukha had turned to the right; the wind which had been at their side again blew in their faces, and to the right, through the snow, loomed something black. It was the bush beside the turning.

"Well, good-by to you!"

"Thanks, Petrukha!"

" 'The storm-clouds veil the sky with darkness!' " shouted Petrukha, and disappeared.

"Quite a poet," said Vasili Andreyitch, and shook the reins.

"Yes, a fine young man, a genuine muzhik," said Nikita.

They drove on.

Nikita, protecting his head by crouching it down between his shoulders, so that his short beard covered up his throat, sat silent, trying not to lose the warmth which the tea had given him. Before him, he saw the straight lines of the shafts, which to his eyes looked like the ruts of the road; he saw the shifting quarters of the horse, with the knotted tail blown off in one direction by the wind; beyond, he saw the high duga-bow between the shafts, and the horse's rocking head and neck, with the floating mane. From time to time he noticed the stakes, and knew that, thus far, they had kept to the road, and he need not concern himself.

Vasili Andreyitch drove on, trusting to the horse to keep to the road. But Mukhortui, although he had rested a little in the village, went unwillingly, and seemed to shirk from the road, so that Vasili Andreyitch had to press him at times.

"Here is a stake on the right, here's another, and there's a third," reckoned Vasili Andreyitch, "and here, in front, is the forest," he thought, examining a dark patch ahead. But that which he took for a forest was only a bush. They passed the bush, drove about fifty yards farther, and there was neither the fourth stake nor the forest.

"We must reach the forest soon," thought Vasili Andreyitch; and buoyed up by the vodka and the tea, he shook the reins. The good, obedient animal responded, and now at an amble, now at an easy trot, made in the direction he was sent, although he knew it was not the way in which he should have been going. Ten minutes went by, still no forest.

"I'm afraid we are astray again!" said Vasili Andreyitch, pulling up.

Nikita silently got out from the sledge, and holding with his hand the flaps of his khalat, which now pressed against him and then flew from him as he stood and turned in the wind, began to tread the snow; first he went to one side, then to the other. Three times he went out of sight altogether. At last he returned, and took the reins from Vasili Andreyitch's hands.

"We must go to the right," he said sternly and peremptorily; and he turned the horse.

"Well, if it must be to the right, let us go to the right," said Vasili Andreyitch, passing over the reins and thrusting his frozen hands into his sleeves.

Nikita did not answer.

"Now then, old fellow, stir yourself," he called to the horse; but Mukhortui, in spite of the shake of the reins, went on only slowly. In places the snow was knee-deep, and the sledge jerked at every movement of the horse.

Nikita took the whip, which hung in front of the sledge, and struck once. The good creature, unused to the knout, sprang forward at a trot, but soon fell again to a slow amble, and then began to walk. Thus they went for five minutes. All was so dark, and so blurred with snow from above and below, that sometimes they could not make out the duga-bow. At times it seemed as if the sledge was standing, and the ground running back. Suddenly the horse stopped short, evidently perceiving something a little distance in front of him. Nikita once more lightly jumped out, throwing down the reins, and went in front to find out what was the matter. But hardly had he taken a pace clear ahead, when his feet slipped, and he went rolling down some steep place.

"Tpru, tpru, tpru!" he said to himself, falling and trying to stop his fall. There was nothing to seize hold of, and he brought up only when his feet plunged into a deep bed of snow which lay in the ravine.

The fringe of drifted snow which hung on the edge of the ravine, disturbed by Nikita's fall, showered down on him, and got into his neck.

"What a way of doing!" cried Nikita, reproachfully addressing the snow and the ravine, as he cleared out his coat-collar.

"Mikit, ha, Mikit," shouted Vasili Andreyitch, from above.

But Nikita did not answer.

He was too much occupied in shaking away the snow, then in looking for the whip, which he lost in rolling down the bank. Having found the whip, he started to climb up the bank where he had rolled down, but it was a perfect impossibility; he slipped back every time; so that he was compelled to go along the foot of the bank to find a way up. About ten yards from the place where he fell, he managed to struggle up again on all fours, and then he turned back along the bank toward the place where the horse should have been. He could not see horse or sledge; but by going with the wind, he heard Vasili Andreyitch's voice and Mukhortui's whinny calling him, before he saw them.

"I'm coming; I'm coming. What are you cackling for!" he said.

Only when he had approached quite near the sledge could he make out the horse and Vasili Andreyitch, who stood close by, and looked gigantic.

"Where the devil have you been hiding? We've got to drive back. We must get back to Grishkino anyway," the master began to rebuke him angrily.

"I should be glad to get there, Vasili Andreyitch, but how are we to do it? Here is a ravine where if we once get in, we shall never come out. I pitched in there in such a way that I could hardly get out."

"Well, assuredly we can't stay here; somewhere we must go," said Vasili Andreyitch.

Nikita made no answer. He sat down on the sledge with his back to the wind, took off his boots and emptied them of snow; then, with a little straw which he took from the sledge, he stopped from the inside a gap in the left boot.

Vasili Andreyitch was silent, as if leaving everything to Nikita alone. Having got his boots on, Nikita drew his feet into the sledge, put on his mittens again, took the reins, and turned the horse along the ravine. But they had not driven a hundred paces when the horse stopped again. Another ravine confronted him.

Nikita got out again and began to explore the snow. He was gone a long while. At last he reappeared on the side opposite to that on which he started.

"Andreyitch, are you alive?" he called.

"Here!" shouted Vasili Andreyitch. "What is the matter?"

"I can't make anything out, it is too dark; except some ravines. We must drive to windward again."

They set off once more; Nikita explored again, stumbling through the snow. Again he sat down, again he crept forward, and at last, out of breath, he stopped beside the sledge.

"How now?" asked Vasili Andreyitch.

"Well, I'm quite tired out. And the horse is done up."

"What are we to do?"

"Wait a minute."

Nikita moved off again, and soon returned.

"Follow me," he said, going in front of the horse.

Vasili Andreyitch no longer gave orders, but implicitly did what Nikita told him.

"Here, this way!" shouted Nikita, stepping quickly to the right. Seizing Mukhortui by the bridle, he turned him toward a snowdrift

At first the horse resisted; then dashed forward, hoping to leap the drift, but failed, and sank in snow up to the hams.

"Get out!" called Nikita to Vasili Andreyitch, who still sat in the sledge; and taking hold of one shaft, he tried to push the sledge after the horse.

"It's a pretty hard job, brother," he said to Mukhortui, "but it can't be helped. Na! na! Stir yourself! Just a little!" he called out.

The horse leaped forward, once, twice, but failed to clear himself, and sat back again as if thinking out something.

"Well, friend, this is no good," urged Nikita to Mukhortui. "Now, once more!"

Nikita pulled on the shaft again; Vasili Andreyitch did the same on the opposite side. The horse lifted his head, and made a sudden dash.

"Nu! na! You won't sink; don't be afraid," shouted Nikita.

One plunge, a second, a third, and at last the horse was out from the snowdrift, and stood still, breathing heavily and shaking himself clear. Nikita wanted to lead him on farther, but Vasili Andreyitch, in his two shubas, had so lost his breath that he could walk no more, and dropped into the sledge.

"Let me get my breath a little," he said, unbinding the handkerchief with which, at the village, he had tied the collar of his coat.

"We are all right here; you might as well lie down," said Nikita. "I'll lead him along;" and with Vasili Andreyitch in the sledge, he led the horse by the head about ten paces farther, then up a slight rise, and stopped.

The place where Nikita drew up was not in a hollow, where the snow, swept from the drifts and piled up, might perfectly shelter them; but nevertheless it was partly protected from the wind by the edge of the ravine.

There were moments when the wind seemed to become quieter; but these intervals did not last long, and after them the storm, as if to make up for such a rest, rushed on with tenfold vigor, and tore and whirled the more angrily.

Such a gust of wind swept past as Vasili Andreyitch, with recovered breath, got out of the sledge, and went up to Nikita to talk over the situation. They both instinctively bowed themselves, and waited until the stress should be over. Mukhortui laid back his ears and shook his head. When the blast had abated a little, Nikita took off his mittens, stuck them in his girdle, and having breathed a little on his hands, began to undo the strap from the duga-bow.

"Why are you doing that?" asked Vasili Andreyitch.

"I'm taking out the horse. What else can we do? I'm done up," said Nikita, as if apologizing.

"But couldn't we drive somewhere?"

"No, we could not. We should only do harm to the horse. The poor beast is worn out," said Nikita, pointing to the creature, who stood there, with heavily heaving sides, submissively waiting for whatever should come. "We must put up for the night here," he repeated, as if they were at their inn. He began to undo the collar-straps.

The hames fell apart.

"But we shall be frozen, shan't we?" queried Vasili Andreyitch.

"Well, if we are, we cannot help it," said Nikita.

6

In his two shubas, Vasili Andreyitch was quite warm; especially after his exertion in the snowdrift. But a cold shiver ran down his back when he learned that they really had to spend the night where they were. To calm himself, he sat down in the sledge, and got out his cigarettes and matches.

Meanwhile Nikita went on taking out the horse. He undid the belly-band, took away the reins and collar-strap, and laid the duga-bow aside from the shafts; continuing to encourage the horse by speaking to him.

"Now, come out, come out," he said, leading him clear of the shafts. "We must tie you here. I'll put a bit of straw for you, and take off your bridle," he went on, doing as he said. "After a bite, you'll feel ever so much better."

But Mukhortui was not calmed by Nikita's words; uneasily, he shifted his feet, pressed against the sledge, turned his back to the wind, and rubbed his head on Nikita's sleeve.

As if not wholly to reject the treat of straw which Nikita put under his nose, Mukhortui just once seized a wisp out of the sledge, but quickly deciding that there was more important business than to eat straw, he threw it down again, and the wind instantly tore it away and hid it in the snow.

"Now we must make a signal," said Nikita, turning the front of the sledge against the wind; and having tied the shafts together with a strap, he set them on end in front of the sledge. "If the snow covers us, the good folk will see the shafts, and dig us out," said Nikita, slapping his mittens together and pulling them on. "That's what old hands advise."

Vasili Andreyitch had meanwhile opened his shuba, and making a shelter with its folds, he rubbed match after match on the steel box. But his hands trembled, and the kindled matches were blown out by the wind, one after another, some when just struck, others when he thrust them to the cigarette. At last one match burned fully, and lighted up for a moment the fur of his shuba, his hand with the gold ring on the bent forefinger, and the snow-sprinkled straw which stuck out from under the sacking. The cigarette lighted. Twice he eagerly whiffed the smoke, swallowed it, blew it through his mustaches, and would have gone on, but the wind tore away the burning tobacco and sent it whirling after the straw. Even these few whiffs of tobacco-smoke cheered up Vasili Andreyitch.

"Well, we will stop here," he said authoritatively.

"Wait a minute, and I'll make a flag," he said, picking up the handkerchief which he had taken from round his collar and put down in the sledge. Drawing off his gloves, and reaching up, he tied the handkerchief tightly to the strap that held the shafts together.

The handkerchief at once began to beat about wildly; now clinging round a shaft, now streaming out, and cracking like a whip.

"That's a clever piece of work," said Vasili Andreyitch, pleased with what he had done, and getting into the sledge. "We should be warmer together, but there's not room for two," he said.

"I can find a place," said Nikita, "but the horse must be covered; he's sweating, the good fellow. Excuse me," he added, going to the sledge, and drawing the sacking from under Vasili Andreyitch. This he folded, and after taking off the saddle and breeching, covered Mukhortui with it.

"Anyway, it will be a bit warmer, silly," he said, putting the saddle and heavy breeching over the sacking.

"You won't need the cloth, will you? and give me a little straw," said Nikita, coming back to the sledge after he had finished his work.

Taking these from beneath Vasili Andreyitch, Nikita went behind the sledge, dug there a hole in the snow, stuffed in the straw, and pulling down his hat, wrapping his kaftan well around him, and covering himself with the coarse matting, sat down on the straw, leaning against the bark back of the sledge, which kept off the wind and snow.

Vasili Andreyitch shook his head disapprovingly at what Nikita was doing, as he usually found fault with the peasants' ignorance and stupidity; and he began to make his own arrangements for the night.

He smoothed the remaining straw and heaped it thicker under his side; then he thrust his hands into his sleeves, and settled his head in the corner of the sledge sheltered from the wind in front.

He did not feel sleepy. He lay and thought; thought about one thing only, which was the aim, reason, pleasure, and pride of his life: —about how much money he had made, and might make, and how much other men whom he knew had made and possessed, and the means whereby they gained it and were gaining it; and how he, in like manner, might gain a good deal more. The purchase of the Goryatchkin forest was for him an affair of the utmost importance. He counted on making from this transaction as much as ten thousand! And he began mentally to estimate the value of the forest which he had inspected in the autumn so carefully as to count all the trees on two desyatins.

"The oak will make sledge-runners. The small stuff will take care of itself. And there'll be thirty cords of wood to the acre," [1] said he to himself. "At the very worst there'll be a little less than eighty rubles an acre. There are one hundred and fifty acres."

He reckoned it up mentally and saw that it amounted to about twelve thousand rubles; but without his abacus he could not calculate it exactly.

"But for all that, I won't pay ten thousand; say eight thousand; besides, one must allow for the bare spaces. I'll oil the surveyor,—a hundred rubles will do it,—a hundred and fifty, if necessary; he'll deduct about thirteen acres out of the forest. He is sure to sell for eight; three thousand down. Never fear; he will weaken at that," he thought, pressing his forearm on the pocket-book beneath.

"And how we lost our way after we left the turning, God only knows! The forest and the woodman's hut should be near by. I should like to hear the dogs, but they never bark when they're wanted, the cursed brutes."

---

[1] He says, "Thirty sazhen to the desyatin." A cubic sazhen is equivalent to 2.68 cords; a desyatin is 2.7 acres. In his prospective purchase there are fifty-six desyatins.

He opened his collar a little from his ear and tried to listen; all he could hear was the same whistle of the wind, the flapping and cracking of the handkerchief on the shafts, and the pelting of the falling snow on the bark matting of the sledge.

He covered himself again.

"If one had only known this beforehand, we had better have stayed where we were. But no matter, we shall get there tomorrow. It is only a day lost. In this weather, the others won't get there either."

Then he remembered that on the twenty-first he had to receive the price for some gelded rams, from the butcher.

"I wanted to be there myself, for if he doesn't find me, my wife won't know how to receive the money. She's very inexperienced, she doesn't know about the right way of doing things," he continued to reflect, remembering how she had failed in her behavior towards a commissary of police,[1] who had come to pay them a visit the day before, at the feast. "Just a woman, of course. What has she ever seen anywhere? In my father's time, what a house we had! Nothing out of the way, a well-to-do countryman's: a barn and an inn, and that was the whole property. And now in these fifteen years what have I done? A general store, two taverns, a flour-mill, a granary, two farms rented, a house and warehouse all iron-roofed," he remembered proudly. "Not as it was in father's time! Who is known over the whole place?[2] Brekhunof.

"And why is this? Because I know my business, I look after things; not like others, who idle or waste their time in foolishness. I don't sleep at night. Storm or no storm, I start out. And of course, the thing is done. People think it's fun making money. Not at all; you work and rack your brains. You spend your night this way outdoors, and go without sleep! The thoughts whirling in your head are as good as a cushion!" he exclaimed with pride. "They think men get on through luck. Look at the Mironofs, who have their millions, now. Why? They worked. Then God gives. If God only grants me health!"

And the idea that he, also, might become a millionaire like Mironof, who began with nothing, so excited Vasili Andreyitch that he suddenly felt a need to talk to some

[1] *Stanovoï.*

[2] *Kto gremit,* who thunders.

one. But there was no one. . . . If he could only have reached Goryatchkino, he might have talked with the land-owner, and "put spectacles on him."

"Whew! how it blows! It will snow us up so that we can't get out in the morning," he thought, as he listened to the rush of the wind, which blew against the front of the sledge, bending it back, and lashed the snow against the bark matting. He lifted himself and looked out: in the white whirling darkness all he could see was Mukhortui's black head, and his back covered with the fluttering matting, and his thick twisted tail; all around, on every side, in front and behind, was the same monotonous white waving mist, occasionally appearing to grow a little lighter, then again growing thicker and denser.[1]

"I was foolish enough yielding to Nikita," he thought. "We ought to have driven on, we should have come out somewhere. We might have gone back to Grishkino, and stayed at Taras's. Now we must sit here all night. Well, what was I thinking about? Yes, that God gives to the industrious, and not to the lazy, not to loafers and fools. It's time for a smoke, too."

He sat up, got his cigarette-case, and stretched himself flat on his stomach, to protect the light from the wind with the flaps of his coat; but the wind got in and put out one match after another. At last he managed to get a cigarette lit, and he began to smoke. The fact that he succeeded greatly delighted him. Though the wind smoked more of his cigarette than he did, nevertheless he got about three puffs, and felt better.

He again threw himself back in the sledge, wrapped himself up, and returned to his recollections and dreams; very unexpectedly he lost himself and fell asleep.

But suddenly something touched him and woke him up. Whether it was Mukhortui pulling the straw from under him, or something within him that startled him, at all events he awoke, and his heart began to beat so quickly and violently that the sledge seemed to be shaking under him.

He opened his eyes. Everything around was the same as before; only it seemed a little lighter.

"The dawn," he said to himself; "it must be nearly morning."

[1] *Sgushchayushchayasa:* literally, "condensing itself."

But he instantly remembered that the light was only due to the rising of the moon.

He lifted himself, and looked first at the horse. Mukhortui was standing with his back to the wind, and shivering all over. The snow-covered sacking had fallen off on one side; the breeching had slipped down; the snowy head and the fluttering crest and mane, all were now clearly visible.

Vasili Andreyitch bent over the back of the sledge and looked behind. Nikita was still sitting in the old position which he had first taken. The sacking with which he had protected himself and his feet were covered with snow.

"I'm afraid the muzhik will be frozen; his clothes are so wretched. I might be held responsible. I declare they're such senseless people! They truly haven't the slightest forethought!" reflected Vasili Andreyitch; and he was tempted to take the sacking from the horse, to put over Nikita; but it was cold to get out and stir around, and besides, the horse might freeze to death.

"What made me bring him? It is all her stupidity!" thought Vasili Andreyitch, remembering his unattractive wife; and he turned again to his former place in the front of the sledge.

"My uncle once sat in snow all night, like this," he reflected, "and no harm came of it. And Sevastian also was dug out," he went on, remembering another case, "but he was dead, stiff like a frozen carcass. If we had only stopped at Grishkino, nothing would have happened."

Carefully covering himself, so that the warmth of the fur might not be wasted, but might protect his neck, knees, and the soles of his feet, he shut his eyes, trying to sleep again. But however much he tried, this time he could not lose himself; on the contrary, he felt alert and excited. Again he began to count his gains and the debts due to him; again he began to boast of his success, and to feel proud of himself and his position; but he was all the while disturbed by a lurking fear, and by the unpleasant regret that he had not stopped for the night at Grishkino.

"It would have been good to lie on the bench in a warm room!" He turned from side to side several times; he curled himself up trying to find a better position, more sheltered from the wind and snow, but all the time he felt uncomfortable; he rose again and changed his position, crossed his feet, shut his eyes, and lay silent; but either his crossed feet, in their high felt boots, began to ache, or the wind blew in somewhere; and thus lying for a short time, he again began the disagreeable reflection, how comfortably he would have rested in the warm house at Grishkino. Again he rose, changed his position, wrapped himself up, and again tucked himself in.

Once Vasili Andreyitch fancied he heard a distant cock-crow. He felt glad, and threw back his shuba, and strained his ear to listen; but in spite of all his efforts he could hear nothing but the sound of the wind whistling against the shafts, and flapping the handkerchief, and the snow lashing the bark matting of the sledge.

Nikita had been motionless all the time, just as he had sat from the first, not stirring or even answering Vasili Andreyitch, though he spoke to him twice.

"He doesn't care in the least; he must be asleep," Vasili Andreyitch thought angrily, looking behind the sledge at Nikita, deeply covered with snow.

Twenty times Vasili Andreyitch thus rose and lay down. It seemed to him this night would never end.

"It must be near morning now," he thought once as he rose and glanced round him. "Let me look at my watch. I shall freeze if I unbutton my coat; but if I only know it is near morning, I shall feel better. We could begin to harness the horse."

At the bottom of his mind, Vasili Andreyitch knew that it could not be anywhere near morning; but he began to feel more and more afraid, and he chose both to assure himself and to deceive himself. He cautiously undid the hooks of his short shuba, then putting his hand in at the bosom, he felt about until he got at the waistcoat. With great trouble, he drew out his silver watch enameled with flowers, and tried to examine it. Without a light, he could make out nothing.

Again he lay down flat on his elbows and his knees, as when he lighted the cigarette; got the matches, and proceeded to strike. This time he was more careful, and feeling for a match with the largest head, ignited it at the first stroke. When he brought the face of the watch into the light he could not believe his eyes. . . . It was not later than ten minutes past twelve. The whole night was still before him.

"Oh, what a long night!" thought Vasili Andreyitch, feeling the cold run down his back; and buttoning up again and wrapping his shuba round him, he snuggled into the corner of the sledge with the intention of waiting patiently.

Suddenly, above the monotonous roar of the wind, he distinctly heard a new and a living sound. It grew gradually louder, and became quite clear; then began to die away with equal regularity. There could be no doubt it was a wolf. And this wolf was so near, that down the wind one could hear how he changed his cry by the movement of his jaws. Vasili Andreyitch turned back his collar and listened attentively. Mukhortui listened likewise, pricking up his ears, and when the wolf had ceased his chant he shifted his feet, and neighed warningly.

After this Vasili Andreyitch not only was unable to sleep, but even to keep calm. The more he tried to think of his accounts, of his business, reputation, importance, and property, more and more fear grew upon him; and above all his thoughts, one thought stood out predominantly and penetratingly:—the thought of his rashness in not stopping at Grishkino.

"The forest,—what do I care about the forest? [1] There is plenty of business without that, thank God! Ah, if we had only stayed for the night!" said he to himself. "They say drunken men soon freeze to death," he thought, "and I have had some drink."

Then testing his own sensations, he felt that he began to shiver, either from cold or fear. He tried to wrap himself up and to lie down, as before; but he could not any longer do that. He could not stay in one position, wanted to rise, to do something so as to suppress his gathering fears, against which he felt helpless. Again he got his cigarettes and matches; but only three of the latter remained, and these were bad ones. All three rubbed away without lighting.

"The devil take you, curse you!" he objurgated, himself not knowing whom or what, and he threw away the cigarette. He was about to throw away the matchbox also, but stayed his hand, and thrust it into his pocket instead. He was so agitated that he could no longer remain in his place. He got out of the sledge, and, standing with his back to the wind, set his girdle again, tightly, and low down.

[1] *Bog s nim, s lyesom:* literally, "God with it, with the forest."

"What is the use of lying down? It is only waiting for death; much better mount the horse and get away!" the thought suddenly flashed into his mind. "The horse will not stand still with some one on his back. It's all the same to *him*,—thinking of Nikita,—if he does die. What sort of a life has he? He does not care much even about his life, but, as for me,—thank God, I have something to live for!" . . .

Untying the horse from the sledge, he threw the reins over his neck, and tried to mount, but his shubas and his boots were so heavy that he failed. Then he clambered on the sledge, and tried to mount from that; but the sledge tilted under his weight, and he failed again. At last, on a third attempt, he backed the horse to the sledge, and, cautiously balancing on the edge, got his body across the horse's back. Lying thus for a moment, he pushed himself once, twice, and finally threw one leg over and seated himself, supporting his feet on the loose breeching straps in place of stirrups. The shaking of the sledge roused Nikita, and he got up; Vasili Andreyitch thought he was speaking.

"Listen to you, fool? What, must I die in this way, for nothing?" exclaimed Vasili Andreyitch. Tucking under his knees the loose skirts of his shuba, he turned the horse round, and rode away from the sledge in the direction where he expected to find the forest and the keeper's hut.

7

Nikita had not stirred since he had covered himself with the matting and taken his seat behind the sledge. Like all men who live with nature, and are acquainted with poverty, he was patient, and could wait for hours, even days, without growing restless or irritated. When his master called him, he heard, but made no answer, because he did not want to stir. Although he still felt the warmth from the tea he had taken, and from the exercise of struggling through the snowdrifts, he knew the warmth would not last long, and that he could not warm himself again by moving about, for he was exhausted, and felt as a horse does when, in spite of the whip, it stops, and its master perceives that it must have food before it can work again. His foot, the one in the torn boot, was numb, and he could no longer feel his great toe. And, moreover, his whole body kept growing colder and colder.

The thought that he might and in all probability would die that night came upon him, but this thought did not seem especially unpleasant or especially awful. It did not seem to him especially unpleasant, because his life had not been a perpetual festival, but rather an incessant round of toil of which he was beginning to weary. And this thought did not seem to him especially awful, because, beyond the masters whom he served here, like Vasili Andreyitch, he felt himself dependent upon the Great Master; [1] upon Him who had sent him into this life, and he knew that even after death he must remain in the power of that Master, and that that Master would not treat him badly.

"Is it a pity to leave what you are practised in, and used to? Well, what's to be done about it? You must get used to new things as well."

"Sins?" he thought, and recollected his drunkenness, the money wasted in drink, his ill-treatment of his wife, his profanity, neglect of church and of the fasts, and all things for which the priest reprimanded him at the confessional. "Of course, these are sins. But then, did I bring them on myself? Whatever I am, I suppose God made me so. Well, and about these sins? How can one help it?"

Thus ran his reflections, and after he had considered what might happen to him that night, he let it have the go-by, and gave himself up to whatever notions and memories came of their own accord into his mind. He remembered Marfa's visit, and the drunkenness among the peasants, and his own abstinence from drink; then he recalled how they had started on their present journey; Taras's izba, and the talk about the break-up of the family; that reminded him of his own lad; then he thought of Mukhortui, with the sacking over him for warmth; and his master, rolling round in the sledge, and making it creak.

"I suppose he is vexed and angry because he started out," said Nikita to himself. "A man who lives such a life as his does not want to die; not like people of my kind."

And all these recollections and thoughts interwove and jumbled themselves in his brain, until he fell asleep.

[1] *Glavnui Khozyaïn*, "Master-in-chief."

When Vasili Andreyitch mounted the horse, he twisted aside the sledge, and the back of it, against which Nikita was leaning, slid away, and one of the runner-ends struck him in the side. Nikita awoke, and was compelled to change his position. Straightening his legs with difficulty, and throwing off the snow which covered them, he got up. Instantly an agonizing cold penetrated his whole frame. On making out what was happening, he wanted Vasili Andreyitch to leave him the sacking, which was no longer needed for the horse, so that he might put it round himself.

But Vasili Andreyitch did not wait, and disappeared in the mist of snow.

Thus left alone, Nikita considered what he should do. He felt that he had not strength enough to start off in search of some house; and it was no longer possible for him to sit down in his former place, for it was already covered with snow; and he knew he could not get warm in the sledge, having nothing to cover him. There seemed no warmth at all from his kaftan and shuba. It was a bitter moment. He felt as cold as if he had only his shirt on. "Our Father, who art in Heaven," he repeated; and the consciousness that he was not alone but that Some One heard him and would not desert him comforted him. He drew a deep sigh, and keeping the matting over his head, he crept into the sledge and lay down in the place where his master had lain.

But he could not possibly keep warm in the sledge. At first he shivered all over, then the shivering ceased, and, little by little, he began to lose consciousness. Whether he was dying, or falling asleep, he knew not; but he was as ready for the one as for the other.

8

Meanwhile Vasili Andreyitch, using his feet and the straps of the harness, urged the horse in the direction where he, for some cause, expected to find the forest and the forester's hut. The snow blinded his eyes, and the wind, it seemed, was bent on staying him; but with head bent forward, and all the time pulling up his shuba between him and the cold pad, on which he could not settle himself, he kept urging on the horse. The dark bay, though with difficulty, obediently ambled on in the direction to which he was turned.

For five minutes he rode on; as it seemed to him, in a straight line; seeing nothing but the horse's head and the white waste, and hearing only the whistling of the wind about the horse's ears and collar of his own shuba.

Suddenly a dark patch showed in front of him. His heart began to beat with joy, and he rode on toward the object, already seeing in it the walls of village houses. But the dark patch was not stationary, it kept moving, and it was not a village but a patch of tall mugwort, growing on a strip of land and protruding through the snow, and shaking desperately under the blast of the wind which bent their heads all in one direction and whistled through them.

The sight of this mugwort tormented by the pitiless wind somehow made Vasili Andreyitch tremble, and he started to ride away hastily; not perceiving that in approaching the patch of mugwort, he had quite turned out of his first direction, and that now he was heading the opposite way, though he still supposed that he was riding toward where the forester's hut should be. But the horse seemed always to make toward the right, and so Vasili Andreyitch had to guide it toward the left.

Again a dark patch appeared before him; again he rejoiced, believing that now surely this was a village. But once more it was a patch of tall mugwort, once more the dry grass was shaking desperately, and, as before, frightening Vasili Andreyitch. But it could not be the same patch of grass, for near it was a horse-track, now disappearing in the snow. Vasili Andreyitch stopped, bent down, and looked carefully; a horse-track, not yet snow-covered; it could only be the hoof-prints of his own horse. He had evidently gone round in a small circle.

"And I shall perish in this way," he thought.

To overcome his terror, he urged on the horse with still greater energy, peering into the white mist of snow, wherein he saw nothing but flitting and fitful points of light which vanished the instant he looked at them. Once he thought he heard either the barking of dogs or the howling of wolves, but the sounds were so faint and indistinct, that he could not be sure whether he had heard them or imagined them; and he stopped and began to strain his ears and listen.

Suddenly a terrible, deafening cry beat upon his ears, and everything began to tremble and quake about him. Vasili Andreyitch seized the horse's neck, but that also shook, and the terrible cry grew still more frightful. For some seconds, Vasili Andreyitch could not collect himself, or understand what had happened. It was only this: Mukhortui, whether to encourage himself or to call for help, had neighed, loudly and resonantly.

"Tfu! Plague take you! You cursed brute, how you frightened me!" said Vasili Andreyitch to himself. But even when he understood the cause of his terror, he could not shake it off.

"I must consider and steady my nerves," he said to himself again, and saw at the same time he could not regain his self-control, but kept urging forward the horse without noting that he was now going with the wind, instead of against it. Especially when the horse walked slowly, his body, where it was exposed and where it touched the pad, was freezing and ached. His hands and legs shook and he was short of breath. He could see that he was likely to perish in the midst of this horrible snowy waste, and he could see no way of rescue. He forgot all about the forester's hut, and desired one thing only,—to get back to the sledge, that he might not perish alone, like that mugwort in the midst of the terrible waste of snow.

Suddenly the horse stumbled under him, caught in a snowdrift, and began to plunge, and fell on his side. Vasili Andreyitch jumped off as he did so, dragging with him the breeching on which his foot was supported, and turned the pad round by holding to it as he jumped.

As soon as Vasili Andreyitch was off his back, the horse struggled to his feet, plunged forward one leap and then another, and neighing again, with the sacking and breeching trailing after him, disappeared, leaving Vasili Andreyitch alone in the snowdrift.

He pressed on in pursuit of the horse, but the snow was so deep, and his shubas were so heavy, that after he had gone not more than twenty paces, sinking over the knee at each step, he was out of breath, and stopped.

"The forest, the sheep, the farms, the shop, the taverns,

the iron-roofed house and granary, my son!" thought he, "how can I leave them all? What does this really mean! It cannot be!"

These words flashed through his mind. Then somehow or other he recalled the wind-shaken mugwort which he had ridden past twice, and such a panic seized him that he lost all sense of the reality of what was happening. He asked himself, "Is not this all a dream?"—and tried to wake up. But there was nothing to wake up from! It was actual snow lashing his face and covering him and be-numbing his right hand, from which he had dropped the glove; and it was a real desert in which he was now alone, like that mugwort, waiting for inevitable, speedy, and in-comprehensible death.

"Queen in heaven, St. Nicholas,[1] teacher of temper-ance!"

He recalled the Te Deums of the day; the shrine with the black image in a golden chasuble; the tapers which he sold for the shrine, and which, when they were at once returned to him hardly touched by the flame, he used to put back into the store-chest.[2] And he began to implore that same Nicholas—the miracle-worker—to save him, vowing to the saint a Te Deum and tapers.

But in some way, here, he clearly and without a doubt realized that the image, chasuble, tapers, priests, masses, though they were all very important and necessary in their place, in the church, were of no service to him now; and that between those tapers and Te Deums, and his present disastrous plight, there could be no possible connection.

"I must not give up," he said to himself, "I must fol-low the horse's tracks, or they, too, will be snowed over." This idea struck him, and he made on. "He'll get away if I don't overtake him. But I mustn't hurry or else I shall be worse off and perish still more miserably."

But notwithstanding his resolution to walk quietly, he kept hurrying on, running, falling down every minute, rising and falling again. The hoof-prints were already al-

---

[1] *Svyatitelyu otche Mikolaye.* A semi-Slavonic form; literally, "Bishop Father Nikolai."

[2] It was a part of Vasili Andreyitch's duties as *tserkovnui starosta* to sell the candles which are abundantly used in the Russian service and which, after the mass, are returned and often resold, thus providing no small revenue.—ED.

most indistinguishable where the snow was not deep. "I am lost!" thought Vasili Andreyitch, "if I lose this track and don't overtake the horse."

But at that instant, casting a glance in front, he saw something dark. It was Mukhortui, and not merely Mukhortui, but the sledge, and the shafts with the handkerchief.

Mukhortui, with the pad twisted round to one side, and the trailed breeching and sacking, was standing, not in his former place, but nearer to the shafts; and was shaking his head, which was drawn down by the bridle beneath his feet.

It turned out that Vasili Andreyitch had stuck in the same ravine into which he and Nikita had previously plunged; that the horse had led him back to the sledge, and that he had dismounted at not more than fifty paces from the place where the sledge lay.

9

Vasili Andreyitch struggled back to the sledge, and clutched hold of it, and stood so, motionless for a long time, trying to calm himself and to get back his breath. There was no sign of Nikita in his former place, but something covered with snow was lying in the sledge, and Vasili Andreyitch conjectured that it was Nikita. Vasili Andreyitch's terror had now altogether disappeared; if he felt any fear, it was of that state of terror which he had experienced when on the horse, and especially when he was alone in the snowdrift. By any and every means, he must keep away that terror; and in order to keep it away it was necessary for him to do something, to occupy himself with something.

Accordingly, the first thing he did was to turn his back to the wind and throw open his shuba. As soon as he felt a little rested, he shook out the snow from his boots and from his left-hand glove,—the right-hand glove was lost beyond recovery and was undoubtedly already buried somewhere deep in the snow,—then he bound up his girdle again, tight and low-down, as he always did when he was going out of his shop to buy grain from the peasants' carts. He tightened his belt and prepared for action. The first thing which appeared to him necessary to do was to free the horse's leg. So Vasili Andreyitch did this; then, clearing the bridle, he tied Mukhortui to the iron cramp in front of the sledge, as before, and walking round the horse's quarters, he adjusted the pad, the breeching, and the sacking.

But as he did this, he perceived a movement in the sledge, and Nikita's head rose out of the snow that covered it. Obviously with great difficulty, the half-frozen peasant rose and sat up; and in a strange fashion, as if he were driving away flies, waved his hand before his face. He waved his hand and said something which Vasili Andreyitch interpreted as a call to himself.

Vasili Andreyitch left the sack unadjusted, and went to the sledge.

"What is the matter with you?" he asked. "What are you saying?"

"I am dy-y-ing, that's what's the matter," said Nikita, brokenly, struggling for speech. "Give what I have earned to the lad. Or to the wife; it's all the same."

"What, are you really frozen?" asked Vasili Andreyitch.

"I can feel I've got my death. Forgive . . . for Christ's sake . . ." said Nikita, in a sobbing voice, continuing to wave his hand before his face, as if driving away flies.

Vasili Andreyitch stood for half a minute silent and motionless; then suddenly, with the same resolution with which he used to strike hands over a good bargain, he took a step back, turned up the sleeves of his shuba, and using both hands, began to rake the snow from off Nikita and the sledge. When he had brushed out, Vasili Andreyitch quickly took off his girdle, opened out his shuba, and moving Nikita with a push, he lay down on him, covering him not only with the fur coat, but with the full length of his own body, which glowed with warmth.

Adjusting with his hands the skirts of his coat, so as to come between Nikita and the bark matting of the sledge, and tucking the tail of the coat between his knees, Vasili Andreyitch lay flat, with his head against the bark matting in the sledge-front; and now he no longer could hear either the stirring of the horse or the whistling of the wind; all he could hear was Nikita's breathing. At first, and for a long time, Nikita lay without a sign; then he gave a loud sigh, and moved.

"Ah, there you are! And yet you say 'die.' Lie still, get warm, and somehow we shall . . ." began Vasili Andreyitch.

But, to his own surprise, he could not speak: because his eyes were filled with tears, and his lower jaw began to quiver violently. He said no more—only gulped down something which rose in his throat.

"I was well scared, that is clear, and how weak I feel!" he thought of himself. But this weakness not only was not unpleasant to him, but rather gave him a peculiar and hitherto unknown delight.

"That's what we are!" he said to himself, experiencing a strange triumph and emotion. He lay quiet for some time, wiping his eyes with the fur of his shuba and tucking under his knees the right skirt, which the wind kept turning up.

He felt a passionate desire to let some one else know of his happy condition.

"Mikita!" he said.

"It's comfortable, it's warm," came an answer from below.

"So it is, friend! I was nearly lost. And you would have been frozen, and I should have . . ."

But here again his face began to quiver, and his eyes once more filled with tears, and he could say no more.

"Well, never mind," he thought, "I know well enough about myself, what I know."

And he kept quiet. Thus he lay for a long time.

Nikita warmed him from below, and the fur coat warmed him from above; but his hands, with which he held the coat-skirts down on both sides of Nikita, and his feet, from which the wind kept lifting the shuba, began to freeze. Especially cold was his right hand, unprotected by a glove. But he did not think either of his legs or of his hands. He thought only of how to warm the muzhik who lay beneath him.

Several times he looked at the horse, and saw that his back was uncovered, and the sacking and breeching were hanging down nearly to the snow. He ought to get up and

cover the horse; but he could not bring himself to leave
Nikita for even a moment, and so disturb that happy situation in which he felt himself; he now no longer had any
sense of terror.

"Never fear, we shan't lose him this time," he said to
himself, about his way of warming Nikita, and with the
same boastfulness as he used to speak of his buying and
selling.

Thus Vasili Andreyitch continued lying an hour and
then another and then a third, but he was unconscious of
the passage of time.

At first his thoughts were filled with impressions of the
snow-storm, the shafts of the sledge, the horse under the
duga-bow, all in confusion before his eyes; he remembered Nikita, lying under him; then mingling with these
recollections rose others, of the festival, his wife, the commissary of police, the taper-box; then again of Nikita, this
time lying under the taper-box. Then came apparitions of
peasants selling and buying, and white walls, the iron-
roofed houses, with Nikita lying underneath; then all was
confused, one thing blending with another; and, like the
colors in the rainbow, uniting in one white light, all the
different impressions fused into one nothing; and he fell
asleep.

For a long time he slept dreamlessly; but before daybreak visions visited him again. It seemed to him that he
was once more standing beside the taper-box, and Tikhon's
wife was asking him for a five-kopek candle for the festi-
val-day; he wanted to take the taper and give it to her, but
he could not move his hands, which hung down, thrust
tightly into his pockets. He wanted to walk round the box,
but his feet would not move; his goloshes, new and shiny,
had grown to the stone floor, and he could neither move
them, nor take out his feet.

All at once the box ceased to be a taper-box, and turned
into a bed; and Vasili Andreyitch sees himself lying, face
downward, on the taper-box, and yet it is his own bed in
his own house. And thus he lies and is unable to get up;
and yet he must get up, because Ivan Matveyitch, the commissary of police, will soon come for him, and he must go
with Ivan Matveyitch either to bargain for the forest, or to
set the breeching right on Mukhortui.

He asks his wife: —

"Well, Mikolavna,[1] has he not come yet?"

"No," she says, "he has not."

He hears some one drive up to the front steps. It must be he. No, he has gone past.

"Mikolavna, Mikolavna! what, has he not come yet?"

"No."

And he lies on the bed and is still unable to rise, and is still waiting. And this waiting is painful, and yet pleasant.

All at once, his joy is fulfilled: the expected one has come; not Ivan Matveyitch, the stanovoï, but some one else, and yet the one for whom he has been waiting. He has come, and he calls to him; and he that called is he who has bidden him lie down on Nikita.

And Vasili Andreyitch is glad because that one has visited him.

"I am coming," he cries joyfully. And the cry awakens him!

He wakes; but wakes an entirely different person from what he had been when he fell asleep. He wants to rise, and cannot; to move his arm, and cannot,—his leg, and he cannot do that. He wants to turn his head, and cannot do even so much. He is surprised but not at all disturbed by this. He divines that this is death, and is not at all disturbed even by that. And he remembers that Nikita is lying under him, and that he has got warm, and is alive; and it seems to him that he is Nikita, and Nikita is he; that his life is not in himself, but in Nikita. He makes an effort to listen, and hears Nikita's breathing, even his slight snoring.

"Nikita is alive, and therefore I also am alive!" he says to himself, triumphantly.

He remembers his money, his shop, his house, his purchases and sales, the Mironofs' millions; and it is hard for him to understand why that man called Vasili Brekhunof had troubled himself with all those things with which he had troubled himself.

"Well, he did not know what it was all about," he thinks, concerning this Vasili Brekhunof. "I did not know; but now I do know. No mistake this time; *now I know.*"

[1] Mikolavna, rustic form of Nikolayevna, "daughter of Nikolaï"; the patronymic used familiarly without the given name.

And again he hears the summons of that one who had before called him.

"I am coming, I am coming," he says with his whole joy-thrilled being. And he feels himself free, with nothing to encumber him more.

And nothing more, in this world, was seen, or heard, or felt by Vasili Andreyitch.

Round about the storm still eddied. The same whirlwinds of snow covered the dead Vasili Andreyitch's shuba, and Mukhortui, all of a tremble, and the sledge, now hardly to be seen, with Nikita lying in the bottom of it, kept warm beneath his dead master.

10

Just before morning Nikita awoke. He was aroused by the cold again creeping along his back. He had dreamt that he was driving from the mill with a cartload of his master's flour, and that in crossing the brook, as he went past the bridge, the cart got stuck. And he sees himself go beneath the cart, and lift it, straightening up his back. But, wonderful!—the cart does not stir, it sticks to his back, so that he can neither lift it nor get out from under it. It was crushing his loins. And how cold it was! He must get away somehow.

"There! Stop!" he cries to whoever it is that presses his back with the load. "Take the sacks out!"

But the cart still presses him, always colder and colder; and suddenly a peculiar knocking awakes him completely, and he remembers everything. The cold cart,—that was his dead and frozen master, lying upon him. The knocking was from Mukhortui, who had struck twice on the sledge with his hoofs.

"Andreyitch, eh, Andreyitch!" calls Nikita, softly, straightening his back, and already having a suspicion of the truth.

But Andreyitch does not answer, and his body and legs are hard, and cold, and heavy, like iron weights.

"He must be dead. May his be the Kingdom of Heaven!" thinks Nikita.

He turns his head, digs with his hand through the snow about him, and opens his eyes. It is daylight. The wind still whistles through the shafts, and the snow is still falling; but with a difference, not lashing upon the bark matting, as before, but silently covering the sledge and horse, ever deeper and deeper; and the horse's breathing and stirring are no more to be heard.

"He must be frozen, too," thinks Nikita.

And, in fact, those hoof-strokes on the sledge were the last struggles of Mukhortui, by that time quite benumbed, to keep on his legs.

"God, Father, it seems Thou callest me as well," says Nikita, to himself. "Let Thy holy will be done. But it is hard. . . . Still you can't die twice, and you must die once. If it would only come quicker!" . . .

And he draws in his arm again, shutting his eyes; and he loses consciousness, with the conviction that this time he is really going to die altogether.

At dinner-time on the next day, the peasants with their shovels dug out Vasili Andreyitch and Nikita, only seventy yards from the road, and half a verst from the village. The snow had hidden the sledge, but the shafts and the handkerchief were still visible. Mukhortui, up to his belly in snow, with the breeching and sacking trailing from his back, stood all whitened, his dead head pressed in on the apple of his throat; his nostrils were fringed with icicles, his eyes filled with frost and frozen round as with tears. In that one night he had become so thin, that he was nothing but skin and bones.

Vasili Andreyitch was stiffened like a frozen carcass, and he lay with his legs spread apart, just as he was when they rolled him off Nikita. His prominent hawk-eyes were frozen, and his open mouth under his clipped mustache was filled with snow.

But Nikita, though chilled through, was alive. When he was roused, he imagined he was already dead, and that what they were doing with him was happening, not in this world, but in another. When he heard the shouts of the peasants who were digging him out and rolling the frozen Vasili Andreyitch from him he was surprised, at first, to think that in the other world, also, peasants should be shouting so, and that they had the same kind of a body. But when he understood that he was still here, in this world, he was rather sorry than glad; especially when he realized that the toes of both his feet were frozen.

Nikita lay in the hospital for two months. They cut off three toes from him, and the others recovered, so that he was able to work. For twenty years more he went on living, first as a farm-laborer, latterly as a watchman. He died at home, just as he wished, only this year,—laid under the holy images, with a lighted wax taper in his hands.

Before his death, he asked forgiveness from his old wife, and forgave her for the cooper; he took leave of his son and the grandchildren; and went away truly pleased that, in dying, he released his son and daughter-in-law from the added burden of his keep, and that he himself was, this time, really going out of a life grown wearisome to him, into that other one which with every passing year had grown clearer and more desirable to him.

Whether he is better off, or worse off, there, in the place where he awoke after that real death, whether he was disappointed or found things there just as he expected, is what we shall all of us soon learn.

1895

THE DUEL

THE DUEL

by *Anton Chekhov*

1

It was eight o'clock in the morning—the time when the officers, the local officials, and the visitors usually took their morning dip in the sea after the hot, stifling night, and then went into the pavilion to drink tea or coffee. Ivan Andreitch Laevsky, a thin, fair young man of twenty-eight, wearing the cap of a clerk in the Ministry of Finance and with slippers on his feet, coming down to bathe, found a number of acquaintances on the beach, and among them his friend Samoylenko, the army doctor.

With his big cropped head, short neck, his red face, his big nose, his shaggy black eyebrows and grey whiskers, his stout puffy figure and his hoarse military bass, this Samoylenko made on every newcomer the unpleasant impression of a gruff bully; but two or three days after making his acquaintance, one began to think his face extraordinarily good-natured, kind, and even handsome. In spite of his clumsiness and rough manner, he was a peaceable man, of infinite kindliness and goodness of heart, always ready to be of use. He was on familiar terms with everyone in the town, lent everyone money, doctored everyone, made matches, patched up quarrels, arranged picnics at which he cooked *shashlik* and an awfully good soup of grey mullets. He was always looking after other people's affairs and trying to interest someone on their behalf, and was always delighted about something. The general opinion about him was that he was without faults of character. He had only two weaknesses: he was ashamed of his own good nature, and tried to disguise it by a surly expression and an assumed gruffness; and he liked his assistants and his soldiers to call him "Your Excellency," although he was only a civil councillor.

"Answer one question for me, Alexandr Daviditch," Laevsky began, when both he and Samoylenko were in the water up to their shoulders. "Suppose you had loved a woman and had been living with her for two or three years, and then left off caring for her, as one does, and began to feel that you had nothing in common with her. How would you behave in that case?"

"It's very simple. 'You go where you please, madam'— and that would be the end of it."

"It's easy to say that! But if she has nowhere to go? A woman with no friends or relations, without a farthing, who can't work . . ."

"Well? Five hundred roubles down or an allowance of twenty-five roubles a month—and nothing more. It's very simple."

"Even supposing you have five hundred roubles and can pay twenty-five roubles a month, the woman I am speaking of is an educated woman and proud. Could you really bring yourself to offer her money? And how would you do it?"

Samoylenko was going to answer, but at that moment a big wave covered them both, then broke on the beach and rolled back noisily over the shingle. The friends got out and began dressing.

"Of course, it is difficult to live with a woman if you don't love her," said Samoylenko, shaking the sand out of his boots. "But one must look at the thing humanely, Vanya. If it were my case, I should never show a sign that I did not love her, and I should go on living with her till I died."

He was at once ashamed of his own words; he pulled himself up and said:

"But for aught I care, there might be no females at all. Let them all go to the devil!"

The friends dressed and went into the pavilion. There Samoylenko was quite at home, and even had a special cup and saucer. Every morning they brought him on a tray a cup of coffee, a tall cut glass of iced water, and a tiny glass of brandy. He would first drink the brandy, then the hot coffee, then the iced water, and this must have been very nice, for after drinking it his eyes looked moist with pleasure, he would stroke his whiskers with both hands, and say, looking at the sea:

"A wonderfully magnificent view!"

After a long night spent in cheerless, unprofitable thoughts which prevented him from sleeping, and seemed to intensify the darkness and sultriness of the night, Laevsky felt listless and shattered. He felt no better for the bathe and the coffee.

"Let us go on with our talk, Alexandr Daviditch," he said. "I won't make a secret of it; I'll speak to you openly as to a friend. Things are in a bad way with Nadyezhda Fyodorovna and me . . . a very bad way! Forgive me for forcing my private affairs upon you, but I must speak out."

Samoylenko, who had a misgiving of what he was going to speak about, dropped his eyes and drummed with his fingers on the table.

"I've lived with her for two years and have ceased to love her," Laevsky went on; "or, rather, I realized that I never had felt any love for her. . . . These two years have been a mistake."

It was Laevsky's habit as he talked to gaze attentively at the pink palms of his hands, to bite his nails, or to pinch his cuffs. And he did so now.

"I know very well you can't help me," he said. "But I tell you, because unsuccessful and superfluous people like me find their salvation in talking. I have to generalize about everything I do. I'm bound to look for an explanation and justification of my absurd existence in somebody else's theories, in literary types—in the idea that we, upper-class Russians, are degenerating, for instance, and so on. Last night, for example, I comforted myself by thinking all the time: 'Ah, how true Tolstoy is, how mercilessly true!' And that did me good. Yes, really, brother, he is a great writer, say what you like!"

Samoylenko, who had never read Tolstoy and was intending to do so every day of his life, was a little embarrassed, and said:

"Yes, all other authors write from imagination, but he writes straight from nature."

"My God!" sighed Laevsky; "how distorted we all are by civilization! I fell in love with a married woman and she with me. . . . To begin with, we had kisses, and calm evenings, and vows, and Spencer, and ideals, and interests in common. . . . What a deception! We really ran away from her husband, but we lied to ourselves and made out that we ran away from the emptiness of the life of the educated class. We pictured our future like this: to begin with, in the Caucasus, while we were getting to know the people and the place, I would put on the Government uniform and enter the service; then at our leisure we would pick out a plot of ground, would toil in the sweat of our brow, would have a vineyard and a field, and so on. If you were in my place, or that zoologist of yours, Von Koren, you might live with Nadyezhda Fyodorovna for thirty years, perhaps, and might leave your heirs a rich vineyard and three thousand acres of maize; but I felt like a bankrupt from the first day. In the town you have insufferable heat, boredom, and no society; if you go out into the country, you fancy poisonous spiders, scorpions, or snakes lurking under every stone and behind every bush, and beyond the fields—mountains and the desert. Alien people, an alien country, a wretched form of civilization—all that is not so easy, brother, as walking on the Nevsky Prospect in one's fur coat, arm-in-arm with Nadyezhda Fyodorovna, dreaming of the sunny South. What is needed here is a life and death struggle, and I'm not a fighting man. A wretched neurasthenic, an idle gentleman. . . . From the first day I knew that my dreams of a life of labour and of a vineyard were worthless. As for love, I ought to tell you that living with a woman who has read Spencer and has followed you to the ends of the earth is no more interesting than living with any Anfissa or Akulina. There's the same smell of ironing, of powder, and of medicines, the same curl-papers every morning, the same self-deception."

"You can't get on in the house without an iron," said Samoylenko, blushing at Laevsky's speaking to him so openly of a lady he knew. "You are out of humour to-day, Vanya, I notice. Nadyezhda Fyodorovna is a splendid woman, highly educated, and you are a man of the highest intellect. Of course, you are not married," Samoylenko went on, glancing round at the adjacent tables, "but that's not your fault; and besides . . . one ought to be above conventional prejudices and rise to the level of modern ideas. I believe in free love myself, yes. . . . But to my thinking, once you have settled together, you ought to go on living together all your life."

"Without love?"

"I will tell you directly," said Samoylenko. "Eight years ago there was an old fellow, an agent, here—a man of very great intelligence. Well, he used to say that the great thing in married life was patience. Do you hear, Vanya? Not love, but patience. Love cannot last long. You have lived two years in love, and now evidently your married life has reached the period when, in order to preserve equilibrium, so to speak, you ought to exercise all your patience. . . ."

"You believe in your old agent; to me his words are meaningless. Your old man could be a hypocrite; he could exercise himself in the virtue of patience, and, as he did so, look upon a person he did not love as an object indispensable for his moral exercises; but I have not yet fallen so low. If I want to exercise myself in patience, I will buy dumb-bells or a frisky horse, but I'll leave human beings alone."

Samoylenko asked for some white wine with ice. When they had drunk a glass each, Laevsky suddenly asked:

"Tell me, please, what is the meaning of softening of the brain?"

"How can I explain it to you? . . . It's a disease in which the brain becomes softer . . . as it were, dissolves."

"Is it curable?"

"Yes, if the disease is not neglected. Cold douches, blisters. . . . Something internal, too."

"Oh! . . . Well, you see my position; I can't live with her: it is more than I can do. While I'm with you I can be philosophical about it and smile, but at home I lose heart completely; I am so utterly miserable, that if I were told, for instance, that I should have to live another month with her, I should blow out my brains. At the same time, parting with her is out of the question. She has no friends or relations; she cannot work, and neither she nor I has any money. . . . What could become of her? To whom could she go? There is nothing one can think of. . . . Come, tell me, what am I to do?"

"H'm! . . ." growled Samoylenko, not knowing what to answer. "Does she love you?"

"Yes, she loves me in so far as at her age and with her temperament she wants a man. It would be as difficult for her to do without me as to do without her powder or her curl-papers. I am for her an indispensable, integral part of her boudoir."

Samoylenko was embarrassed.

"You are out of humour to-day, Vanya," he said. "You must have had a bad night."

"Yes, I slept badly. . . . Altogether, I feel horribly out of sorts, brother. My head feels empty; there's a sinking at my heart, a weakness. . . . I must run away."

"Run where?"

"There, to the North. To the pines and the mushrooms, to people and ideas. . . . I'd give half my life to bathe now in some little stream in the province of Moscow or Tula; to feel chilly, you know, and then to stroll for three hours even with the feeblest student, and to talk and talk endlessly. . . . And the scent of the hay! Do you remember it? And in the evening, when one walks in the garden, sounds of the piano float from the house; one hears the train passing. . . ."

Laevsky laughed with pleasure; tears came into his eyes, and to cover them, without getting up, he stretched across the next table for the matches.

"I have not been in Russia for eighteen years," said Samoylenko. "I've forgotten what it is like. To my mind, there is not a country more splendid than the Caucasus."

"Vereshtchagin has a picture in which some men condemned to death are languishing at the bottom of a very deep well. Your magnificent Caucasus strikes me as just like that well. If I were offered the choice of a chimney-sweep in Petersburg or a prince in the Caucasus, I should choose the job of chimney-sweep."

Laevsky grew pensive. Looking at his stooping figure, at his eyes fixed dreamily on one spot, at his pale, perspiring face and sunken temples, at his bitten nails, at the slipper which had dropped off his heel, displaying a badly darned sock, Samoylenko was moved to pity, and probably because Laevsky reminded him of a helpless child, he asked: "Is your mother living?"

"Yes, but we are on bad terms. She could not forgive me for this affair."

Samoylenko was fond of his friend. He looked upon

Laevsky as a good-natured fellow, a student, a man with no nonsense about him, with whom one could drink, and laugh, and talk without reserve. What he understood in him he disliked extremely. Laevsky drank a great deal and at unsuitable times; he played cards, despised his work, lived beyond his means, frequently made use of unseemly expressions in conversation, walked about the streets in his slippers, and quarrelled with Nadyezhda Fyodorovna before other people—and Samoylenko did not like this. But the fact that Laevsky had once been a student in the Faculty of Arts, subscribed to two fat reviews, often talked so cleverly that only a few people understood him, was living with a well-educated woman—all this Samoylenko did not understand, and he liked this and respected Laevsky, thinking him superior to himself.

"There is another point," said Laevsky, shaking his head. "Only it is between ourselves. I'm concealing it from Nadyezhda Fyodorovna for the time. . . . Don't let it out before her. . . . I got a letter the day before yesterday, telling me that her husband has died from softening of the brain."

"The Kingdom of Heaven be his!" sighed Samoylenko. "Why are you concealing it from her?"

"To show her that letter would be equivalent to 'Come to church to be married.' And we should first have to make our relations clear. When she understands that we can't go on living together, I will show her the letter. Then there will be no danger in it."

"Do you know what, Vanya," said Samoylenko, and a sad and imploring expression came into his face, as though he were going to ask him about something very touching and were afraid of being refused. "Marry her, my dear boy!"

"Why?"

"Do your duty to that splendid woman! Her husband is dead, and so Providence itself shows you what to do!"

"But do understand, you queer fellow, that it is impossible. To marry without love is as base and unworthy of a man as to perform mass without believing in it."

"But it's your duty to."

"Why is it my duty?" Laevsky asked irritably.

"Because you took her away from her husband and made yourself responsible for her."

"But now I tell you in plain Russian, I don't love her!"

"Well, if you've no love, show her proper respect, consider her wishes. . . ."

" 'Show her respect, consider her wishes,' " Laevsky mimicked him. "As though she were some Mother Superior! . . . You are a poor psychologist and physiologist if you think that living with a woman one can get off with nothing but respect and consideration. What a woman thinks most of is her bedroom."

"Vanya, Vanya!" said Samoylenko, overcome with confusion.

"You are an elderly child, a theorist, while I am an old man in spite of my years, and practical, and we shall never understand one another. We had better drop this conversation. Mustapha!" Laevsky shouted to the waiter. "What's our bill?"

"No, no . . ." the doctor cried in dismay, clutching Laevsky's arm. "It is for me to pay. I ordered it. Make it out to me," he cried to Mustapha.

The friends got up and walked in silence along the seafront. When they reached the boulevard, they stopped and shook hands at parting.

"You are awfully spoilt, my friend!" Samoylenko sighed. "Fate has sent you a young, beautiful, cultured woman, and you refuse the gift, while if God were to give me a crooked old woman, how pleased I should be if only she were kind and affectionate! I would live with her in my vineyard and . . ."

Samoylenko caught himself up and said: "And she might get the samovar ready for me there, the old hag."

After parting with Laevsky he walked along the boulevard. When, bulky and majestic, with a stern expression on his face, he walked along the boulevard in his snow-white tunic and superbly polished boots, squaring his chest, decorated with the Vladimir cross on a ribbon, he was very much pleased with himself, and it seemed as though the whole world were looking at him with pleasure. Without turning his head, he looked to each side and thought that the boulevard was extremely well laid out; that the young cypress-trees, the eucalyptuses, and the ugly, anæmic palm-trees were very handsome and would in time give abundant shade; that the Circassians were an honest and hospitable people.

"It's strange that Laevsky does not like the Caucasus," he thought, "very strange."

Five soldiers, carrying rifles, met him and saluted him. On the right side of the boulevard the wife of a local official was walking along the pavement with her son, a schoolboy.

"Good-morning, Marya Konstantinovna," Samoylenko shouted to her with a pleasant smile.

"Have you been to bathe? Ha, ha, ha! . . . My respects to Nikodim Alexandritch!"

And he went on, still smiling pleasantly, but seeing an assistant of the military hospital coming towards him, he suddenly frowned, stopped him, and asked:

"Is there anyone in the hospital?"

"No one, Your Excellency."

"Eh?"

"No one, Your Excellency."

"Very well, run along. . . ."

Swaying majestically, he made for the lemonade stall, where sat a full-bosomed old Jewess, who gave herself out to be a Georgian, and said to her as loudly as though he were giving the word of command to a regiment:

"Be so good as to give me some soda-water!"

2

Laevsky's not loving Nadyezhda Fyodorovna showed itself chiefly in the fact that everything she said or did seemed to him a lie, or equivalent to a lie, and everything he read against women and love seemed to him to apply perfectly to himself, to Nadyezhda Fyodorovna and her husband. When he returned home, she was sitting at the window, dressed and with her hair done, and with a preoccupied face was drinking coffee and turning over the leaves of a fat magazine; and he thought the drinking of coffee was not such a remarkable event that she need put on a preoccupied expression over it, and that she had been wasting her time doing her hair in a fashionable style, as there was no one here to attract and no need to be attractive. And in the magazine he saw nothing but falsity. He thought she had dressed and done her hair so as to look handsomer, and was reading in order to seem clever.

"Will it be all right for me to go to bathe to-day?" she said.

"Why? There won't be an earthquake whether you go or not, I suppose. . . ."

"No, I only ask in case the doctor should be vexed."

"Well, ask the doctor, then; I'm not a doctor."

On this occasion what displeased Laevsky most in Nadyezhda Fyodorovna was her white open neck and the little curls at the back of her head. And he remembered that when Anna Karenin got tired of her husband, what she disliked most of all was his ears, and thought: "How true it is, how true!"

Feeling weak and as though his head were perfectly empty, he went into his study, lay down on his sofa, and covered his face with a handkerchief that he might not be bothered by the flies. Despondent and oppressive thoughts always about the same thing trailed slowly across his brain like a long string of waggons on a gloomy autumn evening, and he sank into a state of drowsy oppression. It seemed to him that he had wronged Nadyezhda Fyodorovna and her husband, and that it was through his fault that her husband had died. It seemed to him that he had sinned against his own life, which he had ruined, against the world of lofty ideas, of learning, and of work, and he conceived that wonderful world as real and possible, not on this sea-front with hungry Turks and lazy mountaineers sauntering upon it, but there in the North, where there were operas, theatres, newspapers, and all kinds of intellectual activity. One could only there—not here—be honest, intelligent, lofty, and pure. He accused himself of having no ideal, no guiding principle in life, though he had a dim understanding now what it meant. Two years before, when he fell in love with Nadyezhda Fyodorovna, it seemed to him that he had only to go with her as his wife to the Caucasus, and he would be saved from vulgarity and emptiness; in the same way now, he was convinced that he had only to part from Nadyezhda Fyodorovna and to go to Petersburg, and he would get everything he wanted.

"Run away," he muttered to himself, sitting up and biting his nails. "Run away!"

He pictured in his imagination how he would go aboard the steamer and then would have some lunch, would drink some cold beer, would talk on deck with ladies, then would get into the train at Sevastopol and set off. Hurrah for freedom! One station after another would flash by, the air would keep growing colder and keener, then the birches and the fir-trees, then Kursk, Moscow. . . . In the restaurants cabbage soup, mutton with kasha, sturgeon, beer, no more Asiaticism, but Russia, real Russia. The passengers in the train would talk about trade, new singers, the Franco-Russian *entente;* on all sides there would be the feeling of keen, cultured, intellectual, eager life. . . . Hasten on, on! At last Nevsky Prospect, and Great Morskaya Street, and then Kovensky Place, where he used to live at one time when he was a student, the dear grey sky, the drizzling rain, the drenched cabmen. . . .

"Ivan Andreitch!" someone called from the next room. "Are you at home?"

"I'm here," Laevsky responded. "What do you want?"

"Papers."

Laevsky got up languidly, feeling giddy, walked into the other room, yawning and shuffling with his slippers. There, at the open window that looked into the street, stood one of his young fellow-clerks, laying out some government documents on the window-sill.

"One minute, my dear fellow," Laevsky said softly, and he went to look for the ink; returning to the window, he signed the papers without looking at them, and said: "It's hot!"

"Yes. Are you coming to-day?"

"I don't think so. . . . I'm not quite well. Tell Sheshkovsky that I will come and see him after dinner."

The clerk went away. Laevsky lay down on his sofa again and began thinking:

"And so I must weigh all the circumstances and reflect on them. Before I go away from here I ought to pay up my debts. I owe about two thousand roubles. I have no money. . . . Of course, that's not important; I shall pay part now, somehow, and I shall send the rest, later, from Petersburg. The chief point is Nadyezhda Fyodorovna. . . . First of all we must define our relations. . . . Yes."

A little later he was considering whether it would not be better to go to Samoylenko for advice.

"I might go," he thought, "but what use would there be in it? I shall only say something inappropriate about boudoirs, about women, about what is honest or dishonest. What's the use of talking about what is honest or dishonest, if I must make haste to save my life, if I am suffocating in this cursed slavery and am killing myself? . . . One must realize at last that to go on leading the life I do is something so base and so cruel that everything else seems petty and trivial beside it. To run away," he muttered, sitting down, "to run away."

The deserted seashore, the insatiable heat, and the monotony of the smoky lilac mountains, ever the same and silent, everlastingly solitary, overwhelmed him with depression, and, as it were, made him drowsy and sapped his energy. He was perhaps very clever, talented, remarkably honest; perhaps if the sea and the mountains had not closed him in on all sides, he might have become an excellent Zemstvo leader, a statesman, an orator, a political writer, a saint. Who knows? If so, was it not stupid to argue whether it were honest or dishonest when a gifted and useful man—an artist or musician, for instance—to escape from prison, breaks a wall and deceives his jailers? Anything is honest when a man is in such a position.

At two o'clock Laevsky and Nadyezhda Fyodorovna sat down to dinner. When the cook gave them rice and tomato soup, Laevsky said:

"The same thing every day. Why not have cabbage soup?"

"There are no cabbages."

"It's strange. Samoylenko has cabbage soup and Marya Konstantinovna has cabbage soup, and only I am obliged to eat this mawkish mess. We can't go on like this, darling."

As is common with the vast majority of husbands and wives, not a single dinner had in earlier days passed without scenes and fault-finding between Nadyezhda Fyodorovna and Laevsky; but ever since Laevsky had made up his mind that he did not love her, he had tried to give way to Nadyezhda Fyodorovna in everything, spoke to her gently and politely, smiled, and called her "darling."

"This soup tastes like liquorice," he said, smiling; he made an effort to control himself and seem amiable, but could not refrain from saying: "Nobody looks after the housekeeping. . . . If you are too ill or busy with reading, let me look after the cooking."

In earlier days she would have said to him, "Do by all means," or, "I see you want to turn me into a cook"; but now she only looked at him timidly and flushed crimson.

"Well, how do you feel to-day?" he asked kindly.

"I am all right to-day. There is nothing but a little weakness."

"You must take care of yourself, darling. I am awfully anxious about you."

Nadyezhda Fyodorovna was ill in some way. Samoylenko said she had intermittent fever, and gave her quinine; the other doctor, Ustimovitch, a tall, lean, unsociable man, who used to sit at home in the daytime, and in the evenings walk slowly up and down on the sea-front coughing, with his hands folded behind him and a cane stretched along his back, was of opinion that she had a female complaint, and prescribed warm compresses. In old days, when Laevsky loved her, Nadyezhda Fyodorovna's illness had excited his pity and terror; now he saw falsity even in her illness. Her yellow, sleepy face, her lustreless eyes, her apathetic expression, and the yawning that always followed her attacks of fever, and the fact that during them she lay under a shawl and looked more like a boy than a woman, and that it was close and stuffy in her room—all this, in his opinion, destroyed the illusion and was an argument against love and marriage.

The next dish given him was spinach with hard-boiled eggs, while Nadyezhda Fyodorovna, as an invalid, had jelly and milk. When with a preoccupied face she touched the jelly with a spoon and then began languidly eating it, sipping milk, and he heard her swallowing, he was possessed by such an overwhelming aversion that it made his head tingle. He recognized that such a feeling would be an insult even to a dog, but he was angry, not with himself but with Nadyezhda Fyodorovna, for arousing such a feeling, and he understood why lovers sometimes murder their mistresses. He would not murder her, of course, but if he had been on a jury now, he would have acquitted the murderer.

"*Merci*, darling," he said after dinner, and kissed Nadyezhda Fyodorovna on the forehead.

Going back into his study, he spent five minutes in

walking to and fro, looking at his boots; then he sat down
on his sofa and muttered:

"Run away, run away! We must define the position and
run away!"

He lay down on the sofa and recalled again that Nadyezhda Fyodorovna's husband had died, perhaps, by his
fault.

"To blame a man for loving a woman, or ceasing to love
a woman, is stupid," he persuaded himself, lying down and
raising his legs in order to put on his high boots. "Love and
hatred are not under our control. As for her husband,
maybe I was in an indirect way one of the causes of his
death; but again, is it my fault that I fell in love with his
wife and she with me?"

Then he got up, and finding his cap, set off to the lodgings of his colleague, Sheshkovsky, where the Government
clerks met every day to play *vint* and drink beer.

"My indecision reminds me of Hamlet," thought Laevsky on the way. "How truly Shakespeare describes it! Ah,
how truly!"

3

For the sake of sociability and from sympathy for the hard
plight of newcomers without families, who, as there was
not an hotel in the town, had nowhere to dine, Dr. Samoylenko kept a sort of table d'hôte. At this time there were
only two men who habitually dined with him: a young
zoologist called Von Koren, who had come for the summer
to the Black Sea to study the embryology of the medusa,
and a deacon called Pobyedov, who had only just left the
seminary and been sent to the town to take the duty of the
old deacon who had gone away for a cure. Each of them
paid twelve roubles a month for their dinner and supper,
and Samoylenko made them promise to turn up at two
o'clock punctually.

Von Koren was usually the first to appear. He sat down
in the drawing-room in silence, and taking an album from

the table, began attentively scrutinizing the faded photographs of unknown men in full trousers and top-hats, and ladies in crinolines and caps. Samoylenko only remembered a few of them by name, and of those whom he had forgotten he said with a sigh: "A very fine fellow, remarkably intelligent!" When he had finished with the album, Von Koren took a pistol from the whatnot, and screwing up his left eye, took deliberate aim at the portrait of Prince Vorontsov, or stood still at the looking-glass and gazed a long time at his swarthy face, his big forehead, and his black hair, which curled like a Negro's, and his shirt of dull-coloured cotton with big flowers on it like a Persian rug, and the broad leather belt he wore instead of a waistcoat. The contemplation of his own image seemed to afford him almost more satisfaction than looking at photographs or playing with the pistols. He was very well satisfied with his face, and his becomingly clipped beard, and the broad shoulders, which were unmistakable evidence of his excellent health and physical strength. He was satisfied, too, with his stylish get-up, from the cravat, which matched the colour of his shirt, down to his brown boots.

While he was looking at the album and standing before the glass, at that moment, in the kitchen and in the passage near, Samoylenko, without his coat and waistcoat, with his neck bare, excited and bathed in perspiration, was bustling about the tables, mixing the salad, or making some sauce, or preparing meat, cucumbers, and onion for the cold soup, while he glared fiercely at the orderly who was helping him, and brandished first a knife and then a spoon at him.

"Give me the vinegar!" he said. "That's not the vinegar —it's the salad oil!" he shouted, stamping. "Where are you off to, you brute?"

"To get the butter, Your Excellency," answered the flustered orderly in a cracked voice.

"Make haste; it's in the cupboard! And tell Daria to put some fennel in the jar with the cucumbers! Fennel! Cover the cream up, gaping laggard, or the flies will get into it!"

And the whole house seemed resounding with his shouts. When it was ten or fifteen minutes to two the deacon would come in; he was a lanky young man of twenty-two, with long hair, with no beard and a hardly perceptible moustache. Going into the drawing-room, he crossed himself before the ikon, smiled, and held out his hand to Von Koren.

"Good-morning," the zoologist said coldly. "Where have you been?"

"I've been catching sea-gudgeon in the harbour."

"Oh, of course. . . . Evidently, deacon, you will never be busy with work."

"Why not? Work is not like a bear; it doesn't run off into the woods," said the deacon, smiling and thrusting his hands into the very deep pockets of his white cassock.

"There's no one to whip you!" sighed the zoologist.

Another fifteen or twenty minutes passed and they were not called to dinner, and they could still hear the orderly running into the kitchen and back again, noisily treading with his boots, and Samoylenko shouting:

"Put it on the table! Where are your wits? Wash it first."

The famished deacon and Von Koren began tapping on the floor with their heels, expressing in this way their impatience like the audience at a theatre. At last the door opened and the harassed orderly announced that dinner was ready! In the dining-room they were met by Samoylenko, crimson in the face, wrathful, perspiring from the heat of the kitchen; he looked at them furiously, and with an expression of horror, took the lid off the soup tureen and helped each of them to a plateful; and only when he was convinced that they were eating it with relish and liked it, he gave a sigh of relief and settled himself in his deep arm-chair. His face looked blissful and his eyes grew moist. . . . He deliberately poured himself out a glass of vodka and said:

"To the health of the younger generation."

After his conversation with Laevsky, from early morning till dinner Samoylenko had been conscious of a load at his heart, although he was in the best of humours; he felt sorry for Laevsky and wanted to help him. After drinking a glass of vodka before the soup, he heaved a sigh and said:

"I saw Vanya Laevsky to-day. He is having a hard time of it, poor fellow! The material side of life is not encouraging for him, and the worst of it is all this psychology is too much for him. I'm sorry for the lad."

"Well, that is a person I am not sorry for," said Von

Koren. "If that charming individual were drowning, I would push him under with a stick and say, 'Drown, brother, drown away.' . . ."

"That's untrue. You wouldn't do it."

"Why do you think that?" The zoologist shrugged his shoulders. "I'm just as capable of a good action as you are."

"Is drowning a man a good action?" asked the deacon, and he laughed.

"Laevsky? Yes."

"I think there is something amiss with the soup . . ." said Samoylenko, anxious to change the conversation.

"Laevsky is absolutely pernicious and is as dangerous to society as the cholera microbe," Von Koren went on. "To drown him would be a service."

"It does not do you credit to talk like that about your neighbour. Tell us: what do you hate him for?"

"Don't talk nonsense, doctor. To hate and despise a microbe is stupid, but to look upon everybody one meets without distinction as one's neighbour, whatever happens —thanks very much, that is equivalent to giving up criticism, renouncing a straightforward attitude to people, washing one's hands of responsibility, in fact! I consider your Laevsky a blackguard; I do not conceal it, and I am perfectly conscientious in treating him as such. Well, you look upon him as your neighbour—and you may kiss him if you like: you look upon him as your neighbour, and that means that your attitude to him is the same as to me and to the deacon; that is no attitude at all. You are equally indifferent to all."

"To call a man a blackguard!" muttered Samoylenko, frowning with distaste—"that is so wrong that I can't find words for it!"

"People are judged by their actions," Von Koren continued. "Now you decide, deacon. . . . I am going to talk to you, deacon. Mr. Laevsky's career lies open before you, like a long Chinese puzzle, and you can read it from beginning to end. What has he been doing these two years that he has been living here? We will reckon his doings on our fingers. First, he has taught the inhabitants of the town to play *vint:* two years ago that game was unknown here! now they all play it from morning till late at night, even the women and the boys. Secondly, he has taught the residents to drink beer, which was not known here either; the inhabitants are indebted to him for the knowledge of various sorts of spirits, so that now they can distinguish Kospelov's vodka from Smirnov's No. 21, blindfold. Thirdly, in former days, people here made love to other men's wives in secret, from the same motives as thieves steal in secret and not openly; adultery was considered something they were ashamed to make a public display of. Laevsky has come as a pioneer in that line; he lives with another man's wife openly. . . . Fourthly . . ."

Von Koren hurriedly ate up his soup and gave his plate to the orderly.

"I understood Laevsky from the first month of our acquaintance," he went on, addressing the deacon. "We arrived here at the same time. Men like him are very fond of friendship, intimacy, solidarity, and all the rest of it, because they always want company for *vint,* drinking, and eating; besides, they are talkative and must have listeners. We made friends—that is, he turned up every day, hindered me working, and indulged in confidences in regard to his mistress. From the first he struck me by his exceptional falsity, which simply made me sick. As a friend I pitched into him, asking him why he drank too much, why he lived beyond his means and got into debt, why he did nothing and read nothing, why he had so little culture and so little knowledge; and in answer to all my questions he used to smile bitterly, sigh, and say: 'I am a failure, a superfluous man'; or: 'What do you expect, my dear fellow, from us, the débris of the serf-owning class?' or: 'We are degenerate. . . .' Or he would begin a long rigmarole about Onyegin, Petchorin, Byron's Cain, and Bazarov, of whom he would say: 'They are our fathers in flesh and in spirit.' So we are to understand that it was not his fault that Government envelopes lay unopened in his office for weeks together, and that he drank and taught others to drink, but Onyegin, Petchorin, and Turgenev, who had invented the failure and the superfluous man, were responsible for it. The cause of his extreme dissoluteness and unseemliness lies, do you see, not in himself, but somewhere outside in space. And so—an ingenious idea!—it is not only he who is dissolute, false, and disgusting, but we . . . 'we men of the eighties,' 'we the spiritless, nervous offspring of the serf-owning class'; 'civilization has crippled us' . . . in fact, we are to understand that such a great man as Laevsky is great even in his fall: that his dissoluteness, his lack of culture and of moral purity, is a phenomenon of natural history, sanctified by inevitability; that the causes of it are world-wide, elemental; and that we ought to hang up a lamp before Laevsky, since he is the fated victim of the age, of influences, of heredity, and so on. All the officials and their ladies were in ecstasies when they listened to him, and I could not make out for a long time what sort of man I had to deal with, a cynic or a clever rogue. Such types as he, on the surface intellectual with a smattering of education and a great deal of talk about their own nobility, are very clever in posing as exceptionally complex natures."

"Hold your tongue!" Samoylenko flared up. "I will not allow a splendid fellow to be spoken ill of in my presence!"

"Don't interrupt, Alexandr Daviditch," said Von Koren coldly; "I am just finishing. Laevsky is by no means a complex organism. Here is his moral skeleton: in the morning, slippers, a bathe, and coffee; then till dinner-time, slippers, a constitutional, and conversation; at two o'clock slippers, dinner, and wine; at five o'clock a bathe, tea and wine, then *vint* and lying; at ten o'clock supper and wine; and after midnight sleep and *la femme*. His existence is confined within this narrow programme like an egg within its shell. Whether he walks or sits, is angry, writes, rejoices, it may all be reduced to wine, cards, slippers, and women. Woman plays a fatal, overwhelming part in his life. He tells us himself that at thirteen he was in love; that when he was a student in his first year he was living with a lady who had a good influence over him, and to whom he was indebted for his musical education. In his second year he bought a prostitute from a brothel and raised her to his level—that is, took her as his kept mistress, and she lived with him for six months and then ran away back to the brothel-keeper, and her flight caused him much spiritual suffering. Alas! his sufferings were so great that he had to leave the university and spend two years at home doing nothing. But this was all for the best. At home he made friends with a widow who advised him to leave the Faculty of Jurisprudence and go into the Faculty of Arts. And so he did. When he had taken his degree, he fell passionately in love with his present . . . what's

her name? . . . married lady, and was obliged to flee
with her here to the Caucasus for the sake of his ideals,
he would have us believe, seeing that . . . to-morrow,
if not to-day, he will be tired of her and flee back again to
Petersburg, and that, too, will be for the sake of his ideals."

"How do you know?" growled Samoylenko, looking angrily at the zoologist. "You had better eat your dinner."

The next course consisted of boiled mullet with Polish
sauce. Samoylenko helped each of his companions to a
whole mullet and poured out the sauce with his own hand.
Two minutes passed in silence.

"Woman plays an essential part in the life of every
man," said the deacon. "You can't help that."

"Yes, but to what degree? For each of us woman means
mother, sister, wife, friend. To Laevsky she is everything,
and at the same time nothing but a mistress. She—that is,
cohabitation with her—is the happiness and object of his
life; he is gay, sad, bored, disenchanted—on account of
woman; his life grows disagreeable—woman is to blame;
the dawn of a new life begins to glow, ideals turn up—
and again look for the woman. . . . He only derives enjoyment from books and pictures in which there is
woman. Our age is, to his thinking, poor and inferior to
the forties and the sixties only because we do not know
how to abandon ourselves obliviously to the passion and
ecstasy of love. These voluptuaries must have in their
brains a special growth of the nature of sarcoma, which
stifles the brain and directs their whole psychology. Watch
Laevsky when he is sitting anywhere in company. You notice: when one raises any general question in his presence,
for instance, about the cell or instinct, he sits apart, and
neither speaks nor listens; he looks languid and disillusioned; nothing has any interest for him, everything is vulgar and trivial. But as soon as you speak of male and female—for instance, of the fact that the female spider,
after fertilization, devours the male—his eyes glow with
curiosity, his face brightens, and the man revives, in fact.
All his thoughts, however noble, lofty, or neutral they may
be, they all have one point of resemblance. You walk along
the street with him and meet a donkey, for instance. . . .
'Tell me, please,' he asks, 'what would happen if you mated
a donkey with a camel?' And his dreams! Has he told you
of his dreams? It is magnificent! First, he dreams that he

is married to the moon, then that he is summoned before the police and ordered to live with a guitar . . ."

The deacon burst into resounding laughter; Samoylenko frowned and wrinkled up his face angrily so as not to laugh, but could not restrain himself, and laughed.

"And it's all nonsense!" he said, wiping his tears. "Yes, by Jove, it's nonsense!"

4

The deacon was very easily amused, and laughed at every trifle till he got a stitch in his side, till he was helpless. It seemed as though he only liked to be in people's company because there was a ridiculous side to them, and because they might be given ridiculous nicknames. He had nick-named Samoylenko "the tarantula," his orderly "the drake," and was in ecstasies when on one occasion Von Koren spoke of Laevsky and Nadyezhda Fyodorovna as "Japanese monkeys." He watched people's faces greedily, listened without blinking, and it could be seen that his eyes filled with laughter and his face was tense with expectation of the moment when he could let himself go and burst into laughter.

"He is a corrupt and depraved type," the zoologist continued, while the deacon kept his eyes riveted on his face, expecting he would say something funny. It is not often one can meet with such a nonentity. In body he is inert, feeble, prematurely old, while in intellect he differs in no respect from a fat shopkeeper's wife who does nothing but eat, drink, and sleep on a feather-bed, and who keeps her coachman as a lover."

The deacon began guffawing again.

"Don't laugh, deacon," said Von Koren. "It grows stupid, at last. I should not have paid attention to his insignificance," he went on, after waiting till the deacon had left off laughing; "I should have passed him by if he were not so noxious and dangerous. His noxiousness lies first of all in the fact that he has great success with women, and so threatens to leave descendants—that is, to present the world with a dozen Laevskys as feeble and as depraved as himself. Secondly, he is in the highest degree contaminating. I have spoken to you already of *vint* and beer. In another year or two he will dominate the whole Caucasian coast. You know how the mass, especially its middle stratum, believe in intellectuality, in a university education, in gentlemanly manners, and in literary language. Whatever filthy thing he did, they would all believe that it was as it should be, since he is an intellectual man, of liberal ideas and university education. What is more, he is a failure, a superfluous man, a neurasthenic, a victim of the age, and that means he can do anything. He is a charming fellow, a regular good sort, he is so genuinely indulgent to human weaknesses; he is compliant, accommodating, easy, and not proud; one can drink with him and gossip and talk evil of people. . . . The masses, always inclined to anthropomorphism in religion and morals, like best of all the little gods who have the same weaknesses as themselves. Only think what a wide field he has for contamination! Besides, he is not a bad actor and is a clever hypocrite, and knows very well how to twist things round. Only take his little shifts and dodges, his attitude to civilization, for instance. He has scarcely sniffed at civilization, yet: 'Ah, how we have been crippled by civilization! Ah, how I envy those savages, those children of nature, who know nothing of civilization!' We are to understand, you see, that at one time, in ancient days, he has been devoted to civilization with his whole soul, has served it, has sounded it to its depths, but it has exhausted him, disillusioned him, deceived him; he is a Faust, do you see?—a second Tolstoy. . . . As for Schopenhauer and Spencer, he treats them like small boys and slaps them on the shoulder in a fatherly way: 'Well, what do you say, old Spencer?' He has not read Spencer, of course, but how charming he is when with light, careless irony he says of his lady friend: 'She has read Spencer!' And they all listen to him, and no one cares to understand that this charlatan has not the right to kiss the sole of Spencer's foot, let alone speak about him in that tone! Sapping the foundations of civilization, of authority, of other people's altars, spattering them with filth, winking jocosely at them only to justify and conceal one's own rottenness and moral poverty is only possible for a very vain, base, and nasty creature."

"I don't know what it is you expect of him, Kolya," said Samoylenko, looking at the zoologist, not with anger now, but with a guilty air. "He is a man the same as everyone else. Of course, he has his weaknesses, but he is abreast of modern ideas, is in the service, is of use to his country. Ten years ago there was an old fellow serving as agent here, a man of the greatest intelligence . . . and he used to say . . ."

"Nonsense, nonsense!" the zoologist interrupted. "You say he is in the service; but how does he serve? Do you mean to tell me that things have been done better because he is here, and the officials are more punctual, honest, and civil? On the contrary, he has only sanctioned their slackness by his prestige as an intellectual university man. He is only punctual on the 20th of the month, when he gets his salary; on the other days he lounges about at home in slippers and tries to look as if he were doing the Government a great service by living in the Caucasus. No, Alexandr Daviditch, don't stick up for him. You are insincere from beginning to end. If you really loved him and considered him your neighbour, you would above all not be indifferent to his weaknesses, you would not be indulgent to them, but for his own sake would try to make him innocuous."

"That is?"

"Innocuous. Since he is incorrigible, he can only be made innocuous in one way. . . ." Von Koren passed his finger round his throat. "Or he might be drowned . . .," he added. "In the interests of humanity and in their own interests, such people ought to be destroyed. They certainly ought."

"What are you saying?" muttered Samoylenko, getting up and looking with amazement at the zoologist's calm, cold face. "Deacon, what is he saying? Why—are you in your senses?"

"I don't insist on the death penalty," said Von Koren. "If it is proved that it is pernicious, devise something else. If we can't destroy Laevsky, why then, isolate him, make him harmless, send him to hard labour."

"What are you saying!" said Samoylenko in horror. "With pepper, with pepper," he cried in a voice of despair, seeing that the deacon was eating stuffed aubergines without pepper. "You with your great intellect, what are you saying! Send our friend, a proud intellectual man, to penal servitude!"

"Well, if he is proud and tries to resist, put him in fetters!"

Samoylenko could not utter a word, and only twiddled his fingers; the deacon looked at his flabbergasted and really absurd face, and laughed.

"Let us leave off talking of that," said the zoologist. "Only remember one thing, Alexandr Daviditch: primitive man was preserved from such as Laevsky by the struggle for existence and by natural selection; now our civilization has considerably weakened the struggle and the selection, and we ought to look after the destruction of the rotten and worthless for ourselves; otherwise, when the Laevskys multiply, civilization will perish and mankind will degenerate utterly. It will be our fault."

"If it depends on drowning and hanging," said Samoylenko, "damnation take your civilization, damnation take your humanity! Damnation take it! I tell you what: you are a very learned and intelligent man and the pride of your country, but the Germans have ruined you. Yes, the Germans! The Germans!"

Since Samoylenko had left Dorpat, where he had studied medicine, he had rarely seen a German and had not read a single German book, but, in his opinion, every harmful idea in politics or science was due to the Germans. Where he had got this notion he could not have said himself, but he held it firmly.

"Yes, the Germans!" he repeated once more. "Come and have some tea."

All three stood up, and putting on their hats, went out into the little garden, and sat there under the shade of the light green maples, the pear-trees, and a chestnut-tree. The zoologist and the deacon sat on a bench by the table, while Samoylenko sank into a deep wicker chair with a sloping back. The orderly handed them tea, jam, and a bottle of syrup.

It was very hot, thirty degrees Réaumur in the shade. The sultry air was stagnant and motionless, and a long spider-web, stretching from the chestnut-tree to the ground, hung limply and did not stir.

The deacon took up the guitar, which was constantly

lying on the ground near the table, tuned it, and began singing softly in a thin voice:

"Gathered round the tavern were the seminary lads,"

but instantly subsided, overcome by the heat, mopped his brow and glanced upwards at the blazing blue sky. Samoylenko grew drowsy; the sultry heat, the stillness and the delicious afterdinner languor, which quickly pervaded all his limbs, made him feel heavy and sleepy; his arms dropped at his sides, his eyes grew small, his head sank on his breast. He looked with almost tearful tenderness at Von Koren and the deacon, and muttered:

"The younger generation. . . . A scientific star and a luminary of the Church. . . . I shouldn't wonder if the long-skirted alleluia will be shooting up into a bishop; I dare say I may come to kissing his hand. . . . Well . . . please God. . . ."

Soon a snore was heard. Von Koren and the deacon finished their tea and went out into the street.

"Are you going to the harbour again to catch seagudgeon?" asked the zoologist.

"No, it's too hot."

"Come and see me. You can pack up a parcel and copy something for me. By the way, we must have a talk about what you are to do. You must work, deacon. You can't go on like this."

"Your words are just and logical," said the deacon. "But my laziness finds an excuse in the circumstances of my present life. You know yourself that an uncertain position has a great tendency to make people apathetic. God only knows whether I have been sent here for a time or permanently. I am living here in uncertainty, while my wife is vegetating at her father's and is missing me. And I must confess my brain is melting with the heat."

"That's all nonsense," said the zoologist. "You can get used to the heat, and you can get used to being without the deaconess. You mustn't be slack; you must pull yourself together."

5

Nadyezhda Fyodorovna went to bathe in the morning, and her cook, Olga, followed her with a jug, a copper basin, towels, and a sponge. In the bay stood two unknown steamers with dirty white funnels, obviously foreign cargo vessels. Some men dressed in white and wearing white shoes were walking along the harbour, shouting loudly in French, and were answered from the steamers. The bells were ringing briskly in the little church of the town.

"To-day is Sunday!" Nadyezhda Fyodorovna remembered with pleasure.

She felt perfectly well, and was in a gay holiday humour. In a new loose-fitting dress of coarse thick tussore silk, and a big wide-brimmed straw hat which was bent down over her ears, so that her face looked out as though from a basket, she fancied she looked very charming. She thought that in the whole town there was only one young, pretty, intellectual woman, and that was herself, and that she was the only one who knew how to dress herself cheaply, elegantly, and with taste. That dress, for example, cost only twenty-two roubles, and yet how charming it was! In the whole town she was the only one who could be attractive, while there were numbers of men, so they must all, whether they would or not, be envious of Laevsky.

She was glad that of late Laevsky had been cold to her, reserved and polite, and at times even harsh and rude; in the past she had met all his outbursts, all his contemptuous, cold or strange incomprehensible glances, with tears, reproaches, and threats to leave him or to starve herself to death; now she only blushed, looked guiltily at him, and was glad he was not affectionate to her. If he had abused her, or threatened her, it would have been better and pleasanter, since she felt hopelessly guilty towards him. She felt she was to blame, in the first place, for not sympathizing with the dreams of a life of hard work, for the sake of which he had given up Petersburg and had come here to the Caucasus, and she was convinced that he had been angry with her of late for precisely that. When she was travelling to the Caucasus, it seemed that she would find here on the first day a cosy nook by the sea, a snug little garden with shade, with birds, with little brooks, where she could grow flowers and vegetables, rear ducks and hens, entertain her neighbours, doctor poor peasants and distribute little books amongst them. It had turned out that the Caucasus was nothing but bare mountains, forests, and huge valleys, where it took a long time and a great deal of effort to find anything and settle down; that there were no neighbours of any sort; that it was very hot and one might be robbed. Laevsky had been in no hurry to obtain a piece of land; she was glad of it, and they seemed to be in a tacit compact never to allude to a life of hard work. He was silent about it, she thought, because he was angry with her for being silent about it.

In the second place, she had without his knowledge during those two years bought various trifles to the value of three hundred roubles at Atchmianov's shop. She had bought the things by degrees, at one time materials, at another time silk or a parasol, and the debt had grown imperceptibly.

"I will tell him about it to-day . . .," she used to decide, but at once reflected that in Laevsky's present mood it would hardly be convenient to talk to him of debts.

Thirdly, she had on two occasions in Laevsky's absence received a visit from Kirilin, the police captain: once in the morning when Laevsky had gone to bathe, and another time at midnight when he was playing cards. Remembering this, Nadyezhda Fyodorovna flushed crimson, and looked round at the cook as though she might overhear her thoughts. The long, insufferably hot, wearisome days, beautiful languorous evenings and stifling nights, and the whole manner of living, when from morning to night one is at a loss to fill up the useless hours, and the persistent thought that she was the prettiest young woman in the town, and that her youth was passing and being wasted, and Laevsky himself, though honest and idealistic, always the same, always lounging about in his slippers, biting his nails, and wearying her with his caprices, led by degrees to her becoming possessed by desire, and as though she were mad, she thought of nothing else day and night. Breathing, looking, walking, she felt nothing but desire. The sound of the sea told her she must love; the darkness of evening—the same; the mountains—the same. . . . And when Kirilin began paying her attentions, she had neither the power nor the wish to resist, and surrendered to him. . . .

Now the foreign steamers and the men in white reminded her for some reason of a huge hall; together with the shouts of French she heard the strains of a waltz, and her bosom heaved with unaccountable delight. She longed to dance and talk French.

She reflected joyfully that there was nothing terrible about her infidelity. Her soul had no part in her infidelity; she still loved Laevsky, and that was proved by the fact that she was jealous of him, was sorry for him, and missed him when he was away. Kirilin had turned out to be very mediocre, rather coarse though handsome; everything was broken off with him already and there would never be anything more. What had happened was over; it had nothing to do with anyone, and if Laevsky found it out he would not believe in it.

There was only one bathing-house for ladies on the sea-front; men bathed under the open sky. Going into the bathing-house, Nadyezhda Fyodorovna found there an elderly lady, Marya Konstantinovna Bityugov, and her daughter Katya, a schoolgirl of fifteen; both of them were sitting on a bench undressing. Marya Konstantinovna was a good-natured, enthusiastic, and genteel person, who talked in a drawling and pathetic voice. She had been a governess until she was thirty-two, and then had married Bityugov, a Government official—a bald little man with his hair combed on to his temples and with a very meek disposition. She was still in love with him, was jealous, blushed at the word "love," and told everyone she was very happy.

"My dear," she cried enthusiastically, on seeing Nadyezhda Fyodorovna, assuming an expression which all her acquaintances called "almond-oily." "My dear, how delightful that you have come! We'll bathe together—that's enchanting!"

Olga quickly flung off her dress and chemise, and began undressing her mistress.

"It's not quite so hot to-day as yesterday?" said Nad-

yezhda Fyodorovna, shrinking at the coarse touch of the
naked cook. "Yesterday I almost died of the heat."

"Oh yes, my dear; I could hardly breathe myself. Would
you believe it? I bathed yesterday three times! Just imagine, my dear, three times! Nikodim Alexandritch was
quite uneasy."

"Is it possible to be so ugly?" thought Nadyezhda Fyodorovna, looking at Olga and the official's wife; she
glanced at Katya and thought: "The little girl's not badly
made."

"Your Nikodim Alexandritch is very charming!" she
said. "I'm simply in love with him."

"Ha, ha, ha!" cried Marya Konstantinovna, with a
forced laugh; "that's quite enchanting."

Free from her clothes, Nadyezhda Fyodorovna felt a
desire to fly. And it seemed to her that if she were to wave
her hands she would fly upwards. When she was undressed, she noticed that Olga looked scornfully at her
white body. Olga, a young soldier's wife, was living with
her lawful husband, and so considered herself superior
to her mistress. Marya Konstantinovna and Katya were
afraid of her, and did not respect her. This was disagreeable, and to raise herself in their opinion, Nadyezhda Fyodorovna said:

"At home, in Petersburg, summer villa life is at its
height now. My husband and I have so many friends! We
ought to go and see them."

"I believe your husband is an engineer?" said Marya
Konstantinovna timidly.

"I am speaking of Laevsky. He has a great many acquaintances. But unfortunately his mother is a proud aris-
tocrat, not very intelligent. . . ."

Nadyezhda Fyodorovna threw herself into the water
without finishing; Marya Konstantinovna and Katya made
their way in after her.

"There are so many conventional ideas in the world,"
Nadyezhda Fyodorovna went on, "and life is not so easy
as it seems."

Marya Konstantinovna, who had been a governess in
aristocratic families and who was an authority on social
matters, said:

"Oh yes! Would you believe me, my dear, at the Garatynskys' I was expected to dress for lunch as well as for din-

ner, so that, like an actress, I received a special allowance for my wardrobe in addition to my salary."

She stood between Nadyezhda Fyodorovna and Katya as though to screen her daughter from the water that washed the former.

Through the open doors looking out to the sea they could see someone swimming a hundred paces from their bathing-place.

"Mother, it's our Kostya," said Katya.

"Ach, ach!" Marya Konstantinovna cackled in her dismay. "Ach, Kostya!" she shouted. "Come back! Kostya, come back!"

Kostya, a boy of fourteen, to show off his prowess before his mother and sister, dived and swam farther, but began to be exhausted and hurried back, and from his strained and serious face it could be seen that he could not trust his own strength.

"The trouble one has with these boys, my dear!" said Marya Konstantinovna, growing calmer. "Before you can turn round, he will break his neck. Ah, my dear, how sweet it is, and yet at the same time how difficult, to be a mother! One's afraid of everything."

Nadyezdha Fyodorovna put on her straw hat and dashed out into the open sea. She swam some thirty feet and then turned on her back. She could see the sea to the horizon, the steamers, the people on the sea-front, the town; and all this, together with the sultry heat and the soft, transparent waves, excited her and whispered that she must live, live. . . . A sailing-boat darted by her rapidly and vigorously, cleaving the waves and the air; the man sitting at the helm looked at her, and she liked being looked at. . . .

After bathing, the ladies dressed and went away together.

"I have fever every alternate day, and yet I don't get thin," said Nadyezhda Fyodorovna, licking her lips, which were salt from the bathe, and responding with a smile to the bows of her acquaintances. "I've always been plump, and now I believe I'm plumper than ever."

"That, my dear, is constitutional. If, like me, one has no constitutional tendency to stoutness, no diet is of any use. . . . But you've wetted your hat, my dear."

"It doesn't matter; it will dry."

Nadyezhda Fyodorovna saw again the men in white who were walking on the sea-front and talking French; and again she felt a sudden thrill of joy, and had a vague memory of some big hall in which she had once danced, or of which, perhaps, she had once dreamed. And something at the bottom of her soul dimly and obscurely whispered to her that she was a petty, common, miserable, worthless woman. . . .

Marya Konstantinovna stopped at her gate and asked her to come in and sit down for a little while.

"Come in, my dear," she said in an imploring voice, and at the same time she looked at Nadyezhda Fyodorovna with anxiety and hope; perhaps she would refuse and not come in!

"With pleasure," said Nadyezhda Fyodorovna, accepting. "You know how I love being with you!"

And she went into the house. Marya Konstantinovna sat her down and gave her coffee, regaled her with milk rolls, then showed her photographs of her former pupils, the Garatynskys, who were by now married. She showed her, too, the examination reports of Kostya and Katya. The reports were very good, but to make them seem even better, she complained, with a sigh, how difficult the lessons at school were now. . . . She made much of her visitor, and was sorry for her, though at the same time she was harassed by the thought that Nadyezhda Fyodorovna might have a corrupting influence on the morals of Kostya and Katya, and was glad that her Nikodim Alexandritch was not at home. Seeing that in her opinion all men are fond of "women like that," Nadyezhda Fyodorovna might have a bad effect on Nikodim Alexandritch too.

As she talked to her visitor, Marya Konstantinovna kept remembering that they were to have a picnic that evening, and that Von Koren had particularly begged her to say nothing about it to the "Japanese monkeys"—that is, Laevsky and Nadyezhda Fyodorovna; but she dropped a word about it unawares, crimsoned, and said in confusion:

"I hope you will come too!"

6

It was agreed to drive about five miles out of town on the road to the south, to stop near a *duhan* at the junction of two streams—the Black River and the Yellow River—and to cook fish soup. They started out soon after five. Foremost of the party in a char-à-banc drove Samoylenko and Laevsky; they were followed by Marya Konstanti-novna, Nadyezhda Fyodorovna, Katya and Kostya, in a coach with three horses, carrying with them the crock-ery and a basket with provisions. In the next carriage came the police captain, Kirilin, and the young Atchmia-nov, the son of the shopkeeper to whom Nadyezhda Fyo-dorovna owed three hundred roubles; opposite them, hud-dled up on the little seat with his feet tucked under him, sat Nikodim Alexandritch, a neat little man with hair combed on to his temples. Last of all came Von Koren and the deacon; at the deacon's feet stood a basket of fish.

"R-r-right!" Samoylenko shouted at the top of his voice when he met a cart or a mountaineer riding on a donkey.

"In two years' time, when I shall have the means and the people ready, I shall set off on an expedition," Von Koren was telling the deacon. "I shall go by the sea-coast from Vladivostok to the Behring Straits, and then from the Straits to the mouth of the Yenisei. We shall make the map, study the fauna and the flora, and make de-tailed geological, anthropological, and ethnographical re-searches. It depends upon you to go with me or not."

"It's impossible," said the deacon.

"Why?"

"I'm a man with ties and a family."

"Your wife will let you go; we will provide for her. Bet-ter still if you were to persuade her for the public benefit to go into a nunnery; that would make it possible for you to become a monk, too, and join the expedition as a priest. I can arrange it for you."

The deacon was silent.

"Do you know your theology well?" asked the zoologist.

"No, rather badly."

"H'm! . . . I can't give you any advice on that score, because I don't know much about theology myself. You give me a list of books you need, and I will send them to you from Petersburg in the winter. It will be necessary for you to read the notes of religious travellers, too; among them are some good ethnologists and Oriental scholars. When you are familiar with their methods, it will be easier for you to set to work. And you needn't waste your time till you get the books; come to me, and we will study the compass and go through a course of meteorology. All that's indispensable."

"To be sure . . ." muttered the deacon, and he laughed. "I was trying to get a place in Central Russia, and my uncle, the head priest, promised to help me. If I go with you I shall have troubled them for nothing."

"I don't understand your hesitation. If you go on being an ordinary deacon, who is only obliged to hold a service on holidays, and on the other days can rest from work, you will be exactly the same as you are now in ten years' time, and will have gained nothing but a beard and moustache; while on returning from this expedition in ten years' time you will be a different man, you will be enriched by the consciousness that something has been done by you."

From the ladies' carriage came shrieks of terror and delight. The carriages were driving along a road hollowed in a literally overhanging precipitous cliff, and it seemed to everyone that they were galloping along a shelf on a steep wall, and that in a moment the carriages would drop into the abyss. On the right stretched the sea; on the left was a rough brown wall with black blotches and red veins and with climbing roots; while on the summit stood shaggy fir-trees bent over, as though looking down in terror and curiosity. A minute later there were shrieks and laughter again: they had to drive under a huge overhanging rock.

"I don't know why the devil I'm coming with you," said Laevsky. "How stupid and vulgar it is! I want to go to the North, to run away, to escape; but here I am, for some reason, going to this stupid picnic."

"But look, what a view!" said Samoylenko as the horses turned to the left, and the valley of the Yellow River came into sight and the stream itself gleamed in the sunlight, yellow, turbid, frantic.

"I see nothing fine in that, Sasha," answered Laevsky. "To be in continual ecstasies over nature shows poverty of imagination. In comparison with what my imagination can give me, all these streams and rocks are trash, and nothing else."

The carriages now were by the bank of the stream. The high mountain banks gradually grew closer, the valley shrank together and ended in a gorge; the rocky mountain round which they were driving had been piled together by nature out of huge rocks, pressing upon each other with such terrible weight, that Samoylenko could not help gasping every time he looked at them. The dark and beautiful mountain was cleft in places by narrow fissures and gorges from which came a breath of dewy moisture and mystery; through the gorges could be seen other mountains, brown, pink, lilac, smoky, or bathed in vivid sunlight. From time to time as they passed a gorge they caught the sound of water falling from the heights and splashing on the stones.

"Ach, the damned mountains!" sighed Laevsky. "How sick I am of them!"

At the place where the Black River falls into the Yellow, and the water black as ink stains the yellow and struggles with it, stood the Tatar Kerbalay's *duhan,* with the Russian flag on the roof and with an inscription written in chalk: "The Pleasant Duhan." Near it was a little garden, enclosed in a hurdle fence, with tables and chairs set out in it, and in the midst of a thicket of wretched thorn-bushes stood a single solitary cypress, dark and beautiful.

Kerbalay, a nimble little Tatar in a blue shirt and a white apron, was standing in the road, and, holding his stomach, he bowed low to welcome the carriages, and smiled, showing his glistening white teeth.

"Good-evening, Kerbalay," shouted Samoylenko. "We are driving on a little further, and you take along the samovar and chairs! Look sharp!"

Kerbalay nodded his shaven head and muttered something, and only those sitting in the last carriage could hear: "We've got trout, your Excellency."

"Bring them, bring them!" said Von Koren.

Five hundred paces from the *duhan* the carriages stopped. Samoylenko selected a small meadow round which there were scattered stones convenient for sitting on, and a fallen tree blown down by the storm with roots overgrown by moss and dry yellow needles. Here there was a fragile wooden bridge over the stream, and just opposite on the other bank there was a little barn for drying maize, standing on four low piles, and looking like the hut on hen's legs in the fairy tale; a little ladder sloped from its door.

The first impression in all was a feeling that they would never get out of that place again. On all sides, wherever they looked, the mountains rose up and towered above them, and the shadows of evening were stealing rapidly, rapidly from the *duhan* and dark cypress, making the narrow winding valley of the Black River narrower and the mountains higher. They could hear the river murmuring and the unceasing chirrup of the grasshoppers.

"Enchanting!" said Marya Konstantinovna, heaving deep sighs of ecstasy. "Children, look how fine! What peace!"

"Yes, it really is fine," assented Laevsky, who liked the view, and for some reason felt sad as he looked at the sky and then at the blue smoke rising from the chimney of the *duhan*. "Yes, it is fine," he repeated.

"Ivan Andreitch, describe this view," Marya Konstantinovna said tearfully.

"Why?" asked Laevsky. "The impression is better than any description. The wealth of sights and sounds which everyone receives from nature by direct impression is ranted about by authors in a hideous and unrecognizable way."

"Really?" Von Koren asked coldly, choosing the biggest stone by the side of the water, and trying to clamber up and sit upon it. "Really?" he repeated, looking directly at Laevsky. "What of 'Romeo and Juliet'? Or, for instance, Pushkin's 'Night in the Ukraine'? Nature ought to come and bow down at their feet."

"Perhaps," said Laevsky, who was too lazy to think and

oppose him. "Though what is 'Romeo and Juliet' after all?" he added after a short pause. "The beauty of poetry and holiness of love are simply the roses under which they try to hide its rottenness. Romeo is just the same sort of animal as all the rest of us."

"Whatever one talks to you about, you always bring it round to . . ." Von Koren glanced round at Katya and broke off.

"What do I bring it round to?" asked Laevsky.

"One tells you, for instance, how beautiful a bunch of grapes is, and you answer: 'Yes, but how ugly it is when it is chewed and digested in one's stomach!' Why say that? It's not new, and . . . altogether it is a queer habit."

Laevsky knew that Von Koren did not like him, and so was afraid of him, and felt in his presence as though everyone were constrained and someone were standing behind his back. He made no answer and walked away, feeling sorry he had come.

"Gentlemen, quick march for brush wood for the fire!" commanded Samoylenko.

They all wandered off in different directions, and no one was left but Kirilin, Atchmianov, and Nikodim Alexandritch. Kerbalay brought chairs, spread a rug on the ground, and set a few bottles of wine.

The police captain, Kirilin, a tall, good-looking man, who in all weathers wore his great-coat over his tunic, with his haughty deportment, stately carriage, and thick, rather hoarse voice, looked like a young provincial chief of police; his expression was mournful and sleepy, as though he had just been waked against his will.

"What have you brought this for, you brute?" he asked Kerbalay, deliberately articulating each word. "I ordered you to give us *kvarel,* and what have you brought, you ugly Tatar? Eh? What?"

"We have plenty of wine of our own, Yegor Alekseitch," Nikodim Alexandritch observed, timidly and politely.

"What? But I want us to have my wine, too; I'm taking part in the picnic and I imagine I have full right to contribute my share. I im-ma-gine so! Bring ten bottles of *kvarel.*"

"Why so many?" asked Nikodim Alexandritch, in wonder, knowing Kirilin had no money.

"Twenty bottles! Thirty!" shouted Kirilin.

"Never mind, let him," Atchmianov whispered to Nikodim Alexandritch; "I'll pay."

Nadyezhda Fyodorovna was in a light-hearted, mischievous mood; she wanted to skip and jump, to laugh, to shout, to tease, to flirt. In her cheap cotton dress with blue pansies on it, in her red shoes and the same straw hat, she seemed to herself little, simple, light, ethereal as a butterfly. She ran over the rickety bridge and looked for a minute into the water, in order to feel giddy; then, shrieking and laughing, ran to the other side to the drying-shed, and she fancied that all the men were admiring her, even Kerbalay. When in the rapidly falling darkness the trees began to melt into the mountains and the horses into the carriages, and a light gleamed in the windows of the *duhan,* she climbed up the mountain by the little path which zigzagged between stones and thorn-bushes and sat on a stone. Down below, the camp-fire was burning. Near the fire, with his sleeves tucked up, the deacon was moving to and fro, and his long black shadow kept describing a circle round it; he put on wood, and with a spoon tied to a long stick he stirred the cauldron. Samoylenko, with a copper-red face, was fussing round the fire just as though he were in his own kitchen, shouting furiously:

"Where's the salt, gentlemen? I bet you've forgotten it. Why are you all sitting about like lords while I do all the work?"

Laevsky and Nikodim Alexandritch were sitting side by side on the fallen tree looking pensively at the fire. Marya Konstantinovna, Katya, and Kostya were taking the cups, saucers, and plates out of the baskets. Von Koren, with his arms folded and one foot on a stone, was standing on a bank at the very edge of the water, thinking about something. Patches of red light from the fire moved together with the shadows over the ground near the dark human figures, and quivered on the mountain, on the trees, on the bridge, on the drying-shed; on the other side the steep, scooped-out bank was all lighted up and glimmering in the stream, and the rushing turbid water broke its reflection into little bits.

The deacon went for the fish which Kerbalay was cleaning and washing on the bank, but he stood still half-way and looked about him.

"My God, how nice it is!" he thought. "People, rocks, the fire, the twilight, a monstrous tree—nothing more, and yet how fine it is!"

On the further bank some unknown persons made their appearance near the drying-shed. The flickering light and the smoke from the campfire puffing in that direction made it impossible to get a full view of them all at once, but glimpses were caught now of a shaggy hat and a grey beard, now of a blue shirt, now of a figure, ragged from shoulder to knee, with a dagger across the body; then a swarthy young face with black eyebrows, as thick and bold as though they had been drawn in charcoal. Five of them sat in a circle on the ground, and the other five went into the drying-shed. One was standing at the door with his back to the fire, and with his hands behind his back was telling something, which must have been very interesting, for when Samoylenko threw on twigs and the fire flared up, and scattered sparks and threw a glaring light on the shed, two calm countenances with an expression on them of deep attention could be seen, looking out of the door, while those who were sitting in a circle turned round and began listening to the speaker. Soon after, those sitting in a circle began softly singing something slow and melodious, that sounded like Lenten Church music. . . . Listening to them, the deacon imagined how it would be with him in ten years' time, when he would come back from the expedition: he would be a young priest and monk, an author with a name and a splendid past; he would be consecrated an archimandrite, then a bishop; and he would serve mass in the cathedral; in a golden mitre he would come out into the body of the church with the ikon on his breast, and blessing the mass of the people with the triple and the double candelabra, would proclaim: "Look down from Heaven, O God, behold and visit this vineyard which Thy Hand has planted," and the children with their angel voices would sing in response: "Holy God. . . ."

"Deacon, where is that fish?" he heard Samoylenko's voice.

As he went back to the fire, the deacon imagined the Church procession going along a dusty road on a hot July day; in front the peasants carrying the banners and the women and children the ikons, then the boy choristers and the sacristan with his face tied up and a straw in his hair, then in due order himself, the deacon, and behind him the priest wearing his *calotte* and carrying a cross, and behind them, tramping in the dust, a crowd of peasants—men, women, and children; in the crowd his wife and the priest's wife with kerchiefs on their heads. The choristers sing, the babies cry, the corncrakes call, the lark carols. . . . Then they make a stand and sprinkle the herd with holy water. . . . They go on again, and then kneeling pray for rain. Then lunch and talk. . . .

"And that's nice too . . ." thought the deacon.

7

Kirilin and Atchmianov climbed up the mountain by the path. Atchmianov dropped behind and stopped, while Kirilin went up to Nadyezhda Fyodorovna.

"Good-evening," he said, touching his cap.

"Good-evening."

"Yes!" said Kirilin, looking at the sky and pondering.

"Why 'yes'?" asked Nadyezhda Fyodorovna after a brief pause, noticing that Atchmianov was watching them both.

"And so it seems," said the officer, slowly, "that our love has withered before it has blossomed, so to speak. How do you wish me to understand it? Is it a sort of coquetry on your part, or do you look upon me as a nincompoop who can be treated as you choose?"

"It was a mistake! Leave me alone!" Nadyezhda Fyodorovna said sharply, on that beautiful, marvellous evening, looking at him with terror and asking herself with bewilderment, could there really have been a moment when that man attracted her and had been near to her?

"So that's it!" said Kirilin; he thought in silence for a few minutes and said: "Well, I'll wait till you are in a better humour, and meanwhile I venture to assure you I am a gentleman, and I don't allow anyone to doubt it. Adieu!"

He touched his cap again and walked off, making his

way between the bushes. After a short interval Atchmianov approached hesitatingly.

"What a fine evening!" he said with a slight Armenian accent.

He was nice-looking, fashionably dressed, and behaved unaffectedly like a well-bred youth, but Nadyezhda Fyodorovna did not like him because she owed his father three hundred roubles; it was displeasing to her, too, that a shopkeeper had been asked to the picnic, and she was vexed at his coming up to her that evening when her heart felt so pure.

"The picnic is a success altogether," he said, after a pause.

"Yes," she agreed, and as though suddenly remembering her debt, she said carelessly: "Oh, tell them in your shop that Ivan Andreitch will come round in a day or two and will pay three hundred roubles. . . . I don't remember exactly what it is."

"I would give another three hundred if you would not mention that debt every day. Why be prosaic?"

Nadyezhda Fyodorovna laughed; the amusing idea occurred to her that if she had been willing and sufficiently immoral she might in one minute be free from her debt. If she, for instance, were to turn the head of this handsome young fool! How amusing, absurd, wild it would be really! And she suddenly felt a longing to make him love her, to plunder him, throw him over, and then to see what would come of it.

"Allow me to give you one piece of advice," Atchmianov said timidly. "I beg you to beware of Kirilin. He says horrible things about you everywhere."

"It doesn't interest me to know what every fool says of me," Nadyezhda Fyodorovna said coldly, and the amusing thought of playing with handsome young Atchmianov suddenly lost its charm.

"We must go down," she said; "they're calling us."

The fish soup was ready by now. They were ladling it out by platefuls, and eating it with the religious solemnity with which this is only done at a picnic; and everyone thought the fish soup very good, and thought that at home they had never eaten anything so nice. As is always the case at picnics, in the mass of dinner napkins, parcels, useless greasy papers fluttering in the wind, no one knew where was his glass or where his bread. They poured the wine on the carpet and on their own knees, spilt the salt, while it was dark all round them and the fire burnt more dimly, and everyone was too lazy to get up and put wood on. They all drank wine, and even gave Kostya and Katya half a glass each. Nadyezhda Fyodorovna drank one glass and then another, got a little drunk and forgot about Kirilin.

"A splendid picnic, an enchanting evening," said Laevsky, growing lively with the wine. "But I should prefer a fine winter to all this. 'His beaver collar is silver with hoar-frost.' "

"Everyone to his taste," observed Von Koren.

Laevsky felt uncomfortable; the heat of the camp-fire was beating upon his back, and the hatred of Von Koren upon his breast and face: this hatred on the part of a decent, clever man, a feeling in which there probably lay hid a well-grounded reason, humiliated him and enervated him, and unable to stand up against it, he said in a propitiatory tone:

"I am passionately fond of nature, and I regret that I'm not a naturalist. I envy you."

"Well, I don't envy you, and don't regret it," said Nadyezhda Fyodorovna. "I don't understand how anyone can seriously interest himself in beetles and ladybirds while the people are suffering."

Laevsky shared her opinion. He was absolutely ignorant of natural science, and so could never reconcile himself to the authoritative tone and the learned and profound air of the people who devoted themselves to the whiskers of ants and the claws of beetles, and he always felt vexed that these people, relying on these whiskers, claws, and something they called protoplasm (he always imagined it in the form of an oyster), should undertake to decide questions involving the origin and life of man. But in Nadyezhda Fyodorovna's words he heard a note of falsity, and simply to contradict her he said: "The point is not the ladybirds, but the deductions made from them."

8

It was late, eleven o'clock, when they began to get into the carriages to go home. They took their seats, and the only ones missing were Nadyezhda Fyodorovna and Atchmianov, who were running after one another, laughing, the other side of the stream.

"Make haste, my friends," shouted Samoylenko.

"You oughn't to give ladies wine," said Von Koren in a low voice.

Laevsky, exhausted by the picnic, by the hatred of Von Koren, and by his own thoughts, went to meet Nadyezhda Fyodorovna, and when, gay and happy, feeling light as a feather, breathless and laughing, she took him by both hands and laid her head on his breast, he stepped back and said dryly:

"You are behaving like a . . . cocotte."

It sounded horribly coarse, so that he felt sorry for her at once. On his angry, exhausted face she read hatred, pity and vexation with himself, and her heart sank at once. She realized instantly that she had gone too far, had been too free and easy in her behaviour, and overcome with misery, feeling herself heavy, stout, coarse, and drunk, she got into the first empty carriage together with Atchmianov. Laevsky got in with Kirilin, the zoologist with Samoylenko, the deacon with the ladies, and the party set off.

"You see what the Japanese monkeys are like," Von Koren began, rolling himself up in his cloak and shutting his eyes. "You heard she doesn't care to take an interest in beetles and ladybirds because the people are suffering. That's how all the Japanese monkeys look upon people like us. They're a slavish, cunning race, terrified by the whip and the fist for ten generations; they tremble and burn incense only before violence; but let the monkey into a free state where there's no one to take it by the collar, and it relaxes at once and shows itself in its true colours. Look how bold they are in picture galleries, in museums, in theatres, or when they talk of science: they puff themselves out and get excited, they are abusive and critical . . . they are bound to criticize—it's the sign of the slave. You listen: men of the liberal professions are more often sworn at than pickpockets—that's because three-quarters of society are made up of slaves, of just such monkeys. It never happens that a slave holds out his hand to you and sincerely says 'Thank you' to you for your work."

"I don't know what you want," said Samoylenko, yawning; "the poor thing, in the simplicity of her heart, wanted to talk to you of scientific subjects, and you draw a conclusion from that. You're cross with him for something or other, and with her, too, to keep him company. She's a splendid woman."

"Ah, nonsense! An ordinary kept woman, depraved and vulgar. Listen Alexandr Daviditch; when you meet a simple peasant woman, who isn't living with her husband, who does nothing but giggle, you tell her to go and work. Why are you timid in this case and afraid to tell the truth? Simply because Nadyezhda Fyodorovna is kept, not by a sailor, but by an official."

"What am I to do with her?" said Samoylenko, getting angry. "Beat her or what?"

"Not flatter vice. We curse vice only behind its back, and that's like making a long nose at it round a corner. I am a zoologist or a sociologist, which is the same thing; you are a doctor; society believes in us; we ought to point out the terrible harm which threatens it and the next generation from the existence of ladies like Nadyezhda Ivanovna."

"Fyodorovna," Samoylenko corrected. "But what ought society to do?"

"Society? That's its affair. To my thinking the surest and most direct method is—compulsion *Manu militari* she ought to be returned to her husband; and if her husband won't take her in, then she ought to be sent to penal servitude or some house of correction."

"Ouf!" sighed Samoylenko. He paused and asked quietly: "You said the other day that people like Laevsky ought to be destroyed. . . . Tell me, if you . . . if the State or society commissioned you to destroy him, could you . . . bring yourself to it?"

"My hand would not tremble."

9

When they got home, Laevsky and Nadyezhda Fyodorovna went into their dark, stuffy, dull rooms. Both were silent. Laevsky lighted a candle, while Nadyezhda Fyodorovna sat down, and without taking off her cloak and hat, lifted her melancholy, guilty eyes to him.

He knew that she expected an explanation from him, but an explanation would be wearisome, useless and exhausting, and his heart was heavy because he had lost control over himself and been rude to her. He chanced to feel in his pocket the letter which he had been intending every day to read to her, and thought if he were to show her that letter now, it would turn her thoughts in another direction.

"It is time to define our relations," he thought. "I will give it her; what is to be will be."

He took out the letter and gave it her.

"Read it. It concerns you."

Saying this, he went into his own room and lay down on the sofa in the dark without a pillow. Nadyezhda Fyodorovna read the letter, and it seemed to her as though the ceiling were falling and the walls were closing in on her. It seemed suddenly dark and shut in and terrible. She crossed herself quickly three times and said:

"Give him peace, O Lord . . . give him peace. . . ."

And she began crying.

"Vanya," she called. "Ivan Andreitch!"

There was no answer. Thinking that Laevsky had come in and was standing behind her chair, she sobbed like a child, and said:

"Why did you not tell me before that he was dead? I wouldn't have gone to the picnic; I shouldn't have laughed so horribly. . . . The men said horrid things to me. What a sin, what a sin! Save me, Vanya, save me. . . . I have been mad. . . . I am lost. . . ."

Laevsky heard her sobs. He felt stifled and his heart was beating violently. In his misery he got up, stood in the middle of the room, groped his way in the dark to an easy-chair by the table, and sat down.

"This is a prison . . ." he thought. "I must get away. . . . I can't bear it."

It was too late to go and play cards; there were no restaurants in the town. He lay down again and covered his ears that he might not hear her sobbing, and he suddenly remembered that he could go to Samoylenko. To avoid going near Nadyezhda Fyodorovna, he got out of the window into the garden, climbed over the garden fence, and went along the street. It was dark. A steamer, judging by its lights, a big passenger one, had just come in. . . . He heard the clank of the anchor chain. A red light was moving rapidly from the shore in the direction of the steamer: it was the Customs boat going out to it.

"The passengers are asleep in their cabins . . ." thought Laevsky, and he envied the peace of mind of other people.

The windows in Samoylenko's house were open. Laevsky looked in at one of them, then in at another; it was dark and still in the rooms.

"Alexandr Daviditch, are you asleep?" he called. "Alexandr Daviditch!"

He heard a cough and an uneasy shout:

"Who's there? What the devil?"

"It is I, Alexandr Daviditch; excuse me."

A little later the door opened; there was a glow of soft light from the lamp, and Samoylenko's huge figure appeared, all in white, with a white nightcap on his head.

"What now?" he asked, scratching himself and breathing hard from sleepiness. "Wait a minute; I'll open the door directly."

"Don't trouble; I'll get in at the window. . . ."

Laevsky climbed in at the window, and when he reached Samoylenko, seized him by the hand.

"Alexandr Daviditch," he said in a shaking voice, "save me! I beseech you, I implore you. Understand me! My position is agonizing. If it goes on for another two days I shall strangle myself like . . . like a dog."

"Wait a bit. . . . What are you talking about exactly?"

"Light a candle."

"Oh . . . oh! . . ." sighed Samoylenko, lighting a candle. "My God! My God! . . . Why, it's past one, brother."

"Excuse me, but I can't stay at home," said Laevsky,

feeling great comfort from the light and the presence of Samoylenko. "You are my best, my only friend, Alexandr Daviditch. . . . You are my only hope. For God's sake, come to my rescue, whether you want to or not. I must get away from here, come what may! . . . Lend me the money!"

"Oh, my God, my God! . . ." sighed Samoylenko, scratching himself. "I was dropping asleep and I hear the whistle of the steamer, and now you . . . Do you want much?"

"Three hundred roubles at least. I must leave her a hundred, and I need two hundred for the journey. . . . I owe you about four hundred already, but I will send it you all . . . all. . . ."

Samoylenko took hold of both his whiskers in one hand, and standing with his legs wide apart, pondered.

"Yes . . ." he muttered, musing. "Three hundred. . . . Yes. . . . But I haven't got so much. I shall have to borrow it from someone."

"Borrow it, for God's sake!" said Laevsky, seeing from Samoylenko's face that he wanted to lend him the money and certainly would lend it. "Borrow it, and I'll be sure to pay you back. I will send it from Petersburg as soon as I get there. You can set your mind at rest about that. I'll tell you what, Sasha," he said, growing more animated; "let us have some wine."

"Yes . . . we can have some wine, too."

They both went into the dining-room.

"And how about Nadyezhda Fyodorovna?" asked Samoylenko, setting three bottles and a plate of peaches on the table. "Surely she's not remaining?"

"I will arrange it all, I will arrange it all," said Laevsky, feeling an unexpected rush of joy. "I will send her the money afterwards and she will join me. . . . Then we will define our relations. To your health, friend."

"Wait a bit," said Samoylenko. "Drink this first. . . . This is from my vineyard. This bottle is from Navaridze's vineyard and this one is from Ahatulov's. . . . Try all three kinds and tell me candidly. . . . There seems a little acidity about mine. Eh? Don't you taste it?"

"Yes. You have comforted me, Alexandr Daviditch. Thank you. . . . I feel better."

"Is there any acidity?"

"Goodness only knows, I don't know. But you are a splendid, wonderful man!"

Looking at his pale, excited, good-natured face, Samoylenko remembered Von Koren's view that men like that ought to be destroyed, and Laevsky seemed to him a weak, defenceless child, whom any one could injure and destroy.

"And when you go, make it up with your mother," he said. "It's not right."

"Yes, yes; I certainly shall."

They were silent for a while. When they had emptied the first bottle, Samoylenko said:

"You ought to make it up with Von Koren too. You are both such splendid, clever fellows, and you glare at each other like wolves."

"Yes, he's a fine, very intelligent fellow," Laevsky assented, ready now to praise and forgive everyone. "He's a remarkable man, but it's impossible for me to get on with him. No! Our natures are too different. I'm an indolent, weak, submissive nature. Perhaps in a good minute I might hold out my hand to him, but he would turn away from me . . . with contempt."

Laevsky took a sip of wine, walked from corner to corner and went on, standing in the middle of the room:

"I understand Von Koren very well. His is a resolute, strong, despotic nature. You have heard him continually talking of 'the expedition,' and it's not mere talk. He wants the wilderness, the moonlit night: all around in little tents, under the open sky, lie sleeping his sick and hungry Cossacks, guides, porters, doctor, priest, all exhausted with their weary marches, while only he is awake, sitting like Stanley on a camp-stool, feeling himself the monarch of the desert and the master of these men. He goes on and on and on, his men groan and die, one after another, and he goes on and on, and in the end perishes himself, but still is monarch and ruler of the desert, since the cross upon his tomb can be seen by the caravans for thirty or forty miles over the desert. I am sorry the man is not in the army. He would have made a splendid military genius. He would not have hesitated to drown his cavalry in the river and make a bridge out of dead bodies. And such hardihood is more needed in war than any kind of fortification or strategy. Oh, I understand him perfectly! Tell me: why is he wasting his substance here? What does he want here?"

"He is studying the marine fauna."

"No, no, brother, no!" Laevsky sighed. "A scientific man who was on the steamer told me the Black Sea was poor in animal life, and that in its depths, thanks to the abundance of sulphuric hydrogen, organic life was impossible. All the serious zoologists work at the biological station at Naples or Villefranche. But Von Koren is independent and obstinate: he works on the Black Sea because nobody else is working there; he is at loggerheads with the university, does not care to know his comrades and other scientific men because he is first of all a despot and only secondly a zoologist. And you'll see he'll do something. He is already dreaming that when he comes back from his expedition he will purify our universities from intrigue and mediocrity, and will make the scientific men mind their p's and q's. Despotism is just as strong in science as in the army. And he is spending his second summer in this stinking little town because he would rather be first in a village than second in a town. Here he is a king and an eagle; he keeps all the inhabitants under his thumb and oppresses them with his authority. He has appropriated everyone, he meddles in other people's affairs; everything is of use to him, and everyone is afraid of him. I am slipping out of his clutches, he feels that and hates me. Hasn't he told you that I ought to be destroyed or sent to hard labour?"

"Yes," laughed Samoylenko.

Laevsky laughed too, and drank some wine.

"His ideals are despotic too," he said, laughing, and biting a peach. "Ordinary mortals think of their neighbour —me, you, man in fact—if they work for the common weal. To Von Koren men are puppets and nonentities, too trivial to be the object of his life. He works, will go for his expedition and break his neck there, not for the sake of love for his neighbour, but for the sake of such abstractions as humanity, future generations, an ideal race of men. He exerts himself for the improvement of the human race, and we are in his eyes only slaves, food for the cannon, beasts of burden; some he would destroy or stow away in Siberia, others he would break by discipline, would, like Araktcheev, force them to get up and go to bed to the sound of the drum; would appoint eunuchs to preserve our chastity and morality, would order them to fire at anyone who steps out of the circle of our narrow conservative morality; and all this in the name of the improvement of the human race. . . . And what is the human race? Illusion, mirage . . . despots have always been illusionists. I understand him very well, brother. I appreciate him and don't deny his importance; this world rests on men like him, and if the world were left only to such men as us, for all our good-nature and good intentions, we should make as great a mess of it as the flies have of that picture. Yes."

Laevsky sat down beside Samoylenko, and said with genuine feeling: "I'm a foolish, worthless, depraved man. The air I breathe, this wine, love, life in fact—for all that, I have given nothing in exchange so far but lying, idleness, and cowardice. Till now I have deceived myself and other people; I have been miserable about it, and my misery was cheap and common. I bow my back humbly before Von Koren's hatred because at times I hate and despise myself."

Laevsky began again pacing from one end of the room to the other in excitement, and said:

"I'm glad I see my faults clearly and am conscious of them. That will help me to reform and become a different man. My dear fellow, if only you knew how passionately, with what anguish, I long for such a change. And I swear to you I'll be a man! I will! I don't know whether it is the wine that is speaking in me, or whether it really is so, but it seems to me that it is long since I have spent such pure and lucid moments as I have just now with you."

"It's time to sleep, brother," said Samoylenko.

"Yes, yes. . . . Excuse me; I'll go directly."

Laevsky moved hurriedly about the furniture and windows, looking for his cap.

"Thank you," he muttered, sighing. "Thank you. . . . Kind and friendly words are better than charity. You have given me new life."

He found his cap, stopped, and looked guiltily at Samoylenko.

"Alexandr Daviditch," he said in an imploring voice.

"What is it?"

"Let me stay the night with you, my dear fellow!"

"Certainly. . . . Why not?"

Laevsky lay down on the sofa, and went on talking to the doctor for a long time.

10

Three days after the picnic, Marya Konstantinovna unexpectedly called on Nadyezhda Fyodorovna, and without greeting her or taking off her hat, seized her by both hands, pressed them to her breast and said in great excitement:

"My dear, I am deeply touched and moved: our dear kind-hearted doctor told my Nikodim Alexandritch yesterday that your husband was dead. Tell me, my dear . . . tell me, is it true?"

"Yes, it's true; he is dead," answered Nadyezhda Fyodorovna.

"That is awful, awful, my dear! But there's no evil without some compensation; your husband was no doubt a noble, wonderful, holy man, and such are more needed in Heaven than on earth."

Every line and feature in Marya Konstantinovna's face began quivering as though little needles were jumping up and down under her skin; she gave an almond-oily smile and said, breathlessly, enthusiastically:

"And so you are free, my dear. You can hold your head high now, and look people boldly in the face. Henceforth God and man will bless your union with Ivan Andreitch. It's enchanting. I am trembling with joy, I can find no words. My dear, I will give you away. . . . Nikodim Alexandritch and I have been so fond of you, you will allow us to give our blessing to your pure, lawful union. When, when do you think of being married?"

"I haven't thought of it," said Nadyezhda Fyodorovna, freeing her hands.

"That's impossible, my dear. You have thought of it, you have."

"Upon my word, I haven't," said Nadyezhda Fyodorovna, laughing. "What should we be married for? I see no necessity for it. We'll go on living as we have lived."

"What are you saying!" cried Marya Konstantinovna in horror. "For God's sake, what are you saying!"

"Our getting married won't make things any better. On the contrary, it will make them even worse. We shall lose our freedom."

"My dear, my dear, what are you saying!" exclaimed Marya Konstantinovna, stepping back and flinging up her hands. "You are talking wildly! Think what you are saying. You must settle down!"

"'Settle down.' How do you mean? I have not lived yet, and you tell me to settle down."

Nadyezhda Fyodorovna reflected that she really had not lived. She had finished her studies in a boarding-school and had been married to a man she did not love; then she had thrown in her lot with Laevsky, and had spent all her time with him on this empty, desolate coast, always expecting something better. Was that life?

"I ought to be married though," she thought, but remembering Kirilin and Atchmianov she flushed and said:

"No, it's impossible. Even if Ivan Andreitch begged me to on his knees—even then I would refuse."

Marya Konstantinovna sat on the sofa for a minute in silence, grave and mournful, gazing fixedly into space; then she got up and said coldly:

"Good-bye, my dear! Forgive me for having troubled you. Though it's not easy for me, it's my duty to tell you that from this day all is over between us, and, in spite of my profound respect for Ivan Andreitch, the door of my house is closed to you henceforth."

She uttered these words with great solemnity and was herself overwhelmed by her solemn tone. Her face began quivering again; it assumed a soft almond-oily expression. She held out both hands to Nadyezhda Fyodorovna, who was overcome with alarm and confusion, and said in an imploring voice:

"My dear, allow me if only for a moment to be a mother or an elder sister to you! I will be as frank with you as a mother."

Nadyezhda Fyodorovna felt in her bosom warmth, gladness, and pity for herself, as though her own mother had really risen up and were standing before her. She impul-

sively embraced Marya Konstantinovna and pressed her
face to her shoulder. Both of them shed tears. They sat
down on the sofa and for a few minutes sobbed without
looking at one another or being able to utter a word.

"My dear child," began Marya Konstantinovna, "I will
tell you some harsh truths, without sparing you."

"For God's sake, for God's sake, do!"

"Trust me, my dear. You remember of all the ladies
here, I was the only one to receive you. You horrified me
from the very first day, but I had not the heart to treat
you with disdain like all the rest. I grieved over dear,
good Ivan Andreitch as though he were my son—a young
man in a strange place, inexperienced, weak, with no
mother; and I was worried, dreadfully worried. . . . My
husband was opposed to our making his acquaintance, but
I talked him over . . . persuaded him. . . . We began receiving Ivan Andreitch, and with him, of course, you.
If we had not, he would have been insulted. I have a
daughter, a son. . . . You understand the tender mind, the
pure heart of childhood . . . 'whoso offendeth one of these
little ones.' . . . I received you into my house and trembled for my children. Oh, when you become a mother, you
will understand my fears. And everyone was surprised
at my receiving you, excuse my saying so, as a respectable
woman, and hinted to me . . . well, of course, slanders,
suppositions. . . . At the bottom of my heart I blamed
you, but you were unhappy, flighty, to be pitied, and my
heart was wrung with pity for you."

"But why, why?" asked Nadyezhda Fyodorovna, trembling all over. "What harm have I done anyone?"

"You are a terrible sinner. You broke the vow you made
your husband at the altar. You seduced a fine young man,
who perhaps had he not met you might have taken a lawful partner for life from a good family in his own circle,
and would have been like everyone else now. You have
ruined his youth. Don't speak, don't speak, my dear! I
never believe that man is to blame for our sins. It is always the woman's fault. Men are frivolous in domestic
life; they are guided by their minds, and not by their
hearts. There's a great deal they don't understand; woman
understands it all. Everything depends on her. To her
much is given and from her much will be required. Oh,

my dear, if she had been more foolish or weaker than man on that side, God would not have entrusted her with the education of boys and girls. And then, my dear, you entered on the path of vice, forgetting all modesty; any other woman in your place would have hidden herself from people, would have sat shut up at home, and would only have been seen in the temple of God, pale, dressed all in black and weeping, and everyone would have said in genuine compassion: 'O Lord, this erring angel is coming back again to Thee. . . .' But you, my dear, have forgotten all discretion; have lived openly, extravagantly; have seemed to be proud of your sin; you have been gay and laughing, and I, looking at you, shuddered with horror, and have been afraid that thunder from Heaven would strike our home while you were sitting with us. My dear, don't speak, don't speak," cried Marya Konstantinovna, observing that Nadyezhda Fyodorovna wanted to speak. "Trust me, I will not deceive you, I will not hide one truth from the eyes of your soul. Listen to me, my dear. . . . God marks great sinners, and you have been marked out: only think—your costumes have always been appalling."

Nadyezhda Fyodorovna, who had always had the highest opinion of her costumes, left off crying and looked at her with surprise.

"Yes, appalling," Marya Konstantinovna went on. "Anyone could judge of your behaviour from the elaboration and gaudiness of your attire. People laughed and shrugged their shoulders as they looked at you, and I grieved, I grieved. . . . And forgive me, my dear; you are not nice in your person! When we met in the bathing-place, you made me tremble. Your outer clothing was decent enough, but your petticoat, your chemise. . . . My dear, I blushed! Poor Ivan Andreitch! No one ever ties his cravat properly, and from his linen and his boots, poor fellow! one can see he has no one at home to look after him. And he is always hungry, my darling, and of course, if there is no one at home to think of the samovar and the coffee, one is forced to spend half one's salary at the pavilion. And it's simply awful, awful in your home! No one else in the town has flies, but there's no getting rid of them in your rooms: all the plates and dishes are black with them. If you look at the windows and the chairs, there's noth-

ing but dust, dead flies, and glasses. . . . What do you
want glasses standing about for? And, my dear, the
table's not cleared till this time in the day. And one's
ashamed to go into your bedroom: underclothes flung
about everywhere, india-rubber tubes hanging on the
walls, pails and basins standing about. . . . My dear! A
husband ought to know nothing, and his wife ought to be
as neat as a little angel in his presence. I wake up every
morning before it is light, and wash my face with cold
water that my Nikodim Alexandritch may not see me
looking drowsy."

"That's all nonsense," Nadyezhda Fyodorovna sobbed.
"If only I were happy, but I am so unhappy!"

"Yes, yes; you are very unhappy!" Marya Konstantinovna sighed, hardly able to restrain herself from weeping. "And there's terrible grief in store for you in the
future! A solitary old age, ill-health; and then you will
have to answer at the dread judgment seat. . . . It's awful,
awful. Now fate itself holds out to you a helping hand,
and you madly thrust it from you. Be married, make haste
and be married!"

"Yes, we must, we must," said Nadyezhda Fyodorovna;
"but it's impossible!"

"Why?"

"It's impossible. Oh, if only you knew!"

Nadyezhda Fyodorovna had an impulse to tell her
about Kirilin, and how the evening before she had met
handsome young Atchmianov at the harbour, and how
the mad, ridiculous idea had occurred to her of cancelling
her debt for three hundred; it had amused her very
much, and she returned home late in the evening feeling
that she had sold herself and was irrevocably lost. She
did not know herself how it had happened. And she longed
to swear to Marya Konstantinovna that she would certainly pay that debt, but sobs and shame prevented her
from speaking. "I am going away," she said. "Ivan Andreitch may stay, but I am going."

"Where?"

"To Russia."

"But how will you live there? Why, you have nothing."

"I will do translation, or . . . or I will open a library. . . ."

"Don't let your fancy run away with you, my dear. You

must have money for a library. Well, I will leave you
now, and you calm yourself and think things over, and
to-morrow come and see me, bright and happy. That will
be enchanting! Well, good-bye, my angel. Let me kiss you."

Marya Konstantinovna kissed Nadyezhda Fyodorovna
on the forehead, made the sign of the cross over her, and
softly withdrew. It was getting dark, and Olga lighted
up in the kitchen. Still crying, Nadyezhda Fyodorovna
went into the bedroom and lay down on the bed. She
began to be very feverish. She undressed without getting
up, crumpled up her clothes at her feet, and curled herself up under the bedclothes. She was thirsty, and there
was no one to give her something to drink.

"I'll pay it back!" she said to herself, and it seemed to
her in delirium that she was sitting beside some sick
woman, and recognized her as herself. "I'll pay it back.
It would be stupid to imagine that it was for money I . . .
I will go away and send him the money from Petersburg.
At first a hundred . . . then another hundred . . . and
then the third hundred. . . ."

It was late at night when Laevsky came in.

"At first a hundred . . ." Nadyezhda Fyodorovna said
to him, "then another hundred . . ."

"You ought to take some quinine," he said, and thought,
"To-morrow is Wednesday; the steamer goes and I am
not going in it. So I shall have to go on living here till
Saturday."

Nadyezhda Fyodorovna knelt up in bed.

"I didn't say anything just now, did I?" she asked, smiling and screwing up her eyes at the light.

"No, nothing. We shall have to send for the doctor
to-morrow morning. Go to sleep."

He took his pillow and went to the door. Ever since he
had finally made up his mind to go away and leave Nadyezhda Fyodorovna, she had begun to raise in him pity
and a sense of guilt; he felt a little ashamed in her presence, as though in the presence of a sick or old horse
whom one has decided to kill. He stopped in the doorway
and looked round at her.

"I was out of humour at the picnic and said something
rude to you. Forgive me, for God's sake!"

Saying this, he went off to his study, lay down, and
for a long while could not get to sleep.

Next morning when Samoylenko, attired, as it was a holiday, in full-dress uniform with epaulettes on his shoulders and decorations on his breast, came out of the bedroom after feeling Nadyezhda Fyodorovna's pulse and looking at her tongue, Laevsky, who was standing in the doorway, asked him anxiously: "Well? Well?"

There was an expression of terror, of extreme uneasiness, and of hope on his face.

"Don't worry yourself; there's nothing dangerous," said Samoylenko; "it's the usual fever."

"I don't mean that." Laevsky frowned impatiently. "Have you got the money?"

"My dear soul, forgive me," he whispered, looking round at the door and overcome with confusion. "For God's sake, forgive me! No one has anything to spare, and I've only been able to collect by five- and by ten-rouble notes. . . . Only a hundred and ten in all. To-day I'll speak to someone else. Have patience."

"But Saturday is the latest date," whispered Laevsky, trembling with impatience. "By all that's sacred, get it by Saturday! If I don't get away by Saturday, nothing's any use, nothing! I can't understand how a doctor can be without money!"

"Lord have mercy on us!" Samoylenko whispered rapidly and intensely, and there was positively a breaking note in his throat. "I've been stripped of everything; I am owed seven thousand, and I'm in debt all round. Is it my fault?"

"Then you'll get it by Saturday? Yes?"

"I'll try."

"I implore you, my dear fellow! So that the money may be in my hands by Friday morning!"

Samoylenko sat down and prescribed solution of quinine and kalii bromati and tincture of rhubarb, tincturæ gentianæ, aquæ fœniculi—all in one mixture, added some pink syrup to sweeten it, and went away.

11

"You look as though you were coming to arrest me," said Von Koren, seeing Samoylenko coming in, in his full-dress uniform.

"I was passing by and thought: 'Suppose I go in and pay my respects to zoology,'" said Samoylenko, sitting down at the big table, knocked together by the zoologist himself out of plain boards. "Good-morning, holy father," he said to the deacon, who was sitting in the window, copying something. "I'll stay a minute and then run home to see about dinner. It's time. . . . I'm not hindering you?"

"Not in the least," answered the zoologist, laying out over the table slips of paper covered with small writing. "We are busy copying."

"Ah! . . . Oh, my goodness, my goodness! . . ." sighed Samoylenko. He cautiously took up from the table a dusty book on which there was lying a dead dried spider, and said: "Only fancy, though; some little green beetle is going about its business, when suddenly a monster like this swoops down upon it. I can fancy its terror."

"Yes, I suppose so."

"Is poison given it to protect it from its enemies?"

"Yes, to protect it and enable it to attack."

"To be sure, to be sure. . . . And everything in nature, my dear fellows, is consistent and can be explained," sighed Samoylenko; "only I tell you what I don't understand. You're a man of very great intellect, so explain it to me, please. There are, you know, little beasts no bigger than rats, rather handsome to look at, but nasty and immoral in the extreme, let me tell you. Suppose such a little beast is running in the woods. He sees a bird; he catches it and devours it. He goes on and sees in the grass a nest of eggs; he does not want to eat them—he is not hungry, but yet he tastes one egg and scatters the others out of the nest with his paw. Then he meets a frog and begins to play with it; when he has tormented the frog he goes on licking himself and meets a beetle; he crushes the beetle with his paw . . . and so he spoils and destroys everything on his way. . . . He creeps into other beasts' holes, tears up the anthills, cracks the snail's shell. If he meets a rat, he fights with it; if he meets a snake or a mouse, he must strangle it; and so the whole day long. Come, tell me: what is the use of a beast like that? Why was he created?"

"I don't know what animal you are talking of," said Von Koren; "most likely one of the insectivora. Well, he got hold of the bird because it was incautious; he broke the nest of eggs because the bird was not skilful, had made the nest badly and did not know how to conceal it. The frog probably had some defect in its colouring or he would not have seen it, and so on. Your little beast only destroys the weak, the unskilful, the careless—in fact, those who have defects which nature does not think fit to hand on to posterity. Only the cleverer, the stronger, the more careful and developed survive; and so your little beast, without suspecting it, is serving the great ends of perfecting creation."

"Yes, yes, yes. . . . By the way, brother," said Samoylenko carelessly, "lend me a hundred roubles."

"Very good. There are some very interesting types among the insectivorous mammals. For instance, the mole is said to be useful because he devours noxious insects. There is a story that some German sent William I. a fur coat made of moleskins, and the Emperor ordered him to be reproved for having destroyed so great a number of useful animals. And yet the mole is not a bit less cruel than your little beast, and is very mischievous besides, as he spoils meadows terribly."

Von Koren opened a box and took out a hundred-rouble note.

"The mole has a powerful thorax, just like the bat," he went on, shutting the box; "the bones and muscles are tremendously developed, the mouth is extraordinarily powerfully furnished. If it had the proportions of an elephant, it would be an all-destructive, invincible animal. It is interesting when two moles meet underground; they begin at once as though by agreement digging a little platform; they need the platform in order to have a battle more conveniently. When they have made it they enter upon a ferocious struggle and fight till the weaker one falls. Take the hundred roubles," said Von Koren, dropping his voice, "but only on condition that you're not borrowing it for Laevsky."

"And if it were for Laevsky," cried Samoylenko, flaring up, "what is that to you?"

"I can't give it to you for Laevsky. I know you like lending people money. You would give it to Kerim, the brigand, if he were to ask you; but, excuse me, I can't assist you in that direction."

"Yes, it is for Laevsky I am asking it," said Samoylenko, standing up and waving his right arm. "Yes! For Laevsky! And no one, fiend or devil, has a right to dictate to me how to dispose of my own money. It doesn't suit you to lend it me? No?"

The deacon began laughing.

"Don't get excited, but be reasonable," said the zoologist. "To shower benefits on Mr. Laevsky is, to my thinking, as senseless as to water weeds or to feed locusts."

"To my thinking, it is our duty to help our neighbours!" cried Samoylenko.

"In that case, help that hungry Turk who is lying under the fence! He is a workman and more useful and indispensable than your Laevsky. Give him that hundred-rouble note! Or subscribe a hundred roubles to my expedition!"

"Will you give me the money or not? I ask you!"

"Tell me openly: what does he want money for?"

"It's not a secret; he wants to go to Petersburg on Saturday."

"So that is it!" Von Koren drawled out. "Aha! . . . We understand. And is she going with him, or how is it to be?"

"She's staying here for the time. He'll arrange his affairs in Petersburg and send her the money, and then she'll go."

"That's smart!" said the zoologist, and he gave a short tenor laugh. "Smart, well planned."

He went rapidly up to Samoylenko, and standing face to face with him, and looking him in the eyes, asked: "Tell me now honestly: is he tired of her? Yes? tell me: is he tired of her? Yes?"

"Yes," Samoylenko articulated, beginning to perspire.

"How repulsive it is!" said Von Koren, and from his face it could be seen that he felt repulsion. "One of two things, Alexandr Daviditch: either you are in the plot with him, or, excuse my saying so, you are a simpleton. Surely you must see that he is taking you in like a child in the most shameless way? Why, it's as clear as day that he wants to get rid of her and abandon her here. She'll be left a burden on you. It is as clear as day that you will have to send her to Petersburg at your expense. Surely your fine friend can't have so blinded you by his dazzling qualities that you can't see the simplest thing?"

"That's all supposition," said Samoylenko, sitting down.

"Supposition? But why is he going alone instead of taking her with him? And ask him why he doesn't send her off first. The sly beast!"

Overcome with sudden doubts and suspicions about his friend, Samoylenko weakened and took a humbler tone.

"But it's impossible," he said, recalling the night Laevsky had spent at his house. "He is so unhappy!"

"What of that? Thieves and incendiaries are unhappy too!"

"Even supposing you are right . . ." said Samoylenko, hesitating. "Let us admit it. . . . Still, he's a young man in a strange place . . . a student. We have been students, too, and there is no one but us to come to his assistance."

"To help him to do abominable things, because he and you at different times have been at universities, and neither of you did anything there! What nonsense!"

"Stop; let us talk it over coolly. I imagine it will be possible to make some arrangement. . . ." Samoylenko reflected, twiddling his fingers. "I'll give him the money, you see, but make him promise on his honour that within a week he'll send Nadyezhda Fyodorovna the money for the journey."

"And he'll give you his word of honour—in fact, he'll shed tears and believe in it himself; but what's his word of honour worth? He won't keep it, and when in a year or two you meet him on the Nevsky Prospect with a new mistress on his arm, he'll excuse himself on the ground that he has been crippled by civilization, and that he is made after the pattern of Rudin. Drop him, for God's sake! Keep away from the filth; don't stir it up with both hands!"

Samoylenko thought for a minute and said resolutely:

"But I shall give him the money all the same. As you please. I can't bring myself to refuse a man simply on an assumption."

"Very fine, too. You can kiss him if you like."

"Give me the hundred roubles, then," Samoylenko asked timidly.

"I won't."

A silence followed. Samoylenko was quite crushed; his face wore a guilty, abashed, and ingratiating expression, and it was strange to see this pitiful, childish, shamefaced countenance on a huge man wearing epaulettes and orders of merit.

"The bishop here goes the round of his diocese on horseback instead of in a carriage," said the deacon, laying down his pen. "It's extremely touching to see him sit on his horse. His simplicity and humility are full of Biblical grandeur."

"Is he a good man?" asked Von Koren, who was glad to change the conversation.

"Of course! If he hadn't been a good man, do you suppose he would have been consecrated a bishop?"

"Among the bishops are to be found good and gifted men," said Von Koren. "The only drawback is that some of them have the weakness to imagine themselves statesmen. One busies himself with Russification, another criticizes the sciences. That's not their business. They had much better look into their consistory a little."

"A layman cannot judge of bishops."

"Why so, deacon? A bishop is a man just the same as you or I."

"The same, but not the same." The deacon was offended and took up his pen. "If you had been the same, the Divine Grace would have rested upon you, and you would have been bishop yourself; and since you are not bishop, it follows you are not the same."

"Don't talk nonsense, deacon," said Samoylenko dejectedly. "Listen to what I suggest," he said, turning to Von Koren. "Don't give me that hundred roubles. You'll be having your dinners with me for three months before the winter, so let me have the money beforehand for three months."

"I won't."

Samoylenko blinked and turned crimson; he mechanically drew towards him the book with the spider on it and looked at it, then he got up and took his hat.

Von Koren felt sorry for him.

"What it is to have to live and do with people like this," said the zoologist, and he kicked a paper into the corner with indignation. "You must understand that this is not kindness, it is not love, but cowardice, slackness, poison! What's gained by reason is lost by your flabby good-for-nothing hearts! When I was ill with typhoid as a schoolboy, my aunt in her sympathy gave me pickled mushrooms to eat, and I very nearly died. You, and my aunt too, must understand that love for man is not to be found in the heart or the stomach or the bowels, but here!"

Von Koren slapped himself on the forehead.

"Take it," he said, and thrust a hundred-rouble note into his hand.

"You've no need to be angry, Kolya," said Samoylenko mildly, folding up the note. "I quite understand you, but . . . you must put yourself in my place."

"You are an old woman, that's what you are."

The deacon burst out laughing.

"Hear my last request, Alexandr Daviditch," said Von Koren hotly. "When you give that scoundrel the money, make it a condition that he takes his lady with him, or sends her on ahead, and don't give it him without. There's no need to stand on ceremony with him. Tell him so, or, if you don't, I give you my word I'll go to his office and kick him downstairs, and I'll break off all acquaintance with you. So you'd better know it."

"Well! To go with her or send her on beforehand will be more convenient for him," said Samoylenko. "He'll be delighted indeed. Well, good-bye."

He said good-bye affectionately and went out, but before shutting the door after him, he looked round at Von Koren and, with a ferocious face, said:

"It's the Germans who have ruined you, brother! Yes! The Germans!"

12

Next day, Thursday, Marya Konstantinovna was celebrating the birthday of her Kostya. All were invited to come at midday and eat pies, and in the evening to drink chocolate. When Laevsky and Nadyezhda Fyodorovna arrived in the evening, the zoologist, who was already sitting in the drawing-room, drinking chocolate, asked Samoylenko:

"Have you talked to him?"

"Not yet."

"Mind now, don't stand on ceremony. I can't understand the insolence of these people! Why, they know perfectly well the view taken by this family of their cohabitation, and yet they force themselves in here."

"If one is to pay attention to every prejudice," said Samoylenko, "one could go nowhere."

"Do you mean to say that the repugnance felt by the masses for illicit love and moral laxity is a prejudice?"

"Of course it is. It's prejudice and hate. When the soldiers see a girl of light behaviour, they laugh and whistle; but just ask them what they are themselves."

"It's not for nothing they whistle. The fact that girls strangle their illegitimate children and go to prison for it, and that Anna Karenin flung herself under the train, and that in the villages they smear the gates with tar, and that you and I, without knowing why, are pleased by Katya's purity, and that every one of us feels a vague craving for pure love, though he knows there is no such love—is all that prejudice? That is the one thing, brother, which has survived intact from natural selection, and, if it were not for that obscure force regulating the relations of the sexes, the Laevskys would have it all their own way, and mankind would degenerate in two years."

Laevsky came into the drawing-room, greeted everyone, and shaking hands with Von Koren, smiled ingratiatingly. He waited for a favourable moment and said to Samoylenko:

"Excuse me, Alexandr Daviditch, I must say two words to you."

Samoylenko got up, put his arm round Laevsky's waist, and both of them went into Nikodim Alexandritch's study.

"To-morrow's Friday," said Laevsky, biting his nails. "Have you got what you promised?"

"I've only got two hundred. I'll get the rest to-day or to-morrow. Don't worry yourself."

"Thank God . . ." sighed Laevsky, and his hands began trembling with joy. "You are saving me, Alexandr Daviditch, and I swear to you by God, by my happiness and anything you like, I'll send you the money as soon as I arrive. And I'll send you my old debt too."

"Look here, Vanya . . ." said Samoylenko, turning crimson and taking him by the button. "You must forgive my meddling in your private affairs, but . . . why shouldn't you take Nadyezhda Fyodorovna with you?"

"You queer fellow. How is that possible? One of us must stay, or our creditors will raise an outcry. You see, I owe seven hundred or more to the shops. Only wait, and I will send them the money. I'll stop their mouths, and then she can come away."

"I see. . . . But why shouldn't you send her on first?"

"My goodness, as though that were possible!" Laevsky was horrified. "Why, she's a woman; what would she do there alone? What does she know about it? That would only be a loss of time and a useless waste of money."

"That's reasonable . . ." thought Samoylenko, but remembering his conversation with Von Koren, he looked down and said sullenly: "I can't agree with you. Either go with her or send her first; otherwise . . . otherwise I won't give you the money. Those are my last words. . . ."

He staggered back, lurched backwards against the door, and went into the drawing room, crimson, and overcome with confusion.

"Friday . . . Friday," thought Laevsky, going back into the drawing-room. "Friday. . . ."

He was handed a cup of chocolate; he burnt his lips and tongue with the scalding chocolate and thought: "Friday . . . Friday. . . ."

For some reason he could not get the word "Friday" out of his head; he could think of nothing but Friday, and the only thing that was clear to him, not in his brain but somewhere in his heart, was that he would not get off on Saturday. Before him stood Nikodim Alexandritch, very neat, with his hair combed over his temples, saying:

"Please take something to eat. . . ."

Marya Konstantinovna showed the visitors Katya's school report and said, drawling:

"It's very, very difficult to do well at school nowadays! So much is expected . . ."

"Mamma!" groaned Katya, not knowing where to hide her confusion at the praises of the company.

Laevsky, too, looked at the report and praised it. Scripture, Russian language, conduct, fives and fours, danced before his eyes, and all this, mixed with the haunting refrain of "Friday," with the carefully combed locks of Nikodim Alexandritch and the red cheeks of Katya, produced on him a sensation of such immense overwhelming boredom that he almost shrieked with despair and asked himself: "Is it possible, is it possible I shall not get away?"

They put two card tables side by side and sat down to play post. Laevsky sat down too.

"Friday . . . Friday . . ." he kept thinking, as he smiled and took a pencil out of his pocket. "Friday. . . ."

He wanted to think over his position, and was afraid to think. It was terrible to him to realize that the doctor had detected him in the deception which he had so long and carefully concealed from himself. Every time he thought of his future he would not let his thoughts have full rein. He would get into the train and set off, and thereby the problem of his life would be solved, and he did not let his thoughts go farther. Like a far-away dim light in the fields, the thought sometimes flickered in his mind that in one of the side-streets of Petersburg, in the remote future, he would have to have recourse to a tiny lie in order to get rid of Nadyezhda Fyodorovna and pay his debts; he would tell a lie only once, and then a completely new life would begin. And that was right: at the price of a small lie he would win so much truth.

Now when by his blunt refusal the doctor had crudely hinted at his deception, he began to understand that he would need deception not only in the remote future, but to-day, and to-morrow, and in a month's time, and perhaps up to the very end of his life. In fact, in order to get away he would have to lie to Nadyezhda Fyodorovna, to his creditors, and to his superiors in the Service; then, in order to get money in Petersburg, he would have to lie to his mother, to tell her that he had already broken with Nadyezhda Fyodorovna; and his mother would not give him more than five hundred roubles, so he had already deceived the doctor, as he would not be in a position to pay him back the money within a short time. Afterwards when Nadyezhda Fyodorovna came to Petersburg, he would have to resort to a regular series of deceptions, little and big, in order to get free of her; and again there would be tears, boredom, a disgusting existence, remorse, and so there would be no new life. Deception and nothing more. A whole mountain of lies rose before Laevsky's imagination. To leap over it at one bound and not to do his lying piecemeal, he would have to bring himself to stern, uncompromising action; for instance, to getting up without saying a word, putting on his hat, and at once setting off without money and without explanation. But Laevsky felt that was impossible for him.

"Friday, Friday . . ." he thought. "Friday. . . ."

They wrote little notes, folded them in two, and put them in Nikodim Alexandritch's old top-hat. When there were a sufficient heap of notes, Kostya, who acted the part of postman, walked round the table and delivered them. The deacon, Katya, and Kostya, who received amusing notes and tried to write as funnily as they could, were highly delighted.

"We must have a little talk," Nadyezhda Fyodorovna read in a little note; she glanced at Marya Konstantinovna, who gave her an almond-oily smile and nodded.

"Talk of what?" thought Nadyezhda Fyodorovna. "If one can't tell the whole, it's no use talking."

Before going out for the evening she had tied Laevsky's cravat for him, and that simple action filled her soul with tenderness and sorrow. The anxiety in his face, his absent-minded looks, his pallor, and the incomprehensible change that had taken place in him of late, and the fact that she had a terrible revolting secret from him, and the fact that her hands trembled when she tied his cravat—all this seemed to tell her that they had not long left to be together. She looked at him as though he were an ikon, with terror and penitence, and thought: "Forgive, forgive."

Opposite her was sitting Atchmianov, and he never took his black, love-sick eyes off her. She was stirred by passion; she was ashamed of herself, and afraid that even her misery and sorrow would not prevent her from yielding to impure desire to-morrow, if not to-day—and that, like a drunkard, she would not have the strength to stop herself.

She made up her mind to go away that she might not continue this life, shameful for herself, and humiliating for Laevsky. She would beseech him with tears to let her go; and if he opposed her, she would go away secretly. She would not tell him what had happened; let him keep a pure memory of her.

"I love you, I love you, I love you," she read. It was from Atchmianov.

She would live in some far remote place, would work and send Laevsky, "anonymously," money, embroidered shirts, and tobacco, and would return to him only in old age or if he were dangerously ill and needed a nurse. When in his old age he learned what were her reasons for leaving him and refusing to be his wife, he would appreciate her sacrifice and forgive.

"You've got a long nose." That must be from the deacon or Kostya.

Nadyezhda Fyodorovna imagined how, parting from Laevsky, she would embrace him warmly, would kiss his hand, and would swear to love him all her life, all her life, and then, living in obscurity among strangers, she would every day think that somewhere she had a friend, someone she loved—a pure, noble, lofty man who kept a pure memory of her.

"If you don't give me an interview to-day, I shall take measures, I assure you on my word of honour. You can't treat decent people like this; you must understand that." That was from Kirilin.

20

Laevsky received two notes; he opened one and read: "Don't go away, my darling."

"Who could have written that?" he thought. "Not Samoylenko, of course. And not the deacon, for he doesn't know I want to go away. Von Koren, perhaps?"

The zoologist bent over the table and drew a pyramid. Laevsky fancied that his eyes were smiling.

"Most likely Samoylenko . . . has been gossiping," thought Laevsky.

In the other note, in the same disguised angular handwriting with long tails to the letters, was written: "Somebody won't go away on Saturday."

"A stupid gibe," thought Laevsky. "Friday, Friday. . . ."

Something rose in his throat. He touched his collar and coughed, but instead of a cough a laugh broke from his throat.

"Ha-ha-ha!" he laughed. "Ha-ha-ha! What am I laughing at? Ha-ha-ha!"

He tried to restrain himself, covered his mouth with his hand, but the laugh choked his chest and throat, and his hand could not cover his mouth.

"How stupid it is!" he thought, rolling with laughter. "Have I gone out of my mind?"

The laugh grew shriller and shriller, and became something like the bark of a lap-dog. Laevsky tried to get up from the table, but his legs would not obey him and his right hand was strangely, without his volition, dancing on the table, convulsively clutching and crumpling up the bits of paper. He saw looks of wonder, Samoylenko's grave, frightened face, and the eyes of the zoologist full of cold irony and disgust, and realized that he was in hysterics.

"How hideous, how shameful!" he thought, feeling the warmth of tears on his face. ". . . Oh, oh, what a disgrace! It has never happened to me. . . ."

They took him under his arms, and supporting his head

from behind, led him away; a glass gleamed before his eyes and knocked against his teeth, and the water was spilt on his breast; he was in a little room, with two beds in the middle, side by side, covered by two snow-white quilts. He dropped on one of the beds and sobbed.

"It's nothing, it's nothing," Samoylenko kept saying; "it does happen . . . it does happen. . . ."

Chill with horror, trembling all over and dreading something awful, Nadyezhda Fyodorovna stood by the bedside and kept asking:

"What is it? What is it? For God's sake, tell me."

"Can Kirilin have written him something?" she thought.

"It's nothing," said Laevsky, laughing and crying; "go away, darling."

His face expressed neither hatred nor repulsion: so he knew nothing; Nadyezhda Fyodorovna was somewhat reassured, and she went into the drawing-room.

"Don't agitate yourself, my dear!" said Marya Konstantinovna, sitting down beside her and taking her hand. "It will pass. Men are just as weak as we poor sinners. You are both going through a crisis. . . . One can so well understand it! Well, my dear, I am waiting for an answer. Let us have a little talk."

"No, we are not going to talk," said Nadyezhda Fyodorovna, listening to Laevsky's sobs. "I feel depressed. . . . You must allow me to go home."

"What do you mean, what do you mean, my dear?" cried Marya Konstantinovna in alarm. "Do you think I could let you go without supper? We will have something to eat, and then you may go with my blessing."

"I feel miserable . . ." whispered Nadyezhda Fyodorovna, and she caught at the arm of the chair with both hands to avoid falling.

"He's got a touch of hysterics," said Von Koren gaily, coming into the drawing-room, but seeing Nadyezhda Fyodorovna, he was taken aback and retreated.

When the attack was over, Laevsky sat on the strange bed and thought.

"Disgraceful! I've been howling like some wretched girl! I must have been absurd and disgusting. I will go away by the back stairs. . . . But that would seem as though I took my hysterics too seriously. I ought to take it as a joke. . . ."

He looked in the looking-glass, sat there for some time, and went back into the drawing-room.

"Here I am," he said, smiling; he felt agonizingly ashamed, and he felt others were ashamed in his presence. "Fancy such a thing happening," he said, sitting down. "I was sitting here, and all of a sudden, do you know, I felt a terrible piercing pain in my side . . . unendurable, my nerves could not stand it, and . . . and it led to this silly performance. This is the age of nerves; there is no help for it."

At supper he drank some wine, and, from time to time, with an abrupt sigh rubbed his side as though to suggest that he still felt the pain. And no one, except Nadyezhda Fyodorovna, believed him, and he saw that.

After nine o'clock they went for a walk on the boulevard. Nadyezhda Fyodorovna, afraid that Kirilin would speak to her, did her best to keep all the time beside Marya Konstantinovna and the children. She felt weak with fear and misery, and felt she was going to be feverish; she was exhausted and her legs would hardly move, but she did not go home, because she felt sure that she would be followed by Kirilin or Atchmianov or both at once. Kirilin walked behind her with Nikodim Alexandritch, and kept humming in an undertone:

"I don't al-low people to play with me: I don't al-low it."

From the boulevard they went back to the pavilion and walked along the beach, and looked for a long time at the phosphorescence on the water. Von Koren began telling them why it looked phosphorescent.

14

"It's time I went to my *vint*. . . . They will be waiting for me," said Laevsky. "Good-bye, my friends."

"I'll come with you; wait a minute," said Nadyezhda Fyodorovna, and she took his arm.

They said good-bye to the company and went away. Kirilin took leave too, and saying that he was going the same way, went along beside them.

"What will be, will be," thought Nadyezhda Fyodorovna. "So be it. . . ."

And it seemed to her that all the evil memories in her head had taken shape and were walking beside her in the darkness, breathing heavily, while she, like a fly that had fallen into the inkpot, was crawling painfully along the pavement and smirching Laevsky's side and arm with blackness.

If Kirilin should do anything horrid, she thought, not he but she would be to blame for it. There was a time when no man would have talked to her as Kirilin had done, and she had torn up her security like a thread and destroyed it irrevocably—who was to blame for it? Intoxicated by her passions she had smiled at a complete stranger, probably just because he was tall and a fine figure. After two meetings she was weary of him, had thrown him over, and did not that, she thought now, give him the right to treat her as he chose?

"Here I'll say good-bye to you, darling," said Laevsky. "Ilya Mihalitch will see you home."

He nodded to Kirilin, and, quickly crossing the boulevard, walked along the street to Sheshkovsky's, where there were lights in the windows, and then they heard the gate bang as he went in.

"Allow me to have an explanation with you," said Kirilin. "I'm not a boy, not some Atchkasov or Latchkasov, Zatchkasov. . . . I demand serious attention."

Nadyezhda Fyodorovna's heart began beating violently. She made no reply.

"The abrupt change in your behaviour to me I put down at first to coquetry," Kirilin went on; "now I see that you don't know how to behave with gentlemanly people. You simply wanted to play with me, as you are playing with that wretched Armenian boy; but I'm a gentleman and I insist on being treated like a gentleman. And so I am at your service. . . ."

"I'm miserable," said Nadyezhda Fyodorovna beginning to cry, and to hide her tears she turned away.

"I'm miserable too," said Kirilin, "but what of that?"

Kirilin was silent for a space, then he said distinctly and emphatically:

"I repeat, madam, that if you do not give me an interview this evening, I'll make a scandal this very evening."

"Let me off this evening," said Nadyezhda Fyodorovna, and she did not recognize her own voice, it was so weak and pitiful.

"I must give you a lesson. . . . Excuse me for the roughness of my tone, but it's necessary to give you a lesson. Yes, I regret to say I must give you a lesson. I insist on two interviews—to-day and to-morrow. After to-morrow you are perfectly free and can go wherever you like with anyone you choose. To-day and to-morrow."

Nadyezhda Fyodorovna went up to her gate and stopped.

"Let me go," she murmured, trembling all over and seeing nothing before her in the darkness but his white tunic. "You're right: I'm a horrible woman. . . . I'm to blame, but let me go . . . I beg you." She touched his cold hand and shuddered. "I beseech you. . . ."

"Alas!" sighed Kirilin, "alas! it's not part of my plan to let you go; I only mean to give you a lesson and make you realize. And what's more, madam, I've too little faith in women."

"I'm miserable. . . ."

Nadyezhda Fyodorovna listened to the even splash of the sea, looked at the sky studded with stars, and longed to make haste and end it all, and get away from the cursed sensation of life, with its sea, stars, men, fever.

"Only not in my home," she said coldly. "Take me somewhere else."

"Come to Muridov's. That's better."

"Where's that?"

"Near the old wall."

She walked quickly along the street and then turned into the side-street that led towards the mountains. It was dark. There were pale streaks of light here and there on the pavement, from the lighted windows, and it seemed to her that, like a fly, she kept falling into the ink and crawling out into the light again. At one point he stumbled, almost fell down and burst out laughing.

"He's drunk," thought Nadyezhda Fyodorovna. "Never mind. . . . Never mind. . . . So be it."

Atchmianov, too, soon took leave of the party and followed Nadyezhda Fyodorovna to ask her to go for a row. He went to her house and looked over the fence: the windows were wide open, there were no lights.

"Nadyezhda Fyodorovna!" he called.

A moment passed, he called again.

"Who's there?" he heard Olga's voice.

"Is Nadyezhda Fyodorovna at home?"

"No, she has not come in yet."

"Strange . . . very strange," thought Atchmianov, feeling very uneasy. "She went home. . . ."

He walked along the boulevard, then along the street, and glanced in at the windows of Sheshkovsky's. Laevsky was sitting at the table without his coat on, looking attentively at his cards.

"Strange, strange," muttered Atchmianov, and remembering Laevsky's hysterics, he felt ashamed. "If she is not at home, where is she?"

He went to Nadyezhda Fyodorovna's lodgings again, and looked at the dark windows.

"It's a cheat, a cheat . . ." he thought, remembering that, meeting him at midday at Marya Konstantinovna's, she had promised to go in a boat with him that evening.

The windows of the house where Kirilin lived were dark, and there was a policeman sitting asleep on a little bench at the gate. Everything was clear to Atchmianov when he looked at the windows and the policeman. He made up his mind to go home, and set off in that direction, but somehow found himself near Nadyezhda Fyodorovna's lodgings again. He sat down on the bench near the gate and took off his hat, feeling that his head was burning with jealousy and resentment.

The clock in the town church only struck twice in the twenty-four hours—at midday and midnight. Soon after it struck midnight he heard hurried footsteps.

"To-morrow evening then, again at Muridov's," Atchmianov heard, and he recognized Kirilin's voice. "At eight o'clock; good-bye!"

Nadyezhda Fyodorovna made her appearance near the garden. Without noticing that Atchmianov was sitting on the bench, she passed beside him like a shadow, opened the gate, and leaving it open, went into the house. In her own room she lighted the candle and quickly undressed, but instead of getting into bed, she sank on her knees before a chair, flung her arms round it, and rested her head on it.

It was past two when Laevsky came home.

15

Having made up his mind to lie, not all at once but piecemeal, Laevsky went soon after one o'clock next day to
Samoylenko to ask for the money that he might be sure
to get off on Saturday. After his hysterical attack, which
had added an acute feeling of shame to his depressed state
of mind, it was unthinkable to remain in the town. If
Samoylenko should insist on his conditions, he thought
it would be possible to agree to them and take the money,
and next day, just as he was starting, to say that Nadyezhda Fyodorovna refused to go. He would be able to
persuade her that evening that the whole arrangement
would be for her benefit. If Samoylenko, who was obviously under the influence of Von Koren, should refuse the
money altogether or make fresh conditions, then he, Laevsky, would go off that very evening in a cargo vessel, or
even in a sailing-boat, to Novy Athon or Novorossiisk,
would send from there an humiliating telegram, and
would stay there till his mother sent him the money for
the journey.

When he went into Samoylenko's, he found Von Koren
in the drawing-room. The zoologist had just arrived for
dinner, and, as usual, was turning over the album and
scrutinizing the gentlemen in top-hats and the ladies in
caps.

"How very unlucky!" thought Laevsky, seeing him.
"He may be in the way. Good-morning."

"Good-morning," answered Von Koren, without looking at him.

"Is Alexandr Daviditch at home?"

"Yes, in the kitchen."

Laevsky went into the kitchen, but seeing from the
door that Samoylenko was busy over the salad, he went
back into the drawing-room and sat down. He always
had a feeling of awkwardness in the zoologist's presence,
and now he was afraid there would be talk about his attack of hysterics. There was more than a minute of si-

lence. Von Koren suddenly raised his eyes to Laevsky and asked:

"How do you feel after yesterday?"

"Very well indeed," said Laevsky, flushing. "It really was nothing much. . . ."

"Until yesterday I thought it was only ladies who had hysterics, and so at first I thought you had St. Vitus's dance."

Laevsky smiled ingratiatingly, and thought:

"How indelicate on his part! He knows quite well how unpleasant it is for me. . . ."

"Yes, it was a ridiculous performance," he said, still smiling. "I've been laughing over it the whole morning. What's so curious in an attack of hysterics is that you know it is absurd, and are laughing at it in your heart, and at the same time you sob. In our neurotic age we are the slaves of our nerves; they are our masters and do as they like with us. Civilization has done us a bad turn in that way. . . ."

As Laevsky talked, he felt it disagreeable that Von Koren listened to him gravely, and looked at him steadily and attentively as though studying him; and he was vexed with himself that in spite of his dislike of Von Koren, he could not banish the ingratiating smile from his face.

"I must admit, though," he added, "that there were immediate causes for the attack, and quite sufficient ones too. My health has been terribly shaky of late. To which one must add boredom, constantly being hard up . . . the absence of people and general interests. . . . My position is worse than a governor's."

"Yes, your position is a hopeless one," answered Von Koren.

These calm, cold words, implying something between a jeer and an uninvited prediction, offended Laevsky. He recalled the zoologist's eyes the evening before, full of mockery and disgust. He was silent for a space and then asked, no longer smiling:

"How do you know anything of my position?"

"You were only just speaking of it yourself. Besides, your friends take such a warm interest in you, that I am hearing about you all day long."

"What friends? Samoylenko, I suppose?"

"Yes, he too."

"I would ask Alexandr Daviditch and my friends in general not to trouble so much about me."

"Here is Samoylenko; you had better ask him not to trouble so much about you."

"I don't understand your tone," Laevsky muttered, suddenly feeling as though he had only just realized that the zoologist hated and despised him, and was jeering at him, and was his bitterest and most inveterate enemy.

"Keep that tone for someone else," he said softly, unable to speak aloud for the hatred with which his chest and throat were choking, as they had been the night before with laughter.

Samoylenko came in in his shirt-sleeves, crimson and perspiring from the stifling kitchen.

"Ah, you here?" he said. "Good-morning, my dear boy. Have you had dinner? Don't stand on ceremony. Have you had dinner?"

"Alexandr Daviditch," said Laevsky, standing up, "though I did appeal to you to help me in a private matter, it did not follow that I released you from the obligation of discretion and respect for other people's private affairs."

"What's this?" asked Samoylenko, in astonishment.

"If you have no money," Laevsky went on, raising his voice and shifting from one foot to the other in his excitement, "don't give it; refuse it. But why spread abroad in every back street that my position is hopeless, and all the rest of it? I can't endure such benevolence and friend's assistance where there's a shillings-worth of talk for a ha'p'orth of help! You can boast of your benevolence as much as you please, but no one has given you the right to gossip about my private affairs!"

"What private affairs?" asked Samoylenko, puzzled and beginning to be angry. "If you've come here to be abusive, you had better clear out. You can come again afterwards!"

He remembered the rule that when one is angry with one's neighbour, one must begin to count a hundred, and one will grow calm again; and he began rapidly counting.

"I beg you not to trouble yourself about me," Laevsky went on. "Don't pay any attention to me, and whose business is it what I do and how I live? Yes, I want to go away. Yes, I get into debt, I drink, I am living with another man's wife, I'm hysterical, I'm ordinary. I am not so profound as some people, but whose business is that? Respect other people's privacy."

"Excuse me, brother," said Samoylenko, who had counted up to thirty-five, "but . . ."

"Respect other people's individuality!" interrupted Laevsky. "This continual gossip about other people's affairs, this sighing and groaning and everlasting prying, this eavesdropping, this friendly sympathy . . . damn it all! They lend me money and make conditions as though I were a schoolboy! I am treated as the devil knows what! I don't want anything," shouted Laevsky, staggering with excitement and afraid that it might end in another attack of hysterics. "I shan't get away on Saturday, then," flashed through his mind. "I want nothing. All I ask of you is to spare me your protecting care. I'm not a boy, and I'm not mad, and I beg you to leave off looking after me."

The deacon came in, and seeing Laevsky pale and gesticulating, addressing his strange speech to the portrait of Prince Vorontsov, stood still by the door as though petrified.

"This continual prying into my soul," Laevsky went on, "is insulting to my human dignity, and I beg these volunteer detectives to give up their spying! Enough!"

"What's that . . . what did you say?" said Samoylenko, who had counted up to a hundred. He turned crimson and went up to Laevsky.

"It's enough," said Laevsky, breathing hard and snatching up his cap.

"I'm a Russian doctor, a nobleman by birth, and a civil councillor," said Samoylenko emphatically. "I've never been a spy, and I allow no one to insult me!" he shouted in a breaking voice, emphasizing the last word. "Hold your tongue!"

The deacon, who had never seen the doctor so majestic, so swelling with dignity, so crimson and so ferocious, shut his mouth, ran out into the entry and there exploded with laughter.

As though through a fog, Laevsky saw Von Koren get up and, putting his hands in his trouser-pockets, stand still in an attitude of expectancy, as though waiting to see what would happen. This calm attitude struck Laevsky as insolent and insulting to the last degree.

"Kindly take back your words," shouted Samoylenko.

Laevsky, who did not by now remember what his words were, answered:

"Leave me alone! I ask for nothing. All I ask is that you and German upstarts of Jewish origin should let me alone! Or I shall take steps to make you! I will fight you!"

"Now we understand," said Von Koren, coming from behind the table. "Mr. Laevsky wants to amuse himself with a duel before he goes away. I can give him that pleasure. Mr. Laevsky, I accept your challenge."

"A challenge," said Laevsky, in a low voice, going up to the zoologist and looking with hatred at his swarthy brow and curly hair. "A challenge? By all means! I hate you! I hate you!"

"Delighted. To-morrow morning early near Kerbalay's. I leave all details to your taste. And now, clear out!"

"I hate you," Laevsky said softly, breathing hard. "I have hated you a long while! A duel! Yes!"

"Get rid of him, Alexandr Daviditch, or else I'm going," said Von Koren. "He'll bite me."

Von Koren's cool tone calmed the doctor; he seemed suddenly to come to himself, to recover his reason; he put both arms round Laevsky's waist, and, leading him away from the zoologist, muttered in a friendly voice that shook with emotion:

"My friends . . . dear, good . . . you've lost your tempers and that's enough . . . and that's enough, my friends."

Hearing his soft, friendly voice, Laevsky felt that something unheard of, monstrous, had just happened to him, as though he had been nearly run over by a train; he almost burst into tears, waved his hand, and ran out of the room.

"To feel that one is hated, to expose oneself before the man who hates one, in the most pitiful, contemptible, helpless state. My God, how hard it is!" he thought a little while afterwards as he sat in the pavilion, feeling as though his body were scarred by the hatred of which he had just been the object.

"How coarse it is, my God!"

Cold water with brandy in it revived him. He vividly pictured Von Koren's calm, haughty face; his eyes the day before, his shirt like a rug, his voice, his white hand; and heavy, passionate, hungry hatred rankled in his breast and clamoured for satisfaction. In his thoughts he felled Von Koren to the ground, and trampled him underfoot. He remembered to the minutest detail all that had happened, and wondered how he could have smiled ingratiatingly to that insignificant man, and how he could care for the opinion of wretched petty people whom nobody knew, living in a miserable little town which was not, it seemed, even on the map, and of which not one decent person in Petersburg had heard. If this wretched little town suddenly fell into ruins or caught fire, the telegram with the news would be read in Russia with no more interest than an advertisement of the sale of second-hand furniture. Whether he killed Von Koren next day or left him alive, it would be just the same, equally useless and uninteresting. Better to shoot him in the leg or hand, wound him, then laugh at him, and let him, like an insect with a broken leg lost in the grass—let him be lost with his obscure sufferings in the crowd of insignificant people like himself.

Laevsky went to Sheshkovsky, told him all about it, and asked him to be his second; then they both went to the superintendent of the postal telegraph department, and asked him, too, to be a second, and stayed to dinner with him. At dinner there was a great deal of joking and laughing. Laevsky made jests at his own expense, saying he hardly knew how to fire off a pistol, calling himself a royal archer and William Tell.

"We must give this gentleman a lesson . . ." he said.

After dinner they sat down to cards. Laevsky played, drank wine, and thought that duelling was stupid and senseless, as it did not decide the question but only complicated it, but that it was sometimes impossible to get on without it. In the given case, for instance, one could not, of course, bring an action against Von Koren. And this duel was so far good in that it made it impossible for Laevsky to remain in the town afterwards. He got a little drunk and interested in the game, and felt at ease.

But when the sun had set and it grew dark, he was possessed by a feeling of uneasiness. It was not fear at the thought of death, because while he was dining and playing cards, he had for some reason a confident belief that the duel would end in nothing; it was dread at the thought of something unknown which was to happen next morning for the first time in his life, and dread of the coming night. . . . He knew that the night would be long and sleepless, and that he would have to think not only of Von Koren and his hatred, but also of the mountain of lies which he had to get through, and which he had not strength or ability to dispense with. It was as though he had been taken suddenly ill; all at once he lost all interest in the cards and in people, grew restless, and began asking them to let him go home. He was eager to get into bed, to lie without moving, and to prepare his thoughts for the night. Sheshkovsky and the postal superintendent saw him home and went on to Von Koren's to arrange about the duel.

Near his lodgings Laevsky met Atchmianov. The young man was breathless and excited.

"I am looking for you, Ivan Andreitch," he said. "I beg you to come quickly. . . ."

"Where?"

"Someone wants to see you, someone you don't know, about very important business; he earnestly begs you to come for a minute. He wants to speak to you of something. . . . For him it's a question of life and death. . . ."

In his excitement Atchmianov spoke in a strong Armenian accent.

"Who is it?" asked Laevsky.

"He asked me not to tell you his name."

"Tell him I'm busy; to-morrow, if he likes. . . ."

"How can you!" Atchmianov was aghast. "He wants to tell you something very important for you . . . very important! If you don't come something dreadful will happen."

"Strange . . ." muttered Laevsky, unable to understand why Atchmianov was so excited and what mysteries there could be in this dull, useless little town.

"Strange," he repeated in hesitation. "Come along, though; I don't care."

Atchmianov walked rapidly on ahead and Laevsky followed him. They walked down a street, then turned into an alley.

"What a bore this is!" said Laevsky.

"One minute, one minute . . . it's near."

Near the old rampart they went down a narrow alley

between two empty enclosures, then they came into a sort of large yard and went towards a small house.

"That's Muridov's, isn't it?" asked Laevsky.

"Yes."

"But why we've come by the back yards I don't understand. We might have come by the street; it's nearer. . . ."

"Never mind, never mind. . . ."

It struck Laevsky as strange, too, that Atchmianov led him to a back entrance, and motioned to him as though bidding him go quietly and hold his tongue.

"This way, this way . . ." said Atchmianov, cautiously opening the door and going into the passage on tiptoe. "Quietly, quietly, I beg you . . . they may hear."

He listened, drew a deep breath and said in a whisper:

"Open that door, and go in . . . don't be afraid."

Laevsky, puzzled, opened the door and went into a room with a low ceiling and curtained windows.

There was a candle on the table.

"What do you want?" asked someone in the next room. "Is it you, Muridov?"

Laevsky turned into that room and saw Kirilin, and beside him Nadyezhda Fyodorovna.

He didn't hear what was said to him; he staggered back, and did not know how he found himself on the street. His hatred for Von Koren and his uneasiness—all had vanished from his soul. As he went home he waved his right arm awkwardly and looked carefully at the ground under his feet, trying to step where it was smooth. At home in his study he walked backwards and forwards, rubbing his hands, and awkwardly shrugging his shoulders and neck, as though his jacket and shirt were too tight; then he lighted a candle and sat down to the table. . . .

16

"The 'humane studies' of which you speak will only satisfy human thought when, as they advance, they meet the exact sciences and progress side by side with them. Whether

they will meet under a new microscope, or in the mono-
logues of a new Hamlet, or in a new religion, I do not
know, but I expect the earth will be covered with a crust
of ice before it comes to pass. Of all humane learning the
most durable and living is, of course, the teaching of
Christ; but look how differently even that is interpreted!
Some teach that we must love all our neighbours but make
an exception of soldiers, criminals, and lunatics. They allow the first to be killed in war, the second to be isolated
or executed, and the third they forbid to marry. Other
interpreters teach that we must love all our neighbours
without exception, with no distinction of *plus* or *minus*.
According to their teaching, if a consumptive or a murderer or an epileptic asks your daughter in marriage, you
must let him have her. If *crêtins* go to war against the
physically and mentally healthy, don't defend yourselves.
This advocacy of love for love's sake, like art for art's
sake, if it could have power, would bring mankind in the
long run to complete extinction, and so would become the
vastest crime that has ever been committed upon earth.
There are very many interpretations, and since there are
many of them, serious thought is not satisfied by any one
of them, and hastens to add its own individual interpreta-
tion to the mass. For that reason you should never put a
question on a philosophical or so-called Christian basis; by
so doing you only remove the question further from solution."

The deacon listened to the zoologist attentively, thought
a little, and asked:

"Have the philosophers invented the moral law which is
innate in every man, or did God create it together with the
body?"

"I don't know. But that law is so universal among all
peoples and all ages that I fancy we ought to recognize
it as organically connected with man. It is not invented,
but exists and will exist. I don't tell you that one day it
will be seen under the microscope, but its organic connection is shown, indeed, by evidence: serious affections of
the brain and all so-called mental diseases, to the best of
my belief, show themselves first of all in the perversion of
the moral law."

"Good. So then, just as our stomach bids us eat, our
moral sense bids us love our neighbours. Is that it? But

our natural man through self-love opposes the voice of conscience and reason, and this gives rise to many brain-racking questions. To whom ought we to turn for the solution of those questions if you forbid us to put them on the philosophic basis?"

"Turn to what little exact science we have. Trust to evidence and the logic of facts. It is true it is but little, but, on the other hand, it is less fluid and shifting than philosophy. The moral law, let us suppose, demands that you love your neighbour. Well? Love ought to show itself in the removal of everything which in one way or another is injurious to men and threatens them with danger in the present or in the future. Our knowledge and the evidence tells us that the morally and physically abnormal are a menace to humanity. If so you must struggle against the abnormal; if you are not able to raise them to the normal standard, you must have strength and ability to render them harmless—that is, to destroy them."

"So love consists in the strong overcoming the weak."

"Undoubtedly."

"But you know the strong crucified our Lord Jesus Christ," said the deacon hotly.

"The fact is that those who crucified Him were not the strong but the weak. Human culture weakens and strives to nullify the struggle for existence and natural selection; hence the rapid advancement of the weak and their predominance over the strong. Imagine that you succeeded in instilling into bees humanitarian ideas in their crude and elementary form. What would come of it? The drones who ought to be killed would remain alive, would devour the honey, would corrupt and stifle the bees, resulting in the predominance of the weak over the strong and the degeneration of the latter. The same process is taking place now with humanity; the weak are oppressing the strong. Among savages untouched by civilization the strongest, cleverest, and most moral takes the lead; he is the chief and the master. But we civilized men have crucified Christ, and we go on crucifying Him, so there is something lacking in us. . . . And that something one ought to raise up in ourselves, or there will be no end to these errors."

"But what criterion have you to distinguish the strong from the weak?"

"Knowledge and evidence. The tuberculous and the scrofulous are recognized by their diseases, and the insane and the immoral by their actions."

"But mistakes may be made!"

"Yes, but it's no use to be afraid of getting your feet wet when you are threatened with the deluge!"

"That's philosophy," laughed the deacon.

"Not a bit of it. You are so corrupted by your seminary philosophy that you want to see nothing but fog in everything. The abstract studies with which your youthful head is stuffed are called abstract just because they abstract your minds from what is obvious. Look the devil straight in the eye, and if he's the devil, tell him he's the devil, and don't go calling to Kant or Hegel for explanations."

The zoologist paused and went on:

"Twice two's four, and a stone's a stone. Here to-morrow we have a duel. You and I will say it's stupid and absurd, that the duel is out of date, that there is no real difference between the aristocratic duel and the drunken brawl in the pot-house, and yet we shall not stop, we shall go there and fight. So there is some force stronger than our reasoning. We shout that war is plunder, robbery, atrocity, fratricide; we cannot look upon blood without fainting; but the French or the Germans have only to insult us for us to feel at once an exaltation of spirit; in the most genuine way we shout 'Hurrah!' and rush to attack the foe. You will invoke the blessing of God on our weapons, and our valour will arouse universal and general enthusiasm. Again it follows that there is a force, if not higher, at any rate stronger, than us and our philosophy. We can no more stop it than that cloud which is moving upwards over the sea. Don't be hypocritical, don't make a long nose at it on the sly; and don't say, 'Ah, old-fashioned, stupid! Ah, it's inconsistent with Scripture!' but look it straight in the face, recognize its rational lawfulness, and when, for instance, it wants to destroy a rotten, scrofulous, corrupt race, don't hinder it with your pilules and misunderstood quotations from the Gospel. Leskov has a story of a conscientious Danila who found a leper outside the town and fed and warmed him in the name of love and of Christ. If that Danila had really loved humanity, he would have dragged the leper as far as possible from the town, and would have flung him in a pit, and would have gone to save the healthy. Christ, I hope, taught us a rational, intelligent, practical love."

"What a fellow you are!" laughed the deacon. "You don't believe in Christ. Why do you mention His name so often?"

"Yes, I do believe in Him. Only, of course, in my own way, not in yours. Oh, deacon, deacon!" laughed the zoologist; he put his arm round the deacon's waist, and said gaily: "Well? Are you coming with us to the duel to-morrow?"

"My orders don't allow it, or else I should come."

"What do you mean by 'orders'?"

"I have been consecrated. I am in a state of grace."

"Oh, deacon, deacon," repeated Von Koren, laughing, "I love talking to you."

"You say you have faith," said the deacon. "What sort of faith is it? Why, I have an uncle, a priest, and he believes so that when in time of drought he goes out into the fields to pray for rain, he takes his umbrella and leather overcoat for fear of getting wet through on his way home. That's faith! When he speaks of Christ, his face is full of radiance, and all the peasants, men and women, weep floods of tears. He would stop that cloud and put all those forces you talk about to flight. Yes . . . faith moves mountains."

The deacon laughed and slapped the zoologist on the shoulder.

"Yes . . ." he went on; "here you are teaching all the time, fathoming the depths of the ocean, dividing the weak and the strong, writing books and challenging to duels—and everything remains as it is; but, behold! some feeble old man will mutter just one word with a holy spirit, or a new Mahomet, with a sword, will gallop from Arabia, and everything will be topsy-turvy, and in Europe not one stone will be left standing upon another."

"Well, deacon, that's on the knees of the gods."

"Faith without works is dead, but works without faith are worse still—mere waste of time and nothing more."

The doctor came into sight on the sea-front. He saw the deacon and the zoologist, and went up to them.

"I believe everything is ready," he said, breathing hard.

"Govorovsky and Boyko will be the seconds. They will start at five o'clock in the morning. How it has clouded over," he said, looking at the sky. "One can see nothing; there will be rain directly."

"I hope you are coming with us?" said the zoologist.

"No, God preserve me; I'm worried enough as it is. Ustimovitch is going instead of me. I've spoken to him already."

Far over the sea was a flash of lightning, followed by a hollow roll of thunder.

"How stifling it is before a storm!" said Von Koren. "I bet you've been to Laevsky already and have been weeping on his bosom."

"Why should I go to him?" answered the doctor in confusion. "What next?"

Before sunset he had walked several times along the boulevard and the street in the hope of meeting Laevsky. He was ashamed of his hastiness and the sudden outburst of friendliness which had followed it. He wanted to apologize to Laevsky in a joking tone, to give him a good talking to, to soothe him and to tell him that the duel was a survival of medieval barbarism, but that Providence itself had brought them to the duel as a means of reconciliation; that the next day, both being splendid and highly intelligent people, they would, after exchanging shots, appreciate each other's noble qualities and would become friends. But he could not come across Laevsky.

"What should I go and see him for?" repeated Samoylenko. "I did not insult him; he insulted me. Tell me, please, why he attacked me. What harm had I done him? I go into the drawing-room, and, all of a sudden, without the least provocation: 'Spy!' There's a nice thing! Tell me, how did it begin? What did you say to him?"

"I told him his position was hopeless. And I was right. It is only honest men or scoundrels who can find an escape from any position, but one who wants to be at the same time an honest man and a scoundrel—it is a hopeless position. But it's eleven o'clock, gentlemen, and we have to be up early to-morrow."

There was a sudden gust of wind; it blew up the dust on the sea-front, whirled it round in eddies, with a howl that drowned the roar of the sea.

"A squall," said the deacon. "We must go in, our eyes are getting full of dust."

As they went, Samoylenko sighed and, holding his hat, said:

"I suppose I shan't sleep to-night."

"Don't you agitate yourself," laughed the zoologist. "You can set your mind at rest; the duel will end in nothing. Laevsky will magnanimously fire into the air—he can do nothing else; and I dare say I shall not fire at all. To be arrested and lose my time on Laevsky's account—the game's not worth the candle. By the way, what is the punishment for duelling?"

"Arrest, and in the case of the death of your opponent a maximum of three years' imprisonment in the fortress."

"The fortress of St. Peter and St. Paul?"

"No, in a military fortress, I believe."

"Though this fine gentleman ought to have a lesson!"

Behind them on the sea, there was a flash of lightning, which for an instant lighted up the roofs of the houses and the mountains. The friends parted near the boulevard. When the doctor disappeared in the darkness and his steps had died away, Von Koren shouted to him:

"I only hope the weather won't interfere with us to-morrow!"

"Very likely it will! Please God it may!"

"Good-night!"

"What about the night? What do you say?"

In the roar of the wind and the sea and the crashes of thunder, it was difficult to hear.

"It's nothing," shouted the zoologist, and hurried home.

17

"Upon my mind, weighed down with woe,
  Crowd thoughts, a heavy multitude:
  In silence memory unfolds
  Her long, long scroll before my eyes.
  Loathing and shuddering I curse
  And bitterly lament in vain,

And bitter though the tears I weep
I do not wash those lines away."

PUSHKIN.

Whether they killed him next morning, or mocked at him
—that is, left him his life—he was ruined, anyway.
Whether this disgraced woman killed herself in her shame
and despair, or dragged on her pitiful existence, she was
ruined, anyway.

So thought Laevsky as he sat at the table late in the
evening, still rubbing his hands. The windows suddenly
blew open with a bang; a violent gust of wind burst into
the room, and the papers fluttered from the table. Laevsky
closed the windows and bent down to pick up the papers.
He was aware of something new in his body, a sort of
awkwardness he had not felt before, and his movements
were strange to him. He moved timidly, jerking with his
elbows and shrugging his shoulders; and when he sat
down to the table again, he again began rubbing his
hands. His body had lost its suppleness.

On the eve of death one ought to write to one's nearest
relation. Laevsky thought of this. He took a pen and wrote
with a tremulous hand:

"Mother!"

He wanted to write to beg his mother, for the sake of
the merciful God in whom she believed, that she would
give shelter and bring a little warmth and kindness into
the life of the unhappy woman who, by his doing, had
been disgraced and was in solitude, poverty, and weakness, that she would forgive and forget everything, everything, everything, and by her sacrifice atone to some extent
for her son's terrible sin. But he remembered how his
mother, a stout, heavily-built old woman in a lace cap, used
to go out into the garden in the morning, followed by her
companion with the lap-dog; how she used to shout in a peremptory way to the gardener and the servants, and how
proud and haughty her face was—he remembered all this
and scratched out the word he had written.

There was a vivid flash of lightning at all three windows, and it was followed by a prolonged, deafening roll
of thunder, beginning with a hollow rumble and ending
with a crash so violent that all the window-panes rattled.
Laevsky got up, went to the window, and pressed his fore-

head against the pane. There was a fierce, magnificent storm. On the horizon lightning-flashes were flung in white streams from the storm-clouds into the sea, lighting up the high, dark waves over the far-away expanse. And to right and to left, and, no doubt, over the house too, the lightning flashed.

"The storm!" whispered Laevsky; he had a longing to pray to someone or to something, if only to the lightning or the storm-clouds. "Dear storm!"

He remembered how as a boy he used to run out into the garden without a hat on when there was a storm, and how two fair-haired girls with blue eyes used to run after him, and how they got wet through with the rain; they laughed with delight, but when there was a loud peal of thunder, the girls used to nestle up to the boy confidingly, while he crossed himself and made haste to repeat: "Holy, holy, holy. . . ." Oh, where had they vanished to! In what sea were they drowned, those dawning days of pure, fair life? He had no fear of the storm, no love of nature now; he had no God. All the confiding girls he had ever known had by now been ruined by him and those like him. All his life he had not planted one tree in his own garden, nor grown one blade of grass; and living among the living, he had not saved one fly; he had done nothing but destroy and ruin, and lie, lie. . . .

"What in my past was not vice?" he asked himself, trying to clutch at some bright memory as a man falling down a precipice clutches at the bushes.

School? The university? But that was a sham. He had neglected his work and forgotten what he had learnt. The service of his country? That, too, was a sham, for he did nothing in the Service, took a salary for doing nothing, and it was an abominable swindling of the State for which one was not punished.

He had no craving for truth, and had not sought it; spellbound by vice and lying, his conscience had slept or been silent. Like a stranger, like an alien from another planet, he had taken no part in the common life of men, had been indifferent to their sufferings, their ideas, their religion, their sciences, their strivings, and their struggles. He had not said one good word, not written one line that was not useless and vulgar; he had not done his fellows one ha'p'orth of service, but had eaten their bread, drunk their wine, seduced their wives, lived on their thoughts, and to justify his contemptible, parasitic life in their eyes and in his own, he had always tried to assume an air of being higher and better than they. Lies, lies, lies. . . .

He vividly remembered what he had seen that evening at Muridov's, and he was in an insufferable anguish of loathing and misery. Kirilin and Atchmianov were loathsome, but they were only continuing what he had begun; they were his accomplices and his disciples. This young weak woman had trusted him more than a brother, and he had deprived her of her husband, of her friends and of her country, and had brought her here—to the heat, to fever, and to boredom; and from day to day she was bound to reflect, like a mirror, his idleness, his viciousness and falsity—and that was all she had had to fill her weak, listless, pitiable life. Then he had grown sick of her, had begun to hate her, but had not had the pluck to abandon her, and he had tried to entangle her more and more closely in a web of lies. . . . These men had done the rest.

Laevsky sat at the table, then got up and went to the window; at one minute he put out the candle and then he lighted it again. He cursed himself aloud, wept and wailed, and asked forgiveness; several times he ran to the table in despair, and wrote:

"Mother!"

Except his mother, he had no relations or near friends; but how could his mother help him? And where was she? He had an impulse to run to Nadyezhda Fyodorovna, to fall at her feet, to kiss her hands and feet, to beg her forgiveness; but she was his victim, and he was afraid of her as though she were dead.

"My life is ruined," he repeated, rubbing his hands. "Why am I still alive, my God! . . ."

He had cast out of heaven his dim star; it had fallen, and its track was lost in the darkness of night. It would never return to the sky again, because life was given only once and never came a second time. If he could have turned back the days and years of the past, he would have replaced the falsity with truth, the idleness with work, the boredom with happiness; he would have given back purity to those whom he had robbed of it. He would have found God and goodness, but that was as impossible as to put back the fallen star into the sky, and because it was impossible he was in despair.

When the storm was over, he sat by the open window and thought calmly of what was before him. Von Koren would most likely kill him. The man's clear, cold theory of life justified the destruction of the rotten and the useless; if it changed at the crucial moment, it would be the hatred and the repugnance that Laevsky inspired in him that would save him. If he missed his aim or, in mockery of his hated opponent, only wounded him, or fired in the air, what could he do then? Where could he go?

"Go to Petersburg?" Laevsky asked himself. But that would mean beginning over again the old life which he cursed. And the man who seeks salvation in change of place like a migrating bird would find nothing anywhere, for all the world is alike to him. Seek salvation in men? In whom and how? Samoylenko's kindness and generosity could no more save him than the deacon's laughter or Von Koren's hatred. He must look for salvation in himself alone, and if there were no finding it, why waste time? He must kill himself, that was all. . . .

He heard the sound of a carriage. It was getting light. The carriage passed by, turned, and crunching on the wet sand, stopped near the house. There were two men in the carriage.

"Wait a minute; I'm coming directly," Laevsky said to them out of the window. "I'm not asleep. Surely it's not time yet?"

"Yes, it's four o'clock. By the time we get there . . ."

Laevsky put on his overcoat and cap, put some cigarettes in his pocket, and stood still hesitating. He felt as though there was something else he must do. In the street the seconds talked in low voices and the horses snorted, and this sound in the damp, early morning, when everybody was asleep and light was hardly dawning in the sky, filled Laevsky's soul with a disconsolate feeling which was like a presentiment of evil. He stood for a little, hesitating, and went into the bedroom.

Nadyezhda Fyodorovna was lying stretched out on the bed, wrapped from head to foot in a rug. She did not stir, and her whole appearance, especially her head, suggested an Egyptian mummy. Looking at her in silence, Laevsky mentally asked her forgiveness, and thought that if the heavens were not empty and there really were a God, then He would save her; if there were no God, then she had better perish—there was nothing for her to live for.

All at once she jumped up, and sat up in bed. Lifting her pale face and looking with horror at Laevsky, she asked:

"Is it you? Is the storm over?"

"Yes."

She remembered; put both her hands to her head and shuddered all over.

"How miserable I am!" she said. "If only you knew how miserable I am! I expected," she went on, half closing her eyes, "that you would kill me or turn me out of the house into the rain and storm, but you delay . . . delay . . ."

Warmly and impulsively he put his arms round her and covered her knees and hands with kisses. Then when she muttered something and shuddered with the thought of the past, he stroked her hair, and looking into her face, realized that this unhappy, sinful woman was the one creature near and dear to him, whom no one could replace.

When he went out of the house and got into the carriage he wanted to return home alive.

18

The deacon got up, dressed, took his thick gnarled stick and slipped quietly out of the house. It was dark, and for the first minute when he went into the street, he could not even see his white stick. There was not a single star in the sky, and it looked as though there would be rain again. There was a smell of wet sand and sea.

"It's to be hoped that the mountaineers won't attack us," thought the deacon, hearing the tap of the stick on the pavement, and noticing how loud and lonely the taps sounded in the stillness of the night.

When he got out of town, he began to see both the road and his stick. Here and there in the black sky there were dark cloudy patches, and soon a star peeped out and timidly blinked its one eye. The deacon walked along the high rocky coast and did not see the sea; it was slumbering below, and its unseen waves broke languidly and heavily on the shore, as though sighing "Ouf!" and how slowly! One wave broke—the deacon had time to count eight steps; then another broke, and six steps; later a third. As before, nothing could be seen, and in the darkness one could hear the languid, drowsy drone of the sea. One could hear the infinitely far-away, inconceivable time when God moved above chaos.

The deacon felt uncanny. He hoped God would not punish him for keeping company with infidels, and even going to look at their duels. The duel would be nonsensical, bloodless, absurd, but however that might be, it was a heathen spectacle, and it was altogether unseemly for an ecclesiastical person to be present at it. He stopped and wondered—should he go back? But an intense, restless curiosity triumphed over his doubts, and he went on.

"Though they are infidels, they are good people, and will be saved," he assured himself. "They are sure to be saved," he said aloud, lighting a cigarette.

By what standard must one measure men's qualities, to judge rightly of them? The deacon remembered his enemy, the inspector of the clerical school, who believed in God, lived in chastity, and did not fight duels; but he used to feed the deacon on bread with sand in it, and on one occasion almost pulled off the deacon's ear. If human life was so artlessly constructed that everyone respected this cruel and dishonest inspector who stole the Government flour, and his health and salvation were prayed for in the schools, was it just to shun such men as Von Koren and Laevsky, simply because they were unbelievers? The deacon was weighing this question, but he recalled how absurd Samoylenko had looked yesterday, and that broke the thread of his ideas. What fun they would have next day! The deacon imagined how he would sit under a bush and look on, and when Von Koren began boasting next day at dinner, he, the deacon, would begin laughing and telling him all the details of the duel.

"How do you know all about it?" the zoologist would ask.

"Well, there you are! I stayed at home, but I know all about it."

It would be nice to write a comic description of the duel. His father-in-law would read it and laugh. A good story, told or written, was more than meat and drink to his father-in-law.

The valley of the Yellow River opened before him. The stream was broader and fiercer for the rain, and instead of murmuring as before, it was raging. It began to get light. The grey, dingy morning, and the clouds racing towards the west to overtake the storm-clouds, the mountains girt with mist, and the wet trees, all struck the deacon as ugly and sinister. He washed at the brook, repeated his morning prayer, and felt a longing for tea and hot rolls, with sour cream, which were served every morning at his father-in-law's. He remembered his wife and the "Days past Recall," which she played on the piano. What sort of woman was she? His wife had been introduced, betrothed, and married to him all in one week: he had lived with her less than a month when he was ordered here, so that he had not had time to find out what she was like. All the same, he rather missed her.

"I must write her a nice letter . . ." he thought. The flag on the *duhan* hung limp, soaked by the rain, and the *duhan* itself with its wet roof seemed darker and lower than it had been before. Near the door was standing a cart; Kerbalay, with two mountaineers and a young Tatar woman in trousers—no doubt Kerbalay's wife or daughter—were bringing sacks of something out of the *duhan*, and putting them on maize straw in the cart.

Near the cart stood a pair of asses hanging their heads. When they had put in all the sacks, the mountaineers and the Tatar woman began covering them over with straw, while Kerbalay began hurriedly harnessing the asses.

"Smuggling, perhaps," thought the deacon.

Here was the fallen tree with the dried pine-needles, here was the blackened patch from the fire. He remembered the picnic and all its incidents, the fire, the singing of the mountaineers, his sweet dreams of becoming a bishop, and of the Church procession. . . . The Black River had grown blacker and broader with the rain. The deacon walked cautiously over the narrow bridge, which by now was reached by the topmost crests of the dirty water, and went up through the little copse to the drying-shed.

"A splendid head," he thought, stretching himself on the straw, and thinking of Von Koren. "A fine head—God grant him health; only there is cruelty in him. . . ."

Why did he hate Laevsky and Laevsky hate him? Why were they going to fight a duel? If from their childhood they had known poverty as the deacon had; if they had been brought up among ignorant, hard-hearted, grasping, coarse and ill-mannered people who grudged you a crust of bread, who spat on the floor and hiccoughed at dinner and at prayers; if they had not been spoilt from childhood by the pleasant surroundings and the select circle of friends they lived in—how they would have rushed at each other, how readily they would have overlooked each other's shortcomings and would have prized each other's strong points! Why, how few even outwardly decent people there were in the world! It was true that Laevsky was flighty, dissipated, queer, but he did not steal, did not spit loudly on the floor; he did not abuse his wife and say, "You'll eat till you burst, but you don't want to work"; he would not beat a child with reins, or give his servants stinking meat to eat—surely this was reason enough to be indulgent to him? Besides, he was the chief sufferer from his failings, like a sick man from his sores. Instead of being lead by boredom and some sort of misunderstanding to look for degeneracy, extinction, heredity, and other such incomprehensible things in each other, would they not do better to stoop a little lower and turn their hatred and anger where whole streets resounded with moanings from coarse ignorance, greed, scolding, impurity, swearing, the shrieks of women. . . .

The sound of a carriage interrupted the deacon's thoughts. He glanced out of the door and saw a carriage and in it three persons: Laevsky, Sheshkovsky, and the superintendent of the post-office.

"Stop!" said Sheshkovsky.

All three got out of the carriage and looked at one another.

"They are not here yet," said Sheshkovsky, shaking the mud off. "Well? Till the show begins, let us go and find a suitable spot; there's not room to turn round here."

They went further up the river and soon vanished from sight. The Tatar driver sat in the carriage with his head resting on his shoulder and fell asleep. After waiting ten minutes the deacon came out of the drying-shed, and taking off his black hat that he might not be noticed, he began threading his way among the bushes and strips of maize along the bank, crouching and looking about him. The grass and maize were wet, and big drops fell on his head from the trees and bushes. "Disgraceful!" he muttered, picking up his wet and muddy skirt. "Had I realized it, I would not have come."

Soon he heard voices and caught sight of them. Laevsky was walking rapidly to and fro in the small glade with bowed back and hands thrust in his sleeves; his seconds were standing at the water's edge, rolling cigarettes.

"Strange," thought the deacon, not recognizing Laevsky's walk; "he looks like an old man. . . ."

"How rude it is of them!" said the superintendent of the post-office, looking at his watch. "It may be learned manners to be late, but to my thinking it's hoggish."

Sheshkovsky, a stout man with a black beard, listened and said:

"They're coming!"

19

"It's the first time in my life I've seen it! How glorious!" said Von Koren, pointing to the glade and stretching out his hands to the east. "Look: green rays!"

In the east behind the mountains rose two green streaks of light, and it really was beautiful. The sun was rising.

"Good-morning!" the zoologist went on, nodding to Laevsky's seconds. "I'm not late, am I?"

He was followed by his seconds, Boyko and Govorovsky, two very young officers of the same height, wearing white tunics, and Ustimovitch, the thin, unsociable doctor; in one hand he had a bag of some sort, and in the other had, as usual, a cane which he held behind him. Laying the bag on the ground and greeting no one, he put the other hand, too, behind his back and began pacing up and down the glade.

Laevsky felt the exhaustion and awkwardness of a man

who is soon perhaps to die, and is for that reason an object of general attention. He wanted to be killed as soon as possible or taken home. He saw the sunrise now for the first time in his life; the early morning, the green rays of light, the dampness, and the men in wet boots, seemed to him to have nothing to do with his life, to be superfluous and embarrassing. All these had no connection with the night he had been through, with his thoughts and his feeling of guilt, and so he would have gladly gone away without waiting for the duel.

Von Koren was noticeably excited and tried to conceal it, pretending that he was more interested in the green light than anything. The seconds were confused, and looked at one another as though wondering why they were here and what they were to do.

"I imagine, gentlemen, there is no need for us to go further," said Sheshkovsky. "This place will do."

"Yes, of course," Von Koren agreed.

A silence followed. Ustimovitch, pacing to and fro, suddenly turned sharply to Laevsky and said in a low voice, breathing into his face:

"They have very likely not told you my terms yet. Each side is to pay me fifteen roubles, and in the case of the death of one party, the survivor is to pay thirty."

Laevsky was already acquainted with the man, but now for the first time he had a distinct view of his lustreless eyes, his stiff moustaches, and wasted, consumptive neck; he was a money-grubber, not a doctor; his breath had an unpleasant smell of beef.

"What people there are in the world!" thought Laevsky, and answered: "Very good."

The doctor nodded and began pacing to and fro again, and it was evident he did not need the money at all, but simply asked for it from hatred. Everyone felt it was time to begin, or to end what had been begun, but instead of beginning or ending, they stood about, moved to and fro and smoked. The young officers, who were present at a duel for the first time in their lives, and even now hardly believed in this civilian and to their thinking, unnecessary duel, looked critically at their tunics and stroked their sleeves. Sheshkovsky went up to them and said softly: "Gentlemen, we must use every effort to prevent this duel; they ought to be reconciled."

He flushed crimson and added:

"Kirilin was at my rooms last night complaining that Laevsky had found him with Nadyezhda Fyodorovna, and all that sort of thing."

"Yes, we know that too," said Boyko.

"Well, you see, then . . . Laevsky's hands are trembling and all that sort of thing . . . he can scarcely hold a pistol now. To fight with him is as inhuman as to fight a man who is drunk or who has typhoid. If a reconciliation cannot be arranged, we ought to put off the duel, gentlemen, or something. . . . It's such a sickening business, I can't bear to see it."

"Talk to Von Koren."

"I don't know the rules of duelling, damnation take them, and I don't want to either; perhaps he'll imagine Laevsky funks it and has sent me to him, but he can think what he likes—I'll speak to him."

Sheshkovsky hesitatingly walked up to Von Koren with a slight limp, as though his leg had gone to sleep; and as he went towards him, clearing his throat, his whole figure was a picture of indolence.

"There's something I must say to you, sir," he began, carefully scrutinizing the flowers on the zoologist's shirt. "It's confidential. I don't know the rules of duelling, damnation take them, and I don't want to, and I look on the matter not as a second and that sort of thing, but as a man, and that's all about it."

"Yes. Well?"

"When seconds suggest reconciliation they are usually not listened to; it is looked upon as a formality. *Amour propre* and all that. But I humbly beg you to look carefully at Ivan Andreitch. He's not in a normal state, so to speak, to-day—not in his right mind, and a pitiable object. He has had a misfortune. I can't endure gossip. . . ."

Sheshkovsky flushed crimson and looked round.

"But in view of the duel, I think it necessary to inform you, Laevsky found his madam last night at Muridov's with . . . another gentleman."

"How disgusting!" muttered the zoologist; he turned pale, frowned, and spat loudly. "Tfoo!"

His lower lip quivered, he walked away from Sheshkovsky, unwilling to hear more, and as though he had accidentally tasted something bitter, spat loudly again, and for the first time that morning looked with hatred at Laevsky. His excitement and awkwardness passed off; he tossed his head and said aloud:

"Gentlemen, what are we waiting for, I should like to know? Why don't we begin?"

Sheshkovsky glanced at the officers and shrugged his shoulders.

"Gentlemen," he said aloud, addressing no one in particular. "Gentlemen, we propose that you should be reconciled."

"Let us make haste and get the formalities over," said Von Koren. "Reconciliation has been discussed already. What is the next formality? Make haste, gentlemen, time won't wait for us."

"But we insist on reconciliation all the same," said Sheshkovsky in a guilty voice, as a man compelled to interfere in another man's business; he flushed, laid his hand on his heart, and went on: "Gentlemen, we see no grounds for associating the offence with the duel. There's nothing in common between duelling and offences against one another of which we are sometimes guilty through human weakness. You are university men and men of culture, and no doubt you see in the duel nothing but a foolish and out-of-date formality, and all that sort of thing. That's how we look at it ourselves, or we shouldn't have come, for we cannot allow that in our presence men should fire at one another, and all that." Sheshkovsky wiped the perspiration off his face and went on: "Make an end to your misunderstanding, gentlemen; shake hands, and let us go home and drink to peace. Upon my honour, gentlemen!"

Von Koren did not speak. Laevsky, seeing that they were looking at him, said:

"I have nothing against Nikolay Vassilitch; if he considers I'm to blame, I'm ready to apologize to him."

Von Koren was offended.

"It is evident, gentlemen," he said, "you want Mr. Laevsky to return home a magnanimous and chivalrous figure, but I cannot give you and him that satisfaction. And there is no need to get up early and drive eight miles out of town simply to drink to peace, to have breakfast, and to explain to me that the duel is an out-of-date formality. A duel is a duel, and there is no need to make it more false and stupid than it is in reality. I want to fight!"

A silence followed. Boyko took a pair of pistols out of a box; one was given to Von Koren and one to Laevsky, and then there followed a difficulty which afforded a brief amusement to the zoologist and the seconds. It appeared that of all the people present not one had ever in his life been at a duel, and no one knew precisely how they ought to stand, and what the seconds ought to say and do. But then Boyko remembered and began, with a smile, to explain.

"Gentlemen, who remembers the description in Lermontov?" asked Von Koren, laughing. "In Turgenev, too, Bazarov had a duel with someone. . . ."

"There's no need to remember," said Ustimovitch impatiently. "Measure the distance, that's all."

And he took three steps as though to show how to measure it. Boyko counted out the steps while his companion drew his sabre and scratched the earth at the extreme points to mark the barrier. In complete silence the opponents took their places.

"Moles," the deacon thought, sitting in the bushes.

Sheshkovsky said something, Boyko explained something again, but Laevsky did not hear—or rather heard, but did not understand. He cocked his pistol when the time came to do so, and raised the cold, heavy weapon with the barrel upwards. He forgot to unbutton his overcoat, and it felt very tight over his shoulder and under his arm, and his arm rose as awkwardly as though the sleeve had been cut out of tin. He remembered the hatred he had felt the night before for the swarthy brow and curly hair, and felt that even yesterday at the moment of intense hatred and anger he could not have shot a man. Fearing that the bullet might somehow hit Von Koren by accident, he raised the pistol higher and higher, and felt that this too obvious magnanimity was indelicate and anything but magnanimous, but he did not know how else to do and could do nothing else. Looking at the pale, ironically smiling face of Von Koren, who evidently had been convinced from the beginning that his opponent would fire in the air, Laevsky thought that, thank God, everything would be over directly, and all that he had to do was to press the trigger rather hard. . . .

He felt a violent shock on the shoulder; there was the sound of a shot and an answering echo in the mountains: ping-ting!

Von Koren cocked his pistol and looked at Ustimovitch, who was pacing as before with his hands behind his back, taking no notice of anyone.

"Doctor," said the zoologist, "be so good as not to move to and fro like a pendulum. You make me dizzy."

The doctor stood still. Von Koren began to take aim at Laevsky.

"It's all over!" thought Laevsky.

The barrel of the pistol aimed straight at his face, the expression of hatred and contempt in Von Koren's attitude and whole figure, and the murder just about to be committed by a decent man in broad daylight, in the presence of decent men, and the stillness and the unknown force that compelled Laevsky to stand still and not to run—how mysterious it all was, how incomprehensible and terrible!

The moment while Von Koren was taking aim seemed to Laevsky longer than a night: he glanced imploringly at the seconds; they were pale and did not stir.

"Make haste and fire," thought Laevsky, and felt that his pale, quivering, and pitiful face must arouse even greater hatred in Von Koren.

"I'll kill him directly," thought Von Koren, aiming at his forehead, with his finger already on the catch. "Yes, of course I'll kill him. . . ."

"He'll kill him!" A despairing shout was suddenly heard somewhere very close at hand.

A shot rang out at once. Seeing that Laevsky remained standing where he was and did not fall, they all looked in the direction from which the shout had come, and saw the deacon. With pale face and wet hair sticking to his forehead and his cheeks, wet through and muddy, he was standing in the maize on the further bank, smiling rather queerly and waving his wet hat. Sheshkovsky laughed with joy, burst into tears, and moved away. . . .

20

A little while afterwards, Von Koren and the deacon met near the little bridge. The deacon was excited; he breathed hard, and avoided looking in people's faces. He felt ashamed both of his terror and his muddy, wet garments.

"I thought you meant to kill him . . ." he muttered. "How contrary to human nature it is! How utterly unnatural it is!"

"But how did you come here?" asked the zoologist.

"Don't ask," said the deacon, waving his hand. "The evil one tempted me, saying: 'Go, go. . . .' So I went and almost died of fright in the maize. But now, thank God, thank God. . . . I am awfully pleased with you," muttered the deacon. "Old Grandad Tarantula will be glad. . . . It's funny, it's too funny! Only I beg of you most earnestly don't tell anybody I was there, or I may get into hot water with the authorities. They will say: 'The deacon was a second.' "

"Gentlemen," said Von Koren, "the deacon asks you not to tell anyone you've seen him here. He might get into trouble."

"How contrary to human nature it is!" sighed the deacon. "Excuse my saying so, but your face was so dreadful that I thought you were going to kill him."

"I was very much tempted to put an end to that scoundrel," said Von Koren, "but you shouted close by, and I missed my aim. The whole procedure is revolting to anyone who is not used to it, and it has exhausted me, deacon. I feel awfully tired. Come along. . . ."

"No, you must let me walk back. I must get dry, for I am wet and cold."

"Well, as you like," said the zoologist, in a weary tone, feeling dispirited, and, getting into the carriage, he closed his eyes. "As you like. . . ."

While they were moving about the carriages and taking their seats, Kerbalay stood in the road, and, laying his hands on his stomach, he bowed low, showing his teeth;

he imagined that the gentry had come to enjoy the beau-
ties of nature and drink tea, and could not understand why
they were getting into the carriages. The party set off in
complete silence and only the deacon was left by the
duhan.

"Come to the *duhan,* drink tea," he said to Kerbalay.
"Me wants to eat."

Kerbalay spoke good Russian, but the deacon imagined
that the Tatar would understand him better if he talked to
him in broken Russian. "Cook omelette, give cheese. . . ."

"Come, come, father," said Kerbalay, bowing. "I'll give
you everything. . . . I've cheese and wine. . . . Eat what
you like."

"What is 'God' in Tatar?" asked the deacon, going into
the *duhan.*

"Your God and my God are the same," said Kerbalay,
not understanding him. "God is the same for all men, only
men are different. Some are Russian, some are Turks,
some are English—there are many sorts of men, but God
is one."

"Very good. If all men worship the same God, why do
you Mahomedans look upon Christians as your everlasting
enemies?"

"Why are you angry?" said Kerbalay, laying both hands
on his stomach. "You are a priest; I am a Mussulman: you
say, 'I want to eat'—I give it you. . . . Only the rich man
distinguishes your God from my God; for the poor man it
is all the same. If you please, it is ready."

While this theological conversation was taking place at
the *duhan,* Laevsky was driving home thinking how dreadful it had been driving there at daybreak, when the roads,
the rocks, and the mountains were wet and dark, and the
uncertain future seemed like a terrible abyss, of which one
could not see the bottom; while now the raindrops hanging
on the grass and on the stones were sparkling in the sun
like diamonds, nature was smiling joyfully, and the terrible future was left behind. He looked at Sheshkovsky's
sullen, tear-stained face, and at the two carriages ahead
of them in which Von Koren, his seconds, and the doctor
were sitting, and it seemed to him as though they were
all coming back from a graveyard in which a wearisome,
insufferable man who was a burden to others had just
been buried.

"Everything is over," he thought of his past, cautiously touching his neck with his fingers.

On the right side of his neck was a small swelling, of the length and breadth of his little finger, and he felt a pain, as though someone had passed a hot iron over his neck. The bullet had bruised it.

Afterwards, when he got home, a strange, long, sweet day began for him, misty as forgetfulness. Like a man released from prison or from hospital, he stared at the long-familiar objects and wondered that the tables, the windows, the chairs, the light, and the sea stirred in him a keen, childish delight such as he had not known for long, long years. Nadyezhda Fyodorovna, pale and haggard, could not understand his gentle voice and strange movements; she made haste to tell him everything that had happened to her. . . . It seemed to her that very likely he scarcely heard and did not understand her, and that if he did know everything he would curse her and kill her, but he listened to her, stroked her face and hair, looked into her eyes and said:

"I have nobody but you. . . ."

Then they sat a long while in the garden, huddled close together, saying nothing, or dreaming aloud of their happy life in the future, in brief, broken sentences, while it seemed to him that he had never spoken at such length or so eloquently.

21

More than three months had passed.

The day came that Von Koren had fixed on for his departure. A cold, heavy rain had been falling from early morning, a north-east wind was blowing, and the waves were high on the sea. It was said that the steamer would hardly be able to come into the harbour in such weather. By the time-table it should have arrived at ten o'clock in the morning, but Von Koren, who had gone on to the sea-front at midday and again after dinner, could see nothing through the field-glass but grey waves and rain covering the horizon.

Towards the end of the day the rain ceased and the wind began to drop perceptibly. Von Koren had already made up his mind that he would not be able to get off that day, and had settled down to play chess with Samoylenko; but after dark the orderly announced that there were lights on the sea and that a rocket had been seen.

Von Koren made haste. He put his satchel over his shoulder, and kissed Samoylenko and the deacon. Though there was not the slightest necessity, he went through the rooms again, said good-bye to the orderly and the cook, and went out into the street, feeling that he had left something behind, either at the doctor's or his lodging. In the street he walked beside Samoylenko, behind them came the deacon with a box, and last of all the orderly with two portmanteaus. Only Samoylenko and the orderly could distinguish the dim lights on the sea. The others gazed into the darkness and saw nothing. The steamer had stopped a long way from the coast.

"Make haste, make haste," Von Koren hurried them. "I am afraid it will set off."

As they passed the little house with three windows, into which Laevsky had moved soon after the duel, Von Koren could not resist peeping in at the window. Laevsky was sitting, writing, bent over the table, with his back to the window.

"I wonder at him!" said the zoologist softly, "What a screw he has put on himself!"

"Yes, one may well wonder," said Samoylenko. "He sits from morning till night, he's always at work. He works to pay off his debts. And he lives, brother, worse than a beggar!"

Half a minute of silence followed. The zoologist, the doctor, and the deacon stood at the window and went on looking at Laevsky.

"So he didn't get away from here, poor fellow," said Samoylenko. "Do you remember how hard he tried?"

"Yes, he has put a screw on himself," Von Koren repeated. "His marriage, the way he works all day long for his daily bread, a new expression in his face, and even in his walk—it's all so extraordinary that I don't know what to call it."

The zoologist took Samoylenko's sleeve and went on with emotion in his voice:

"You tell him and his wife that when I went away I was full of admiration for them and wished them all happiness . . . and I beg him, if he can, not to remember evil against me. He knows me. He knows that if I could have foreseen this change, then I might have become his best friend."

"Go in and say good-bye to him."

"No, that wouldn't do."

"Why? God knows, perhaps you'll never see him again." The zoologist reflected, and said:

"That's true."

Samoylenko tapped softly at the window. Laevsky started and looked round.

"Vanya, Nikolay Vassilitch wants to say good-bye to you," said Samoylenko. "He is just going away."

Laevsky got up from the table, and went into the passage to open the door. Samoylenko, the zoologist, and the deacon went into the house.

"I can only come for one minute," began the zoologist, taking off his goloshes in the passage, and already wishing he had not given way to his feelings and come in, uninvited. "It is as though I were forcing myself on him," he thought, "and that's stupid."

"Forgive me for disturbing you," he said as he went into the room with Laevsky, "but I'm just going away, and I had an impulse to see you. God knows whether we shall ever meet again."

"I am very glad to see you. . . . Please come in," said Laevsky, and he awkwardly set chairs for his visitors as though he wanted to bar their way, and stood in the middle of the room, rubbing his hands.

"I should have done better to have left my audience in the street," thought Von Koren, and he said firmly: "Don't remember evil against me, Ivan Andreitch. To forget the past is, of course, impossible—it is too painful, and I've not come here to apologize or to declare that I was not to blame. I acted sincerely, and I have not changed my conviction since then. . . . It is true that I see, to my great delight, that I was mistaken in regard to you, but it's easy to make a false step even on a smooth road, and, in fact, it's the natural human lot: if one is not mistaken in the main, one is mistaken in the details. Nobody knows the real truth."

"No, no one knows the truth," said Laevsky.

"Well, good-bye. . . . God give you all happiness."

Von Koren gave Laevsky his hand; the latter took it and bowed.

"Don't remember evil against me," said Von Koren. "Give my greetings to your wife, and say I am very sorry not to say good-bye to her."

"She is at home."

Laevsky went to the door of the next room, and said:

"Nadya, Nikolay Vassilitch wants to say good-bye to you."

Nadyezhda Fyodorovna came in; she stopped near the doorway and looked shyly at the visitors. There was a look of guilt and dismay on her face, and she held her hands like a schoolgirl receiving a scolding.

"I'm just going away, Nadyezhda Fyodorovna," said Von Koren, "and have come to say good-bye."

She held out her hand uncertainly while Laevsky bowed.

"What pitiful figures they are, though!" thought Von Koren. "The life they are living does not come easy to them. I shall be in Moscow and Petersburg; can I send you anything?" he asked.

"Oh!" said Nadyezhda Fyodorovna, and she looked anxiously at her husband. "I don't think there's anything. . . ."

"No, nothing . . ." said Laevsky, rubbing his hands. "Our greetings."

Von Koren did not know what he could or ought to say, though as he went in he thought he would say a very great deal that would be warm and good and important. He shook hands with Laevsky and his wife in silence, and left them with a depressed feeling.

"What people!" said the deacon in a low voice, as he walked behind them. "My God, what people! Of a truth, the right hand of God has planted this vine! Lord! Lord! One man vanquishes thousands and another tens of thousands. Nikolay Vassilitch," he said ecstatically, "let me tell you that to-day you have conquered the greatest of man's enemies—pride."

"Hush, deacon! Fine conquerors we are! Conquerors ought to look like eagles, while he's a pitiful figure, timid, crushed; he bows like a Chinese idol, and I, I am sad. . . ."

They heard steps behind them. It was Laevsky, hurrying

after them to see him off. The orderly was standing on the
quay with the two portmanteaus, and at a little distance
stood four boatmen.

"There is a wind, though. . . . Brrr!" said Samoylenko.
"There must be a pretty stiff storm on the sea now! You
are not going off at a nice time, Kolya."

"I'm not afraid of sea-sickness."

"That's not the point. . . . I only hope these rascals
won't upset you. You ought to have crossed in the agent's
sloop. Where's the agent's sloop?" he shouted to the boatmen.

"It has gone, Your Excellency."

"And the Customs-house boat?"

"That's gone, too."

"Why didn't you let us know?" said Samoylenko angrily.
"You dolts!"

"It's all the same, don't worry yourself . . ." said Von
Koren. "Well, good-bye. God keep you."

Samoylenko embraced Van Koren and made the sign of
the cross over him three times.

"Don't forget us, Kolya. . . . Write. . . . We shall look out
for you next spring."

"Good-bye, deacon," said Von Koren, shaking hands with
the deacon. "Thank you for your company and for your
pleasant conversation. Think about the expedition."

"Oh Lord, yes! to the ends of the earth," laughed the
deacon. "I've nothing against it."

Von Koren recognized Laevsky in the darkness, and held
out his hand without speaking. The boatmen were by now
below, holding the boat, which was beating against the
piles, though the breakwater screened it from the breakers.
Von Koren went down the ladder, jumped into the boat,
and sat at the helm.

"Write!" Samoylenko shouted to him. "Take care of
yourself!"

"No one knows the real truth," thought Laevsky, turning up the collar of his coat and thrusting his hands into
his sleeves.

The boat turned briskly out of the harbour into the
open sea. It vanished in the waves, but at once from a
deep hollow glided up on to a high breaker, so that they
could distinguish the men and even the oars. The boat

moved three yards forward and was sucked two yards back.

"Write!" shouted Samoylenko; "it's devilish weather for you to go in."

"Yes, no one knows the real truth . . ." thought Laevsky, looking wearily at the dark, restless sea.

"It flings the boat back," he thought; "she makes two steps forward and one step back; but the boatmen are stubborn, they work the oars unceasingly, and are not afraid of the high waves. The boat goes on and on. Now she is out of sight, but in half an hour the boatmen will see the steamer lights distinctly, and within an hour they will be by the steamer ladder. So it is in life. . . . In the search for truth man makes two steps forward and one step back. Suffering, mistakes, and weariness of life thrust them back, but the thirst for truth and stubborn will drive them on and on. And who knows? Perhaps they will reach the real truth at last."

"Go—o—od-by—e," shouted Samoylenko.

"There's no sight or sound of them," said the deacon. "Good luck on the journey!"

It began to spot with rain.

1891

THE LAUREL DOSTOYEVSKY
Introductions by Ernest J. Simmons

CRIME AND PUNISHMENT

One of the most compelling novels in all literature by the man André Gide called "the greatest of all novelists." 75c

THE HOUSE OF THE DEAD

Dostoyevsky's unforgettable account of a man condemned to ten years of penal servitude for murdering his wife, based on the author's own prison experiences. 50c

THE POSSESSED

An outstanding treatment of political conspiracy. Includes the rarely published Tikhon chapter in a brilliant new translation. 95c

NOTES FROM UNDERGROUND, POOR PEOPLE and THE FRIEND OF THE FAMILY

Three short novels which illustrate the remarkable diversity and range of Dostoyevsky's genius. 75c

A RAW YOUTH

The story of a young rebel. Uprooted, disillusioned, and with a tendency toward corruption, he presents a brilliant parallel to the conflicts of today's youth. 95c

THE BROTHERS KARAMAZOV

The Constance Garnett translation in an authoritative modern abridgment by Edmund Fuller 60c

THE IDIOT

One of the best portraits in all fiction of a rare and difficult subject: the good, truly moral man. 95c

If you cannot obtain copies of these titles at your local bookseller, just send the price (plus 10c per copy for handling and postage) to Dell Books, Box 2291, Grand Central Post Office, New York, N.Y. 10017. No postage or handling charge is required on any order of five or more books.